HEARTWOOD

Chonrad, Lord of Barle, comes to the fortified temple of Heartwood for the Congressus peace talks, which Heartwood's holy knights have called in an attempt to stave off war in Anguis. But the Arbor, Heartwood's holy tree, is failing, and because the land and its people are one, it is imperative the nations try to make peace.

After the Veriditas, or annual Greening Ceremony, the Congressus takes place. The talks do not go well and tempers are rising when an army of warriors emerges from the river. After a fierce battle, the Heartwood knights discover that the water warriors have stolen the Arbor's heart. For the first time in history, its leaves begin to fall...

The knights divide into seven groups and begin an epic quest to retrieve the Arbor, and save the land.

FREYA ROBERTSON

HEARTWOOD

The Elemental Wars
Book I

ANGRY
ROBOT

ANGRY ROBOT
A member of the Osprey Group

Lace Market House,
54-56 High Pavement,
Nottingham
NG1 1HW
UK

Angry Robot / Osprey Publishing
PO Box 3985
New York
NY 10185-3985
USA

www.angryrobotbooks.com
Lucky seven

An Angry Robot paperback original 2013

Cover art by Alejandro Colucci
Map by Steve Luxton
Set in Meridien by EpubServices

Distributed in the United States by Random House, Inc., New York

ISBN: 978 0 85766 386 3
Ebook ISBN: 978 0 85766 387 0

Printed in the United States of America

9 8 7 6 5 4 3 2 1

To Chris, the heart of Heartwood,
who provided the inspiration and ideas for so much of the story,
the best son a mother could have.

And to Tony, the king of history,
the cleverest man I've ever met, a talented DM,
my adventuring partner in the worlds of fantasy,
and the love of my life.

THE LAND OF ANGUIS – YEARS AND DAYS

An Anguis year consists of 240 days separated into eight seasons, each of which is divided into two Moons of 15 days as follows:

Moon (15 days)	Season
Old	The Darkening
Dead	"
Holly	The Sleep
Berry	"
Lamb	The Stirring
Bud	"
Hare	The Awakening
High	"
Flower	The Flourishing
Birth	"
Bright	The Shining
Green	"
Hay	The Harvest
Apple	"
Leaf	The Falling
High	"

Each day is 18 hours long. A typical Heartwood day is divided as follows (times vary from season to season):

Campana (Bell)	Day Activity	Night Activity
Primus	Sunrise meal	Sunset meal
Secundus	Light Service	Dark Service
Tertius	Chapter House	Bed
Quartus	Weapons Practice	
Quintus	Free time	
Sextus	High meal	
Septimus	Day Service	
Octavus	Reading/studying/weapons	Night vigil
Nonus	"	"

CHRONOLOGY OF ANGUIS HISTORY

Century   Important Events

Pre-Oculus

500	Quercetum written
400	Early Temple over the Arbor
300	The Great Quake – Early Temple collapses
200	Komis invasion and their defeat
100	First Famine

Post-Oculus

0	Oculus – he writes his Rule and builds Heartwood's stone Temple
100	Missionaries spread his new ideas to all lands
200	Growth of the Universities, development of the Castellum
300	New wave of religious orders – religious diversity
400	First Religious Wars. Isenbard's Wall built
500	Heartwood begins to help patrol the Wall
600	Hurricanes and floods
700	The Second Famine
800	Second Religious Wars, then peace. Isenbard's Wall refortified
900	The Great Famine and Pestilence
1000	Present day

"Understanding in the soul is like the Veriditas of the branches and the leaves of the tree."

Hildegard von Bingen

PART ONE

CHAPTER ONE

I

The belt hung from a hook in the doorway of a tent, weighed down by a bulging leather pouch. Gold coins shone at the top where the tie had loosened – an open invitation to the light-fingered.

The boy's gaze alighted on it like a bird. He paused amidst the busy traffic on the main road into Heartwood, stepping out of the way of the carts and huge battle steeds that threatened to trample him.

He glanced around to make sure no one was looking and sidled over. A blue Wulfengar banner flew from the top of the tent, and he pulled a face at it as he reached out to take the pouch.

A large, strong hand clamped on his shoulder, and he jumped in fright. The hand belonged to a sturdy Wulfengar lord, his bristling face dark as thunderclouds.

"Laxonian." The Wulfian sneered, and he spat on the page's red tabard. "I might have guessed."

He raised his right hand to strike the young lad. The page twisted, however, and wrenched himself away from the knight's grip. Like an arrow, he sped off into the crowd. For a moment, he thought the Wulfian would let him go, but then shouts and curses echoed behind him, and he realised the knight was hot on his trail.

He risked a glance over his shoulder, and fear slashed through him like a blade at the sight of the knight's bulky form barging through the crowds of people towards him. He picked up his pace, but without warning flew straight into a mail-clad knight, solid and firm as a stone wall.

"What's the hurry, lad?" The knight's words tailed off as the Wulfian appeared through the throng.

"He was going to steal my money pouch!" the Wulfian yelled, coming to a halt in front of them.

The page looked up at the knight he had barged into. The knight wore a red tabard over his mail which marked him as a Laxonian, as did his tall stature, his short beard and the light brown hair swept back from his open, honest face. The silver stag embroidered on the tabard marked him as Chonrad, Lord of Barle: a knight whose reputation for fairness and justice was renowned throughout the Seven Lands of Laxony.

"My Lord Bertwald, I think there has been some confusion." Chonrad pushed the page behind him. "This is my lad – I sent him to retrieve a belt from my tent and he must have mistaken it for yours."

Bertwald narrowed his eyes. "You are already wearing a belt."

"Yes," Chonrad said easily, "but the other one has my money pouch on it, and I wanted to purchase some armour from the blacksmith."

"My tent flies a blue pennant," Bertwald snapped. "Is your boy so stupid he cannot tell Laxonian from Wulfian?"

"He is somewhat simple." Chonrad trod on the page's foot when he opened his mouth to protest. "Please forgive his foolishness. And let me fetch you an ale from the drinks tent to compensate for your inconvenience."

Bertwald stepped closer to them. The page shrank away, shuddering at the sight of the knight's greasy beard flecked with food. "I have no intention of partaking of any beverage with a Laxonian." Bertwald's voice was filled with menace. "Nor is this your lad. Do not think you can make a fool out of me, Barle."

"I do not need to," Chonrad said just as quietly. "You are managing well enough on your own."

Bertwald bared his teeth, but glanced up as another knight appeared at Chonrad's shoulder. The page turned to see a towering hulk of a man that dwarfed even the tall Laxonian. By the way he moved in front of the knight, the page decided the man must be his bodyguard.

Bertwald gave a snort. "Peace between our two countries? It is a ridiculous notion. These talks will not last the day."

With that, he turned and marched off back to his tent, knocking people askew as he barged through the crowd.

The page breathed a sigh of relief. Then his heart hammered as Chonrad turned to face him, hands on hips. "Were you trying to steal the money?" he asked in his deep, mellow voice.

"Yes, my lord." The page gulped. Would the bodyguard beat him? He would barely be able to crawl to his bed if that were the case.

Chonrad nodded. "Well, at least your honesty does you credit. Whom do you serve?"

"L-Lord Amerle," stuttered the page.

"Then you are very far from home." Chonrad sighed. "I understand your motivation, but believe me – you do not want to start an incident with Wulfengar today, of all days."

"No, my lord," the page said.

"Go back to your master before he wonders where you are."

"Yes, my lord." The lad's heart lifted as he realised he was not to be beaten.

"And no more stealing."

"Yes, my lord." The page turned to run and then let out a yelp as the leather boot of the bodyguard met his soft behind. He did not stop, however, but slipped quickly into the crowd. He knew when he had been let off lightly.

As he ran, he touched the oak leaf pendant hanging around his neck and thanked the Arbor that Lord Barle had been there to save his life.

••••

II

Chonrad, Lord of Barle and second-in-command to the High Lord of Laxony, smiled wryly as the page skittered off into the crowd. He exchanged a glance with his bodyguard, Fulco, who rolled his eyes and shook his head. Little did the boy know how close he had come to causing the downfall of the Congressus, Chonrad thought as they made their way towards the gatehouse. Bertwald was looking for any excuse to end the peace talks and would have seized the transgression of a Laxonian page with both gleeful hands. The meeting, he thought with a sigh, was doomed to failure. But that did not mean he should not try as hard as he could to get it to work.

He looked up as the Porta loomed over him. The huge gatehouse at the easternmost end of the Heartwood complex towered over the rest of the buildings like an eagle hovering over its prey. For a moment, it blocked out the rising sun, and his mood darkened in keeping as he walked through the gateway into the place that had haunted his dreams for the last thirty-five years.

The solemn Custos – one of the many Custodes guards keeping a careful watch at the bottom of the Porta – saw the golden sash he wore over his armour, which marked him as one of the Congressus dignitaries, and then noticed the silver stag on his tabard. "The Dux would like to see you, Lord Barle," she said. "She is upstairs, on the roof."

Chonrad nodded and, together with Fulco, climbed up the stone stairs that curled inside the left tower, emerging into the open air at the top. There were several people up there, mainly Custodes keeping watch across Heartwood, ready to raise the alarm at the sight of any problems, but it was the knight waiting on the far side of the roof who caught his attention.

He had met Procella once before, when she visited his home town of Vichton on the coast, and he recognised her immediately. Tall and straight-backed with elaborately braided brown hair, she held herself like the stern leader she was, although the smile she gave him was warm.

He walked across to join her. "Dux." He gave her the standard soldier's salute of an arm across his chest, hand clenched over his heart.

"Lord Barle." She returned the salute and then clasped his hand in a firm handshake.

He leaned on the parapet, and she followed his gaze across the vast expanse of the Heartwood estate. He had forgotten how large Heartwood was, having not been there since childhood, and he had thought to find the place smaller than he remembered, as often happens when you revisit somewhere from your youth. But he had been wrong. As he stood there watching the sun's early rays flood the place with light, its very size took his breath away.

The Heartwood Castellum, a huge, stone-built fortified temple, glowed like a jewel amongst the scatter of buildings in the surrounding Baillium. It was an unusual, evocative building: its small, high windows sparkling and twinkling in the sunlight, its domed roof rising above the walls like the sun above the horizon. It was beautiful and strange, and even after all these years it made him mad.

The knight next to him raised an eyebrow. "You look angry," she observed.

"I am."

"Why?"

He glanced across at her. She had declined to wear a ceremonial gown as was usual on the day of the Veriditas religious ceremony and had instead donned a full coat of mail that reached almost to her knees over a thick leather tunic, the hood of mail folded under her braided hair. Her longsword hung in the scabbard on her hips, and she'd tucked her thick breeches into heavy leather boots. Her garb echoed his deep-rooted unease that these peace talks were not going to remain peaceful for long.

"Well?" she prompted.

He glanced over at Fulco, who stood to one side looking politely the other way across the Heartwood estate. Chonrad sighed and glanced back at the bustling Baillium, watching the people ebb and flow across the grounds like waves brushing at a shoreline. No one alive knew what had happened, not even Fulco. Was now really the time to open up the part of him he had kept hidden like a sore since the age of seven?

Procella's eyes were gentle, however, and understanding shone in their depths. And Fulco, he thought wryly, would not be able to tell anyone what he heard; he was mute and communicated with Chonrad via hand signals.

"My parents put me forward for the Allectus," he said eventually. "And Heartwood rejected me."

It was not an easy admission to make. His parents had held high hopes that he would be chosen for the prestigious role of one of Heartwood's Militis knights, and it had been easy for them to convince the seven year-old Chonrad that he would definitely be chosen at the Allectus – the annual selection ceremony. He left Vichton boasting to his friends that he would not return, and it had been a humbling experience for him to have to ride back into town and admit he hadn't been good enough for the holy order.

Everyone else eventually forgot what had happened, but the knowledge that he did not have the indefinable quality needed to become a member of the Exercitus army had stayed with him through his growing years. In fact, he thought, it had probably prompted him to work harder at his soldiering, to prove to himself that he was good enough to have joined them.

"I see." A small smile touched Procella's lips. "It is our loss."

Chonrad shrugged, but her admission pleased him. "Maybe; maybe not." He exchanged a glance with Fulco. At first, the bodyguard made no sign he had heard Chonrad's story, but Chonrad caught the little flick of his fingers. *Fools*, Fulco signed. Clearly, he was not impressed with their rejection of his overlord.

Chonrad turned back to Procella. "Who knows whether the life of the Militis would be suitable for me?"

Now it was Procella's turn to shrug. "It is not so different, I think, from the time you spent in the borderlands."

He thought about it. "Perhaps my life has been similar to yours as Dux. I would think, though, that for the Militis who serve in the Castellum, life is very different."

She caught the barely-disguised resentment behind his tone and her eyebrows rose. "All Militis have to spend at least a year in the Exercitus," she said in what he assumed was the tone she used on those who lay abed in the morning.

"Even so," he replied, unperturbed, "in spite of the fact that Heartwood is like a small city, it still chooses to isolate itself from the rest of Anguis. And that must lead to a strange atmosphere inside its walls?" He made it a Question, although he was sure he knew the answer.

Even if she did agree with him, she didn't know him well enough to admit it. "Would it make it easier for you if I said yes?" she asked crisply. "So you can feel glad you never became a part of its community?"

"Ouch."

Her face softened. "I am sorry. It was not my intention to insult such an important visitor as yourself." Her lips twitched. "But you did ask for it."

He laughed. "I suppose I did." He studied her for a moment, watching as her hand came up to brush back a stray hair from her face. For the first time he saw the small oak leaf tattoo on her left outer wrist. Truth to tell, she fascinated him. He had known a few female knights in his time, but this one... Strong, brave, authoritative, yet strangely compassionate, with very womanly curves beneath all the armour...

"Are you married?" she asked, surprising him.

"I was. Minna died six years ago, in childbirth."

A look passed fleetingly across her face. "I am sorry," she said. "How many children do you have?"

"Two. A girl, six, and a boy, eight." He thought about the look he had nearly missed. Was it to do with his wife dying, or the fact that it was in childbirth? "I never spend as much time with them as I would like," he added wistfully. "Do you wish you had children?"

Her eyebrows rose. He had the feeling she had never been asked that before. "I… sometimes…" She was clearly flustered, and obviously didn't like that unfamiliar emotion. "Families are not permitted in Heartwood," she stated flatly. "It is pointless even to think about the Question."

He noted she had said "families" and not "relationships". "Do you have to take an oath of celibacy?" he asked curiously. He wasn't sure if she would answer him. The religious rituals the Militis undertook were kept very private and nobody outside Heartwood knew very much about them.

She looked back at him. Her eyes were very dark, the colour of polished oak. "No. Heartwood Animism does not demand the impossible from a person." She referred to her religion. "It is accepted that from time to time a knight will need to satisfy his or her bodily needs. We are taught it is better to succumb to your desire than to burn with it."

"That is sensible."

At his amused words, her eyes fixed on him, but she did not smile back. "Equally, however, relationships are discouraged. Passion for a man or woman detracts from the passion we must direct towards our work, and those who cannot contain their feelings are encouraged to leave."

"I see." He spoke gently, understanding the warning behind her words.

He caught Fulco's amused gesture, *Pity!* but chose to ignore it.

Procella nodded at the sky to the west, and he turned to see the faintly pink Light Moon, barely visible as the sun continued its ascent. She smiled at him, and the sheer enjoyment that flooded her face surprised him. "It is nearly time," she said. "You have never seen the Veriditas?"

"Never."

She turned and walked over to the stairwell. "Come on." She winked at him. "You are in for a treat."

III

Together, they began to descend the spiral staircase, Fulco trailing a short distance behind. The stone Porta consisted of two towers joined by a large corridor overlooking a portcullis and drawbridge. It dominated the surrounding landscape. Built to withstand a direct assault, it was really the main fortification in Heartwood, the Castellum itself – even though its walls were six feet thick – meant to be a place to pray than a place to defend. The Porta, however, was solid and substantial, an impenetrable block between high, thick walls that curved around until they met the mountains behind.

Chonrad watched Procella run her fingers lovingly along the stone walls as she descended the steps.

"Did you work in the Porta before you went into the Exercitus?" he asked.

"Yes. I was one of the Custodes and spent a lot of time here. I organised the Watch and looked after maintenance of the defences."

"So what made you join the Exercitus?"

She looked over her shoulder at him. "You are very inquisitive."

"I am interested."

She sighed. "I spent some time training the young Militis at one of the camps in Laxony – they do not come to Heartwood until they reach the age of eighteen. Then I did my service in the Exercitus. All Militis do this; we spend a year away from Heartwood out on Isenbard's Wall, patrolling the borders. The atmosphere between Laxony and Wulfengar was not as good then as it is now, and we were called on constantly to deal with raids and put down rebellions."

"I should think you were in your element there."

She laughed. "I did enjoy it, I must admit. I rose through the ranks and got to know Valens, who was Dux at the time – I think you know him."

Chonrad did indeed know the mighty Valens. A huge knight, incredibly brave and fearless in battle, Valens had made it his business to know the lords of all the lands in Laxony, and most especially those near to the Wall. Chonrad had met him on several occasions, and had been disappointed when he heard Valens was retiring to Heartwood after an injury. Though he had heard much about her, and admired her, Chonrad had yet to learn whether Procella was a worthy successor.

"Do you enjoy being Dux?" he asked.

"Someone has to do it."

He laughed. "That is not an answer."

"It is all you are going to get." She seemed flustered by his Questions.

"I am irritating you." Was it because she did not intimidate him, as he imagined she did most people?

"Not at all. It is just… It is a long time since I have discussed my feelings with anybody. My life is a busy one and does not leave much time for analysing and the discussion of one's emotions."

"I can understand that."

She shot him a glance over her shoulder. "And you unnerve me."

"Why?"

She ran her gaze down him, her eyes alight with something he realised with surprise was interest. "You are an attractive knight. You must be used to making women flustered."

He raised his eyebrows. "I am afraid I have little experience in that area."

She stopped so suddenly he bumped into her, and she turned and looked up at him curiously. "Truly?"

"Well, I do not think of myself as ugly." He knew he was tall and broad-shouldered, with strong features under his light brown beard. "But I am afraid I have not spent a lot of time entertaining. The sword has been my constant companion, not the rose."

"You were married; presumably your wife fell in love with you?"

He thought about his wife. Memories of her stirred up feelings of duty and responsibility rather than affection. He had been sad when she died, but although he had worn a white tunic for the obligatory year, in his heart his mourning had passed long before that. "Minna was a difficult woman, and ours was a marriage of convenience. I am not sure love ever came into it at all."

Procella said nothing, but her dark eyes studied him curiously. Perhaps she thought all marriages involved falling in love. The reality, in his experience, was very different.

They reached the bottom of the stairs and turned into the large room that served as offices for the Watch where they co-ordinated the changing of the guard and the rota for the day. "On your feet!" she barked at the Custos who lounged in his chair, playing idly with a couple of dice. "Have you made your rounds yet?"

"Er, no Dux, sorry…" His face reddened as his eyes flicked from her to Chonrad and back again.

"It is nearly time for the Secundus Campana, so you had best be off."

He scurried down the stairs in front of them, his scabbard clanging on the stone.

She grinned at Chonrad, and he laughed. "You are very scary."

"It is all an act. I am a pussycat really."

"That is not what I have heard." Stories of the new Dux had become almost legend, even in the short time she had been in the role. Most of the knights in the Exercitus were scared of her, and he could understand why. He had also heard she was a sight to be seen in battle: skilled, fearless and experienced, fiercely loyal, someone her soldiers would fight to the death for.

Once again, his interest in her stirred, but he clamped it down firmly. *Distract yourself, Chonrad.* He thought about what she had said to the Custos. "What is the Secundus Campana?" She had spoken in the language of Heartwood, and he did not understand completely what she had said to the guard.

She looked at him with surprise, continuing in Laxonian, "I thought you spoke Heartwood's language?"

"A little of course. But I did not... ah... pay as much attention to my studies as I probably should have."

"You are referring to not being chosen at the Allectus?"

"Actually, no. I was just very bad at school."

She laughed. "The Secundus Campana is the second bell. The Campana rings nine times while the sun is up, marking time for prayer, weapons exercise and meals." She smiled. "I forget most people are unfamiliar with the ways here. I have known them for so long – they are all I can remember, really." She began to descend the stairwell to the next floor.

Chonrad followed her, Fulco trailing behind like a shadow. "Where were you from originally?" he asked, wondering if it was anywhere near his home town.

She looked over her shoulder at him. There was an impish look in her eyes. "I do not know if I should tell you."

"Why not?"

"It might... unnerve you."

He frowned. "What do you mean?"

"I am from Wulfengar."

He stopped dead on the steps and stared at her. She laughed, enjoying the effect her words had had on him, clearly not surprised to see his reaction. Her admission shocked him. In Wulfengar, women were not held in high regard, and it was unknown for them to enter the army, or indeed to sit on any council or hold any office in the land. They were forbidden to attend school or university. Wulfengar men regarded their women as brood mares, figures to satisfy their lust and produce their offspring, to cook their meals and look after them when they returned home at the end of the day.

Needless to say, Procella's position was rather unusual.

"By the oak leaf," said Chonrad. "How did you manage that?"

"My mother's mother was from Laxony." She carried on down the stairs. "My grandfather met her while on a raid across the Wall, and he carried her back with him as a spoil of victory."

Chonrad said nothing. It was an increasing problem, one that angered him greatly.

"I do not think they were that unhappy. She grew to love him, in her way. But she brought up her daughter – my mother, to be strong and independent, and although my father did his best to control her, my mother managed to do the same for me. She was determined I escape the hold of Wulfengar, as she had not, and so, unknown to my father, she took me to Heartwood herself for the Allectus, and left me there when I was chosen."

"That must have been hard."

"It was a long time ago," was all she said.

Reaching the bottom of the steps, they entered the large Watchroom. Usually a large oak door closed it off from the corridor to the north tower. Today, because all shifts of the Custodes were on Watch, they had pushed the doors open. The room now stretched from one tower of the Porta to the other, spanning the length of the wide drawbridge and portcullis below. The place was filled with knights, some arming themselves from the stock of weapons to one side of the room, others checking on the rota sheet where they were supposed to be at specific times of the day. They parted respectfully to let Procella, Chonrad and Fulco through as they crossed to the other tower and descended the final staircase to the outside world.

"Busy today," Chonrad commented, watching as a group of Hanaire visitors, distinguishable by their long fair hair, stopped at the gates to talk to the Custodes who ticked names off their list of invited guests.

"The busiest I have seen it for a long time," Procella agreed. They slipped past the Hanaireans and walked into the Baillium, the large area inside Heartwood's walls. The wide path led straight through the scatter of buildings and temporary tents to the Castellum.

"Everyone has come to see the show," Chonrad murmured. He glanced aside at a large group of Wulfengar knights who sat in front of a tent, swilling ale. Instinctively, his hand fell to the pommel of his sword.

Procella nudged him. "Remember we are here today to talk peace."

"Sorry." He let his hand drop. "But it has been a long time since I stood in the same country as a Wulfengar, let alone the same room."

He looked across at the huge circular Curia, where the Congressus was due to take place after the Veriditas ceremony. It had been a noble effort, he thought, by Heartwood, to try to get as many leaders of the Seven Lands of Laxony, the five lands of Wulfengar, and the lords of Hanaire together to discuss the possibility of a pact. Relations had not been good for some years between the eastern Twelve Lands especially, and things only seemed to be escalating. Heartwood's Exercitus was being called on more and more to try to keep things quiet on Isenbard's Wall, and he knew how thin their resources were being stretched. This was a last ditch attempt on Heartwood's part to try to make peace between the nations.

And he knew Procella was as certain as himself it would fail.

The blue Wulfengar banners waved in the early morning breeze like a flock of small birds hovering above the ground. Chonrad wondered if Procella felt disturbed by the close proximity of all the Laxony and Wulfengar lords. The invitation had specified they were not to bring large armies with them, but each lord had come accompanied by a small contingent of armed men. Having so many knights in such a small area was, he felt, inherently dangerous. He glanced across at Fulco, who pointed his thumb towards the ground with a grimace.

"Did you manage to get a look in the Castellum when you arrived last night?" Procella gestured at the building.

"No." He fell into step beside her, dodging the swishing tail of a horse as the rider headed for the Porta. "It was dark and my knights were tired after the long journey. We set up the tent and went straight to sleep." He did not tell her the main reason he had not visited the Temple – that part of him did not want to go in there, did not want to see the Arbor.

Procella gestured for him to follow her. "Come, I shall show you around the Temple." As she spoke, the sound of a bell rang around the Baillium. Its chime was not harsh on the ears, but it resonated throughout him, deep in his chest.

IV

"Is that the Veriditas beginning?" he asked.

For a moment she looked startled. Then she laughed. "It is odd but I have heard that bell for so many years that now I hardly hear it at all. No, it is not time for the ceremony quite yet. That will start with the Tertius Campana – the third bell."

"Are you missing anything at the moment?" He was aware each bell marked a specific item in the day's agenda.

"No." She turned her face up to the sunshine as they walked. "Usually it would mark the Light Service, but all Services are postponed today for the Congressus."

The Baillium bustled, filled with knights from the three countries and the Militis, but in spite of the commotion Chonrad found he could not draw his gaze away from the Castellum that reared above them, casting a shadow across a large portion of the grounds. He remembered seeing it so many years ago, this tall honey-coloured building, and he could also remember the fluttering in his stomach then, the excitement and anticipation of being chosen at the Allectus. He had been so certain they would choose him.

He could also recall walking away from the Temple after the ceremony and casting a glance back. He remembered the heavy feeling in the pit of his stomach, and the burning sensation behind his eyelids. Heartwood hadn't wanted him then; could it really have changed in all those years?

"I cannot take you inside the western part, of course," said Procella. If she was aware his mood had darkened, she didn't mention it. "That is for the Militis only. But I can show you around the Temple."

He did not reply. Instead, he slowed his walk as the path went over a small bridge, and he leaned over the railings and looked down at the river that splashed merrily beneath. "This is not natural, is it?"

"No." She leaned over next to him. "The channel was dug many years ago to divert water from the Flumen that runs from the mountains, just north of Isenbard's Wall to the sea. Water is diverted here to feed the Arbor and for the use of the Militis. It runs right through the Castellum, out through the Temple and then down here and under the wall to the east of the Porta."

The water shimmered on the stones at the bottom of the channel, momentarily blinding him. He blinked, and for a second thought he saw a shadow in the water, like a face next to his, staring up at him. He blinked again, however, and it vanished. Looking up, he saw a cloud covering the face of the sun and realised it must have been the reflection of this he had seen. More clouds lay hunched on the horizon, dark grey and ominous, and he wondered whether they were going to get rain before the day was out.

They continued walking up the road, picking their way through the piles left by the horses, to where the road met the Quad in front of the main entrance to the Castellum. The Quad was a large square of flagstones, used in pleasant weather for some meetings. But it was too small to hold the Congressus, which was going to take place in the more formal meeting place of the Curia, a large and circular ring of oak trees to one side of the Baillium. The Quad was currently full of people waiting for the start of the Veriditas. Procella pushed through them, heading for the large oak doors. At one point, Chonrad felt her warm, strong grip on his hand, as she made sure he followed.

The doors were closed while they prepared the Temple for the ceremony. But nobody closed the doors to the Dux.

"Come on." She slipped through the gap as one of the Custodes opened the door for her.

"Are you sure?" He looked over his shoulder at the colours of many Wulfengar lords: "Does everyone get a personal tour such as this?"

"No. Only the really important people," she said. "Well, and you, obviously."

His retort vanished as he moved through the crack in the doors, which closed behind him, unfortunately leaving Fulco outside. Instantly, he felt as if he had stepped into another world.

The Temple was vast, much bigger than he remembered. With walls constructed from the amber mountain stone, the Temple had a high ceiling that soared above his head in a huge dome. He craned his neck to look up at the roof. The dome was inlaid with thousands of tiny panes of coloured glass that cast sunlight onto the floor in coloured shapes, as if someone had spilled a basket of jewels across the flagstones.

The Temple floor was divided into a series of concentric rings. The outer ring, the one closest to the thick stone walls, was fronted by a wooden screen with shutters, some of which were open to reveal small cubicles, each with a seat, a prayer cushion and a small table. The whole outer ring was formed from a series of these cubicles, presumably, he guessed, where the Militis spent time between the services if they wish to take private prayer or study.

At the moment, however, access to the cubicles was blocked because in the next ring, the widest one, a series of temporary wooden tiers had been erected to form a circle of seats for the ceremony, like an amphitheatre. Usually, he realised, the Temple must seem even bigger without the seating, and he vaguely remembered the wide-open space from the Allectus. This ring was for visitors, and a low wooden fence at waist height hemmed the inner edge of it, to discourage people from going into the central layers.

He followed Procella across the floor to the fence. The small gate that usually stopped visitors from going any farther lay open, so he followed her through it. The next ring was filled with water, and he realised this was the same stream he had crossed outside. The water was obviously fed into the Temple, where it circled the centre and then continued in a small channel outside.

Procella smiled at him and led him across the bridge.

The second-to-last ring was usually for Militis only. It was obviously much smaller than the huge outer circle and littered with cushions, to save the sore knees of those who came to pray. And the object of their prayers stood in the centre circle, lit by the light of the rising sun.

Chonrad stopped, letting Procella walk forward on her own. She touched her fingers to her heart, lips and forehead in a gesture of veneration. His heart pounded. It had been thirty-five years since he had last set foot in the Temple. But immediately he was taken back to the moment he had stood before the Arbor, and the wonder that had filled him then.

The Arbor was an oak tree, *the* oak tree: the one tree whose roots reached to the centre of the world, and which fed the land with its energy. It was formed, he knew, from the tears of the god Animus, who had cried when he realised he was alone in the universe, and his tears had fallen onto the land and hardened, and formed the Pectoris – the heart of all creation. And the Pectoris had fed the land with Animus's love, and around the Pectoris grew the Arbor. And since time had begun, the Arbor had protected the land, and because the land and the people were one, the Arbor and the people were one.

He could remember his mother telling the story in front of the fire in the cold winter evenings before he went to the Allectus. He remembered lying on his front, listening to his mother's soft voice, and he would stare into the flames and imagine what this wonderful tree was like.

Someone touched his arm, and a soft voice said, "What do you think?"

He cleared his throat. "It is smaller than I remember." He turned and only then realised it wasn't Procella standing next to him but a smaller knight, with long black hair, brown skin and disturbing eyes the colour of beaten gold.

"This is Silva," Procella said, indicating the dark-haired knight. "She is the Keeper of the Arbor. Silva, this is Chonrad of Vichton, Lord of Barle."

"A pleasure," Silva said, although she didn't smile, and her golden eyes glinted.

"I apologise if I insulted the Arbor." He hoped he hadn't caused an international incident. "I was merely... I mean I remember... The last time I came, it seemed bigger... But then I was a child..."

"Calm yourself," Silva said in her strange sing-song voice. "There is no offence taken. In fact you are correct – the Arbor would have been bigger when you were a child, you are not mistaken."

"Is that right? Why?"

Silva arched an eyebrow. "That Question requires a very long and complicated answer."

Procella looked up into its branches. She'd wrapped her arms around her body in a strangely defensive gesture, looking for all the world, he thought, as if she were frightened, although he couldn't imagine the brave Dux ever feeling that emotion.

"From what we understand," Silva said, "the Arbor has been shrinking steadily over the past thousand years. Oculus's records state the height of the tree as being a good third taller than it is now." She sighed heavily. "We think it is because of our disconnection with the land."

"Disconnection?"

"We are taught the land and the Arbor are one, and therefore the people and the Arbor are one, are we not? Well, over the past few hundred years, we have hardly been at one with each other. There has been war after war, followed by floods and famines, and we think this has resulted in a lack of understanding of how to connect with the land, and therefore how to connect to the Arbor."

Chonrad studied the tree as he thought about her words. Oculus, the writer of the Militis's Rule and the founder of the stone Temple that eventually became the Castellum, explained in his writings that three hundred years before his birth – over thirteen hundred years before Chonrad was born – there had been a great earthquake, which had caused the old Temple to collapse. He had written in his *Memoria* that oral tradition stated that early literature had been hidden beneath the rubble, and that maybe important information about how to look after the Arbor had been lost. Oculus had tried to find it, but had not been successful. Was it possible the truth had been buried along with the ancient writings?

He looked over at the two knights who watched him patiently but attentively. "Is that why you called the Congressus?" he asked. "You think the Arbor will continue to shrink unless we finally have peace?"

Procella shrugged. "We do not know. But it is worth a try, do you not think?"

"Are you going to explain your theory at the Congressus?"

"Do you think we should?" Silva asked.

It was Chonrad's turn to shrug. "It might help the Twelve Lands come to a peaceful decision. Without the impetus of this goal..." He did not finish his sentence, but the serious look on their faces meant they had understood: *it might not come to pass.*

He looked once more at Silva, with her dark hair and gold eyes. Recognition suddenly struck him. "You are from Komis!" he blurted before he could stop himself.

••••

V

Silva surveyed him coolly, then nodded. "You are correct. I came to Heartwood at the age of fifteen."

"She is the only person from Komis to have joined the Militis for twenty years," said Procella.

Chonrad nodded with interest. His life in Laxony had led him to have very few dealings with the people of Komis, but he knew them to have a varied and colourful past. Before the time of Oculus, the Komis had been a strong, arrogant race. The King of Komis at the time had been powerful and greedy, and his desire for land had led him to mount an invasion on the eastern lands shortly after the Great Quake. In spite of his vast wealth and power amongst his people, however, he was a bad tactician. When, in a bid to show the strength of his forces, he moved his whole army into the Knife's Edge intending a secret invasion, he met a combined army of eastern knights who swiftly obliterated his troops, leaving barely a person alive. Komis suffered greatly; with nearly all their men of a certain age dead, the population declined swiftly, and the spread of the Pestilence did not help matters. Crop failure in the west was particularly bad during the cold winters of those years, and many also died from hunger. The kingdom shattered, and those who were left withdrew into the great forests to find food and shelter. And there they stayed until the present day, a race of tree-dwellers and guerrilla warriors, as alien to the easterners as a bird underground.

From what he understood, however, the people of Komis had developed a keen understanding of nature through their many generations of living in the forests. He supposed that explained why Silva was Keeper of the Arbor.

Chonrad turned his attention back once more to the Arbor. He felt strangely disappointed. He could not put his finger on it: he wasn't sure if it was due to the fact that the tree was smaller, or if it was something else... Over the years, since the Allectus, he supposed he had built up the Arbor in his mind to be something magnificent and awe-inspiring, something that would make him gasp and instinctively make the traditional sign of reverence Procella had done.

And yet after his initial feeling of wonder, he felt a kind of dull disenchantment, as you might feel when the clouds block the sun on your wedding day. It was just a tree. An old oak tree. And not a very big one. The one outside his castle at Vichton was nearly as big as the Arbor.

Procella was watching his face. She came over, took his hand and pulled him forwards until he stood right underneath the tree, its overhanging branches like a canopy above his head.

"Touch it," she whispered. Lifting his hand, she placed it on the bark.

A shock went through him. The trunk was warm. And beneath the bark, his fingers could detect a slight, slow heartbeat. *The Pectoris*. He looked up at the leaves. There was, of course, no wind inside the Temple. And yet the leaves moved, carrying with them a soft whisper like the sound of the sea.

He looked across at Procella, realisation striking him. "We are just coming out of The Sleep," he said.

"Yes."

"But the leaves have not fallen."

"The Arbor's leaves never fall," Silva said from behind him.

Her words made a shiver run down his back, and he withdrew his hand from the bark. He felt distinctly unsettled by what he had felt there. All trees were living things, and of course the Arbor was no ordinary tree. But still, feeling that heartbeat... It gave him the impression the Arbor was more than just leaves and trunk and branches. Looking up into its branches, he suddenly wondered if it were aware that he was there, if it could see him, could feel him. Did it remember him from the Allectus? What was it thinking? *You should not be here... Why did you come...?* He shivered again and took a step backwards. Although the Arbor was at the root of his religion, and although he wore an oak leaf pendant around his neck and said his prayers at night, he did not feel comfortable standing beneath its branches.

Across the western side of the Temple, a door opened in the wall and several people came through. Chonrad knew this was the wall separating the main part of the Temple from the Domus or living area of the Militis, and realised they had to belong to Heartwood.

They crossed the bridge and came over to the Arbor. One of them he knew: a tall, powerful-looking knight, grey-haired, his face marked with scars, looking even more imposing in full battle armour. Last time Chonrad had seen him, it had been on the Wall, during one of the many skirmishes Wulfengar had been carrying out. Now, however, he walked with a pronounced limp, a testament to the reason why he no longer headed the Exercitus.

Valens was Imperator of Heartwood, leader of both the Exercitus and the Castellum, overlord of the whole holy complex – the top rung of the ladder; a truly powerful position, but a difficult one, Chonrad thought, for a knight used to a life out in the open, in almost constant battle. He wondered how Valens coped with his disability and his confinement to the building. Was he relieved after a life spent on the road? Or did he itch to get back out there?

The Heartwood leader came forward and held out his hand. "Lord Barle," he said in his deep, gruff voice. "It is good to see you once again." He closed his hand on Chonrad's in a firm grip.

"And you, Valens." Chonrad placed his left hand on the Imperator's wrist, and Valens did the same.

"Thank you for coming." Valens released his hand and turned to face the tree, making, as he did so, the same gesture Procella had: putting his hand to his heart, his lips and his forehead.

Chonrad nodded. "You are welcome."

"I just hope it will not have been in vain." Valens sighed.

"You do not have hopes for the Congressus?"

Valens looked him in the eye. "Do you?"

Chonrad said nothing.

"As I thought," Valens said gruffly. He turned to the knight who waited patiently beside him. "Have you met our Abbatis, Dulcis?"

"No." Chonrad came forward and held out his hand. He knew she was in charge of the Domus. "It is a pleasure to meet you, my lady."

"And I you." Dulcis took his hand. She was shorter than Procella, but taller than Silva, and her hair, like Valens's, was grey and hung loose to her waist like a sheet of metal. She wore only light leather armour covered by a knee-length white tunic embroidered with a single oak leaf. "I have heard much about you," she said. "The famous Lord Barle. You have a reputation as a great knight and, more importantly to us today, as a skilled diplomat."

"Peace must be our ultimate aim."

"That is not everyone's belief," she said wryly. She did not say the name Wulfengar; she did not have to.

"I will do my best to aid today's discussions," he said.

"Then that is the best we can hope for." She smiled at him. "I understand we made the mistake many years ago, of turning you away from the Allectus."

Chonrad looked sharply at Procella. She returned his gaze openly, raising an eyebrow. Dulcis caught the look and shook her head. "Nobody told me, Lord Barle, I make it our business to research the lives of those who come to Heartwood. Our records state you came to us at the age of seven." She touched his arm. "It was our loss." She looked over at Valens. "You were not the first – and will not be the last – mistake we have made in choosing the Militis."

He wanted to ask her what she meant, but she was already turning away. Her comment flattered him, although it did not completely remove the resentment he carried deep within him towards Heartwood. It was an old wound that had never healed properly, and it was too late to do anything about it now. He wondered to whom she was referring when she mentioned making a mistake in choosing the Militis. Was it someone he had already met? He would probably never find out, but her words intrigued him.

Dulcis looked up through the dome at the sun's position in the sky. "It will not be long until the Tertius Campana," she observed. "We must bring in our guests."

Silva stayed by the Arbor, but the rest of them walked back towards the outer ring. As they passed over the channel of water, Chonrad glanced down. Once again, he was surprised to see a shadow beneath the surface, a dark shape moving along the bottom of the channel.

"Are there fish in there?" he asked.

Procella stopped and looked back at him. "There is a grille at the top of the channel where it is siphoned off from the Flumen, but occasionally one slips through."

"That must be it then." He dismissed the frisson of unease that made his spine tingle. He had more important things to worry about than shadows. Today could be a beginning, the start of a new peace treaty, the commencement of a new historical era.

Or it could be the end. But he refused to dwell on that.

The Custodes pulled back the huge oak doors, and people filtered in. More Custodes took their places at intervals along the tiers. He knew they would have been present at the Veriditas anyway, but even so, he guessed their strategic placing had more to do with an attempt to keep an eye on the guests than out of a genuine wish to spread out.

Fulco came through, looking anxiously for him, his relief evident when he saw his overlord. His bodyguard took his duties seriously, especially during a time when their enemies were in such close proximity.

The guests filed in, and gradually the tiers filled up. Not everyone who had come to Heartwood would be able to attend the ceremony; there wasn't enough space for all the contingent of each lord, so the leaders of each of the Twelve Lands, the Hanaire lords and their closest followers were brought in first, and then the rank and file took the remaining spaces.

Chonrad had been standing by the doorway, in the shadows, but now Procella beckoned to him. He and Fulco made their way around the tiers to a space a few levels up that had been reserved for them amongst the knights from Barle. She left them there and walked to the front row, where the most senior members of the Heartwood Militis were waiting.

He looked around the Temple at the people seated on the tiers. Although each person sat with people of his or her own land, the Militis had been insightful enough to spread the three countries around the room. Not that he expected trouble during the Veriditas. Whatever tensions there were between the Twelve Lands, they were all followers of Animus, and none wished to defile the Temple by bringing politics and war into its midst.

The Tertius Campana rang from somewhere in the western half of the Castellum, reverberating around the wooden tiers and the stone walls, sounding deep inside his chest.

Gradually, everyone in the Temple fell quiet.

CHAPTER TWO

I

Silva stepped out of the ring of Militis towards the Arbor. The rest of them closed the gap, reaching out to take each other's hands to form a circle. Chonrad saw Procella, Valens and Dulcis, their faces serene as they gazed on the tree that seemed to sway gently in spite of there being no wind.

Silva began speaking, her voice ringing out around the Temple. She spoke in the language of Heartwood, and he did not understand every word, but listened instead to the beauty of the language. Every now and again, the rest of the Militis would chant a line in answer, reinforcing what he realised was a devotional prayer to the tree.

When they had finished the prayer, Dulcis then turned to the rest of the Temple and addressed the crowd. She gave a short speech in the language of Heartwood, and then began again in Laxonian. Chonrad saw the men from Wulfengar stir resentfully at the fact that the translation was first in Laxonian, but they soon quieted as her words echoed around the room.

"My friends," said Dulcis, her hand taking in the whole of the Temple, "I welcome you to Heartwood. May you enjoy your stay in this place of worship, and I hope you will use your time here to meditate by the Arbor and take in the atmosphere of peace and serenity that is generated by our loving tree."

She repeated the words again in the language of Wulfengar, then in Hanairean, and then in Komis, although as far as Chonrad knew, Silva was the only one there from that country.

Then the Militis started to sing. It was a very old hymn, one Chonrad knew from childhood, as did most of the people in the room, obviously, as everyone began to join in. It was in the Heartwood language, but this time he knew what the words meant.

Heart of Arbor, deep inside,
The Pectoris holds the tears that Animus cried.
The roots of the tree lace through the land.
We honour you now as, hand in hand,
We thank you for watching over us all,
So strong and proud, so wide and tall.
Keep us safe and keep us strong.
The land of our fathers, where we belong.

It was nothing more than a simple verse, really, like a nursery rhyme with a straightforward tune, and he wondered why they had chosen it. He supposed the main reason was probably that most people would be able to sing along. But he wondered also whether they were purposefully trying to rouse everyone's memories of their childhood and make them think about the feelings they had towards the Arbor, which inevitably changed as one grew older and the problems of the world replaced the aspirations and daydreams of youth.

The song ended and Dulcis began a prayer. As she did so, bowls began to be passed along the lines of guests. Chonrad knew what was in there: Acerbitas, the bitter tea made from oak leaves the Militis drank to remind themselves of how bitter life would be without Animus's love. He accepted the bowl as it was passed to him and sipped a small amount of the tea. He grimaced, passing the bowl to Fulco. It truly was bitter. Fulco pulled a face too as he sipped and signed to Chonrad: *Lovely!* Chonrad glared at him, trying hard not to laugh. This was not the place to have a fit of the giggles.

Just then, the oak doors at the front opened. He craned his neck to see over the heads of the others to observe what was coming through. It didn't matter that he couldn't see, though, because when he heard the high voice of the animal he knew instantly it was a lamb.

Two Custodes led the creature down the pathway and across the bridge to the inner Arbor ring. He hadn't noticed before, but he could now see from his elevated position a circular pattern of stones where the path crossed the inner ring. This was the Sepulchrum – the area of death – where animal sacrifices were made and the dead offered to the tree.

Silva knelt down and took the creature in her arms. The chanting of the Militis grew louder as she grasped the animal's legs and lifted it so it lay on its side. She then pressed down with her knees so it couldn't rise and reached to one side to pick up a large ceremonial knife. Swiftly she cut its throat, and lifted it so its blood ran onto the roots of the tree.

Chonrad's breath caught in his throat. He was both fascinated and appalled by Silva's actions. The viscous red liquid dripped from the twitching lamb's neck and then, as the blood hit the roots, the tree shivered, its leaves rattling like teeth. Silva laid the lamb at the foot of the tree. Then he saw something he had never thought to see, that he did not fully comprehend.

The roots of the tree moved. Like snakes, they lifted themselves out of the earth and crawled towards the lamb. He watched them, unnerved by their slow slide along the ground, unsure what was going to happen next. The lamb, which was nearly dead, twitched feebly as its lifeblood flowed over the ground. The roots curled over the white woollen body and drew it closer to the trunk. Slowly, the animal was absorbed as the Arbor ingested its limp form.

There was a dramatic moment as the tree seemed to wait. If it had been a person, Chonrad felt it would be standing with its head tipped back and its face to the sun, arms spread wide to take in as much of the light as possible.

And then there was a dramatic movement – Chonrad could only think of it as a spurt of growth, as the tree grew taller, its branches lengthening and buds appearing on the twigs, which quickly unfurled to reveal new, bright green leaves. Everyone in the Temple cheered and rose to their feet, clapping and shouting their approval that the ceremony had worked, and Animus had accepted their offering. He rose with them, not wishing to seem irreligious, but in truth his stomach had been turned by the event.

He took his seat again as the Militis joined hands once again for the final ritual. Everyone bent their heads, but Chonrad found his gaze drawn up to where the sun filtered through the coloured glass in the roof, and he wished fervently he was outside in the fresh air.

The Veriditas ended with a closing prayer. Even if he had been able to understand Dulcis, however, he wouldn't have been able to concentrate on what she was saying. The mix of emotions he had felt when watching the ceremony combined inside him with the nervousness and anticipation of the coming Congressus, and his head buzzed as his brain kept switching from thinking about the Arbor to what was going to happen next.

He wasn't the only one getting jumpy either. Even as Dulcis finished and the Militis gave a final chant, the noise in the Temple grew louder as everyone began talking at once, and there was general shifting in the seats. As the sound of the Quartus Campana rang through the Castellum, the Militis left the inner ring and headed down the central path towards the oak doors, and gradually everyone began to file out.

Chonrad waited until the crowd had died down, then made his way outside, Fulco following. The sun was now high in the sky, and he blinked as he came out into the Quad, the fresh air and the noise of the crowd a vivid contrast to the quietness and coolness of the Temple.

There was to be a short interval for lunch before the Congressus began. Heartwood had erected a special food tent for the visitors, and so he decided to make his way there to grab a snack before he went to the Curia. He walked along the central pathway, counting off the roads as he did so.

The Baillium was constructed in a similar fashion to the Temple, with roads in a series of concentric rings around the central Castellum. Buildings of all shapes and sizes filled the space in between.

To the rear, nearest to the steep backdrop of the mountains, were the workshops: the fullers, weavers, dyers and blacksmiths who made the clothing, weapons and armour for Heartwood, with the furnaces near to the river for cooling the metal.

Around the sides were the stables, chicken houses, cow and pig pens, the grain stores, the armoury, the offices for the steward who dealt with the business side of things, lodgings for the Exercitus when they were at home, and the two huge arenas where the Militis carried out their Exerceo, or daily weapons and riding practice.

At the front of the Baillium was the Curia meeting place on the south side, and also the Hospitalia, or visitors' lodgings. However these were nowhere near big enough to accommodate all the visitors present this weekend, and brightly coloured tents filled the grassed areas.

The place heaved with people. Chonrad picked his way carefully through the horse dung, turned at the second ring road and threaded through the tents on the south side of the complex to find the large one flying Heartwood's flag – a gold-coloured banner, emblazoned with a green oak leaf. The tent was huge, a scarlet monstrosity stretched between about a hundred tent poles, but already, through the pinned-up tent flaps, he could see it was busy.

At the entrance to the tent, a long table had been set up with trays of cold meats, loaves of bread, bowls of fruit and huge pitchers of ale. Leaning over, he grabbed a chicken leg and, leaving Fulco to fill up a plate several inches high with food, he ducked under the flap of the tent.

Inside, he looked around, recognising a lot of the faces. The other lords of Laxony were already there, as well as the High Lord, Hariman, busy tucking into what looked like a whole loaf of bread. Few Wulfengar were there, however. He recognised Grimbeald, Lord of the Highlands, the land furthest from the Wall, but none of the others were present, and Raedwulf, High Lord of Wulfengar, was conspicuous by his absence. Grimbeald looked decidedly uncomfortable there on his own, Chonrad thought with not a little amusement, the Wulfian was obviously regretting his decision to go there rather than to his own tent.

The four High Council members of Hanaire were all present, though, distinguishable by their height and their bright blond hair, clad in mail topped with the green tunic of Hanaire. The rest of the people present were all Militis, armoured and serious, the oak leaf tattoo clear on the outside of their left wrists.

Chonrad saw Procella talking to Valens, along with two heavyset male Militis that were so alike he knew they must be twins. They were both young knights, probably late twenties, he thought, and both had the same bright blue eyes and curly brown hair with an intriguing lock that fell into exactly the same place on their forehead. He walked over to join them, picking up a tankard of ale along the way.

II

Procella smiled as he came up. "Well, Lord Barle? Did you enjoy the ceremony?"

"Er, yes," Chonrad said, not about to admit his real thoughts to the Militis. "It was... interesting."

One of the twins nodded. "I have seen twenty-one Veriditas ceremonies now, and they never fail to move me."

Valens introduced the knights with a twinkle in his eye. "These are Gavius and Gravis, Custodes at Heartwood."

"Which is which?" asked Chonrad. He realised the jest had been planned when all four of them answered in unison, "It doesn't matter!"

"This is obviously a standing joke to tease visitors with," Chonrad said good-naturedly.

One of the twins shrugged. "Yes and no. Truly we sometimes think we were one person in the womb who was by some miracle of nature divided at birth."

"But, if you really want to know," said the other twin, "I'm Gravis, and I have the Heartwood tattoo on my left wrist."

"But mine is on my right," said Gavius. "It is the only way to tell us apart."

"Well, I am the stronger knight."

"And I have the better sense of humour," the other rejoined. Chonrad laughed as they walked off to get some food, bickering good-naturedly.

He looked around the room. "I see the men of Wulfengar have decided to dine alone," he said to Valens and Procella in a lower voice.

Valens shrugged. "As was expected. We did of course extend the invitation to all parties but we did not really think they would accept." He inclined his head towards Grimbeald. "Except for him."

"Why is he here?" Chonrad studied the Lord of the Highlands as he talked stiffly to one of the Militis. Grimbeald was short and thickset, with a full head of dark brown hair and a long, bushy beard to match. Chonrad knew the man was younger than himself, but thought the Wulfian looked much older. He was almost as wide as he was tall, in his armour, but in spite of being in a room where almost everyone was taller than him, he still radiated power.

"The Highlands have always been the most affable towards Laxony," said Procella.

"But he must realise it makes his own position vulnerable, dining with the 'enemy'," said Chonrad.

Valens shrugged. "From what I understand, there is not a lot in the Highlands apart from sheep and hills. I do not know that the other Lords of the Five are pounding on his door."

Chonrad's retort was cut short as a young woman Militis came up and touched Valens gently on the arm. "Valens? Dulcis says we should start heading for the Curia shortly."

"Of course." Valens indicated Chonrad. "Have you met the Lord Barle? Chonrad, this is Beata. She is one of the deans at Heartwood."

Chonrad was surprised, but polite enough to hide it as he shook her hand. She seemed very young to be a Dean. There were four at Heartwood, responsible for the general welfare of the Militis, a person to whom they could take their grievances and general day-to-day problems of living in a cloistered community.

Her handshake was firm, however, and as he looked at her face more closely, he saw fine lines around her eyes and mouth, and one or two grey hairs amongst the brown. Maybe she wasn't as young as he'd first suspected. She turned to talk to Procella, and he observed her strong profile with its slightly upturned nose, her full mouth and deep grey eyes. Did she know how beautiful she was? Probably not; the Militis were not raised to be interested in their physical appearance. However, she could have taken on any one of the powdered and rouged women at the court of Barle in a beauty pageant.

He hid a smile as he thought what she might say if he told her that. Dressed in full mail over a thick leather tunic, her light brown hair tied tightly at the nape of her neck, her appearance was clearly not the most important thing on her mind that day.

"Shall we go?" asked Valens.

Chonrad nodded, grabbing a buttered piece of bread from the table and munching on it as he followed Valens out of the tent. Fulco put his plate down hurriedly and followed him out, snatching up a piece of pork as he did so and continuing to eat as they walked. As they joined the main road, the Quintus

Campana rang, and all over Heartwood, people started heading
for the Curia.

The road to the Curia was lined with a series of poles decorated
with the flags of all the countries and lords visiting that day.
Chonrad joined the throng, finding himself next to Grimbeald at
one point, and he nodded a greeting to him. Grimbeald nodded
back, but didn't smile. The atmosphere seemed to be changing,
Chonrad thought. There had been an almost exultant feel in the
air during the Veriditas, and lunch had had a jovial informality
to it. Now, however, everyone's voices were hushed, and a
seriousness settled on the crowd like a heavy blanket. He looked
up at the sky, not surprised to see clouds moving over the face
of the sun, which had now passed its zenith. It looked like they
were in for a storm. He just hoped the thundery atmosphere
wasn't reflected inside the Curia.

The Curia was an interesting building, if you could call it that.
It consisted of a very large ring of oak trees whose branches
had grown over the centre and had knitted together to make a
roof. Because the oak trees had not yet budded and the roof was
presently just a mesh of bare branches, a canopy of cloth had
been erected in case of rain.

As in the Temple, a channel of water had been cut around
the inner edge of the oak trees. A removable floor made from
wooden boards slotted together had been erected over the grass
in the centre. On this twenty podiums had been placed, each
topped with a single flag.

This, then, thought Chonrad, was where the lords of the
Twelve Lands, the four lords of Hanaire, and presumably four
Militis, would stand. Heartwood clearly intended the Congressus
to be a small affair, and had sectioned off the areas outside the
ring of trees with large, colourful screens to stop the rest of their
visitors watching. Several stern Custodes stood at the entrance
to the Curia, and clearly they were only going to let the sixteen
leaders and Militis pass.

Chonrad was allowed to enter, although Fulco had to remain outside, much to his disgust, but Chonrad reassured him he would call if he was needed. After all, it wasn't fair for him to have a bodyguard and no one else. He walked through the oaks and across a steady plank that covered part of the water channel to the wooden floor, seeing the red Laxonian flag with his silver stag embroidered in the middle pinned above one of the podiums, and went over and stood behind it. The five Wulfengar lords were already there, faces ominously stony, and as he took his place, the last two Laxonian lords arrived to take theirs. The four Hanaire Council members came in together and each stood behind his or her banner. The Militis were the last to arrive, coming in at the end.

Valens, Dulcis, Procella, and one other male Militis Chonrad had not yet met came in and took the empty podiums that flew with the gold flags embroidered with the green oak leaf. He looked with interest at the knight whose name he didn't know – he had only one arm, the left cut off at the elbow, the loose sleeve of his tunic sewn up.

Several other Militis, include Beata and the twins, stationed themselves around the edge of the ring, presumably as a deterrent against any violence that might break out. He looked around him and saw he had been placed beside the lords of the two lands that stood either side of the Isenbard Wall: the Wulfengar Lord of the Lowlands, Leofric, and the Laxonian Lord of Hannon, Ogier. Heartwood was obviously hoping he would be able to intercede between the two should tempers rise.

Valens raised his hand. The room gradually fell quiet.

"Welcome," he said, his voice ringing out through the Curia. To Chonrad's surprise, he spoke in Laxonian. "I thank you all for taking the time to come to Heartwood for this Congressus, which we hope will bring peace to our lands. I know not all of you can speak Heartwood, so I have chosen to use the language of the majority of the lords present – that of Laxony."

He opened his mouth to carry on, but before he could go any further, one of the Wulfengar lords stepped forward from his podium across the other side of the circle from Chonrad. It was Bertwald, the same knight he had already had dealings with that morning. Chonrad assumed he was going to object to the use of his enemy's language, but instead he announced in a loud voice, "You might as well stop there, Imperator. For I will take no further part in these talks while these podiums are filled with *women*." He practically spat the last word.

He spoke in Wulfian, but Chonrad knew the language well enough to understand what he had said. He stared in disbelief as whispers and then shouts of indignation began to rise from around the Curia. He had known Bertwald was opposed to these talks, but he had not expected such an open and aggressive confrontation so early in the proceedings. He looked across at Procella, who stood next to the Wulfian lord's podium. Her eyes had narrowed and her right hand rested on the pommel of her sword, the Heartwood tattoo on her left clearly visible from across the room.

Valens stepped down slowly from his podium onto the centre of the wooden floor. He raised his hand to ask for quiet and voices quickly hushed those who were talking, so they could hear what the Heartwood leader had to say in return.

"Bertwald, Lord of the Flatlands, you knew before you came that women stand in Heartwood alongside the men." He did not mention the same was true in Laxony and Hanaire, although he looked pointedly around the circle, taking in the women who were present.

"I did not think they stood so close," said Bertwald, and his lips curved in a sneer.

III

Procella twitched, but Valens shot her a look and she stayed where she was. Her eyes, however, were like sharp knives aimed at the

Wulfengar knight. Chonrad wondered if the Wulfian knights had planned this together, but noticed the High Lord Raedwulf wore a frown. Had Bertwald taken the initiative without advice from the others?

Valens stood tall and imposing in the centre of the room, and Chonrad was reminded that the Imperator had led the Exercitus for many years, and was renowned as a skilled diplomat and mediator.

"Lord Bertwald," Valens said clearly. "In Heartwood we do not distinguish between men and women when we choose the Militis. Our knights are chosen for their skill in battle, for their bravery and their holy manner. Not their sex."

"Yes, yes," said Bertwald. "As if their pretty *pawes* were of no consequence at all."

His use of the Wulfian swearword for a woman's private parts was like a match put to the wick of a candle. Suddenly it seemed everyone moved at once.

Procella was on Bertwald before he even blinked. As she moved, Chonrad saw Leofric next to him put his hand on his sword and make as if to step down from his podium. Unsheathing his own sword with a sharp sing of steel, Chonrad covered the short distance between them in a heartbeat and flicked the blade around until the point rested on the soft hollow at the base of Leofric's throat. "Do not even think about it," he warned.

Once he was assured that Leofric had got his message, he looked around. The scuffle was pretty much over. Valens still stood in the centre of the floor, his face as thunderous as the rainclouds gathering overhead, but around him, everyone else had moved. A startled Grimbeald looked down the sharp end of a Militis sword, care of one of the twins – Chonrad couldn't see his tattoo and therefore wasn't sure which one, although, as he remembered, it didn't really matter. The Wulfengar Lord of the Flatlands, Kyneburg, had been sandwiched between two Hanaire Council members and they had moved in swiftly to disarm him, kicking his sword across the tiles. Raedwulf was facing the other Militis twin and also the Heartwood knight Chonrad had not yet been introduced to. Though they had not gone as far as disarming him, the two longswords at his throat made it clear what would happen if he should try to draw his own.

And Bertwald lay flat on his stomach on the floor with Procella's knee in his back and her small dagger pressed just under his ear lobe, pushing so hard on his skin a red line of blood had appeared. He was clearly struggling to escape her grip, but even as he did so, she tightened her hold on the arm she had twisted behind his back and he cried out in pain and stopped resisting. She leaned close to him and spoke softly, but Chonrad still heard her words: "You think to better this *pawes* in combat? Think again, *flantor*." A smile twitched on Chonrad's lips. Clearly the Wulfengar idiot was unable to best her in colloquial vocabulary, either.

"Enough!" Valens's voice boomed around the Curia. It coincided almost exactly with a roll of thunder, as if the very weather itself agreed with him. He flicked his hand at Procella, who pushed herself to her feet and then, burying a hand in Bertwald's mail, hauled him up by the neck.

Valens strode over to him. "People have travelled across Anguis for weeks to take part in this Congressus," he snapped. "You will not, I repeat – *not!* – ruin it within the first five minutes!"

Bertwald put a hand to his neck and, when it came away with blood, cast a murderous glance at Procella. Before he could speak, however, Raedwulf put out his hands and, resting them on the two swords in front of him, pushed them down so he could step forward. "Bertwald does not speak for all Wulfengar lords," he said clearly so all could hear him. "We have many problems to solve today, and making peace is going to be difficult. But not impossible. We do wish to talk about it."

He looked at Bertwald. "I warned you of this before we came. Your position in the Flatlands has long been tenuous, but I have overlooked your regular incursions into the Plains, your repeated raids on my land, because I did not want to fight a civil war as well as a national one. But now you have gone too far." He nodded to Procella. "You have my permission to take him and place him under arrest in the Porta. When we leave I will take him back with me, and he will be dealt with according to the law of Wulfengar." He did not say what this would mean for Bertwald, but looking at the latter's face, Chonrad thought it unlikely that it involved riches and a castle on the coast.

Procella looked at Valens, who nodded. She grabbed Bertwald's arm ready to march him to the doors. He spun on her and declared angrily, "Don't touch me, *pawes*!"

Wincing, Valens brought his hand up to massage his forehead and Chonrad rolled his eyes as Procella's arm drew back and her fist met Bertwald's chin with a resounding clunk. The Wulfengar outcast fell heavily to the floor and lay there unmoving.

Shaking her hand, the knuckles now bright red, Procella beckoned to the two Custodes who were standing guard at the doorway. They came over and picked up the limp body, carrying him out of the Curia.

Procella's eye caught Chonrad's as she made her way back to her podium. He didn't dare smile, but he saw her lips twitch briefly, and knew she had recognised his admiration.

Everyone went back to their own podiums. Valens, his hands behind his back, his face serious, waited for the voices to die down. Then he began again.

"Where was I…?" he said wryly. "Oh, yes. As I was saying… Welcome to you all. We have asked you to come to Heartwood today to take part in a discussion about resources, and the movement of those resources throughout the lands.

"As you all know, there has been a steady decline over the past few years in the quality of the harvests, due to several unfortunate, unforeseeable issues – mainly bad weather, with too much rain in The Shining, and The Sleep hit exceptionally hard. This has combined with a widespread crop disease that has eradicated almost half of Laxonian wheat yields. There has also been a deadly cow sickness, which has taken a good quarter of our cows in all corners of the lands. Food, my friends, is in short supply, and we can only envisage it growing rarer."

One of the Hanaire Council members spoke up. "We need better lines of communication," he stated. "If we do not know this is happening, we cannot address the problem."

"That is not the main issue here," said Raedwulf. "The issue is there is just not enough food to go round. There is little we can do about that."

The High King of Laxony, Hariman, frowned and said: "There is always something we can do. There are always those who have more and others who have less. It is a Question of evening out the provisions so they are more equally distributed."

Before Raedwulf could give an angry retort, Valens stated, "Part of the problem is the continuing aggression between the Twelve Lands. While there is war, trade and travel can only occur at a minimum, which means the grain from Laxony and the meat from Wulfengar are not exchanging hands. That is why we have to talk peace."

"We are not at war," said Raedwulf.

"Are we not?" Hariman's gaze was challenging.

Raedwulf stared at him, then looked back at Valens. "We are not at war," he repeated, "but I can see how it might look that way. The repeated taking of our trade vessels in Laxonian waters…"

"…by pirate vessels," Hariman stated.

"So you say," snapped Raedwulf. "But what proof do we have you are not keeping the spoils?"

"What proof do you have that we are?"

Raedwulf glowered. "If piracy is rife off the Laxonian coast, why have you done nothing about it?"

"We have! We have increased the manning in our shore forts, and we have doubled the Coastal Watch, but we have a very long coastline and cannot cover every inch of every beach in Laxony all the time." Hariman was clearly exasperated. "We have spies operating in the coastal towns, trying to find out where the smugglers are working from, but so far the people are keeping quiet. And our navy is not strong like yours; we do not have your ship-building skills."

"That is because you can but stretch your legs and walk from Laxony to the mainland," said Raedwulf enviously, clearly not believing the Laxonian High Lord.

Hariman threw his hands up in defeat and looked to Valens, his face expressing his frustration.

Valens held up a hand. "Perhaps we could talk later about measures that can be adopted by both countries to solve this problem. But for now I would like to continue to address the problem of the poor."

Raedwulf gripped the sides of his podium with both hands. Chonrad frowned. The Wulfengar leader looked grim, as if he were about to tell Valens that someone close to him had died.

IV

"We have no more food to go around, Valens. Our stores are depleted – our stock is virtually nil! We have nothing left to share. And therefore..." he paused slightly, whether for effect or whether because he genuinely didn't want to continue, Chonrad didn't know. "We are going to have to cease the Charitas."

There was a collective gasp from around the Curia. Valens went rigid. Chonrad's heart sank.

Everyone throughout the Twelve Lands and Hanaire who owned land was instructed to give a tenth of what they made to Heartwood and its temples throughout Anguis. This was the law, but it was also more than that; it was recognition by all to the service that the Militis carried out for them with the Arbor. Heartwood itself had no land outside its walls; it owned some milk cows and goats, pigs and chickens, but not enough to feed the whole of the Militis, and there was nowhere inside the Baillium to grow grain. Luckily the majority of their wheat came from Laxony, but Chonrad knew they would sorely miss the sacks of oats and barley, and the barrels of fish Wulfengar wagons brought to them with each new Moon.

Hariman's face was aghast. "You cannot do that. It is the law."

Raedwulf had grown pale, but his mouth was firm as he said: "This decision has not been taken lightly. And it need not be a permanent one. But we must look to our own first."

Valens began arguing with him, the two of them coming down from their podiums to face each other across the floor as the first drops of rain began to fall on the cloth roof. Most people's attention was fixed on them, everyone realising this decision by Raedwulf marked a new low in the relationships between Laxony, Wulfengar and Heartwood.

However, Chonrad's attention was suddenly distracted by Procella. She wasn't watching the rapidly escalating argument that was ensuing. She was watching the ring of water around the edge of the floor and frowning. What was she staring at during this crucial moment? Chonrad's eyes flicked back to Valens impatiently, but he couldn't help looking back at where she stood transfixed at her podium.

Suddenly she looked up, and to his surprise she stared straight at him. "The water," she mouthed, pointing at the ring.

He looked behind him into the channel.

The water, which usually moved slowly, its surface with barely a ripple, was bubbling.

Looking closer, he could see shadowy shapes under the surface, the same as he had seen earlier, only this time there were more, crowded together. Was it just the reflection of the people in the Curia? But immediately he knew that wasn't the case. Apprehension rose inside him.

Turning, he saw Procella leaving her podium and, one eye on the channel, moving down towards Valens. So far the Imperator hadn't seen her; he was almost shouting at Raedwulf now, the two of them standing so close you couldn't walk between them.

"Valens," she said cautiously, backing towards him. He ignored her, continuing to shout at the Wulfengar High Lord.

"Valens," she said more urgently. Around the Curia, other people had started to notice the movement in the water and voices began to rise.

"Valens!" she yelled. With one fluid movement, she drew her longsword. Chonrad sucked the breath in between his teeth – it was not a good move in a place where tempers were escalating and the Wulfengar lords flinched as she drew her weapon, sensing they had been betrayed.

But even as he wondered at her action, he saw what she had seen, and his hand quickly went to his own sword. He slid the steel blade out of the scabbard, yelling, "Raid! Raid!"

If he had not seen it with his own eyes, he would not have believed it. Out of the water, figures were rising, huge figures, taller and broader than any he had seen in his life, and Chonrad was not small for a Laxonian. Yells echoed around the Curia as everyone finally realised what had caught Procella's eye in the first place, and he heard rather than saw the singing of steel as all weapons were drawn.

He stared at the warrior in front of him as he stepped out of the water onto the floor of the Curia. Towering over him, the warrior's skin was green as grass in sunlight, although his hair was darker, the colour of a forest river, where it curled beneath the bottom of his helmet. This looked as if it were made of gold, although that metal was too soft for such a piece of armour.

His arms were bare, but his chest was covered with a huge breastplate made from, it seemed, tiny shells interlinked with thread, and underneath he wore a short tunic made from some sort of thick cloth. His legs and feet were bare, but the size of his thigh and calf muscles made Chonrad blink.

The warrior came forward quickly, and Chonrad had no time to think. On the defensive immediately, he raised his sword to counter the other's slicing cut across his body, the steel blades meeting with an ear-piercing ring. Up close, the warrior's eyes shone through the visor like two glowing green jewels. Through the helmet he heard the warrior say something angrily, but he couldn't understand the words and he grunted in reply, using all his weight to throw the warrior back. With his left hand he quickly reached up and pulled his mail hood over his head. He was immediately glad he had done so; the warrior's next parry glanced off his own upraised sword and struck the top of his left shoulder, jarring the bone, but failing to break through.

Combat was rarely won on the defensive, and Chonrad knew he had to step up his game. All around him he could hear the sounds of battle, and briefly wondered if any had fallen, but there was no time to dwell on the matter, for the warrior was coming for him again. This time, however, he planted his feet firmly and was the first to swing, a right-handed thrust at the warrior's left side. It was parried neatly, but Chonrad followed it with a quick swing to his left, and the blade cut into the warrior's upper arm, sinking deep into the flesh. Chonrad waiting for the howl of pain, but to his amazement none came; the warrior pulled himself back so the blade sliced free, and looked down with what Chonrad could only call interest as thick, dark, green-blue blood oozed out of the wound.

Deep inside, a small sliver of fear embedded itself in his stomach. He thrust at the warrior's chest, but the sword glanced off the hard shell breastplate. He could find no weak spot in the warrior's torso, but his uncovered arms and legs were an obvious target. Flipping his opponent's weapon to one side using the hilt as a lever, he swung the blade round and up, and with all his strength brought it across his body. This time the steel did more than sink into the warrior's flesh; it severed the arm just above the elbow joint, the limb falling to the floor with the sword still clutched tightly in its hand.

The warrior looked at his side, seemingly confused. Chonrad steadied himself, then aimed his blade at the gap between his enemy's breastplate and arm socket, and thrust it in. The blade went in deep, almost up to the hilt. The warrior screeched and shuddered. Then Chonrad watched in shock as the body *melted* – it just dissolved into water, falling in a pool at his feet.

It was only as he looked down that he realised what he had not noticed before: the water level had risen from above the top of the channel to cover the whole floor of the Curia, and he was currently ankle-deep. He turned to cast a quick glance over the scene, his first real look at the battle since it had started. Procella was right in the middle and was clearly in control; feet planted firmly, she swung her blade at the warrior in front of her, and was in no immediate danger. Protecting her back was Valens, and the mighty Imperator also looked dangerous in spite of his war wound. A fierce grimace on his face, he lopped off the head of one of the water warriors even as Chonrad watched, the warrior's head – its helmet still intact – rolling on the floor before it, too, dissolved into the water sloshing around their ankles.

The twins battled it out fiercely to one side, and just in front of him stood Beata, her mail hood still in folds around her neck, her beautiful face flushed and strands of hair sticking to her damp forehead as she thrust and parried. The warrior with one arm was fighting admirably, wielding his sword with practised ease.

Some of the Laxonian lords were visible, but he could not see Hariman, and he wondered if he had fallen. Raedwulf still stood, as did Grimbeald, the Wulfengar lord putting up an excellent fight in spite of his short stature. There were other figures on the floor though, their faces beneath the water, and it was too early to tell whether they were winning or losing the fight.

Briefly, he wondered where Fulco was. Surely if his bodyguard had heard the sounds of battle, he would have come running. Were these water warriors also outside in the Baillium?

It was then he saw Dulcis off to one side of the Curia, defending herself valiantly against a huge warrior, his enormous frame towering over her as he slashed down continuously with his mighty sword. Chonrad ran over to her, but he was too late – even as he leapt onto her podium, the warrior lifted his arms back and, with a two-handed blow, slid the tip of the sword into her stomach. She wore only light armour, and the point of the weapon passed easily through the padded tunic and into her body. The warrior pushed until her body touched the hilt and then, with a final and probably unnecessary move, twisted the blade before pulling it out.

Dulcis fell to her knees, her face white, and stared blankly at Chonrad as he ran towards her, only just managing to catch her as she fell to the floor.

V

His battle fury now truly engaged, Chonrad let out a blood-curdling yell before swinging his sword at Dulcis's executor. The warrior had barely enough time to turn round before Chonrad rained down blows upon his body. In spite of the fact that he was several inches taller than Chonrad and a good deal heavier, Chonrad managed to push him back until the warrior tripped on Dulcis's fallen body and toppled backwards, landing with a splash in the water. Chonrad knelt on top of him and, rage giving him extra strength, forced the blade down through the gap above the warrior's mail and below his helmet into the soft flesh below. The warrior shuddered, went rigid and then, with the same strange gurgling scream deep inside him, melted into the water.

Chonrad stood, soaked now from the waist down, but furious and ready to kill. Sword swinging, he went into the fray, knocking aside blades and warriors alike as he sliced a path through the battling bodies.

The water seemed to be coming in waves now, the strength of the liquid making him struggle to keep his feet. However, as in all the battles he had fought in, he became aware of a sense of victory even before it became clear they had won. The number of huge green warriors seemed to be diminishing, and a renewed sense of energy swept through him as the people fighting beside him pushed the enemy back towards the channel of water at the edge. To one side he could see out of the corner of his eye Procella, Valens and one of the twins battling valiantly, and to the other side Grimbeald, a couple of Militis and a Hanaire lord, all sensing the warriors were in decline.

Eventually there were only half a dozen of the water warriors left. They hurriedly exchanged words as they scanned the room and realised their reduced numbers. They seemed to be pressing for a withdrawal. Together they all jumped in, melting into the water before Chonrad's eyes. Within seconds, they were gone.

The Militis, Laxonians, Wulfians and Hanaireans who were still standing watched as the waters around them began to recede, the water withdrawing into the channel, although the floor was flat and there was no obvious gradient to cause the water to flow back. Within about a minute, the floor was clear, and the river channel flowed merrily along in its usual manner.

"Roots of the Arbor," swore one of the twins, his voice loud in the sudden silence that had fallen on the Curia. "What in the name of Animus were they?"

Chonrad gradually lowered his sword to the ground. Everyone did the same, turning to view the floor of the Curia and see what damage had been done.

Immediately, Procella saw Dulcis and, with a cry, ran over to her and knelt by her side. Chonrad walked over to them. "I am sorry," he said. "I saw her go down but I could not get there in time."

Procella bent her head over the Abbatis, and he thought she was crying, but when she lifted her face he saw that anger and not grief was her emotion. Slowly she pushed herself to her feet. Marching into the centre of the circle, she sheathed her sword as she looked about, counting the dead. Chonrad joined her.

Hariman had fallen, as he had feared, and two other Laxonian lords had not survived. Wulfengar had fared little better. Raedwulf, though not yet dead, had received a deep wound to his stomach, and from experience Chonrad knew he would not last the night. Kyneburg and Leofric lay where they had been killed. Only Grimbeald still stood, blood running freely down his face from a cut he had received on his temple.

Of the Militis, Chonrad spotted four knights on the floor. Apart from Dulcis, none were known to him. The twins and Beata were still on their feet, and so were half a dozen others, although several were wounded.

"Has anybody got even the faintest idea what just happened?" asked Valens, looking at the survivors, his hands on his hips. No answers were forthcoming. Eventually he held up his hands in defeat. "We can debate the whys and wherefores of this later – for now we must assess the damage and stop it happening again."

"We should close the culvert outside the walls," said Procella, "stop the flow of water into the Baillium for now. And we should raise the drawbridge – if it has not been done already. That way they will have to attack Heartwood the old way – by siege."

"Good," said Valens. He walked over to the entrance and pushed aside the screens. Chonrad saw the look on his face before he saw the view outside. It was enough to make him run over to look out at the scene.

The rest of the Baillium looked as if a tidal wave had hit it. Tents had been flattened, buildings were in ruins, horses lay dead where they had drowned, and there were bodies all over the place. Rain continued to hammer down on the scene, washing it in a dull grey light.

The rest of those still standing in the Curia joined Valens at the door. They looked out at the detritus, frozen for a moment in shock. Chonrad stared at a limping figure coming towards them and recognised Fulco. He ran towards him, and the two knights clasped hands. "I am glad you are safe," Chonrad said.

Fulco signed something and Chonrad chuckled.

"What did he say?" asked Procella.

"I cannot repeat it here," Chonrad said wryly. "Let us just say it involved a swear word or two."

The knights around him laughed, clearly as relieved as he was that they were alive. Their laughter died away, however, as they continued to survey the scene, seeing the number of people dead or injured. "Why?" Chonrad found himself saying, his brow furrowed as he thought of how devastating the attack had been. "Why did they do it?"

And then, suddenly, Procella jumped as if she had been struck by lightning. "The Arbor!" she shrieked and, before anyone could stop her, she leapt over the dead bodies lying nearest the Curia and sprinted down the road towards the Castellum.

Chonrad was just the beat of a pulse behind her. In the pouring rain they ran to the central road and then turned towards the Temple. His heart thudded, and it was not just from the exertion of the run. Could it have been the Arbor the warriors were after?

Behind him he could hear the pounding of feet as everyone followed, but he and Procella were way ahead. Debris littered the road, bits of tent pole and food and animals and dead people, but there was no time to stop and assess the situation. Together they raced towards the Castellum, and part of him wanted to get there, and part of him didn't.

The rain soon soaked him, but he paid little heed to the wetness on his face, welcoming the coolness. His worst fears were realised, however, as they neared the building and saw the oak doors were open, the entrance encumbered by the bodies of the two dead Custodes who usually guarded the doors. Procella didn't stop, however; she leapt over the fallen knights and Chonrad followed, entering the darkness of the Temple.

He almost ran into her, and Fulco into him, neither realising the one in front had stopped. "What..." he began, his voice faltering as he took in the scene before him.

The place was littered with dead and wounded Militis. He heard Procella's intake of breath as she looked around the room, taking in the number of fallen knights. Heartwood knights prided themselves on their military prowess, and they were a strong and fearless bunch. How many of the water warriors had attacked the Temple to cause such damage?

The waters had obviously risen in here too, because the wooden tiers had been damaged in places, and broken beams littered the floor. Their attention, however, was soon drawn to the tree that stood in the centre of the rings.

Procella walked forward, stopped, then walked forward again. Chonrad followed her slowly. He could not believe what his eyes were seeing.

The Arbor was split in half.

A dozen swords had hacked at the top of the trunk, severing some of the branches and carving a great gouge in the bark so they could get the blades in even deeper. He dreaded to think about the strength of the warriors who had caused such damage. Their continued carving had resulted in the trunk being divided almost to the ground.

Procella stopped and fell to her knees. Suddenly he realised who lay on the floor – it was Silva, and miraculously she was still alive. She was covered in blood though, and he guessed the water warriors had probably left her for dead not realising that in fact some small amount of lifeforce still existed inside her.

Procella cradled Silva's head, brushing back some of the black hair. The disturbing golden eyes flickered and she looked up at the knight crouching over her. "I am sorry," she said in a husky voice.

Procella half-laughed, half-cried as she said: "What do you have to be sorry about?"

"I let them take it," said Silva. She turned her head and spat blood onto the floor before continuing. "I could not stop them. I let them take it, I am sorry."

"Take what?" Chonrad asked, dropping to his knees beside her.

"The Pectoris." Silva dissolved into tears. "The heart of the Arbor is gone!"

Chonrad's eyes met Procella's. Together they looked up at the old oak tree. Its heart taken, the Arbor sagged sadly.

But that wasn't the worst thing of all somehow, in Chonrad's mind.

The worst thing was that the Arbor's leaves were starting to fall.

CHAPTER THREE

I

Nitesco came to his senses slowly, as if he were swimming to the surface from the bottom of a deep pond. He lay on his front, his cheek against the cold stone floor. Slowly, he lifted his head. It pounded as if someone were hitting him repeatedly with a hammer, and when he lifted his hand to touch his brow, it came away scarlet.

Carefully, he pushed himself to a sitting position. Beneath his mail, his padded tunic was soaked, and he shivered with the cold as a cool evening breeze swept through the gap in the Temple wall.

Gap? Nitesco did a double take as he stared at the wooden screen separating the Temple from the Domus. There was a huge hole in the middle. No wonder he could feel a draught.

He looked around, the fog of confusion clouding his thoughts. He sat on the flagstones of the path that ran around the centre Claustrum, the rectangle of grass inside the Domus. Debris littered the normally neat and tended lawn: bits and pieces of wood, occasional chunks of stone, and other items of furniture and personal belongings of the Militis. The lawn itself had been flattened and rent with great furrows from one end to the other, as if it had been clawed with giant fingers.

What had happened here? His brain felt slow and stupid. He had gone to the Veriditas and watched the ceremony, and then when the others had withdrawn for the Congressus, he and Caecus had gone back to the Armorium to continue the cataloguing of the library that they were about halfway through.

Caecus!

It all came back to him in a rush, as if the floodgates of his memory had been opened.

He stumbled through the archway of the covered arcade onto the outer path, tripped over a piece of wood, and fell heavily into the sodden grass, splashing and coughing. The last thing he remembered was a huge green figure standing above him, sword paused ready for the kill, his emerald eyes glowing like green fire from inside the visor of his golden helmet.

And yet, Nitesco puzzled, he wasn't dead. What had happened? He touched the wound on his head again. There was slight swelling and some residual blood, but it wasn't a sword cut, and had probably been caused, he thought, by bumping it on the stones. He looked around the place again, suddenly wary of being attacked, but it was definitely empty of both green warriors and Militis, and there were no shouts or sounds of clashing metal. Although the ground and his clothes were damp, the water had receded and the channel was tinkling away merrily as usual.

His head spun and it took him a moment to steady himself. Then, carefully, he walked into the Armorium.

He felt ashamed to admit he wasn't sure what upset him the most: the sight of Caecus lying on the floor, his mangled body spilled across the flagstones, or the fact that the library had been almost completely destroyed. He stood in the doorway, his stomach knotting as he took in the scene before him.

Most of the wooden bookshelves around the room had collapsed from the force of the water. Their contents had fallen onto the floor and, after being soaked and then dashed against the stone walls, they now formed a large heap of sodden parchment, much of the writing indistinguishable, the beautiful calligraphy – copied down patiently over years by previous Libraris – blurred and smeared into obscurity.

Hot tears poured down his face. He went over to the crumpled body lying in the middle of the floor and knelt beside it. His stomach churned as his eyes passed quickly over the split abdomen, the innards torn and bloated by water and debris. Caecus's nearly-blind eyes were open, the distorted left pupil somehow grotesque in the failing light, and so Nitesco closed the lids gently with his fingertips, breathing a sigh of relief as he did so.

He stood, intending to pick up the body and carry it out to the Arbor, where the tree would welcome the old Militis and swallow his energy, but even as he bent to slide an arm under Caecus's neck, he paused, something catching his eye.

He frowned, squinting at the dark shape on the floor, on the opposite side of the room furthest from the door. What was that? Usually a heavy wooden chest resided there, and had done, he thought, since he had first come to Heartwood. The chest was still there, but it had been lifted by the force of the water and moved a few feet to one side, and now sat askew.

He lay Caecus's head back down gently and stood. The sun had set and it was growing dark in the Claustrum, and he needed light. Where was he to find dry tinder after the flood? But then he saw that by chance the top shelf above where he had been working earlier that afternoon was still intact, and a lamp and tinder box sat upon it. Reaching for the lamp, he quickly lit the wick of the candle. With a shaking hand, he moved cautiously over to the back of the room, stepping over the bent and soggy books and scraps of wood.

It was a hole. Nitesco stared at it, mouth open. The chest had covered part of the paving that Caecus had once speculated had been part of the old Temple destroyed by the Great Quake, as they knew Oculus had built the new Temple on the foundations of the old. The paving had cracked under the weight of either the water or other debris, and it had broken in the middle.

Nitesco bent down next to it and carefully removed the bit of stone sticking up and some of the other pieces of rubble. Instead of an earthen floor beneath, a set of stone steps led downwards into the darkness.

His mouth went dry, and he wet his lips nervously, looking over his shoulder at the darkened doorway. He really should go and get help; it would be ridiculous to go down there on his own. Anything could be down there – animals, even more of those warriors, or, more likely, the steps could be dangerous, and he might slip and fall.

But even though all these thoughts flickered through his mind like the flame that danced at the top of the candle, and even though courage was not one of his best features, Nitesco's heart pounded. He knew, of course, of the stories about documents and other treasures that had been hidden when the old Temple fell. And the thought of marvellous historical mysteries being secreted down there was just too great for his scholarly mind to ignore.

Quickly, he walked back outside and found his sword lying where he had left it, pinned under his body when he fell. Sheathing the blade and holding the light out in front of him, he moved to the edge of the steps and started to descend.

II

Procella seemed unable to move. Chonrad watched her for a while from the shadows, where he sat on a piece of broken bench that had floated against the wall. Fulco cleaned his sword quietly beside him. The others had followed them into the Temple, and most of them stood around the edge of the Arbor now, mouths open in shock, their faces filled with defeat and hopelessness.

Procella's face was composed but pale, and her cheeks were wet, although she did not seem to make any effort to cry; large tears just slid down her face, and he supposed that, soaked from the sweat of battle, the splashing around in the rising waters and the heavy rain, she didn't even notice them.

She had fought valiantly in the battle, and he was full of admiration for the way she handled a sword – better than any other knight he had ever seen, he thought, bar maybe Valens on a good day. She was obviously fearless, courageous, aggressive, commanding and skilled, a true knight, and yet now she seemed lost, like a child at a fair who can't find her mother and, after searching the crowd, decides there is no hope of her being found, and sits forlornly on the floor in despair.

He wanted to understand what she was feeling, but he had had a very different upbringing to hers. And the way he had been rejected at the Allectus had definitely had an impact on his religious views as an adult.

For Chonrad, religion was for other people: for the Militis who served Heartwood; for the scholars who made a living out of debating Animus and the Arbor in the universities; and for the local priests who taught Oculus's *Theories* in the village temples and carried out rituals to comfort the people.

But underlying his basic belief was the resentment that he had grown up with that Heartwood had, basically, rejected him. And that had mentally made him keep his distance from his religion. It was something he wore, like the traditional wooden oak leaf symbol around his neck that could be discarded conveniently and hung around the bedpost when he tired of it.

The same was obviously not true for Procella. She seemed crushed, shattered, as if the sword that had split the tree had also carved through her heart. Religion was a completely different thing to her, he realised; it was as much a part of her as her physical body; it grew within her as mistletoe does within an apple tree, like a parasite, consuming its host, and sometimes killing it.

He wondered what it must be like to have your faith be so big a part of your life it influenced everything you said, everything you did. For the first time, he began to understand the passion behind the work of the Exercitus, and the reasons they had called the Congressus to discuss the failing of the land.

It was almost completely dark in the Temple now, and although there were some quiet murmurings among the visitors, the Militis seemed fixated on the mutilated tree, as if its defacement had somehow sapped their energy. Someone needed to take charge, and at the moment both Valens and Procella were unable to do it.

Chonrad stood and cleared his throat, which sounded very loud in the silence of the room. Faces turned towards him, and he waited until he had their attention before he began.

"My friends," he said, holding out his hands towards them, "this is a terrible time and I beg your forgiveness for interrupting you in your time of grief. But we have much to do and it is nearly dark. We do not know if the water warriors are planning to return, and therefore I think we need to make some preparations before we lose the last threads of light.

"I suggest we form three working parties; Procella, your first aim must be to cut off the river channel at its source and stop the water flowing through Heartwood. Secondly, you must organise a review of the fortifications – are there any weaknesses in the walls; has the Porta withstood the floods? Gather together as many Custodes as you can find and apportion them as you see fit. We must protect ourselves against another attack."

The Dux stood as he spoke and wiped her face clear of tears. She was still pale, but he could see she was grateful someone had taken charge, and she was relieved to have something to do. She nodded, and he turned his attention to Valens.

"I suggest, Imperator, you co-ordinate the gathering of those visitors who have made it through the attack. We need to organise the remaining lords and the closest followers of those who have died for a discussion on what has happened and what has to be done. You need to find a suitable venue and get it cleared and ready for the meeting, by sun-up, if possible."

Valens nodded, taking a deep breath and releasing it slowly. He, too, looked relieved at having a task to which he could turn his attention.

Chonrad turned to the Militis twins, who had been listening and talking amongst themselves at the end of the circle. "The third group has the least enjoyable task, I am afraid," he said, seeing by their faces they knew what was coming. "The dead must be collected and brought here, to the Sepulchrum." He pointed to the large area in front of the Arbor. "The wounded must also be brought together. I suggest maybe in the Hospitium rather than the Infirmaria as there will be more room, and we need to find people with knowledge of herbs and medicines to tend their wounds."

"I can do that," said the female Hanairean High Council member who had been at the Congressus. "I have knowledge of healing."

Chonrad nodded, glad to see everyone pulling together. He had feared the other countries would immediately withdraw to their own lands and leave Heartwood shattered and torn, unable to defend itself against future attacks.

Procella looked at the huge hole in the screen separating the Temple from the Domus. "The Domus needs to be searched," she said hoarsely. "I have not yet been in there, I do not know who... what..."

"I can do that," said Chonrad, "if I am permitted to enter."

Valens smiled wryly. "I think restricted access is the last thing we need to worry about at the moment." He came over and clasped Chonrad's hand. "And anyway, if there is anyone who should have been a Militis and was not, it is you, Chonrad. I know that probably does not mean much to you after Heartwood turned you away, but Dulcis admitted to me on several occasions she wished her predecessor had not done so."

Chonrad smiled. "That is good praise from a knight such as yourself and I thank you for your words."

· Beside them, the Militis that Chonrad had not yet met, the knight with one arm who had been present at the podiums in the Curia, stepped forward. "I will help search the Domus if you wish," he said, in his low, gruff voice.

"This is Dolosus," said Valens, "One of the Deans of Heartwood."

Chonrad shook the knight's remaining hand. He was heavyset and dark-haired, and probably from Wulfengar originally, Chonrad thought. He had eyes so dark brown they were almost black, making him look as if he had no pupils. "I will be glad of your help." Chonrad stifled his wariness. This was not the time to worry about personal opinions.

Beata came up to him. "I will help too," she offered. She had a cut on her cheek and the top of her undyed padded tunic was dark with blood, but the bleeding appeared to have stopped and apart from this she looked fresh and determined.

"The first thing we need is light," said Chonrad. "Where can we get dry lamps?"

"The cupboards at the sides are where we store the candles," said Beata.

They walked over to them, picking their way amongst the rubble. One cupboard was completely destroyed. The doors hung on their hinges and the shelves inside had collapsed, throwing the candles into the water. Chonrad's heart sank as he saw the other cupboard in much the same condition, but when he pulled open a sagging door the very top shelf was still intact. He lifted down the contents. There were six glass lanterns – two had some of the panes broken, but were usable, and there were about a dozen candles.

"That will have to do." Chonrad took down the tinder box. He struck the flint against the steel, igniting the small pile of straw inside, and then lit six of the candles from the resulting flame. Beata placed the candles inside the lanterns and closed the doors.

"Right," said Chonrad, "let us get to work."

Valens, Procella and the twins began to call people to them to ask them to help out in their tasks. Meanwhile, Chonrad, Dolosus and Beata, and Fulco, who had insisted on coming, made their way around the back of the Arbor ring. It was not easy going: the damage here was more extensive as this was where the diverted Flumen channel had run, and rubbish was piled up on either side. Slowly they heaped the broken wooden boards, bits of glass, kneeling cushions, candles, prayer books and other detritus to one side of the Temple, leaving the path to the doorway through to the Domus clear.

As yet, there had been no sounds from inside the Domus. Chonrad drew his sword before placing his hand on the door handle and pushing it open.

He looked around him. He was in a wide corridor made of wood, and when he looked up he could see the walls of both sides of the corridor had been smashed through, as if something heavy had been thrown against them. Directly in front of him was another door, closed. To his right the corridor ran down to another doorway at the far end. To his left, the corridor ended in a flight of steps curving upwards to the first floor of the building.

"Those are the night stairs," Beata whispered. "They lead up to the Dormitory and the Infirmaria, and we use them for the Night Service. I'll go up there, if you like."

"Do you want the lantern?"

She shook her head. "I know the steps by heart." She unsheathed her sword before walking to the bottom of the stairs. Silently, she began to climb.

He turned to Dolosus. "You should lead the way," he murmured; "you know this place better than I."

Dolosus nodded, unsheathed his own sword, stepped across the corridor and opened the door. Slowly, Chonrad and Fulco followed him through.

III

Beata made her way quietly up the night stairs, staying close to the wall as she climbed. It was completely black in the stairwell, but her feet had trodden the stairs in darkness every night for twenty-two years since she had arrived at Heartwood, and she knew each individual step, each crumbling edge and bump in the stone. Her breathing sounded loud in the silence, and she paused several times, sure someone was waiting in front of her. But her passage upwards remained unchallenged, and slowly she climbed to the top of the stairs.

When she got there, the oak door at the top was open, which was very unusual as the cold draught from the stairs made the dormitory cold and all the Militis were instructed from the time they arrived at Heartwood to keep it closed.

She sank into a crouch and waited, her eyes searching the darkness.

Beata was not easily shocked or frightened, and it was her calmness during moments of crisis and her unfailing commonsense that had led to her becoming Dean at the age of twenty-one. But it had been clear to Dulcis that Beata was a natural spiritual leader from a very early age. She had an inborn talent of being able to calm people and worked well with her companions both old and young.

However, in spite of her renowned unflappability, Beata had to admit to being nervous. The hilt of her sword felt clammy in her hands. She wiped them on her breeches before gripping the hilt tightly once again.

It couldn't be the darkness that was unsettling her, she thought. For one thing, the Lamb Moon was high in the sky and the Dormitory – though not brightly lit – glowed with a subtle light; and for another thing, she was used to moving around the Castellum at night. She had been used to years of groping around in the stairwells, finding the stairs with her feet.

No, it was something else... Something indefinable... Was it her just her imagination playing tricks on her, making her think there was something waiting for her in the shadows? Or were her instincts right?

The first floor dormitories consisted of a linked chain of almost circular chambers that formed the lobes of the leaf shape of the Castellum. She had to move through one room to get to the next. She looked around the beds of the first room, wondering if any Militis had been there when the water warriors arrived. The

Custodes, who worked in shifts, slept in the Barracks outside the Castellum; it was mainly the Militis who carried out duties inside the Temple and who held positions in the Domus that slept there. They would have been at the Veriditas, and would probably have gone about their daily business afterwards and not gone up to the Dormitory.

She made her way through to the next room. The bottom edge of the oak leaf was the Infirmaria. There would have been several Militis there. She wondered what had happened to Otium, the Medica, in charge of those too old or unwell to work. A fierce, buxom knight, Otium would have brooked no nonsense and would have defended her patients to the death.

The rooms definitely seemed to be empty. Consisting mainly of beds with the occasional table and chest for clothing, there were no figures, live or otherwise, and no signs of water or battle. At the end, the door to the Infirmaria also lay open. She slid up to the frame, avoiding the patch of moonlight that had spilled across the flagstones.

She peered around the doorway and couldn't stop the gasp that issued from her lips. The first thing that struck her was the blood – it seemed to have been sprayed around the room, over the walls, the beds, the floor; it pooled on the flagstones and had soaked into the bedding. In the bleached light of the Lamb Moon, the room was drained of colour and the blood was like thick black mud. Hardly breathing, she looked at the figures slumped around the room, bits of limbs and piles of innards and bodily fluids. Bile rose in her throat. This was different to the relatively straightforward battle that had occurred in the Curia. This was a *slaughter*.

Then, in the corner, she saw Otium propped up against the wall, her hand pressed tightly to her side, her chest rising and falling rapidly. Beata ran over to her and knelt down in front of her. The Medica's eyes were closed, but when Beata whispered her name they flew open in fear.

"It is only me," said Beata.

Otium stared at her and blinked. She struggled to focus, but eventually she recognised the Dean. "Beata!" Her eyes filled with tears. "Oh, thank the Arbor it is you!"

Beata knew better than to ask what had happened or bring attention to the pile of gore around her. She had to get Otium out of there, and fast. "Come on," she whispered, "you have to get to your feet."

"I cannot..." moaned Otium, and thick, dark blood flowed over her fingers. Her head twisted from side to side and, though her eyes were open, they were hot with fever. "Where is he, where is he?" she asked anxiously.

"Where is who?"

"The water warrior. I got him, Beata, I got him..." She shuddered, and her head rolled back.

"You have to get up," said Beata firmly, placing her hands under the Medica's armpits. She went to lift her. Suddenly however, even though the room was dark, she became aware of a shadow rising over her.

Beata dropped the now unconscious Otium and drew her sword, bracing her feet and raising the blade in the standard defensive stance she had been taught from the age of seven. Her opponent's blade rang on hers, and then, to her surprise, the figure slipped to the floor, breathing harshly.

She waited a moment for him to rise but he stayed down, and so eventually she moved closer. She lowered herself to her knees and leaned over him. He lay on his back, and she could see where Otium had stabbed him – a wound in his armpit that had obviously penetrated deep inside. Dark liquid flooded out of him, covering the flagstones.

Why hadn't he disappeared with the others? She looked around, realising the place wasn't wet – of course, the flood wouldn't have reached to the first floor. He must have come up the stairs and, when the others withdrew, his wound would have stopped him from returning with them.

Curious, she put her hand on his visor and lifted it up.

Of course she had known there was something supernatural about these beings – the way they had reared out of the water, and how they had melted back in; there were no logical explanations for that. But still, she felt a deep shock as she looked at his face.

He was beardless and his skin strangely even, as if made of clay. But it was his eyes that were the most shocking; they opened slowly as she stared at him, and they were not the white orbs she was used to, but small, green flickering lights like marsh fireflies dancing in his sockets.

Reaching out a hand, she touched the skin on the top of his arm, above his wound. It had a strange consistency, firm like muscle, but also pliable; her finger sank into it, and she withdrew it with distaste.

He made a strange, gurgling sound, but she ignored him. She had to find out as much as she could about him before he died or vanished into the water like the others. Pulling out her small dagger, she cut the straps holding together the back and front of his armour and removed the curious breastplate, made from hundreds of tiny shells linked together. Placing it to one side, she looked down at his chest. His skin was flat, with no telltale ridges of ribs or mounds of muscle. The flesh had the same spongy feel as his shoulder.

The strangest thing, however, was that deep inside him, at the point which would have been at the base of his ribs, if he had any, was a round, circular glow. She frowned and pressed down on it with her fingers. He opened his mouth and a strange shriek issued from his lips, though his throat muscles did not move.

Beata had had enough. This thing had murdered her friends in a killing frenzy; even now she could not bear to look around the room at the display of frenetic savagery. Taking her sword, she rested the blade edge-down across his neck, kneeling up so she could put all her weight on it. Grasping a nearby blanket, ignoring the splashes of blood on it, she wrapped it around her left hand and then coolly pressed down on both sides of the sword.

The blade sliced cleanly through the muscle, or whatever it was, until it met the stones below with a clang. For a second she saw dark green blood and broken sinew, and then suddenly his body melted, the skin and bone dissolving and forming a pool on the floor. The green circular glow in the centre of his torso dimmed and then vanished into the floor, and for a moment she was certain she saw the stones beneath glow with its eerie light. Then the glow died, and all that was left was a puddle of water on the flagstones.

She sat back on her heels and looked across at Otium. The Medica's eyes were open, but her chest no longer rose and fell. Beata sighed, went over and closed her eyes. Then, sheathing her own sword, she made her way downstairs.

IV

Dolosus said, "I will take the left side, you take the right." He looked up at the night sky, seeing the Lamb Moon high above him hanging in the sky like a pearl earring. Just above the top of the Castellum he could also see the Dark Moon rising, much smaller than her sister, the two of them ready to take up their nightly dance.

Chonrad and Fulco went into the Armorium, but Dolosus didn't move. He looked around the Domus, feeling an odd mixture of emotions at the damage that had been done.

He had not been a member of Heartwood for as long as most of the Militis, as he hadn't come to the Allectus as was customary. Instead, he had joined the Exercitus on the road when he was twenty-eight after a lifetime spent as an itinerant mercenary fighting for whoever would pay him most. He had had a hard life; he had never known his father, and his mother – who had been a servant to an insignificant Wulfengar lord – had died when he was seven. At the age when he could have been sent for the Allectus, he was eating scraps of food off the floor and cleaning out the stables and the pig sty, the brand of servitude on his hand clear for all to see.

After a while one of the castle guards took pity on him and began to train him to hold a sword and defend himself. This went on for several years without anybody knowing, but when he was twelve the three sons of the Wulfengar lord caught him practising and, after he bested them all in a mock battle, complained to their father. He was beaten soundly, and when he was eventually able to walk again, he decided to leave.

He spent his teenage years moving from town to town, carrying out menial jobs for food, keeping the brand on his hand covered in case the lord should find him and try to bring him back. Eventually he was spotted by the leader of a raiding band who asked him to join them, and that was the beginning of his itinerant lifestyle, always moving, always fighting, believing in nothing but beating the person in front of him.

And then one day he was captured by the Exercitus during a raid, and he found himself in front of Valens. The Dux had been impressed with the raider's skills and for some reason saw something within the young man that reminded him of himself. He asked Dolosus if he would fight instead for the Heartwood army. At the time Dolosus had shrugged – one army was as good as another to him; he did not care which side he fought for. But although the only payment he received in the Exercitus was food and lodgings, and he only planned to stay until the wind changed, he had found in their ranks a purpose and a meaning previously denied to him. He did not fit in easily with the Militis, who disliked his mercenary approach and could not understand his dismissive attitude to their religion. But he kept himself to himself, and gradually they began to accept him. When the cohort he had been placed with eventually returned to Heartwood, Valens suggested he go with them, which he did, and he was finally accepted into the Militis and took his vows on his thirtieth birthday.

He had continued to fight in the Exercitus for another eight years, until he made a foolish mistake one evening and paid a heavy price for it. He had been stationed with a cohort whose responsibility was manning one of the lonely hill forts on the Wall. He could be a difficult man to live with in an enclosed space, and as he did not always understand the camaraderie and religious fervour that characterised the Exercitus knights, his cabin fever had resulted in repeated clashes that led to several warnings by his superior, and he was not in a good mood. He was given a late night shift and, in a show of rebelliousness, got drunk, something completely forbidden while on duty.

The Wulfengar raiders had come out of nowhere, taking those on guard completely by surprise. There had been a quick skirmish, and the raiders had eventually been repelled, but not before Dolosus had had a short and difficult struggle with a Wulfian knight, who had taken advantage of his dulled senses and slow responses. The knight had beaten him back into a corner and then dealt him a heavy blow to the left arm which had gone right through to the bone. The wound had become infected, and the Medica at the nearest town behind the Wall had had to remove the limb just above the elbow.

The most ironic thing was that the hand he had lost was not the one with the brand of servitude on it, but the one with the Heartwood tattoo.

It had been a devastating injury for a knight whose whole life had been spent with a sword in his hand.

He knew he did not belong in Heartwood. The Militis tolerated him because he was one of Valens' favourites, but he could not live off that forever. And he didn't want to. He was nobody's pet, and he didn't like being on a leash. However, so far he had resisted the urge to just leave, knowing it would break Valens's heart.

The large oak door to the Capitulum was shut. Dolosus pulled it open, raising his lantern to scan the interior. This was the room where the Militis gathered at the Tertius Campana for daily readings by Dulcis from the pulpit. The only items of furniture inside were wooden chairs, and although these had been swept up in the flood and many had been broken, no other damage had been done.

He left the room and moved along to the next one, which was the Apotheca, or store room. This had suffered quite extensive damage. Broken bowls and foodstuffs lay scattered on the floor, soggy loaves of bread, tipped-over fruit barrels, dripping pots of honey and empty flagons of ale. He didn't even bother to go in; there was clearly nobody there.

So where was everyone? He left the room, frowning. There should have been lots of Militis around; after the Veriditas the members of Heartwood who weren't involved in the Congressus would mostly have returned to their positions, many of which were in the Castellum itself, such as the Cellarer, the Chamberlain, the Refectorer and the Granarer. Unless they were all outside dealing with the visitors...

He pushed open the door to the Refectorium and stood in the doorway. *Ah*, he thought. *So this is where they all are.*

Bodies had been heaped around the dining room in an untidy tangle of torsos and limbs. Dolosus walked slowly around the room, treading carefully so as not to slip in the blood. His mind puzzled as he moved, wondering who the warriors were, and why they had caused such destruction. He couldn't help but admire the relentless way they had disposed of the trained Militis knights with ease. There had not been so much carnage in the Curia. That made him wonder if the warriors who had attacked them in the Curia had merely had the task of distracting them while the rest of them desecrated the Arbor. Heartwood's best knights had all been in the Curia – Valens, Procella, Beata, all the lords of the Twelve Lands. It didn't make sense that the water warriors hadn't put their strongest force against those warriors unless the main objective was distraction.

"Help..."

Dolosus turned and looked down at the person who had called out at his feet. It was Brevis, the Refectorer. He knelt down to look at him. The Militis had been skewered like a pig. Whoever had done the job knew how to make sure his victim didn't get up again. They had twisted the blade inside Brevis, leaving a gaping, jagged hole out of which spilled greasy grey intestines.

The Refectorer clutched hold of Dolosus's hand with blooded fingers. His face was pale as a bowl of milk, his forehead beaded with sweat. "Help me," he whispered, his other hand clutching his innards and trying to push them back in.

Dolosus extricated his only hand from the other's grip with distaste. "I think you are past help, my friend," he said coolly. Tears ran down Brevis's face. The Refectorer was a large, plump knight who ran his kitchens with a harsh hand. Dolosus had seen him beat the young Militis who served as part of their training on more than one occasion for no reason other than accidentally dropping a piece of food on the floor. He knew Brevis disliked him, and thought less of him because he had come late to Heartwood, as if somehow that tainted him and made him less worthy of being a Militis.

Brevis must have seen the look on his face because his eyes went wide and his mouth opened and closed like a fish. Dolosus leaned back against the table and folded his arms. "I think you will die by sun-up," he said, leaning across and retrieving an unblemished apple from an upturned bowl. "We will soon find out, will we not?"

V

Chonrad decided not to blow out the lantern, now they had gone to the trouble of getting one lit. He didn't think they would find any water warriors. They had got what they came for and retreated, he presumed, as soon as they had it, so he doubted there would be any left hanging around.

Still, he and Fulco proceeded cautiously, keeping to the walls as they made their way around the right side of the colonnade.

It was the first time he – and maybe, he thought, anyone but a Militis – had been inside the living area of Heartwood. He had known the Castellum was shaped like an oak leaf and he could see this layout now as he looked around at the buildings shimmering in the light of the Lamb Moon, high above them.

The centre of the complex was a large lawn, slightly wider at the Temple end than the west end, reflecting the narrowing shape of the oak leaf plan. Flotsam and jetsam littered the lawn, and the beautiful flat grass had been gouged in many places. To either side, rounded buildings formed the lobes of the leaf. In front of these, a covered walkway with arches led through to the lawn. He suspected that usually it would have been a tranquil place, but now it looked deserted and forlorn, like a dog tied up and left for dead.

He made his way around the northern walkway, Fulco following remarkably silently for such a big knight. They stopped outside the first room. Blood stained the floor and the door hung half open. Chonrad pushed it with his sword, waited in the doorway and lifted the lantern.

It was a library, or had been, anyway. Books lay in sodden piles of parchment on the floor, the beautifully scrolled words blurred and smudged. Furniture piled up to the side, and broken pieces of wood, torn books and candles littered the floor.

A body sprawled on the flagstones.

Chonrad went in and bent over the body while Fulco stood in the doorway, keeping guard. The dead knight – an old man – hadn't been wearing armour. His chest and stomach had been gouged out and spilled on the floor, where it had obviously mixed with the water, for there were bits and pieces of flesh and innards all over the place. Chonrad's lips tightened. An elder did not deserve to die in such a way.

He bent to pick up the body, intending to carry it out onto the lawn, and then he saw the faint light emanating from a hole in the corner of the room. He stood and walked over to the hole and looked through. A set of stone steps curved down and around, leading to somewhere he could not see, but the light and the slight shuffling sounds of movement meant someone was down there.

He whistled to Fulco, indicating he was going down. "Stay here, unless I call you," he directed. Fulco nodded, coming over and holding the lantern aloft while Chonrad descended the spiral stone staircase. He did his best to walk quietly, but the steps were covered with loose bits of wood and stone and his feet crunched so much he knew he had no hope of creeping up on anyone. Sure enough, his head was barely below ground level before someone demanded: "Who is that? Who goes there? Tell me who you are!" and a tall, slender youth appeared out of the gloom, sword held aloft.

"Peace, friend," said Chonrad in the language of Heartwood. Then, changing to Laxonian, he continued: "I am Chonrad, Lord of Barle. I mean you no harm."

The tip of the youth's sword lowered to the ground. "I thought you were one of those... whatever they were." He gave a ghost of a smile. "I am Nitesco. I help out – helped out – Caecus, the Libraris."

Holding up his lantern, Chonrad could see the young lad's face looked white and drawn against his long blond hair, and blood marked his temple. "Are you hurt badly?" he asked, descending the last few steps.

The youth touched his head. "No, the bleeding has stopped." He glanced up the staircase. "What is going on up there? I think I have been down here a while."

"The Pectoris has been taken," Chonrad told him. "There are many dead, including Dulcis, I am sorry to tell you."

Nitesco stared at him, shocked. "Arbor's roots..." His mouth tightened. "What a terrible thing. The Pectoris gone... What will happen to the Arbor now?"

"I do not know. We are meeting at sun-up to have a discussion. They are starting to clean up upstairs," said Chonrad. "There are many dead, and there has been a lot of damage to the buildings." He looked around the place. They were in some kind of underground cave. It was dark and airless, and not very big, but filled from floor to ceiling with books, maps and other pieces of parchment. In the middle stood a lectern, on which was spread out a slender book, pages brown with age. "Where are we?" He had never heard of an underground room beneath Heartwood.

In the light of the lantern, Nitesco's green eyes gleamed. "This is the Cavus. It is part of the old Temple, the one destroyed in the Great Quake."

"Did you know it was here?" Chonrad walked around the perimeter of the room, touching the books with his fingertips.

"Not at all and, more importantly, neither did Caecus, as far as I know." For a moment Nitesco looked forlorn at the memory of the sickening death of his mentor and friend. Obviously pushing that thought away, he continued: "And he knew everything about Heartwood."

"Why was it not damaged in the flood?" The books were all dry, Chonrad could see, and the floor remained thick with dust.

"The hole was covered by a flagstone, which was also covered by a chest. I believe the waters moved the chest, and then heaped debris on top of the flagstone. It broke after the waters had receded from the weight of the damp debris."

Chonrad shrugged. This was mildly interesting, but he had more pressing matters on his mind. "We will come down here and investigate further when things are more settled upstairs," he said.

To his surprise, Nitesco shook his head. "No, you do not understand." He indicated the books with his hand. "These all predate the Heartwood we know, the Castellum Temple and Domus. They all predate *Oculus*."

Chonrad frowned. He failed to see the reason for the excitement in Nitesco's eyes. "I understand. I know we have very few documents of that time and therefore…"

"No! We have *no* documents of that time!" urged Nitesco. "The earliest document we have is Oculus's *Rule* and his *Theories* on the Arbor, which record the stories and oral traditions of his days. But this was written three hundred years after the Great Quake. As a historian I was taught that the truth can disappear in one generation."

Chonrad sighed impatiently. "I still do not understand. What are you trying to tell me?"

"That Oculus was wrong!"

"Wrong?"

"Yes, wrong. Well, not completely. But he clearly misunderstood some of the basic concepts of our religion. I do not blame him; he could only piece together the stories he had; it is not his fault. But for a thousand years we have followed his writings – wars are being fought over them, for Arbor's sake!"

He walked over to the lectern and tapped the book that resided there with his long fingers. "This is the *Quercetum*. It was written by the Keepers of the Temple maybe two thousand years ago."

Chonrad nodded. "That is very impressive. And I understand that, as a librarian, these things are important to you." He pointed up the stairs. "But we have just suffered an attack on Heartwood. Incredible beings just sprang from the water fully formed; I do not even know where to start to explain that. And they took the heart of the Arbor, Nitesco, they took the Pectoris. So you can see why a dusty old book holds little fascination for me at the moment." Chonrad moved to walk past the youth up the stone stairs. To his surprise, however, Nitesco moved too, blocking his way.

"You still do not understand," he said firmly. He folded up the Quercetum and clutched it to his chest. "This book holds our history within its pages. It explains it all – who the water warriors are, the truth about the Veriditas, and why the land is failing."

He took the book in both hands and shook it in front of Chonrad's face. "This has the answer to everything!"

CHAPTER FOUR

I

Heartwood spent the dark hours of the night dealing with the after-effects of the attack. Progress was slow, mainly because everyone was dealing with the shock of the fact that not only had a raid been carried out on such an important religious site, but that it had been successful.

Oculus had created the Militis for both the worship and the protection of the Arbor. In a relatively unstable position between two warring countries, it had become clear that some form of defence would be necessary to keep the tree in neutral ground and avoid it being taken over by any other country to use as a tool of control over everyone else. To make the Arbor's holy guardians also knights had therefore been a natural progression, and for a thousand years the Militis had trained the young to become fearless and skilled in battle, even as they took their holy vows.

But the expected attack on Heartwood had never materialised. That was partly why the Exercitus had eventually become peacekeepers, spending more of their time out on Isenbard's Wall and in the lands on either side than in Heartwood itself. The Militis had taken care to never become complacent and their military training was as extensive as ever, but still, an enemy had not set foot inside the Porta for over a thousand years.

Valens took a moment in between his organising of the meeting to go up to the top of the Porta and look over Heartwood. He had been putting on a brave face for the others: slapping backs, congratulating those who had fought bravely against the water warriors, raising spirits and spreading a feeling of strength and resistance among his compatriots, but now, alone and surrounded by darkness, weariness and sadness swept over him.

There were few who had not been injured in some way, and many had died of their wounds in the hours that had already passed since the attack. Those who were still alive were being treated in the Hospitium by the Hanairean High Council member, Fionnghuala, who was skilled in herbs and medicines.

The dead had been taken to the Sepulchrum in front of the Arbor, and left there for the tree to take them in. It had done so, slowly, its roots creeping over the bodies, bringing them into its depths, and those gathered around it had taken some comfort at the fact that it seemed to rejuvenate a little, and maybe the remaining leaves seemed a little less limp afterwards. But Valens had not been able to take his eyes off the massive rent down the centre of the trunk, and the gaping hole in the middle. With its heart taken, how could the Arbor, and therefore the land, hope to survive?

Standing now, looking down on the people moving slowly around the Baillium, despondency swept over him. His role as Imperator was to protect Heartwood and its people, and in this he had failed. He had failed Dulcis, who as Abbatis looked to him to keep Heartwood safe; he had failed Procella, his student, who looked up to him and who had believed him infallible; and he had failed himself, for he had always thought himself invincible, able to overcome any opponent, any army, any enemy, and he realised now he had grossly misjudged his ability.

Footsteps sounded on the stone behind him and he spun, hand to his sword, but it was just Procella, and so he let his hand drop and turned back to look out at the view.

She walked up beside him and leaned on the parapet, looking around at the walls. "I have sorted out the guard," she said.

"Thirteen Custodes are dead. I told a third of the remainder to snatch some sleep and stationed the others around the Baillium and in the Castellum. I have also pulled in some of the Exercitus to take the place of those who have fallen."

Valens nodded. He thought, but didn't say, what was the point of guarding the Castellum now? The Arbor was crippled. Anything they did now was too late. The words "stable door" and "bolted" came to mind.

He sighed and looked over at her. Her brown hair remained twisted in a knot at the base of her neck, but wisps had escaped and hung around her face in light curls. She looked tired but alert, and didn't appear to have suffered any injuries in the battle. She was a good warrior, he thought; the best, a truly deserving heir to the Dux, and she had served him well. He felt ashamed he had failed her.

She turned to meet his gaze, and for the first time she looked uncertain. Her brown eyes looked down hesitantly, then back up at him, beseeching. "I... I want to apologise, Imperator, for failing you. I should have been more prepared for something like this; I should have increased the guard on the Arbor. I truly thought the threat to be more between Wulfengar and Laxony – it did not enter my head there might be danger from outside Heartwood. But a Dux should always be ready for anything, and I was not. I am sorry for letting you down."

Valens stared at her. Her gaze was open and honest; she thought she had made a bad tactical decision, and she was ready to accept the consequences. He had taught her well.

A wry smile twisted his lips. "It is I who has failed you," he said softly. "Some leader I have been – allowing a major invasion in the very place I have sworn to protect – the heart of Heartwood!" He sighed. "In truth, I know, neither of us is to blame. This is not something we could have foreseen. Of course our attention was on the very proximity of the Laxony and Wulfengar visitors – why would it not have been? And the invaders obviously knew that would be the case. Why should we have prepared otherwise? How could we have guessed warriors were going to rise from the water?" He frowned, shaking his head. "How is that possible? I cannot go to the meeting, Procella, for I have no answers, nothing to say. How can I lead when I do not know from where the threat is coming?"

"That is one reason I came up to find you." She laid her hand lightly on his arm. "I have just seen Chonrad – he and Nitesco have found a cave underneath the Armorium. Nitesco has uncovered an old document, so old it predates Oculus. And he says it holds many of the answers, not only to what has happened today, but to what has been happening to the land."

"Truly?" Hope stirred within his chest. He looked down at the Baillium. The clean-up crews were doing a good job; much of the debris – the broken pieces of wood, ripped tents, broken plates and damaged food – had been removed and the bodies had been taken in to the Temple. People were now heading towards the Castellum, and word had obviously spread that there was news, for he could see their pace had quickened, and their faces had lightened.

He breathed in deeply, looking up to see the Lamb Moon hovering above the horizon, the Dark Moon now high in the sky and fading in the early morning sunlight. "I fear for the future, Procella," he admitted. It was not something he would have confessed to anyone else.

She tipped her head, studying him. "Why so?"

He shivered, an early morning breeze ruffling his grey hair. "We are poised on the knife edge of change. I am..." He could not bring himself to say "frightened". "Concerned," he chose eventually. "Though wars come and go, there are certain things that remain stable, that you can rely on." He slapped his hand on the parapet. "This is rock; it is hard; it will not yield to my hand. And water is water, it is liquid, it takes only the form of that in which it is placed, like a bowl. How can it take the shape of a warrior?"

Procella shrugged. "I am no philosopher; I do not understand these things. But you have just said that water takes the form of its container; maybe these beings can temporarily acquire bodies, and their watery form takes their shape." She smiled and held out her hand. "Come, Valens. We shall do no good debating the issue up here. We need to speak to those who are skilled in such matters; we need great thinkers, and people to help us plan what to do next."

"People like Lord Barle?" Valens said impishly. He laughed as she turned her startled gaze on him. "He is a good man. I have known him for some time; he came and fought with us during the Raids of the Falling, five years ago. He is strong, and clever, and kind."

"And I am Militis," she said sharply. "We should not be talking thus."

"As you wish." He bowed his head as she walked away to the stairs. He half regretted his words; he had not meant to make her uncomfortable. It was harder for female Militis, he thought. Most male Militis had sexual encounters throughout their life, but it was easy to remain detached. But women had the risk of becoming pregnant, which would mean they would have to leave Heartwood. And Heartwood was in Procella's blood – she was a knight, she was Militis through and through. He recalled the look on her face when they had found the tree split in half, its heart gone. She was not made for hearth and home, and he knew she would not succumb to mere physical attraction.

II

The meeting was to be held in the Capitulum. They could have gone to the Curia again, but for the Militis the Capitulum was comforting and familiar.

Chonrad watched everyone enter the room. First in were the twins, Gravis and Gavius. They had been moving the bodies to the Arbor all night. Chonrad had averted his eyes when he walked through the Temple to the Capitulum. There was something that disturbed him about the tree when it was feeding.

After the twins came the two Council members of Hanaire that were left – Fionnghuala, who had been busy in the Hospitium, tending to the wounded, and a man, Bearrach, both of them tall with shoulder-length blond hair, their movements elegant and graceful. They nodded to Chonrad before taking their seats on the stone steps around the edge. Chonrad had spoken to them briefly when he returned from the Domus. They had been considering returning to Hanaire before the meeting, eager to sort out their domestic affairs now two other Council members were dead. Chonrad had dissuaded them from leaving, however, convincing them this was not just a Heartwood matter, and not just an eastern matter either; the loss of the Pectoris would have lasting consequences on all four lands, and they would want to be a part of the decision of how to deal with matters. In the end they had agreed, if somewhat reluctantly, and now took their places along with the others.

From Wulfengar, only Grimbeald had survived out of the original five lords, as Raedwald had died during the night. He came in hesitantly, with a couple of his followers, clearly conscious they were the only Wulfians in the place. At least he had come, thought Chonrad, and he admired the lord's courage at walking into a room full of what he had probably been brought up to believe were all enemies.

From Laxony, as well as himself, there were Kenweard of Frennon, Malgara of Dorle and Ogier of Hannon. All three came in and took their places on the stone seats.

Valens and Procella came in together, and then Dolosus with Beata. Chonrad was then surprised to see Silva enter. She had had her wound patched up and, though pale, she was obviously determined to take part in the discussions.

A few other surviving Militis he had not yet met filed in behind her and took their seats. There was a much more informal feeling to this meeting, Chonrad thought. The peoples of the three countries had been brought together by their misfortune. They made quite a sorry bunch; many had bandages around limbs and everyone looked tired, having been up all night. But they were all eager to hear what Nitesco had to say.

Fulco stood quietly beside him. Chonrad had sent him to the Hospitium to get his leg fixed and the bodyguard now had a large bandage around his thigh. He was still limping, but Chonrad knew there was nothing he could do to stop Fulco staying at his side now.

The young Libraris stood in the doorway, clutching the *Quercetum* to his chest. His eyes were wide and he looked nervous but calm, his eyes flicking around the room as he waited for everyone to seat themselves and quieten.

Seeing him standing there, Valens got to his feet and turned to address the room. "My friends," he said, his hand taking in everyone present. "We experienced a terrible tragedy here yesterday. Many of our colleagues and family were killed and, as we know, Heartwood's Arbor has suffered the great loss of its Pectoris, taken by the warriors who attacked us." He sighed. "I have no answers for you – I am as confused and alarmed by what happened here as the rest of you. But I understand Nitesco has uncovered something that might answer some of our Questions and I would now like to ask him to come forward and speak." He turned and beckoned to the waiting Libraris.

Nitesco came forward to the podium at one side of the room and mounted the step. He laid the book he was carrying on the lectern and left it there for a moment, pages shut, his hands resting on top of the leather cover.

"My friends," he began, then stopped as he obviously realised his voice was too soft. He cleared his throat and started again, his voice louder. "My friends. Like you, I was told the story of the Creation as a child. We all know this story because Oculus recorded it in his *Memoria* – his great work on Animus and the

Arbor, which contains the stories he gathered through oral tradition after the Great Quake. The *Memoria* is the foundation of our religion – it is on this we base our rituals and our beliefs, and it is because of different interpretations of this that Wulfengar and Laxony have been bitter enemies for so long.

"However, yesterday the flood revealed a secret beneath Heartwood – the Cavus, a hidden room below the Armorium." There were gasps from around the Capitulum from those who had not yet heard the news. Nitesco nodded. "The Cavus belonged to the time before the Castellum was built – to the first Temple created around the Arbor. I did not know of its existence and neither, I think, did Caecus. I believe it was buried in the Great Quake, and I do not think – from his writings – that Oculus knew of it either." He shrugged. "Of course there has been speculation for centuries that old documents and artefacts lay hidden beneath the Castellum, but it has never been proven."

"What is down there?" someone asked. "Treasures?"

Nitesco smiled. "For me, at least. There are mainly old books and documents." His smile disappeared. "But they are so much more than that."

He lifted the book lying on the lectern in front of him. "This is the Quercetum. It is not complete – it has suffered some damage, but there is enough left to answer many of our Questions about what happened during the attack yesterday. It predates Oculus, predates the first Temple, in fact. And it holds the truth of who we are and where we come from. I must warn you: the information it contains will shock many of you; it will change much of what we think about the Arbor, and Animus, and Oculus, and that will not be easy for us to accept."

A general air of unease settled on the room. Chonrad was intrigued by what Nitesco had found out. What could possibly be in the book that was going to cause such an upset?

"I will read to you," Nitesco said, "and I shall let the words speak for themselves." He opened the front cover of the

Quercetum, the leather cover creaking softly, the pages crackling as he smoothed them out. "The language is quite different from modern Heartwood," he said, "and I shall have to translate, so please forgive me if I struggle at times with the meaning.

"'The Chronicles of the Veriditas,'" he read. "'Once, there were only the elements. Earth, fire, air and water they were, and together they made up the universe. At first, they only consisted of their purest structure, each as intangible as the other, existing in a nameless void of confusion.

"'Slowly, however, the elements began to take form. They became the elementals: shadowy, ethereal beings that still bore the characteristics of their elements, creatures of the dirt, the wind, the heat and the wet. And, after an age spent in the Void, they were filled with hate for each other.

"'For thousands of millennia the Great War raged, and gradually over time some of the elementals became stronger than the others. Fire and air were weakest, and before long their subjugation was complete. They were forced to remain in their purest form, existing only as the breeze in the sky and the flames of the fire that warmed.

"'The battle between earth and water continued for much longer. Eventually, however, earth won.

"'The earth elementals bonded, took shape. They became the rocks and the trees and the things that walked upon them – they formed the beasts of the earth and the flora they ate.'"

Nitesco looked up for a moment and glanced around the room. Chonrad took the opportunity to look around too. Everyone's face showed the same emotions he himself was experiencing: fascination, confusion, denial.

Nitesco swallowed before he continued reading. "'Most of the earth elementals in these lands have forgotten they were spirits at all. And maybe that is not a bad thing, for the time spent in the Void was a time of misery, but our time in Anguis is a time of happiness. And so we live our lives without the knowledge of the

Great Wars, and of our greatest enemies, the water elementals. They are forced to remain bound by the constraints we earth elementals imposed upon them. They churn and seethe at the edges of our existence... But they do not forget. And we must not forget either that they are always planning to take over us earthly beings and condemn the universe to be made of only a single element: water.'"

Nitesco stopped and looked up at the room. For a moment there was deathly silence. Then, everyone started speaking at once.

"What is he suggesting; we are these earth elementals?"

"I have not heard anything like this before, have you?"

"Time in the Void? The Great Wars? It is just a story to frighten children...!"

"And yet it does make a certain sense," murmured Chonrad to himself. He watched the others around the room. Tempers were flaring – the Militis were angry that Nitesco was suggesting Oculus was wrong; he knew they were frightened there was some truth in his words. The Libraris said nothing but merely stood there, resting his hands on the pages; still, his face showed his alarm. He had anticipated this reaction, but it was one thing to imagine people's anger and another to actually experience it.

Chonrad stood and held up his hands. People gradually quieted as they saw him about to speak. "My friends," he said, catching the eye of those he knew and smiling at those he did not. "I understand why this story sounds so incredible. It *is* like a tale we tell our children, of fearsome creatures that come out of the sea at night to take you away if you are bad. But we must not let our beliefs and our prejudices cloud the truth." He gestured towards the *Quercetum*. "I do not know if this is but a story, or if it is true. All I do know is I saw something amazing yesterday, something I cannot explain, and Nitesco here is offering me an explanation. As incredible as it is, I believe we should at least consider it – because we have nothing else to go on."

He looked across at Procella. Her cheek muscles were pronounced and he sensed she was clenching her teeth. Her back was rigidly straight and she emanated disapproval and anger at the blasphemy that one of her own had uttered. She looked over at him and met his gaze and, as she looked into his eyes, her posture softened and her antagonism melted a little. He smiled. He could sense her fear that everything she knew, everything her life had been based on, was a lie, and felt sorry her faith was being tested in this way. But still, wasn't the truth more important than any one religious teaching?

Around the room, people were gradually starting to agree with him. The anger had dampened after he had said they had little else to go on. He could hear their comments: "Well, how else do you explain the water warriors...?", "It is incredible but nobody else is offering a solution...", "I wonder what else the book says?"

Beata was one of the few Militis who didn't seem angry at the revelation. "As most of you know, I came upon one of the water warriors in the Domus," she announced to the room. "I was able to inspect him. It was clear to me he was not like us – his form was different, and his eyes burned like green fire in their sockets. It is obvious these are supernatural creatures. We all saw them disappear into the water. We have to accept the explanation for their presence is not going to seem logical."

To Chonrad's surprise, it was Grimbeald, the only Wulfian lord in the room, who nodded agreement and stood up to speak. "I would like to say something," he said in faltering Laxonian.

III

Grimbeald stood in front of the people in the Capitulum. It was a brave thing to do, thought Chonrad; he knew he wasn't among friends and yet he was still prepared to voice his opinions and make himself heard. The Wulfian lord drew himself up to his full height – some several inches shorter than Chonrad – and lifted his head proudly, shaking his mane of thick brown hair.

"As you know, I am from Wulfengar," he began. "I have been a follower of Exerceo Animism all my life. I was brought up to worship the Arbor, and I have been sound in my faith all these years.

"However, I have also attended the University of Ornestan, at which the learned people of our land discuss our religion and contemplate the most basic Questions of existence – who is Animus, what is the purpose of the Arbor, and how and why are we here?"

There were subtle murmurings around the room, which Chonrad listened to with amusement. Obviously there were many people who had not thought the Wulfian lord to be educated.

"I sat through the lectures and discussions on my faith," continued Grimbeald, "and I learned I must keep my mind open, for religion is but a matter of interpretation of the facts, and if we do not have the correct facts then our interpretation will also be wrong. Therefore I would like to hear more of what your young Libraris has to say, and after I have heard all, I will then make my judgement."

Most people were nodding around the room, the newfound admiration for Grimbeald clear on their faces.

Valens stood and approached the Wulfian lord. "You speak wise words, my friend. It is difficult for us here at Heartwood to remain objective about Animus and the Arbor because it is such a great part of our lives. I think I speak for all the Militis when I say I feel uncomfortable hearing stories that contradict what I have spent my whole life believing and fighting for. But I like to think my heart is large enough to admit I might have been wrong, and to be open to new ideas. What happened here yesterday cannot be swept under the rug; we cannot ignore such a challenge to our fundamental ideas about our religion. If we do we are foolish and it makes a mockery of our faith. So I, too, would like Nitesco to continue. And after he has finished, I suppose we will all have made up our minds."

Nitesco nodded, taking a deep, relieved breath as Valens and Grimbeald sat down. "I think the lords speak wisely," he said. "I believe there is information in here that will help us understand what has been happening, both yesterday with the water warriors, and in general with the failing of our land. I will carry on reading from the *Quercetum*."

He turned the page over, the crackle of the parchment loud in the silence of the room. "This chapter is called 'The Darkwater Lords'," he explained. "This appears to be the name given to the beings that attacked us yesterday."

Nitesco continued to read. "'The Darkwater Lords are spirits who exist in the watery realms out in the oceans. Nobody has ever been able to visit these realms, but it is thought vast cities and whole civilisations exist beneath the waves.

"'As such the Darkwater Lords have no form, but long, long ago, when the Great War had only just ended and the world as we know it was only just forming, there is a story that a group of water spirits forced some earth spirits to give them shape, and they were able to come onto the land and walk upon the ground. They were banished once the Arbor took root, but it must be noted that should the Veriditas fail and the energies cease to flow, it is conceivable that once again the Darkwater Lords may learn to walk among us.'"

Nitesco paused and looked up at the room. A chill went through Chonrad. The Libraris's words implied this was what had occurred – the Veriditas had failed. Somehow, the energy the ceremony raised in the Arbor was not being relayed to the rest of the land, and that must be why, he thought, they were experiencing so many problems with famines and pestilence.

Nitesco cleared his throat, turned the page and continued to read. "'The importance of the flow of energy throughout the lands cannot be overemphasised. The health and strength of the land and its people are directly related to the energy flow from the Arbor.'" Nitesco was becoming more animated, and he waved his hand at the group now as he said, "Now listen to this. 'The Arbor is the conduit through which the love of Animus passes, drawn through the Pectoris, which is our connection to the Creator, at the centre of the tree. The Arbor directs the energy to all four corners of the lands by channelling it down through its roots and along the energy channels which run beneath the earth. However it must be made clear the Arbor is not solely responsible for the flow – the major arteries from the Arbor run to the five Nodes, which continue to conduct the energy through smaller veins so it reaches all parts of the land.'"

He turned the page over, his eyes flicking briefly around the room before continuing. "'The maintenance of the Nodes is of paramount importance – this cannot be stressed enough. The Nodes must be cleansed on a regular basis to remove any residual dark energy and allow the light energy to continue to flow. *Failure to do this will result in failure of the land.*'" Nitesco's final sentence rang around the Capitulum like a warning bell.

There were gasps from around the room. Everywhere people were shocked into standing, wanting to express their confused emotions.

"Can this be true?" asked Valens, his hands on his hips. "It sounds like lunacy."

Procella was laughing. "What and where are these five Nodes? We could go searching for them for months and find out it has all been a figment of someone's imagination."

Another Militis gestured towards the *Quercetum* on the lectern. "We should burn the book and turn our attention to facts, not fiction."

Grimbeald stood then and bellowed, "And what answers do you have for what happened to us yesterday? How can you explain these mysterious Darkwater Lords except by using the information we have just been given?" The other voices gradually fell silent. Procella set her jaw stubbornly but had no reply. Valens just frowned.

Grimbeald turned to face the room. "I have heard rumours about these 'arteries' of energy running beneath the land. There are supposed to be places throughout Anguis where natural energies can be felt, if you are sensitive to such things."

"So now you believe in mystics and wizards?" laughed Kenweard of Frennon, his dislike of the Wulfian lord evident. Chonrad's eyes narrowed – it was not a good time to be pouring scorn on each other.

But Grimbeald did not rise to the bait. "I believe there are many things I do not know," he said calmly. "And I am willing to listen to other people's opinions. Can you make such a statement?"

Chonrad stood as Kenweard opened his mouth to retort. "I think what you say is wise, Lord of the Highlands," he said, stepping in front of Kenweard.

The Lord of Frennon, however, was not going to stand back so easily. "You are not High Lord of Laxony yet," he snapped, reaching out to grasp Chonrad's upper arm.

Chonrad stopped and let his gaze slide down to the fingers clutching hold of his mail. He kept his eyes there until Kenweard reluctantly withdrew his hold. "This is neither the time nor the place to debate the succession," he said quietly, "but I should remind you I *was* Hariman's second in command, and though that does not make me natural successor, I believe in a situation such as this I retain the authority to speak for Laxony until the next High Lord is appointed."

He turned away from Kenweard, trying to hide his anger, and smiled briefly at Grimbeald. "Do you know the locations of any of these Nodes?"

Grimbeald shrugged. "There is one place in Wulfengar that has the reputation of being a place of mystic energy. Couples fornicate there if they are struggling to conceive." There was light laughter around the room. He grinned sheepishly. "It is actually a tomb in the Highlands; an old burial mound covered with grass and sheep. But supposedly it has an 'energy' to it."

Fionnghuala of Hanaire stood, her face alight. "There is a place, too, in Hanaire that has a similar reputation. It is called the Portal – an ancient stone trilithon, built the other side of the Snout Range. It is miles from anywhere and tends to be forgotten about, but it has always had the reputation of being a mystical place."

Valens turned to Chonrad. "What of Laxony? Do you have anything similar there?"

Chonrad frowned. "I can think of nothing in Barle." He turned to the other two Laxonian lords. "What of your lands?"

Kenweard shrugged, clearly not intending to contribute to the conversation after being snubbed. However Malgara of Dorle nodded. "We have the Henge," she said. "A stone circle, built before records began. We know very little of it, but there are lots of myths surrounding it; tales of ghosts and lights and mystical sightings."

Valens was getting caught up in Nitesco's enthusiasm. "That's three!" he exclaimed. "But what of Komis? Surely one of the Nodes must be in that country? How will we find that out?"

"You forget where I come from," a voice said wryly from the back of the group. Everyone turned to see who had spoken.

IV

"Silva!" said Valens joyfully. "Of course, I had forgotten the place of your birth. Do you have many memories of it?"

"Some," she said. Although her face was pale and she was clearly in pain, her voice was strong. "I can remember talk of an ancient carving on a hillside. It was of a naked male with an erect phallus."

There was some muffled laughter around the room, more because of Silva's serious delivery of the fact than of the item itself. Chonrad could see Valens trying not to smile as he said to her, "Was it also a forgotten site?"

"Not really. But then the Komis people have always had a stronger connection to the land than the other three peoples of

Anguis. They have always treated the Green Giant as an energy centre."

Chonrad nodded. "So there are four of the Nodes. What about the fifth?"

Nobody had a reply to that Question. Nitesco shrugged. "If there is one in each land, maybe the fifth is in the Spina Mountains, although I have never heard of a mystical site there."

Nobody else seemed to have either. Valens sighed. "Well, we must think on that a while."

Chonrad frowned. "The problem is, even if we are correct and these places we have mentioned are Nodes, what do we have to do with them to get them working again?"

"I might be able to help there," said Nitesco. He turned over a page in the *Quercetum*. "There is information here about energy flow." He ran his finger down the lines. "Here we go. 'The flow of energy is what keeps the land and its people alive. The Nodes can be seen as physical landmarks around energy centres which act as conduits or conductors of the energy, passing it on throughout the land via a network of veins and arteries. The physical centres must be kept in good condition, as must the energy centres, which should be maintained by regular use of the Veriditas.'"

There was silence for a moment in the Capitulum. Chonrad was puzzled. As far as he knew, the Veriditas was the name of the ceremony performed once a year to the Arbor, but it seemed as if the Quercetum was suggesting it was something else. He looked at Nitesco, who held up a finger, urging him to wait, and turned over the page.

"'The Veriditas, or the Greening, is how we connect ourselves to Animus. The Greening of the Soul is a voluntary surrendering to the power of nature, a Quest for the truth, an opening of oneself to Animus so he can explore our mind and our soul. It completes and confirms the cycles of the seasons and strengthens our connection to the land. The Veriditas should be used at each of the five Nodes to ensure the regular flow of energy between them. It should also be used once a year with the Arbor, when the ceremony should be performed and the selected..." Nitesco's voice tailed off. He looked up at the group of people listening intently to his speech.

"What?" said Valens impatiently. "Selected what?"

In answer, Nitesco picked up the *Quercetum* and turned it round to face his audience. They all gasped – the back cover of the book was missing, as were the last few pages. The story ended with his final words... There was no more.

"That is it?" asked Valens.

"That is it," said Nitesco. "That is all we have to go on." He placed the *Quercetum* on the lectern and stepped down from the podium. "I have been giving some thought to the attack yesterday, and to what I have found out in the *Quercetum*. Would you like to know what I think about it all?"

Valens gestured to the centre of the floor. "If you can throw any light onto this matter, I am sure we would all be very grateful."

Nitesco nodded. "This is what I think. The Great Quake has proved a fundamental influence in the way our lives have been shaped since then. I believe our heritage and our knowledge of how to work with the land were lost when the Quake occurred, and although Oculus did the best job he could in piecing together what he could find out through talking to others, several vital aspects disappeared, and it is these we need to piece together now."

He took a deep breath. "It is my belief the Darkwater Lords will be back." There were murmurings around the room at this comment; clearly it wasn't what everyone wanted to hear. "I might be wrong," he continued, "but it makes sense to think the water elementals have been slowly increasing in power. My guess is they made the attack today because they knew the guard on the Arbor was going to be less than usual as our attention was concentrated on the Congressus and the Curia – not the Temple. They obviously came for the Pectoris. But I believe they will be back to try and take over Heartwood and gain full control of the tree."

"Do you have a view on how long we have?" Valens asked.

Nitesco nodded. "It would seem to me the High Moon would be the ultimate time for them to attack again. Tides are highest at that point and therefore we could assume the Darkwater Lords would be at their strongest then. That gives us..." he did a quick calculation. "About forty-four days before they return."

Forty-four days, thought Chonrad. Suddenly it didn't seem like very long at all.

"I think we should formulate a plan of action," Nitesco continued. "We have four main areas to address. Firstly, we need to think about the five Nodes. It would be wise to find a map of Anguis and ensure as best we can if the sites we have discussed are likely to be four of these Nodes. I can then do some research in the books we have left to see if any other mystical place is mentioned, to try to determine the location of the fifth. Then I think we need to go and visit these Nodes."

"And do what?" said Valens.

"That brings me to my next point," said Nitesco. "We need to have a discussion about the Veriditas. Clearly the ceremony we carry out each year is only a shadow of what it should really constitute. We need to try to work out what we are missing."

"Yes," said Silva. "As I said earlier, the Komis have always had a closer connection with the land than the other peoples of Anguis. Obviously this 'Greening of the Soul' is a merging of energies from the giver – that is the one carrying out the ceremony – to the receiver, which is either a Node or the Arbor itself. I have some idea how that works, but clearly our knowledge in that area is not complete."

"I have something to say about that," said Kenweard, the Laxonian lord. Chonrad looked at him in surprise. Kenweard just shrugged. "A few weeks ago a stranger came to Cuddington Fort, my home city. He called himself a 'Virimage' – a 'green magician', an entertainer of sorts, and he amused the court by carrying out what I thought then to be just magic tricks. But now..."

"I, too, have heard of him," said Malgara of Dorle eagerly. "He visited last year, and stayed a while in Realberg, and then went to Henton. People were talking about him for weeks."

"What sort of tricks does he do?" asked Chonrad. He had not heard of this Virimage.

Malgara and Kenweard exchanged glances, seemingly hesitant to say. Finally Malgara shrugged. "He made flowers appear out of thin air, and acorns fall from the sky. He could make leaves sprout from his ears and nostrils and pulled berries and nuts from his mouth. He was fascinating, but I thought it just a series of clever illusions... until now."

"Perhaps then we need to find this Virimage and ask if he will come to Heartwood and help us," suggested Nitesco.

Valens smiled grimly. "I think in the present circumstances it will be more of a demand than an enquiry. If he can throw light on the Veriditas, he needs to be brought here."

Nitesco nodded. "The next obvious thing that needs to be done is a strengthening of the fortifications in Heartwood. Perhaps a wall around the Arbor, increased guard... Obviously that is your area of expertise," he said to Valens, who nodded in return.

"The last," said the Libraris, "and perhaps most difficult task is the recovery of the Pectoris. Although we can do our best to repair the Arbor and work out the nature of the Veriditas, it is clear that without the heart, our connection to Animus is lost."

The room fell silent. Chonrad grew cold inside. "How can we possibly recover it?" he asked. "Presumably the Darkwater Lords have taken it back to their realm beneath the ocean. How could we possibly travel down there?"

Nitesco took a deep breath and smiled. "This is the most incredible part – and I know that is saying something! But I have been giving some thought to the fact that the water elementals are able to force earth spirits to give them shape. If this is the case, why can we not do the opposite?"

Everyone looked at everyone else. "You mean turn ourselves into water elementals and go under the sea?" said Valens flatly.

Nitesco shrugged. "I would have to do some research. But I think it might be possible."

Chonrad's head was spinning. He glanced around the room. Everyone looked stunned, tired and many were struggling to contain their emotions. He looked over at Valens. "I think maybe it is time for a break, Imperator?" he suggested. "Nobody has slept and we could probably all do with something to eat too. Perhaps we could take some time to think and chat to friends and colleagues, have a rest and then reconvene later in the day to discuss any thoughts that may arise."

Valens nodded. "I think that is a very good idea." He ran his hands through his greying hair. The stubble of his beard was beginning to show through, and Chonrad had seen him rub his leg repeatedly, as if it were beginning to ache. "Let us break and return at... shall we say, Sextus Campana? Please take the time to rest – we have cleared the Custodes Barracks and placed all the dry bedding there, so you are welcome to visit it if you need to sleep. Any food not damaged has been collected and is in the Quad."

He sighed. "Undoubtedly, while we are resting we will be thinking about what has been said here today. We have heard many unusual things, things we would not have considered even possible a few days ago. But in the light of what happened yesterday, I feel we cannot dismiss any notion out of hand. So please, keep your hearts and minds open and think about what we have learned, and what part you can play in securing Heartwood and the land, and by that keeping safe the lives of the people who live there."

••••

V

Chonrad stayed behind with Valens and watched everyone file out, bar Fulco, who refused to leave until Chonrad did. He smiled at Nitesco who, face drawn with exhaustion, picked up the *Quercetum* and left, promising to get some sleep before returning to the Armorium for more research. Chonrad knew if he went to the book room in an hour he would probably find the young Libraris dozing over some parchment or other.

Procella glanced at him but did not stop to talk as she left. She had said very little during the discussion and he could not read what she was thinking. He resolved to go and find her in a short while and make sure she was resting.

The three remaining knights sighed simultaneously, and then laughed as they did so. "Are we growing old?" Valens rubbed his knee more obviously now it was just the three of them in the room. "By the oak leaf, my leg aches."

"Did you wound it further in the attack on the Curia?" Chonrad took a seat on the stone steps.

"No, but I do find physical exercise increasingly makes it sore." Valens came to sit beside him and Fulco sat further down with a sigh, his own wound obviously troubling him. "What do you think of what you have heard today?"

"That we are all elementals, but have just forgotten our ancestry? Honestly?" Chonrad smiled wryly. "I find it all a little fantastic. And yet I have no answers for what I saw yesterday. The way the water warriors just arose from the water, like figures made out of shadows… How can I explain that, except by accepting the information I have learned?"

Valens nodded. Then he yawned. "I simply must get a few hours' sleep," he said. "Are you going to join me in the Barracks?"

"Yes," said Chonrad, his eyes dry and his limbs heavy with tiredness. They all heaved themselves to their feet and walked out of the Capitulum and into the Temple.

As they passed the Arbor, however, Valens stopped. Chonrad

paused beside him, following his gaze to see the roots creeping over the dead bodies laid out on the Sepulchrum, wrapped in white sheets. He turned his back, sickened by the sight.

Valens caught the movement. Walking once more to the entrance, he said, "The Feeding bothers you?"

Chonrad shrugged, following him, but knew his face gave the game away. "It is not something I have been used to."

"I suppose it must seem an unusual sight to those not accustomed to it." Valens pushed open the door to the outside world, flooding the place with light. The three men blinked, going out into the Quad. The sun was out, although light rain still fell from the storm clouds gathered to the east. "It is something I have grown up with since the age of seven." He turned his face up to the sun. The rays shone on his grey hair, turning it silver. "And yet I wonder now whether the ceremonies we have carried out all these years are correct. It is so unsettling finding out everything we have lived for so long has been a lie."

"Not necessarily." Chonrad fell into step beside the Imperator as they walked past the baskets of food collected from around the Baillium. His stomach growled, but he was too tired to eat. He did, however, accept a flagon of ale from a servant. "We do not know yet which stories are true and which are fictitious. Though he did not have all the facts at his disposal, Oculus clearly made the best out of what he could glean."

"I suppose." Valens crossed to the central road and the three knights walked down in the sunlight.

Chonrad began to feel hot in his armour and wondered whether he could risk removing it for a few hours. "Do you think Nitesco was right, and we can expect another attack at the High Moon?"

Valens shrugged. "I have no idea. The theory makes sense though and, in spite of his lack of years, the Libraris seems to know more about what is occurring here than I do."

Chonrad smiled, glancing around as he walked. The Baillium looked a good deal tidier. Most of the debris had been collected and placed in neat piles, the wood separated from the cloth and the cloth from the food, to make it easier to reuse the materials. The grass still had a flattened look to it from the weight of the flood water, but the sun made everything look brighter and less frightening. There was also a beautiful rainbow arching east, which somehow gave him hope things were going to be all right.

They arrived at the Barracks and Chonrad walked into the large building. Makeshift beds had been placed in all the rooms on the ground floor, most of which were filled with sleeping people, exhausted from the night's activities. The twins were fast asleep, heads tipped back as they snored, and Grimbeald, still in his armour, settled between two other Militis, seemingly at ease in his surroundings in spite of being the only Wulfengar present.

Chonrad could not see Procella. Leaving Valens talking to Beata, who had removed her armour briefly and looked much younger and slender in just a linen tunic, he went up to the first floor and searched the beds there too, but still could not find Procella.

He was desperate to lie down and fall asleep, but he knew he would not be able to rest until he made sure she was all right. Leaving the Barracks, he went outside, Fulco yawning away on his heels, and paused for a moment, wondering where she would be. He looked around the Baillium. In the Castellum? Perhaps in front of the Arbor? But no, he had just come from there. Asleep in the dormitory of the Domus? He frowned, looking around, and then the Porta caught his eye. Where would the Dux feel more at home than in the place where she had grown up, at the very centre of Heartwood's defences? He looked up. Sure enough, a small figure at the top of the gatehouse leaned on the parapets and looked out over the Baillium.

Sighing, he walked down the central road towards the Porta, said hello to the Custodes on duty and walked up the stairs. This time, Fulco stayed at the bottom, clearly having found it difficult to climb the steps.

When he got there, Procella was still leaning on the parapet. "I saw you coming," she said flatly, not bothering to turn around. "What do you want?"

Casting one eye up at the rain, he sighed and came over to stand beside her. "To see how you are." He leaned close enough so their mailed arms almost touched.

She didn't move away, but neither did she move closer. She turned her dark brown eyes on him for a moment. He had thought to see them shot through with anger, but to his surprise they were sad, a shimmer of tears hovering like a silver fish below the surface of a river.

He smiled at her. "It is not the end, you know."

"Is it not?" She glared at him. "How would you like it if you found you had wasted your whole life defending a lie?"

Chonrad had meant it was not the end of Heartwood – that they were going to do their best to get back the Pectoris. But she clearly thought he had been referring to Oculus and the revelations in the *Quercetum*.

Impatience flared briefly within him at her self-pity, but he quashed it. This was not the time to tell her to pull herself together and get back on the horse. Like a heated pot of water, she needed to vent some steam, and unfortunately he realised he was the one who was about to get scalded. "That is not really true," he told her. "You have spent your life defending the Arbor, and Heartwood too. I would hardly call that a wasted life."

She dismissed his words with a flick of her hand. "You all like to spend your time in discussion using big words and fancy arguments. You have not dedicated your life to Oculus's lie – you could not understand."

He had met many knights in his time; had marched beside them and joined them in battle. And Procella was a knight through and through. He recognised in her the marks of one born to fight: a matter-of-fact attitude to life and death; a tendency to follow rather than Question, even though she was a leader herself; and a desire to settle matters by strength, rather than diplomacy, although as Dux she would have needed to understand the importance of mediation as opposed to war.

And suddenly he knew the way to make her feel better. "So Oculus was not the great religious leader everyone thought he was," he said. "So what? What difference is that going to make to your life?"

She blinked, puzzled at his change of direction.

"Your job is to protect Heartwood – and that is what you have done admirably since the time you could hold a sword. Where is the lie in that? Heartwood is just the cage around the Arbor, and nobody is disputing the Arbor is still of vital importance to Anguis." He turned to look at her properly. "Are you really telling me it makes a difference to you what is written in one book or another? Or what different philosophers argue happened? I think not. I think the most important thing to you is to feel you have made a difference – that your life has served a purpose, and I would still say that is still the case. As Dux you have prevented war – so far, at any rate – on several occasions. That is no mean feat, and I understand that better than anyone."

A smile curved her lips, and her eyes were now light as polished oak. "You are a strange one, Chonrad, Lord of Barle," she said, her voice husky. "You extract my feelings as if you are wheedling a whelk out of its shell. Nobody has ever had the power to affect me in all my years the way you have since your arrival only two days ago."

He shrugged. She had closed the distance between them so their arms touched and, although they both wore mail, he was sure he could feel the heat of her body. He was very attracted to her, he realised. He admired her strength and her battle skill, and yet clearly her hard exterior encased a tender heart. His eyes rested on her lips, which had parted slightly. He very much wanted to kiss her, and he suspected she would not reject him.

But this was not the time; when she was feeling more her old self she would not forgive him for taking advantage of her when she was vulnerable. "It is a natural skill," was all he said.

She laughed. "Come on. I am sure you are as tired as I am. We have a few hours before we have to meet to discuss what we are to do. Shall we go to the Barracks?"

Chonrad agreed and together they made their way down the stairs, picking up a dozing Fulco at the bottom. They walked through the Porta and along the main road to the Custodes Barracks. By the time they got there, however, the place was full, and there were no beds to be found. So they went outside and, finding a couple of clean blankets, put one on the ground under an oak which was covered with a cloth as a makeshift roof, rolled up another for a pillow and lay down. They were all used to sleeping rough, and though his bones protested more than they used to when he was younger and out on the march, Chonrad knew he would be asleep within minutes.

It was just before he dozed off that Procella turned towards him and cuddled up against his side, her head resting on his shoulder. Surprised, but pleased, he laid his arm gently around her.

Then they fell asleep.

CHAPTER FIVE

I

When Chonrad awoke, Procella was gone. The sun was low in the sky, and the shadows were lengthening. How long had he been asleep? Several hours, he thought. Fulco yawned and stretched when Chonrad poked him with his foot, looking around him with confusion as if he wasn't where he had expected to be. *Dream*, he signed to Chonrad, and Chonrad thought maybe he had imagined himself at home in Vichton, with his wife and children.

They walked over to the Quad. An area had been set aside next to the lavatorium for washing, with large tubs of water and soap. Some of the younger Militis from the Academy were helping the knights and visitors with their ablutions. He asked one of them, "Where have you got the water from? I see the river is no longer flowing."

"We also have a well, in case of emergencies," said the young Militis.

"Thank the Arbor for that!" said Chonrad fervently.

After he had washed and changed his clothes, he and Fulco took some food and drink and joined a group sitting under an oak to eat. The twins, Beata, Silva and Dolosus were discussing the Virimage.

"Even if he can truly do the things Malgara said he could," said Beata, "he might not be aware of its importance."

"He must be conscious there is something odd about being able to pull acorns out of your nose," said Gavius.

She smiled. "I suppose. But the very fact he has used this… gift for entertainment, to make money, suggests he does not take it seriously."

Dolosus shrugged, skilfully placing a piece of chicken on top of a chunk of bread with his one hand. "What else can he do with it? He could hardly start telling people he can make the grass grow. He would be locked away before he could crack a nut."

Chonrad took a swig of ale and wiped his mouth on his sleeve. "What about you?" he asked Silva. "Do you think he is truly able to do these things?"

Silva looked around the group. "I absolutely think he can alter nature."

"How are you so sure?" said Gavius curiously.

For the first time since he had arrived at Heartwood, Chonrad saw her smile. She placed her hands around a small yellow flower that grew in the shade of the tree. "I have never shown anyone this before," she murmured.

She closed her eyes and concentrated. For a few moments nothing happened. Then very slowly the small flower opened its petals like a yellow eye blinking in the sunlight. The stem grew by about a finger's length, and the leaves lengthened and shone green and glossy.

"By the Arbor!" exclaimed Gravis, "how did you do that?"

Silva shrugged. "I am not really sure. You have to concentrate and imagine it growing. I sense it is something to do with the transfer of energy from my hands to the flower, but I could not tell you more than that."

"So you think the Virimage can also do this?" Chonrad asked her.

"Yes, although I suspect, from what Malgara said, that he is far more powerful than I. Perhaps he truly does have the power to heal the Arbor, to seal the crack that has grown." She looked forlorn. "I have tried to work on it, but my small skill has done little to repair the damage."

As she spoke, a bell rang out from the Castellum. "Sextus Campana," said Beata. "Time for the meeting."

They all got up and carried their plates back to the tables, then gradually made their way into the Temple and through to the Capitulum. Four tables had been set up around the room. On one, a large map of Anguis had been spread, and Fionnghuala and Grimbeald were poring over it, discussing the locations of the five Nodes. Another map covered the second table, and Malgara and Kenweard were talking about how to find the Virimage. Nitesco and Procella sat behind a third table covered with piles of parchment and old books talking about the location of Darkwater. On the fourth table was a detailed map of Heartwood's defenses, and Valens stood by this.

The Imperator looked up as the room started filling. "Please come in," he called, welcoming in both the Militis and the visitors who crowded the doorway. "We have set up four working parties. Please join whichever you feel you can contribute to."

Beata went over to Malgara and Kenweard. The twins and Silva joined the discussion on the five Nodes. Several of the Militis went over to help Valens. Chonrad looked at Dolosus, who shrugged and said, "I am up for a dip in the ocean. How about you?"

Procella looked up as the two knights came over. Her eyes met Chonrad's briefly before returning to the map of Anguis in front of her. "Nitesco has been reading through some old myths and fables to find out if there is any mention of possible locations of this Darkwater place," she said.

"Any luck?" Chonrad perched opposite her. On the table a fishing map showed Anguis and the mainland and, between them and to the east, the large expanse of the Bluewater Ocean.

Nitesco put down his papers and stood to lean over the map. "There are a group of islands over here," he said, indicating a scatter of markings right in the middle of the ocean, "that are mentioned several times. They are called the Gantlos Islands, and apparently the people living there have many myths about fish that turn into warriors who come to shore to find women to bear their young."

"They mate with them?" asked Dolosus.

Nitesco shrugged. "So the myth says. Listen." He ferreted under the pile of books and on finding the one he wanted, slid it out and turned to the appropriate page. "It is in a strange dialect," he said. "It is a variant of Wulfian. It says... 'The young women are warned not to go onto the beach at night, for it is then that the warriors come out of the sea. The...'" He paused. "I am not sure what word this is, there is no direct translation. It is like a fusion of the Wulfian word for 'fish' and 'warrior'... anyway, they 'come looking for women in which to plant their seed, and then they disappear into the...' This is one long word – I think it means 'city under the water'... 'and leave the maids to bear and bring up the young. When the offspring are of age, the 'fish warriors' then come ashore and take the young back to the 'city under the water', to raise them in their army, ready for the...'" Nitesco looked up at the others around the table. "This last word is difficult to interpret. The beginning is like the Wulfian word for 'conclusive' but the ending is more like the word for 'crusade'. My best guess is it means 'final battle'."

"Final battle?" A shiver ran down Chonrad's spine. "That is interesting."

Nitesco put the book down and pulled the map towards him again. He took a piece of chalk and began to draw on the parchment. "We have several volumes of tales handed down orally by people from the coast, fisherpeople, who have seen things out on the ocean. There have been sightings of strange creatures who have been described as things like 'half-fish, half-warriors', 'water knights' and 'sea soldiers', in these places." He marked half a dozen crosses on the map. The crosses formed a large, rough circle to the west of the Gantlos Islands. "Interestingly, there are also records of stories related by divers looking for mussels and oysters off the rocks surrounding the islands, of strange things they have seen beneath the ocean."

"What sorts of things?" Chonrad watched Nitesco hunt through the papers for another book.

He pulled a neatly bound volume towards him and opened it at a marked page. "Here, this one has tales from Laxonian coastal villages. One diver talks of 'glittering objects on the bottom of the ocean', another mentions 'stone buildings like great towers in the deep'."

"Does it say where they saw them?" Dolosus asked.

Nitesco nodded and pointed with his chalk right in the middle of the circle of crosses.

"Well, at least we know where to look." Chonrad wondered how long it would take them to get there by boat. "Any ideas on what we do when we get there? How we survive under the water?"

"I'm working on that." Nitesco sat back in his seat, pulling the next pile of books towards him.

Procella sighed. "Perhaps we should talk about what sort of force to take down there, and what exactly we mean to accomplish," she suggested.

"Good idea," said Chonrad, impatient to do something. Fulco pulled up a couple of seats and Dolosus did the same the other side, and they proceeded to begin a discussion on what tactics they should assume for the attack.

II

The four groups talked until the sun had set and the Primus Night Campana rang. Some people moved from one discussion group to another to give their input, others got caught up in what they were researching and stuck with their topic. But after the bell, Valens held up his hand, called for quiet and asked everyone to take a seat.

"My friends," he began. "I think maybe it is time for us to see where we have got to." He looked across at Nitesco, who looked tired but buoyant with the evening's work. "I think you will understand when I say I have elected our Libraris to co-ordinate the four tasks. Perhaps he would care to speak now and summarise our findings for us."

Nitesco nodded and took the floor. "I think we have made great headway tonight. Firstly, I would like to talk about the Veriditas and our search for this Virimage. We have his location over the past few weeks, so it seems he is still in Laxony. Beata has asked to head the search party for the Virimage and hopefully bring him back to Heartwood so he can talk to us about the Veriditas, and maybe help us heal the Arbor."

Nitesco sighed. "We do not know how long it will take. I have speculated we might have until the High Moon before Darkwater attacks again – if I am right, and they do not attack before then, that is still only fourty-four days, and if I am wrong it could be even sooner than that. I do not believe we have time to wait until the Virimage is found before the party going to secure the five Nodes sets off.

"With this in mind, Silva is going to spend some time teaching how to control the energy flow. This will provide those travelling to the Nodes with at least a little knowledge of how to secure the energy centres."

"Is that going to be enough?" Procella frowned. "Is there any point in going all the way to the Nodes without truly knowing how to open them?"

"If we can do nothing else, making sure the sites are clear of debris and structurally sound will be better than nothing," said Nitesco. "Then maybe if the Virimage is found and reveals the answer to how to open the Nodes, we can then send further people to do just that.

"While we are on the subject of the Nodes, it has been decided it makes more sense to have four different people travel to the Nodes than to have one party travelling to all four in succession, as this will save time. We have had four groups of volunteers to undertake this task: Gravis will travel to the Henge in Laxony, Gavius to the Green Giant in Komis, Fionnghuala and Bearrach to the Portal in Hanaire and Grimbeald to the Tumulus in Wulfengar. In the meantime, I will continue my research into the fifth Node."

Valens nodded. "I have decided to stay in Heartwood and oversee the defensive improvements. My injury means I cannot travel far and as my knowledge about the defences here is second only to Procella's. I think I will serve us best if I prepare for a second attack."

Nitesco indicated the Dux. "Finally, Procella, Chonrad and Dolosus have volunteered to lead the descent into Darkwater. We are still exploring ways to do this, but we think we have established it is possible to take the form of a water elemental, and we are in the process of planning a raid on this underwater city."

Procella stood. "Our main aim for this raid is to get the Pectoris back. We are hoping the actions of those securing the Nodes and improving the Arbor will seal off the Darkwater Lords' chances of attacking us again. If for any reason that does not turn out to be the case, we will reassess the situation again when – if – we return, and then plan a further full frontal attack with as many troops as we can muster. But for now it will be a quick foray to try to recover the Arbor's heart."

"How dangerous is it likely to be, or is that a ridiculous Question?" asked Beata.

Chonrad shrugged. "Obviously, any raid into enemy territory is a huge risk. Our aim would be to take a very small party, the three of us and a few others, and disguise ourselves as Darkwater Lords. We will be in and out as quickly as possible. However, there is always the risk of discovery and we have no idea of their numbers. We do know they are greatly skilled in battle. So our plan is to only engage them in an emergency."

"What about the actual process of the descent?" Beata asked. "How much do you know about what that involves?"

"I am still reading about how it works," said Nitesco. "It is a complicated concept and I am not a natural philosopher! From what I understand, each elemental carries within it the strength and properties of its element – therefore earth elementals have physical presence and a connection to Nature, while water elementals are fluid in form and are closely associated to the oceans. However, one element can 'bind' itself to another using special energy bonds – I am still researching this, but it seems to involve 'giving oneself over' to the other elemental, surrendering yourself to it, almost hiding within it, if you like."

"It sounds very dangerous." Beata's eyes flicked to Procella.

Procella pulled a face. "I admit to not liking the idea of 'giving myself over' to a water elemental, whatever that involves. But the Pectoris must be returned. That is not a matter open for debate. If we do not retrieve it, the Arbor will fail. We *must* try, at least."

Valens nodded. The room had grown quiet. He looked around at the knights who were going to risk their lives to save their beloved tree, and sighed. "So when do you all start?"

"We shall spend tomorrow preparing for the journey," said Beata, "and then be off at first light the day after."

Gavius nodded. "Gravis and I are going to accompany Beata as far as Hicton and then we will go our separate ways."

"Fionnghuala and Bearrach will travel north with me to the Neck Pass, and then we will go our own ways, too," said Grimbeald. "We, also, will start the day after tomorrow."

"I am going to pick an assortment of warriors from the Exercitus to come and help us," said Procella. "I suggest we meet up again at first light to decide who is going with whom, and then we will know numbers for organising supplies and horses for the rest of the day."

"That is it, then," said Valens. "Thank you for your time and cooperation, everyone. Please go and eat or rest, and then rejoin us – I suggest in the Quad – at Secundus Campana tomorrow to allocate troops."

Wanting to eat before they slept again, Chonrad and Fulco headed for the Quad tables and helped themselves to a plate of meat and vegetables, and joined Dolosus under the cover of an oak.

For a while they ate in companionable silence, the rain pattering onto the grass around them. Chonrad tried not to look at the limp sleeve hanging at Dolosus' side. "How long have you been Dean?" he asked, swigging down a mouthful of ale.

"Two years," said Dolosus, chewing on a piece of pork.

"Do you like the job?"

Dolosus swallowed and sighed. "The role of a Dean is to provide support to other Militis. I cannot truly say it is a role I was born for."

"Then why do you do it?"

Dolosus licked his fingers, studying Chonrad for a while as if unsure if he could trust him. Chonrad just ate steadily, waiting for him to talk.

"There is not a lot else I can do," Dolosus shrugged eventually.

"Would you not be more suited to the role of a Custos?"

"Valens thought this would be more... challenging."

"Valens?" His food finished, Chonrad pushed his plate away and stretched out his legs. He looked at Dolosus thoughtfully. "He recommended you for Dean?"

Dolosus nodded. "Dulcis was not certain I would be right for the position but he insisted. She was right, of course."

Chonrad wondered if this was the Militis Dulcis had referred to with regret. "Does Valens usually put himself to so much trouble for other knights caught drunk on duty?"

Dolosus met Chonrad's eye. Chonrad raised an eyebrow, refusing to back down. He had done his research – he wasn't going to go on such a dangerous mission without knowing as much as possible about the knights fighting beside him. Dolosus shrugged. "Sometimes I think Valens sees himself in me. I do not know why – I do not think we are anything alike. After the incident on the Wall, he was angry with me. Maybe he hopes to transform me into what he became – a great leader." He shrugged again. "If that is so, then he is in for a great disappointment."

III

Chonrad watched as Dolosus promptly got up and, returning his plate, made his way over to the Barracks. He sat there with Fulco a while longer, too tired to move, thinking about what the Militis had said and watching the rain. It had not stopped since the storm had arrived with the Darkwater Lords. He frowned, looking up at the grey clouds, which showed no signs of clearing. Was the weather actually due to the Darkwater Lords' arrival, or was it a coincidence?

He sighed. He was too tired to think straight and he didn't want to spend another night on the hard ground. He pulled Fulco to his feet and they walked over to the Barracks and went up to the first floor, which was still relatively empty, and found two beds in the corner. They lay down, still fully armoured, and Chonrad looked up at the rain-washed windows and sighed, missing Procella's weight on his shoulder.

When he finally awoke, the sun had risen, although it was still raining and there was no sign of its welcoming rays to warm up the land. He woke Fulco, and they went out to the makeshift lavatorium, had a wash and then helped themselves to a bowl of porridge the Militis had cooking on a huge cauldron over a fire in the Quad.

People were already beginning to assemble and so he hung around, seeing Procella coming down the main road with about thirty or so members of the Exercitus in tow. As they approached, Valens went over to converse with her and then pulled up a low bench and climbed awkwardly onto it, favouring his left leg.

"My friends," he called to gain their attention. "Procella has been recruiting from the Exercitus for those who wish to take part in the tasks. She has divided them up into the relevant groups, so if the Quest Leaders would now like to take their groups away and discuss the Quests with them, you may do so. I know you wish to spend most of the day sorting out supplies and horses and finalising your routes. However, Nitesco here would also like to see those of you on the Node Quests to talk to you about the activation of the Nodes."

He took a list from Procella and proceeded to call out the names of the Exercitus volunteers, allocating them to the Quest Leaders. Chonrad watched to see who she had picked for their descent into Darkwater. Valens called out three names and those Militis stepped forward to join her. One was called Solum; a knight probably from Wulfengar, he thought, with thick dark hair and a rather fierce but intelligent expression. The second was called Hora. A Laxonian, she was tall and slim, and from the way she moved he could see she was fit and agile, almost certainly an excellent knight. The third was called Terreo. Chonrad blinked as he stepped forwards. He was huge! Taller even than Fulco! Almost as broad as he was tall, the brown-haired Militis towered over him, and Chonrad was by no means small himself. He raised an eyebrow as Procella came over to him, smiling. "I didn't know there was giant in Laxonian blood," he said wryly.

She grinned and bent close to whisper to him. "He is not the smartest in the bunch, but he is built like a stone lavatorium and *nothing* gets through him. Do not worry; Solum and Hora have enough brains for all of us put together."

Chonrad nodded, reassured by the company.

The Exercitus allocated, it was time to start preparing for the trips. Chonrad felt at a loss. There was no point making plans for their journey to Darkwater when they weren't even sure if it was possible; they had to wait for Nitesco to find out how to transform them before they could leave. He wandered around for a while, wondering if anyone needed any help, but everyone seemed very busy talking and drawing plans.

As he came around the southern side of the Castellum, he saw an awning had been erected between a couple of oaks, and a group of people sat beneath it. He came nearer to see what was going on, not wanting to interrupt, but when Silva saw him and Fulco, she beckoned them closer. They sat on the cushions at the edge of the group.

The knights around him were those going on the Nodes Quests, about twenty in all. Silva was talking about the power of the Veriditas, and she and Nitesco, who sat beside her, were discussing their views on how to get the Nodes activated.

"The *Quercetum* emphasises the importance of the physical centre of the Node," Nitesco said. "We must not be mistaken in thinking this is only an energy core. It is just as important for you to correct any way in which the site has become dilapidated – that means moving rubble, resetting any fallen stones, cleaning any standing stones, clearing weeds and moss and just generally making the site clear." He looked over at Gravis. "Of course, large fallen standing stones in the Henge will be a problem. It is possible there may be people living nearby who can help. If not, you will just have to do the best you can."

"And now for the Veriditas," said Silva. She shook back her long black hair, and her gold eyes glowed. "I only wish we had been able to find the Virimage before you set out on your journey. But alas, I shall have to share with you the little I know and hope that will help you to activate the Nodes.

"As we all know, Veriditas is a combination of two words – Viridis, which is green, and Veritas, which is truth. Therefore, Veriditas is the process of looking within us and seeing the truth – accepting who we are, and in doing that letting the power of Animus sweep through us to the land. Like this."

She cupped her hands around a small daisy and closed her eyes. Those seated around her strained over others' heads to look. For a moment nothing happened. Then, slowly, the daisy began to grow, its petals unfurling and stretching out as if the sun had come out, its stem lengthening and its leaves greening and glossing under her hands.

Those who had not yet seen Silva do her magic gasped. She opened her eyes and smiled ruefully. "I wish it could be more. And hopefully the Virimage will help us all to increase this flow of energy. But anyway, I will show you what I can. Please, find a flower near you and place your hands over it."

Chonrad looked around, wondering if he was expected to partake in the experiment, saw everyone looking for a flower and shrugged and turned to the small group of daisies beside him. He separated one stem from the others and cupped it in his palms. Fulco stared at him. Chonrad gestured for Fulco to do the same. His bodyguard raised an eyebrow, but did as he was bid.

"Close your eyes," Silva instructed. "Now, I want you to imagine yourself as a vessel, a cup, and the sunlight – if there were any – is the love of Animus streaming down and filling you up. You are being filled with a golden light that runs through your veins and into the flower between your hands. Imagine yourself as made of glass, clear and pure; acknowledge the fact that you have faults, and put them to one side; realise you have done things wrong in the past, and put them to one side. You are clean, wholesome and thoroughly deserving of Animus's love, it runs through you, cleansing, washing out all the imperfections, making you pure and whole once again…"

Chonrad tried to concentrate, but found himself distracted by the tap-tapping of the rain on the awning and the small sounds of people shuffling awkwardly on the grass. He tried to focus on Silva's voice, her low, mellow tone, and he imagined the sun coming out from the clouds and shining on him, pouring the yellow light like butter down on him and through his veins. *Animus loves me*, he said to himself. But did he really believe it?

He opened his eyes cautiously and looked at the flower in his hands. It didn't seem to have changed. Had the petals opened a little? Perhaps it was just his imagination.

Around him, everyone compared what they had produced to their neighbours. Gravis and Grimbeald both stared ruefully at their offerings, declaring no change, as did most of the others in the gathering. Nitesco's daisy appeared to have grown by a finger's height, which made him beam with pleasure. To Chonrad's amazement – and slight indignation – Fulco's also appeared to have bloomed a little, and he scowled at Fulco's superior smile. And then an exclamation made everyone turn and look at Gavius. Chonrad stared. The daisy within the twin's hands had grown to twice its size. The petals had unfurled and glowed white, and the yellow inside was like a small, golden sun. The thick, shiny leaves curled in his fingers.

"Wow," Gavius said.

Gravis pulled a face. "You changed it while we had our eyes closed," he complained. Everyone laughed, dispelling the tension a little. However, Chonrad saw the look that lingered on Gravis's face when he thought no one was looking. Jealousy? Resentment? Chonrad frowned. Maybe the twins' relationship was not as perfect as everyone imagined it to be.

"Very well done," said Silva. "But the rest of you, please do not be despondent. I did not really expect any results today. All I wanted to show you was the technique. Please, practice this as much as possible on your way to the Nodes. It will help you when you get there." She got to her feet. "Now that's the Quartus Campana. That is our weapons practice time, for those of you who wish to join us."

IV

Later, the high meal of the day turned out to be a great party, as if everyone was aware this might be the last time they were all together. Nobody wanted to admit they were nervous or scared about the coming adventures, and wanted instead to forget for a night and enjoy the short time they had left with their friends.

The Hanaireans had brought a small troop of musicians with them to entertain them on the long journey, and so they set themselves up on a small platform to one side of the Quad and played through the night as everyone danced and sang or just sat and listened to the music.

The Quad had been covered with a succession of awnings to keep off the now-constant rain, and the earth floor underneath was spread with rushes gathered from the banks of the Flumen outside Heartwood, mixed with sprigs of rosemary and thyme so the sweet smell of the herbs kept drifting up as people walked or danced across them. Chairs and cushions were scattered to the sides, and tables set up along the southern edge of the Quad on which a feast had been prepared in honour of the adventures about to be undertaken.

"It is a fine spread," said Chonrad to Valens, who stood to one side watching the dancers with a smile.

"We cannot really afford to use so much food, but I could not send everyone away on bread and water," said Valens.

"It would help if Fulco was not eating half of it on his own," Chonrad said wryly, seeing his bodyguard walk past with his usual huge plate of bread and meat.

Valens smiled, then sighed. "Now Wulfengar are refusing to give us the Charitas, our supplies will dwindle even more."

"How long could you withstand a siege?"

Valens thought about it. "We have sacks of wheat, oats and barley in the grain store, which should last us a while, and barrels of salted meat and fish. We have our own vegetable gardens which are still supplying us with a good yield, although obviously it is down from last year, and this continual rain will not help their growth. But we have some put aside for an emergency. We have a few cows, which can supply us with milk and cheese, although not as much as we would like. Our well, at least, should give us water, and anyway with all this rain we should not be short of a drink." He sighed. "We would probably be able to last for a couple of months without having to cut rations drastically. Let us hope it does not come to that."

Chonrad nodded. He saw Valens looking across the Quad at someone and followed his gaze to see Dolosus sitting by himself, a cup of ale in his hand, watching the dancing morosely. Chonrad frowned, intrigued by the Imperator's connection with this Militis. "You are concerned for Dolosus?" he enquired, wondering if Valens would open up.

Valens looked at him. "I think he will perform more than adequately on your Quest."

"That is not what I meant." Chonrad smiled. "I think he means more to you than just another Heartwood knight. Am I right?"

For a moment Valens's face was carefully guarded, but suddenly, as if aware this was the night of nights and everything could end on the morrow, he sighed and nodded. "He is like the son I never had," he admitted. "I was very like him in my youth."

"You were?" Chonrad could not imagine Valens sulky or morose.

Valens smiled. "I suppose you are not aware, but I too came late to Heartwood. I was born in Wulfengar and grew up, like Dolosus, without a true house to call my home. My father was a visiting knight who took a fancy to the serving wench who was my mother, and I never knew him. When she died at the age of twenty-five, I was only nine years old. Nobody wanted me; I was another mouth to feed in a village where food was not in abundance. So I left and went to the nearest city and made a living here and there, helping in smithies mainly. I soon learned all about swords and armour and, like Dolosus, learned how to wield them. And eventually I attached myself to a raiding party. It was through them that I learned of Heartwood, so one day I walked up the gates and asked to join."

"Thank goodness they said yes!"

"Oh, they did not, initially," said Valens mischievously. "But I sat outside and refused to move. Eventually, the old Abbatis came out to see me himself and after speaking to me, agreed to give me a trial. And I have never looked back."

Chonrad nodded. He looked over at Dolosus. "And are you grooming him to take your place one day?"

A frown marred Valens's features and for a moment he didn't answer. "I was getting there... and then he lost his arm. It should not make any difference to a leader, of course, but it has affected him so much; he feels less than a knight, and it has deepened the anger and mistrust that have simmered within him since childhood." He shrugged. "But I will persevere. It is difficult, feeling nobody wants you. He should not have to feel that way."

Chonrad walked to the edge of the awning, looking up at the sky. For a brief moment, the rain had eased, and stars sparkled like a scatter of diamonds on the black velvet cloak of the sky. "The future is so uncertain," he murmured.

"The wheel of time turns continuously," said Valens, joining him. "It is always so. It is only that we are more aware of it at this moment."

Procella came up to them both, breathless, her cheeks flushed. Her eyes glittered, and she winked at Chonrad as she held out a hand. "You are so boring, standing there in the shadows and talking," she exclaimed. "Come and dance."

Chonrad blinked, surprised at her sudden gaiety. But he smiled and took her hand, and let himself be led forwards to the space where people were moving to the music in a beautiful dance like the movement of the stars above their heads.

V

The next morning, Chonrad awoke at first light to hear the rain had started again and was patting away merrily at the windows of the Barracks.

He walked over to one of the tables and helped himself to a large bowl of porridge. Turning, he glanced around at the people in the Quad, looking for a familiar face.

Beata was already there, dressed in full mail, looking fresh and determined as she checked her horse's fittings and filled the small baskets that hung on either side of her saddle with her belongings.

"Travelling light?" said Chonrad with a smile, walking up to her as he ate his porridge.

She turned to face him, her eyes as grey as the storm clouds above their heads, and nodded. "Just a little clothing, my weapons and a few odds and ends."

"If I do not get the chance to say it later, good luck on your Quest," said Chonrad sincerely. "I am sure you will find the Virimage and encourage him to come back."

"Oh, he will be coming back all right," said Beata vehemently, "if I have to drag him by the earlobes."

Chonrad raised an eyebrow, sensing she wasn't jesting. "Can I get you something to eat?" he asked, watching her moving restlessly as she checked and rechecked the contents of the panniers.

She shot him a quick smile. "No, thank you. Too nervous to eat."

As the hour passed and the Secundus Campana rang, the Quad gradually filled up. Chonrad busied himself with helping others to pack belongings into horses' baskets, kept the steeds quiet while the parties moved around getting organised, and generally did whatever he could to stop himself feeling useless. He helped to wrap bread in cloths, roll up blankets, load bags with apples, carry buckets of water from the well and fill up leather water bottles, double-check routes on maps and generally cheer everyone up as tension spread throughout the vicinity and nerves became taut.

At one point Fulco appeared, bleary-eyed and with his hair sticking up, scolding Chonrad with gesticulations for not waking him. Chonrad laughed, but Fulco grabbed his arm and turned him to face him. *You are not to leave my sight*, Fulco signed. *Understand?* Chonrad nodded, holding up his hands and sobering at the serious look on his bodyguard's face. Clearly the tension was even getting to the normally placid Laxonian.

By the Tertius Campana, Fionnghuala and Grimbeald and their parties were ready to leave. Chonrad, Valens and Procella accompanied them to the Porta.

"Good luck," Valens said simply. He had already spoken in depth with them about their Quests, and there was little more advice he could give that would do them any good at this late hour.

The Quest Leaders, and the Militis who were accompanying them, made their way across the drawbridge. Fionnghuala and Grimbeald waited and then nodded at the three knights waiting under the Porta before turning their horses, casting one last look back at the towering gatehouse and the giant oak leaf carved into the stone above the portcullis. They crossed the drawbridge over the moat, the horses' hooves echoing on the wood. Immediately to their left was the beginning of Isenbard's Wall, the tall, towering stone barrier that lay between Wulfengar and Laxony. The gate through the Wall was opened temporarily and they passed through it, crossing over the bridge that spanned the Flumen – the wide river that tumbled to the north of the Wall, and then they were in Wulfengar, and soon they were swallowed up by the dark forest.

"I wonder if we shall see them again," said Valens, his voice rough.

The others didn't answer, too caught up in their own thoughts to reply.

The activity inside the Quad intensified as the other three parties got ready for their journey. By the Quartus Campana, Beata, Gravis, Gavius and their parties were ready to leave.

This time, Chonrad, Valens and Procella walked to the Porta accompanied by most of the others who were staying behind. The Quest Leaders moved through the gatehouse and then paused on their horses, turning to look back at the place that had been more than just their home, Chonrad guessed. For some, it was their whole life, and leaving it now must be terrifying.

Chonrad saw Beata swallow. However, as her horse twitched under her she quieted it immediately and smiled at the crowd waiting to say goodbye.

Gavius just looked excited, his palfrey sensing his eagerness and dancing beneath him. Gravis's expression was blank, and Chonrad could not read what he was thinking.

Valens, who had previously spoken to them all separately, now just put his left hand over his heart, revealing his oak leaf tattoo, and the others did the same. No more words needed to be said.

The parties ambled over the drawbridge, this time turning right on the road leading from the Wall into Laxony. They looked back just once more before the road curled around to the south and out of sight.

The people in the Porta filtered back into the Baillium, leaving Procella, Valens, Chonrad and Fulco.

Chonrad felt a strange nervousness in the pit of his stomach, a feeling of excitement mixed with fear.

Tears shone in Procella's eyes, but did not fall. She met Chonrad's glance and raised her chin. Silently, she walked past him and into the Baillium.

Valens watched her go. He gave one last look over his shoulder at the empty road, then turned and smiled wryly at Chonrad and Fulco.

"And so it begins," he said.

Together, they walked back through the gatehouse, the drawbridge rising slowly behind them.

PART TWO

CHAPTER SIX

I

As the three Quest parties rounded the corner of the woodland and Heartwood disappeared behind the trees, Beata's heart sank and she bit her lip, trying to stop the tears streaming down her face. Pulling the hood of her riding cloak low over her head, she kicked her mare forward until she was at the head of the train and then settled in the seat, relieved no one could see her.

For a brief moment, she let the tears flow. Leaving Heartwood was like leaving a loved one; she felt again the homesickness and loneliness she'd experienced when first arriving at the Castellum at the age of seven. At least then she had understood she was being given a great honour, that she was moving on to something better than the nondescript life she would have led as the third daughter of a relatively poor knight, married off to some local landowner as soon as she was sixteen, condemned to live in a tiny castle in the middle of a field somewhere.

But this time, she did not feel that she was moving on to something better. She was leaving her home and all the people who meant something to her to travel across Anguis, a land filled with unrest and unknown dangers, and for what? To find a phantom, an idea, a dream she wasn't even sure was real.

Why had she volunteered? Valens wouldn't have thought twice if she had said she wanted to stay at Heartwood and help with the defences. He knew she had barely been a mile from the Castellum for years; he had in fact said to her that morning that if she wanted to change her mind, he would not think badly of her because of it. But although tempted to take him up on his offer, her pride would not let her do it.

She had volunteered to go on this Quest because she knew it might help save Heartwood. What was the point in staying in the Castellum with the sword of doom hanging above her head? Would she ever have been able to forgive herself if the Darkwater Lords invaded again and she had done nothing to try and stop them? She was not a person who could fool herself easily – she was completely aware of her faults and looked at herself honestly and openly. And she would not have been able to live with herself if she had not come on this Quest.

Also, unlike Procella, who fought tò defend the stones and mortar of Heartwood and its people, Beata had a much deeper faith that had not been shaken by the revelations of Nitesco and the *Quercetum*. She had listened to the Libraris's words with interest and was not closed to the idea of elementals and a mystical place under the sea, as at least that would explain what had happened that afternoon in the Curia. But she had not had a crisis of faith. She did not see how it would change her love of Animus and her role in life to both worship and defend the Arbor. So what if the fantastic story was true and she wasn't flesh and bone but merely an elemental that had taken physical shape? How did that make the life she had spent pointless? How did it change her thoughts and feelings towards the tree? The answer was that it didn't, and therefore she knew she had to come on this Quest, and do her utmost to save the Arbor, though the journey may be long and the outcome, as yet, uncertain.

She sighed, her emotions calming. It was understandable, she thought, to feel upset and uneasy about leaving the place she had lived in for almost as long as she could remember. She should not judge herself too harshly for her moment of weakness.

Taking a deep breath, she let it out slowly, raising her head and beginning to look at her surroundings. This was an adventure, she thought, an opportunity to explore the world in which she lived, and although it had in fact been forced upon her, it should not dissuade her from getting as much out of the experience as she could.

For this first leg of the journey, she had to stay on the main road leading south until they reached Cherton. Turning slightly in her saddle, she could see behind her the formidable grey barrier of Isenbard's Wall following the line of the hills into the distance, marked by the occasional fortlet, and fronted to the north by the dark blue glitter of the Flumen.

Turning back to face south, on her left the low hills were divided by hedges into large fields, linked by lanes and roads that criss-crossed the region, giving the whole area the look of a giant patchwork quilt. Some fields were brown, newly ploughed and sown with wheat; others were green and dotted with sheep.

To her right reared the formidable Spina Mountains, capped with white in the far distance, grey and intimidating in the foreground. Trees smattered the slopes of the nearest peaks, multiplying at the base of the range, spilling onto the hills in a thick blanket known as the Forest of Blades, which reached out fingers to cut off the road down which they were heading.

She could skirt the forest but it would mean another day's journey to travel first east and then west again to get to Cherton, and it was a day they could ill afford to waste. Ahead, the earthen track disappeared into the woods as if swallowed whole, and she sighed, wishing their journey could have started with a more open and direct route. The Forest of Blades was so called because historically there had always been outlaws hiding in its leafy depths, ready to pounce on unsuspecting travellers. Heartwood periodically scoured the forest to clean it of raiders, but they always seemed to creep back once the holy knights had left.

She looked behind her, checking everyone was following. Gavius and Gravis were close behind, indicating, she thought, they too felt uneasy at straying so far from home. The Exercitus accompanying them, however, had spread out to either side, clearly more comfortable than their Heartwood companions at being out on the open road.

Her eyes flicked over the four of her companions who would be staying with her when the twins went their own ways. Peritus she knew well; they had been in the same Allectus and had grown up under the same Dean. He had eventually left Heartwood to join the Exercitus, but when Procella had brought him to her and told her he would be accompanying her on her journey, she had grasped his arm with pleasure, relieved to see a familiar face, one she knew was trustworthy, a placid and yet solid warrior.

Caelestis and Erubesco were both younger than her, but similar in stature and appearance: tall, slim, female Militis from Laxony, brown haired and lithe, Caelestis skilled with a bow, Erubesco a natural with both sword and dagger. Pleasant and affable, they were also accomplished fighters, and would, Beata thought, be congenial but useful companions.

The last of her group, Fortis, was at least twenty years older than her, and a close friend of Procella, although Beata had never spoken with him much. He was clearly from Wulfengar: sturdily built, rugged and silent, a natural warrior, with powerful muscles and the riding skills of a knight who had spent a lifetime in the saddle. He made Beata nervous. Not, she thought, because he had been particularly aggressive or unfriendly. But his field experience and the fact that he was so well travelled made her wonder if he would be Questioning decisions she made on the road, and whether he would challenge her authority. Still, Procella had placed him with her for a reason, and she hoped he would turn out to be the stalwart rock Procella had insisted he was.

Gavius and Gravis each had four Militis with them also, so there should be safety in numbers.

They were nearly at the forest's edge. Beata reined in her mare, and turned and addressed her companions. "The road narrows ahead," she said, raising her voice to reach those at the back. "We will have to travel no more than two abreast. We must keep on the alert until we pass through this band of forest. This should take us about three hours." She looked at Fortis, who was waiting patiently, his hands loose on the reins so his mount could nibble the grass at the edge of the road. "Perhaps you could bring up the rear," she suggested, hoping he understood she had asked this of him because she trusted him and knew he would stay alert.

"Of course," he said immediately, turning the horse using only his knees so the mount moved to the back of the party. She nodded. She had forgotten the Exercitus were an exceptionally well-trained army, taught to follow commands immediately with no Questions asked. That would undoubtedly come in handy on the journey!

She laid her right hand on the pommel of the sword hanging on her left hip, making sure it was loose in the scabbard, then nudged her horse forwards. Gavius fell in beside her, and Gravis behind him with Caelestis, the others following in a line, Fortis bringing up the rear. Together, the party crossed a ditch marking the boundary of the forest, and entered the canopy of trees.

Almost immediately Beata felt as if she had passed into a different world. She experienced a similar feeling to that when entering the Castellum from the sunny Quad in Heartwood. There she always noticed the coolness of the Temple and the immediate change in sounds, from the call of birds and clash of swords and general busyness of the Baillium, to the high-ceilinged quietness and echoing acoustics in the domed building.

Here, in the forest, she was immediately aware of how alive the place was; from the soft, rushing sound of leaves above her head, to the quiet murmur of the brook running to her left and the occasional rustle of a creature in the undergrowth. Like everyone else from Heartwood, she felt a distinct affinity with trees and there was nothing more familiar to her in the world – other than perhaps the weight of a sword in her hand – than the scratch of bark beneath her fingertips, or the rich smell of loam from the roots. But here was different; she almost felt as if she were inside a giant creature, an animal made from branches and twigs and leaves and bark, which sniffled and snuffled and rustled and twitched as she moved through it. She felt unsettled and nervous, and as the canopy of leaves closed over her head she began to pray fervently she would make it through to the other side.

II

The road running north of Isenbard's Wall from Heartwood swept a wide arc to the east to avoid the Forest of Wings. Fionnghuala knew there was no direct path through the forest, because she had travelled through Wulfengar on her way from Hanaire to Heartwood, and at the time she had been puzzled to find there was no way south other than by the circuitous route that added a good three days to the journey. Nobody at the time had been able to answer her Questions, but now she spurred her horse forwards to catch up with Grimbeald, and asked him why.

He looked to the west at the dark mass of the forest that seemed to watch them broodingly, clustered at the base of the Spina Mountains. "The trees grow too thick and close together," he said, and shivered. "There are many tales of ghosts lurking in the shadows. I would not travel through the forest if you paid me."

Fionnghuala raised her eyebrows, but said nothing as the Wulfian warrior hunched himself forward in his saddle and drew his travelling cloak close around him. She let the horse drop back a little until she rode behind him. He was an enigma to her; she did not understand him at all, and could not read his mood.

She sighed, wishing they were several days forward on their journey, and at the Neck Pass, close to Hanaire. She disliked the five lands of Wulfengar with a passion that was difficult to hide, which was one reason why she was certain Grimbeald resented her company. But she could not change the way she felt. She disliked the men of Wulfengar, so dark and hairy, arrogant and aggressive, domineering and dismissive of any women they encountered. She even disliked the countryside: Wulfengar was a land of rivers and swamps, and most of its travel and trade was conducted by boat. Its roads were under-developed, barely used and made riding a tedious business. And to top it all, because of the abundance of rivers and the swift transport of goods from the coast, fish was the Wulfians' main food, and there was a faint fishy smell about both the men and the land through which they passed.

She longed for Hanaire – a land of hills and dales, forests and streams, a place of balance and peace, where men and women lived as equals, children were a blessing and the extended family was the social unit that kept everyone caring for one another. She did not understand the Wulfian men's desire to oppress their women – in Hanaire the women's special skills such as intuition, empathy and compassion were considered as important as men's aggressiveness and leadership skills, and it was agreed the social unit could not function without a balance of each.

And yet, strangely, Grimbeald did not seem like a typical Wulfian, she thought, observing him where he sat on his horse. He certainly looked like one: squat and muscular with a full head of dark hair and a bushy brown beard, and the fierce expression that most Wulfian men seemed to wear. And yet he was not aggressive, and she knew he played the flute – not a hobby she could imagine would earn him much praise in Wulfian circles. She had also seen him writing on several occasions, and although she had not been able to see what he had written, she sensed the sheer ability to put pen to paper was more than most Wulfian men could – or wanted to – do.

She sighed, unusually despondent. The rain seemed to be getting heavier, and her clothes felt sodden, and her spirits likewise.

"Are you all right?" The voice came from beside her. Her countryman, Bearrach, had ridden closer and looked at her with some concern.

"I am wet," she said flatly, adding, "That is all," not wanting to worry him with her dark mood.

"Everything is going to be all right," he said, and she realised he must be sensing her concern. She smiled at him. He had proved himself a sound and pleasant companion during her time spent away from home. Head of the High Council of Fintaire, the most easterly town in Hanaire, Bearrach was tall, slender and blond in the Hanairean way, steady, reliable, solid: a rock of a man. She had met him before during diplomatic trips from one town to another, and had always been impressed with his polite and deferential manner, and his frank and no-nonsense approach.

He was studying her now, smiling, and there was something in his smile and the crinkling of his eyes that gave her heart a sudden start. He was interested in her. There was no mistaking it. Fionnghuala looked across the damp, miserable landscape, clutching her horse's reins tightly as it stumbled on another ill-made part of the road. Her lips pressed together tightly. She hoped he had not set his sights on her. She was not wife material, and the sooner he realised that, the better.

In less than a day they had reached Redgar, the first town north of the Wall, and although an hour or two of riding time remained, they stopped at the town, everyone in need of rest. On the way down from Hanaire they had not gone into the towns, preferring to keep their distance from the Wulfians, and had camped a mile or so outside, but this time, partly because of the weather and partly because they had Wulfians with them, they went into the town centre and looked for an inn.

Grimbeald led them directly to the Green Oak, which he was obviously familiar with, and went in and booked several rooms for the night. Fionnghuala dismounted from her horse and gathered her travelling bag, then followed the others into the inn a little nervously.

As she walked into the bar, she realised her nerves were justified as she saw every pair of eyes in the room staring at her and the other women in her party. It did not pay to be a woman in Wulfengar, she thought, especially this close to the Wall, where Wulfian feelings ran so much higher than in the scattered northern towns. Bearrach steered her toward some seats by the fire, passing between her and the Wulfians gathered around the tables, drinking ale. In spite of her earlier worries about his feelings for her, she was glad he was there, and that she was surrounded by hardened warriors.

Reaching the fire, they sat in chairs as the serving lad brought over a tray of cups and a couple of jugs of ale. Before they could even pour the drink, however, one of the Wulfian men came over to their party, and her heart sank at the fierce look on his face.

"Women are not welcome in this bar," he spat. "You had best be on your way." Behind him, several more Wulfians rose to their feet, adding their weight to his words.

Grimbeald stood and turned to face him. "They are with me," he said quietly. "Therefore be careful with whom you pick your fight."

The Wulfian turned on him, his heavy features carved into a sneer, his long beard shining with spilt ale. "Any Wulfian who travels with *pawes* is no friend of mine!"

Everyone seemed to move at once. The room was filled with the sing of steel as swords were drawn rapidly, and ale went flying as the Heartwood knights moved to engage the Wulfian warriors who were so incensed at their presence.

Fionnghuala was no warrior herself, but she wore a lightly padded jerkin under her cloak, and she knew how to handle a sword. However, she found herself pushed behind Bearrach as he clashed with a very short and rather ugly Wulfian, and she did not resent it, knowing he could defend himself better than she.

The scuffle was over within minutes. Though the Wulfians had spent their lives on the battlefront, raiding continually across the Wall, they were no match for trained Heartwood Exercitus, and Fionnghuala hardly had time to blink before the Wulfians were all looking at the sharp end of a sword.

Grimbeald pressed his weapon firmly into the neck of the Wulfian who had first spoken, a sliver of blood appearing above the steel blade. "Next time think carefully before you insult us," he growled. The Wulfian spat at him, but said nothing more.

The innkeeper came over, frowning at the knocked over tables and spilt ale. "I think it would be best if you went up to your rooms, and I will serve you there," he said. Clearly, he did not want to pass up the coins that would land in his purse, but he was not happy having the party under his roof.

Grimbeald nodded, and the Heartwood parties pulled back cautiously. But the Wulfians had lost the stomach for a fight and sank to their chairs, muttering curses and casting them angry looks.

Suddenly tired, Fionnghuala followed the others up the stairs to the rooms allocated to them. Dividing into small groups, they settled themselves in the rooms and ate the food hungrily that the innkeeper brought up to them.

After they had eaten, Fionnghuala watched the Heartwood knights who would be accompanying her and Bearrach station themselves on the floor close to the door. It was the first time she had ever been to Redgar, though she had heard a lot about the place from travellers to the region. She felt glad some of the knights would be going with her to the Portal. Suddenly the Quest seemed treacherous, full of pitfalls and dangers she had not contemplated when accepting the task. It would be good to have such trained warriors with her.

And at least she would have Grimbeald accompanying her until the Neck Pass, she thought. She looked to the left at the Wulfian who was lying on the bed next to hers. He was staring at the door, and she thought his face looked rather white beneath his bushy beard.

"Are you all right?" she asked.

He started at her words and turned surprised eyes to her, then looked back at the door. "I thought I saw…" His voice trailed off and he shrugged. "Never mind."

She studied him, seeing the closed look come down over his face like a veil. She could not tell what he was thinking, but still had the feeling he disliked her because of her sex. "Thank you for standing up for us," she said softly.

He looked over at her then. In the light from the candles his eyes were very bright, like two polished stones in his face. "You should not judge all Wulfians the same," he said. Then he turned over on his side away from her and drew the covers over his head.

Fionnghuala sighed. She looked across to her right. Bearrach was watching her, curled up on the bed, although his face was in shadow and she could not see his eyes.

"Good night," he said, confirming he was still awake.

"Good night." She looked over at the door. What had Grimbeald been about to tell her? What had he seen in the doorway?

In the distance, she heard a baby crying, its thin wail cutting through the sound of the rain on the shutters.

Shivering, she closed her eyes and succumbed to sleep.

III

"Unnerving, isn't it?" said Gavius lightly as he nudged his horse towards Beata, the mount prancing nervously beneath his too-tight reins.

She nodded. "I feel like I can hear the trees breathing."

"Perhaps you can." They were both aware, more than the average person in Anguis, of how alive trees were.

She smiled at him. Though she was nervous, her time spent as Dean had meant she always looked to comfort others before searching for comfort herself, and it was instinct now that made her lean over to him and place a light hand on his arm, his mail cold beneath her fingers. "Are you looking forward to your journey to Komis?" she asked, intending to distract him from the strangeness of their surroundings.

He shifted awkwardly and she was reminded that he, like herself, had not been trained to spend more than an hour or so in the saddle. She would have to ensure they stopped regularly to stretch their legs, or they would be unable to walk in the morning. He shrugged. "It should be... an adventure."

Was he nervous? He'd done his Exercitus service, but had chosen to remain in Heartwood, as she had. But whereas she would be travelling in friendly territory, Komis was an unknown country. Although some of its people such as Silva had found their way to the east, they tended to keep themselves to themselves and as such were a puzzle to those from the Twelve Lands and Hanaire alike.

Before long they were in the heart of the forest. The trees had closed behind them, and those in front had yet to thin. They were enclosed in a rich green world, their nostrils filled with the smell of damp earth and decaying leaves underfoot, and the freshness of new growth above them.

The horses were nervous. Bred for the open road, they found this new atmosphere strange and bewildering, and the constant rustling sounds and movement of animals and leaves made the whites of their eyes show, and caused them again and again to startle.

Beata felt much the same. "This forest has eyes," she said to Gavius, whose left hand rested on the pommel of his sword.

Gavius frowned. "I feel it, too. I cannot establish whether it is just because I am unfamiliar with the territory or if – Arbor's roots!" His exclamation came as two figures appeared on the path before him.

Beata's hand went automatically to her sword but the figure in front of her growled. He held a bow, the arrow nocked and pointing straight at her heart, with a bodkin head that would open up the links in her mail and find its way through to her soft flesh. She lifted her hand, looking aside at Gavius, who did the same. Turning in her saddle, she saw several more figures had emerged from the woods and they were now surrounded. The Militis shifted in their seats, but quieted as she gave them a warning look with her eyes.

The bandits were a motley bunch. Their clothes were filthy and badly mended where they had been torn over the years and covered with leaves and mud as camouflage; their hair was wild and their beards matted and flecked with food. She could smell them from up on the horse. Clearly they lived in the woods, probably leaving them only to steal food and other supplies. Outlaws, bandits, call them what you will, they obviously lived by their own rules, and considered themselves above the law.

"We want all the money you have in your purses," one of the outlaws snarled in guttural Laxonian. "If we consider it enough, we will let you continue on your journey. And if not…" He left the answer to their imagination.

Gavius and Gravis, like Beata, carried Laxonian coin to buy food for the journey. She had no intention of giving hers up and was sure that neither did the twins. Still, she was reluctant to attack the outlaws. At Heartwood she had been trained to think defensively rather than to assume attack was the only option, and besides, she did not want to start this journey with bloodshed. Over her shoulder her eyes met Fortis's at the back; his face showed no emotion, and she could not read his thoughts. Did he think she should attack?

She turned back to the outlaw. She sat straight in the saddle and made her voice loud and clear. "We have no intention of giving up any of our possessions," she replied in Laxonian. "We are Heartwood knights – holy warriors, on a Quest of great importance. You will let us through now!"

The outlaws all looked at each other. For a moment she thought she had won. Then her heart sank as they all burst out laughing.

The second outlaw in front of her stepped forward so his sword – cheap-looking and rusty with disuse – nudged her breast. "Give us your money," he demanded, and she could smell the sourness of his breath as he leered at her, saying, "or else my sword won't be the only thing looking to pierce that sweet body."

Beata's eyes narrowed as she understood his meaning. She looked at Gavius, whose face was stony with anger that this imbecile had insulted a holy guardian of the Arbor. She met his gaze openly. An outlaw's weapon could kill as well as a knight's, and she did not want to move unless everyone was ready. But in Gavius's eyes she read what she had hoped – that he was poised to move, just waiting for her nod. Though they were not as battle-experienced as some, they were still knights, trained and practised in the art of war, and she knew instinctively the other Militis would automatically follow her lead.

She raised her left hand, palm upwards. In spite of the fact that she faced forwards, she could feel those in the saddle behind her tense. The outlaws around her shifted impatiently, waiting for a sign of their booty.

She dropped her hand.

Everything happened at once. She drew her cavalry sword – shorter and wider than her infantry weapon – and, using the impetus of the movement, swung the blade in an anticlockwise circle on her horse's left side, the sword coming across and cleanly slicing through the throat of the outlaw who had leapt towards her with a shout as he saw her move.

To her right Gavius pulled sharply on his palfrey's reins, causing the horse to rear up, its hooves thrashing and its whole weight coming down on the other outlaw at the front, crushing him instantly.

Something whistled by her ear and instinctively she kicked her feet free of her stirrups to avoid the arrows and rolled from the saddle, putting the mare's body between her and the outlaws on her left. Behind her Gravis had done the same and together they ducked between the horses and emerged to face the outlaws, standing in the battle stance they had practised every day in the Exerceo since the age of seven.

Arrows whistled past them and Beata saw Caelestis had drawn her own bow and was shooting from her horse, and in front of them an outlaw fell, the shaft sticking out of his throat, his hands clawing at it even as he collapsed. Beata leapt over him, finding courage in the familiarity of the movements she was used to, easily defending herself against the clumsy movements of the bandit in front of her, realising quickly she was by far the more skilled. She parried his weak thrusts, then used the hilt of her sword to lock under his own and put her whole weight into the disarming movement, watching with satisfaction as his blade went flying off into the undergrowth. He turned to flee and she stopped, intending to let him go, but before he could reach the safety of the trees a small blade buried itself in his back and he fell heavily to the ground. She turned to see Fortis watching her, his face impassive, his hand still raised from the throw. She frowned at him. She would have to speak to him about that later.

Looking around she saw the skirmish was over. The outlaws were all dead. Most worryingly, Erubesco had been wounded, shot in the shoulder with an arrow that had embedded itself in her armour, and her pale face glistened with sweat.

Sheathing her sword, Beata ran up to her and caught her as she slid from the saddle. She lowered the knight to the floor and knelt beside her, examining the shaft. The bodkin head had just managed to enter the links in the mail. With careful fingers she pushed aside the broken links, apologising as Erubesco groaned in pain.

"Sorry." She examined the tip of the arrow. "It has not gone in too far. I can still see the head. The mail and the jerkin caught most of the blow. I think I can pull it out." She looked up at the

Militis who stood around her. "Gavius and Gravis, can you move the horses out of the way, just take them a little further ahead to that clearing, and keep your eyes and ears open? Peritus, can you retrieve the small green bag from my horse's side panniers – I have some herbs there that will help the wound to heal?"

Beata waited until Peritus had brought her the bag, then removed from it some of the linen strips she had taken from the Infirmaria in Heartwood. She had not thought she would need them so early in their journey. She folded the strips into a wad and handed it to Peritus, who was kneeling by her side. Then she removed a small, thick wooden stick. Instructing Erubesco to open her mouth, she placed it sideways and closed the knight's jaw so she bit down on it. Then she took a deep breath.

IV

It was a long journey around the Forest of Wings. Grimbeald saw Fionnghuala and her escorts glancing impatiently from time to time at the trees as if wishing they could make them part and reveal a road straight through to the Neck Pass. But the trees remained closed, and the road long and treacherous.

Grimbeald had suggested to Fionnghuala they take the river instead of the road, but the Hanaireans had distrusted the water even before the appearance of the Darkwater Lords, and they stated firmly they would stick to the road in spite of its lack of maintenance. Grimbeald could have left them at Acelstan, as there was a river route from there straight up to the Highlands, but decided instead to stick with them to Karlgan. He could feel the growing tension in the land as the political climate escalated on the Wall; each town they passed through now held groups of Wulfians talking about war. The Heartwood knights were looked on with dislike, and Grimbeald did not want to leave them alone until he had to.

Wulfian attitude to Heartwood had never been benevolent. The Militis were regarded as interferers by the Wulfians in a private relationship between themselves and the Laxonians, and were generally only tolerated because they were the holy guardians of the Arbor. The violent nature of the Wulfians was not a random thing; it was an integral part of their religion. The Wulfian branch of Animism had developed over hundreds of years, until it was as much a part of their lives as the sap was part of the tree, and it was not something that could be talked out of them at one Congressus. And yet they still worshipped the tree, and thus the Heartwood knights had been endured, until now.

Grimbeald had not discussed it with the Congressus, but he had been hearing very disturbing conversations on his journeys across Wulfengar. There was talk of a major invasion of Laxony – which was nothing new, really, and tended to be a general topic of conversation – but, more worryingly, there had also been talk of taking over Heartwood. The Militis were regarded as being too friendly towards the Laxonians, and there were many Wulfians who thought their own priests would be better able to defend the Arbor.

But he had not told Valens about these rumblings. Grimbeald's loyalties were torn. He was not your average, typical Wulfian. His mother had been half Hanairean, and her mother had ensured she was educated in the ways of other people and their beliefs. Grimbeald's mother had done the same with him, and therefore although he had grown up trained as a Wulfian knight by his father, he was not as antagonistic towards Laxony and Heartwood as many of his peers were.

But there was more to his differences than that. Wulfians were generally straightforward men, raised on a diet of aggression, taught that violence was the way to show their love for the Arbor. But Grimbeald did not have the heart of a warrior. Sometimes he fancied that, as a child, someone had crept in to his room in the night, taken out his heart and replaced it with a bard's or an artist's. Instead of seeing violence, he saw beauty everywhere he went. And he enjoyed expressing that beauty through music, writing and painting. But he could not express it openly because he knew he would be chased from Wulfengar before he could sing a note.

And yet sometimes he wanted that to happen. Sometimes he felt life was an elaborate game, a play, and he was a pawn placed on the board and moved by unseen hands, while in his mind he daydreamed about things he was sure very few other Wulfians had ever considered. He would be at a Council meeting, and the room would be filled with Wulfians all talking animatedly, and he would be sitting at the head of the table but his mind would be outside, running through the grasses, or lying by the river and watching the fish dart in and out of the reeds. Because of this he had gained the reputation of being a thinker, a strategist, someone who considered all the options and trusted his head before his heart, which in a strange way was something the passionate and impulsive Wulfians admired. But he had never explained to anyone this was not the case, although now, as he wandered along uncomfortably on his horse and looked across at the elegant Hanaireans talking quietly among themselves, he wondered how different his life would have been if he had escaped at a young age and made his way to his grandmother's land.

But it was a ridiculous notion. He sighed, his hand coming up to touch his bushy beard. He did not appear to have a trace of his grandmother's blood in him – there was absolutely nothing about his appearance to suggest he was in any part Hanairean. Going to Hanaire would have just meant he would be an outcast in two lands – he would not have been able to settle there, to feel at home. No, he lived his life the only way he could – his body in Wulfengar, his mind in the clouds, free even if his physical self wasn't.

Karlgan must be close now, he thought, seeing the Spina Mountains rearing up before him, dusted with white. He looked to the south towards the Forest of Wings, the trees close and forbidding like a trained army. He had not been strictly truthful with Fionnghuala. There *was* a path through the forest from Redgar to Karlgan, and although it was narrow and fraught with obstacles, it would probably have cut off a day or two from their journey. But the forest held many dark memories for Grimbeald, and he had not travelled through it for years. He looked at the trees, at the dark spaces between them, which could hide a thousand pairs of eyes. He had the strange sensation of being watched.

It was not the first time he had felt the presence of an invisible observer. That evening in Redgar, in the room with Fionnghuala, he had thought he saw a figure standing by the door, watching him. He had caught it out of the corner of his eye, but when he turned to look, there was nothing there. But now, staring at the forest, he was sure he could see a person, just visible within the trees. He blinked a few times and suddenly it was only a pattern cast by the branches, a scatter of light against dark, but still he shivered and kicked his heels into his steed, picking up the pace.

They reached Karlgan at midday, or what felt like midday; there was still no sun to guide them.

"I think we will continue on rather than stop here," said Fionnghuala. "There are several huts along the Pass for travellers to stay."

Grimbeald nodded, knowing she felt uncomfortable in Wulfengar, and he did not blame her. "May your Quest be successful," he said, giving her the Heartwood salute.

She smiled and returned it. "And yours, too. Take care, Grimbeald." Turning her horse, she led the party left at the crossroads towards the mountains.

Grimbeald did not stay to watch her disappear into the Pass. He had a long journey still to undertake, and besides, he wished to put as much distance between himself and the Forest of Wings as possible. He cast one last look at it before turning his horse towards the road north. The forest glared at him, resenting him.

The tree branches bent in the wind and formed the figure that watched him, waiting. Then they moved, and the figure was gone.

Grimbeald turned in his seat to check his companions and saw one of the Heartwood knights studying him curiously. Her name was Tenera, and she was very young – maybe not even in her third decade, and shorter than most of the Laxonian female knights, with very long brown hair she wore in braids to her waist. Her snub nose covered with freckles somehow emphasised her youth. He had asked Procella why she had decided to send such a young Militis with him when he really needed strong and experienced warriors, but she had just smiled and said not to judge her knights by their appearance. Grimbeald had found out what she meant when during the brief exchange at the inn in Redgar: Tenera had been the first knight across the tables when the Wulfians all stood up to challenge them. She had disarmed one of them and pinned another to the wall with her sword before the rest of them had time to blink. What she lacked in height, she obviously made up for in agility, and she was clearly skilled in many forms of weaponry, as he could see from the bow she carried across her back.

What took him by surprise now, though, was her searching gaze and quizzical expression. He said nothing, kicking his heels into the horse and guiding it onto the road north, but he was not to escape her curiosity.

She manoeuvred her horse up to his and rode alongside him for a while. The rain had lightened to a steady drizzle, and she tipped back the hood of her cloak so the mist settled on her hair, making it glitter with droplets.

Eventually he looked across at her and gave her his best scowl that would have cowed most Wulfian women. "Do you want something?"

Instead of looking alarmed, however, she merely smiled. "I was wondering if I could ask you a few Questions. We have quite a journey and a big task to complete – it would be nice if I knew a little about you."

"You do not need to know me intimately to be able to complete the Quest."

"True," she agreed. "But it is a long journey, and conversation would help to pass the time."

He turned away, looking ahead at the path that rose gently to meet the hills of the Farmines. He sighed. It was true, he had not been very good company since leaving Heartwood. His men were used to his morose moods, and spoke to him only when spoken to, but the Exercitus spent months, if not years, on the road and would be used to finding ways to pass long journeys.

"Forgive me," he said, "I am not used to spending much time with others."

She cocked her head at him. "That is a strange thing to say. I would have thought conversation and companionship were compulsory for a lord."

He shrugged. "I was not chosen for the role because of my social skills."

"You were chosen for the role?"

"When my father died, I was the strongest candidate for succession and did not have any serious contenders."

"I bet your father would be very proud of you, if he could see you."

His smile faded and he returned his gaze to the road. "Maybe."

He said nothing for a while, and when she spoke she changed the subject, clearly picking up on his reluctance to talk about his father.

"Are you married? I mean, I know Wulfians do not generally believe in marriage, but I have heard that some do get involved with a long-term partner."

"Yes. Well, I was. But my wife died several years ago, and she never bore me a child."

"Oh, I am sorry," she said with sincerity.

He shrugged. "It is one of those things. Wulfian law states that the woman is barren if she cannot bear children, but I have taken my fair share of lovers both before and since my wife, and none has ever had a child." He stopped talking. Why was he opening up like this? He had never spoken to anyone about his wife before.

He looked over at her again. Perhaps it was the "trust me" look in her wide eyes, a dark grey-blue like the sky during a thunderstorm. Or her honest face, with its upturned nose. There was definitely something about her that intrigued him. He had spent most of his life with Wulfian women who, brought up to believe they were inferior beings, had failed to do anything other than satisfy his occasional sexual needs. Even his wife had not been a soulmate – he had always doubted such a thing existed, even though his heart told him the stories bards sang were true. Now, staring at Tenera, he found he could believe it – a woman such as this would be a just companion for him, someone he could finally open up to, and tell of all the fears and worries he had never before shared with anyone.

He felt a stirring in his stomach, a surge of desire, which he quelled quickly, looking away. Even if she was twenty, which he doubted, he was still over fifteen years her senior. And she was Heartwood Militis, a holy knight, bound by vows of chastity and obedience to the Arbor, and she was talking to him now for no other reason than because she was inquisitive and wanted to pass the time.

It was raining heavier now. He pulled the hood of his cloak over his head, trying to discourage further conversation, and he waited for her to do the same.

But she had not finished with him yet. The droplets falling onto her face, she blinked them away from her lashes and said: "So why are you so frightened to go into the Forest of Wings? And who was the figure watching us at the edge of the trees?"

••••

V

"I am going to pull the arrow out now," Beata told Erubesco, whose white face was covered with a sheen of sweat. She leaned her left hand on the knight's breastbone, pushing down, and closed her right hand around the shaft. "Three, two..." Before she finished the countdown she pulled up sharply. Erubesco's body bucked, but the arrow slid out neatly. Beata took the wad of linen from Peritus and pressed it onto the wound. "Lean down on this," she instructed him. Sitting back, she examined the arrowhead. It was intact, the wood unsplintered, which meant none would have been left in the wound. The only problem would be if it had been poisoned in any way.

Peritus had removed the wooden bar from Erubesco's mouth, and Caelestis mopped the sweat from her forehead with some water from her container tipped onto another piece of cloth. Beata took some longer strips of linen from the bag. Taking Peritus's place, she removed the bloodied wad and examined the wound. It looked clean, but it would take time before it was clear whether it had been infected. She opened the small bowl containing yarrow ointment, which was used to treat battlefield wounds. Smearing it thickly on the linen pad, she pressed it onto the wound again before binding it tightly to Erubesco's arm.

Finally she sat back on her heels and washed her hands with a little of the water from the container Caelestis held out to her.

"She will not be able to continue the journey," Fortis said from his position a little behind the others.

"I think that is obvious," Beata said sharply, pushing herself to her feet. "We must be nearing the end of the forest now. That means we are about three hours from Cherton."

"We should go back," said Fortis. "She needs rest and treatment."

"No. We must keep going."

Fortis pushed forward through the others to stand before her. He towered over her, his whole manner imposing and authoritative. "She may die if we do not return."

Beata knew this was a key moment. If she buckled now and did as he suggested, he would think he was in charge of this Quest and would continue to confront her. She wondered whether to take him to one side and speak to him, but from her experience as Dean, she knew a public confrontation would be much more likely to make him realise she would not be pushed around, even if he embarrassed her in front of others.

"And she may die if we go back," she said quietly but forcefully. She indicated the rest of the company and said, "We all have a task to complete and we do not have much time. We cannot keep running home every time we meet misfortune."

His eyes narrowed. "'Running home?' Are you implying cowardice on my part?"

"Of course not," she said smoothly. She touched him lightly on the arm, relieved he didn't pull away. "I know Procella thinks very highly of you, which is why she asked you to accompany me on my Quest." Her use of the personal pronoun was not an accident. "I shall always appreciate your advice – you are a seasoned warrior – the most experienced of us all, I know, so do not think I do not know your worth. But we have to keep moving. Time is of the essence, and we are foolish if we do not think there will be casualties along the way."

He said nothing more, and did not continue to challenge her. She turned away and looked down at Erubesco. "We are going to continue to Cherton, and we shall find a place for you there where you can recover. And maybe eventually somebody travelling to Heartwood will be able to bring you back. Now we have to get you on your horse." She went to motion to Peritus to help her, but Fortis bent and gently lifted up the wounded warrior in his arms. He walked up to her horse and carefully set her astride the saddle.

She was white as milk and covered with sweat, but she smiled at them as she took the reins in her right hand. "I am all right; I can ride."

Beata nodded. "Just signal to whoever is riding beside you if you need to stop. We will ride for an hour and then take a rest."

She looked at Fortis and nodded her thanks to him. He nodded back and, turning, leapt easily astride his horse.

She glanced around at the bodies of the outlaws. There seemed little sense in burying them. Already they had sunk into the undergrowth and were partially covered by the leaves and plants that had sprung back over them.

Sighing, she went back to the mare that stood patiently with the twins and the other horses, and climbed into the saddle. Reaching up, she grabbed a large leaf and, withdrawing her sword, cleaned the blade. Throwing the leaf away, she sheathed the sword. "Eyes and ears," she called to them all. Then, tapping her feet into the mare's sides, she began the journey again.

They were closer to the edge of the wood than they had realised. Within minutes the trees thinned, and soon they emerged into the rainy Hannon landscape. They pulled the hoods of their travelling cloaks over their heads and set off along the mud road, heading south along the edge of the forest.

In the end it took well over four hours to reach the town. They had to stop frequently, for Erubesco grew increasingly unwell, and at one point almost fell from the saddle. From then on Beata put Erubesco on the front of her mare and kept tight arms around her as they rode, but it was slow going, and by the time they arrived at Cherton, everyone was tired.

It was just starting to get dark as the little town loomed out of the rain, nestled at the foot of the hill on top of which was Ogier's castle – the Lord of Hannon who had attended the Congressus at Heartwood. He had left the day after the attack on the Curia, so Beata knew it was likely he would be home. She led the party through the main street of the town, which in spite of the late hour was still busy with carts travelling to and from Hicton to the south and Setbourg to the east, and people going about their daily business.

In the castle, they were met by Ogier himself. "Welcome," he said, clasping her hand with his right and her forearm with his left. "It is good – although rather unusual – to have you visit. Please, come into the Hall, and you can dine and rest while you tell me your story."

The Hall was huge, much bigger than the rooms in Heartwood's Castellum. The ceiling was high and the walls were hung with giant, colourful tapestries depicting scenes of battle and romantic stories. At right angles to the wall between the tapestries were long banners on poles embroidered with the Hannon coat of arms, which fluttered in the breeze as the doors opened and closed. In the centre of the Hall was a large fireplace, the smoke spiralling up to the blackened rafters. Around the Hall were long wooden tables and benches, with a larger table along the raised dais at the end of the hall, the elaborate chairs indicating this was where Ogier and his family usually sat.

Now he took them to the tables around the fire, however, and gestured to the servants to bring food and wine. The party sank gratefully onto the benches, warming themselves in front of the flames. Servants took their cloaks as they unpinned them, and spread them out on the unused tables to dry. Ogier carefully lay Erubesco in front of the fire and called for his wife to come and tend her. Skilled in the arts of herbs and medicines, his wife began work on removing the dressing and cleaning the wound.

As Beata began to tell him about the purpose of the Quests, the servants came out carrying trays of sliced meat, bowls of stew, and bread with pats of butter, and the hungry party helped themselves as the servants poured wine into their goblets. Beata told Ogier all as she ate, not realising how hungry she was until the smell of the roasted meat filled her nostrils.

When she had finished speaking, she felt her eyelids grow heavy. Ogier continued to talk for some time, speaking about the Darkwater Lords and the strange way they had risen out of the water, but eventually he saw she was nearly asleep and laughed, beckoning to the servants to bring blankets. The travellers rolled themselves in them in front of the fire, and most of them were soon asleep.

In spite of her tiredness, however, Beata found herself looking up at the smoke that curled in the rafters. She felt embarrassed and foolish as she thought about how she had pictured herself heading a noble rescue party, riding into a town somewhere and confronting this Virimage, and triumphantly bringing him back to Heartwood to save the day. She had been naïve and idiotic to think the long journey across Laxony would be safe and trouble-free, and could not believe the party had been attacked less than half a day's ride from Heartwood. Luckily, they had been large in number at the time; what would happen when the parties split, and she travelled with the now only three remaining Militis in her group, one of whom would obviously take every chance to Question her authority?

For the first time since the attack in the Curia, the thought entered her head that they might not win this fight. Until now she had assumed they would find and activate the five Nodes; that she would find the Virimage and persuade him to return; Procella and her party would slip into Darkwater and spirit away the Pectoris, and in a few months' time they would look back on this period as a lesson to teach them about being overconfident and that they must always be on their guard.

Now, however, she entertained the possibility actually all four Quests for the Nodes might fail and she might never find the Virimage – if in fact he even existed or was able to help at all – and for the first time she realised just how impossible the descent into Darkwater was, let alone the rescue of an object from the clutches of those powerful and frightening warriors.

And if they could not complete the Quests? She thought about the water warriors overrunning Heartwood, smashing down the walls, tearing apart the Temple and, worse, completely destroying the Arbor. A pain grew deep in her stomach and she rolled over onto her side, away from the others so they could not see the tears glimmering in her eyes.

After a few moments of self-pity, however, her natural resolute character began to reassert itself. She could do nothing more than try to achieve the Quest she had taken on, to the best of her abilities. And she had to trust in the others to do the same.

Sleep finally swept over her, and the last thing she remembered was the acrid smell of the smoke from the fire in her nostrils, and the warm glow of the flames on her back.

The next day, the party arose feeling refreshed and invigorated. Erubesco was able to sit and eat some porridge from a bowl, and Ogier's wife assured Beata the wound did not appear infected, although it would be best if she rested for a while at the Hall. Erubesco was distraught she was going to have to stay behind, and cried silent tears as Beata knelt by her side and told her, but she did not protest and Beata knew she understood why they could not wait for her to get better.

"I have failed you," the injured warrior said softly, her face still pale from the loss of blood.

"Nonsense." Beata dismissed her words with a wave of her hand. "It could have been any one of us – I had an arrow whistle right past my cheek. One inch to the left and it would have gone in one ear and out the other." Still it was a blow to have to leave one of her knights behind. It was possible they were going to have to take the Virimage by force to Heartwood, and as yet she had no idea what sort of person this magician was – he could be tall, strong, powerful, or maybe all three.

"Have you seen him?" she asked Ogier as they walked down the stairs to the stables to retrieve their horses.

"No, although I have had travellers here who have." His stable lads had already brought out their steeds and her horse stood champing at the bit, impatient to be on her way. The horses had been rubbed down and fed well and rested, and seemed as eager to continue the adventure as the Militis. "They all speak of him as a wonderful trickster. Whether or not his skills are genuine, I do not know." He sighed as she put one foot in the stirrup and lifted herself up nimbly into the saddle. "I wish you would agree to take one or more of my knights with you. You are on a dangerous Quest across lands which are not as peaceful as they once were, and safety is greater in numbers."

"I shall have Gavius's and Gravis's company until Hicton," she said with a smile. She had considered his offer, but decided against borrowing his knights, as they were not trained the Heartwood way, and she felt uneasy about accepting the aid of others who may not follow her orders during times of crisis. "Take care of yourself, Ogier."

"And you, fair knight." He laid his hand over his heart in the standard salute and she did the same, turning her horse and leading the way out of the courtyard, scattering chickens and goats as she did so, the mare falling into a quick trot through the gatehouse and along the drawbridge to the road.

CHAPTER SEVEN

I

It was still raining, if anything slightly heavier than the day before, and Beata drew her cloak closely around her and settled into the saddle for the long day's ride. She was glad the cloak was well waterproofed, which kept her mail fairly dry. The knights spread out behind her, and although occasionally Gravis or Gavius rode beside her for a while, generally she stayed ahead on her own, left to her thoughts as the countryside passed beneath her horse's hooves.

That day was a lot less eventful than the previous one, which she wasn't displeased with. After leaving Cherton, the road wound its way through the low hills, passing mostly terracotta-brown fields of ploughed earth, dotted with scarecrows to frighten away the crows that were tempted to eat the seed. Here and there were fields of sheep, and the occasional one of cattle, the cows chewing miserably in the rain.

At one point they crossed a river, and Beata halted on the bridge to look down at the water tumbling beneath the wooden planks. She felt a distinct unease as she gazed at it, remembering the way the Darkwater Lords had sprung from the green channel, taking shape from liquid, and she shivered as she saw how the river had swollen slightly, the water brown from its violent passage from the mountains, crashing and breaking itself on the rocks under the bridge.

Gavius joined her, peering over the wooden handrail. "I wonder how long it will continue to rain," he said. "If this continues, we will drown long before Darkwater invades again."

"Perhaps that is their plan." She shrugged, shuddering as she thought of such a watery death, imagining how it would feel to have lungs full of water, and be unable to breathe. She could think of nothing cheerful to say and touched the mare's sides to encourage her to walk on. She wanted to put the river behind her and would not be disappointed if they did not see another drop of water on this adventure.

The day wore on, and the sun remained hidden behind the clouds, which scudded across the sky in a never-ending river of grey. They stopped after a few hours for some lunch, trying to take shelter beneath a group of oaks that stood by the roadside, but everyone was quiet and nobody felt like talking, and after only half an hour or so they were back on their horses and continuing on their journey.

Some time after this, Gavius moved his palfrey up to ride beside Beata, and she could tell from the way his mouth was moving, as if he was chewing something, that he had something he wanted to say.

"Spit it out, Gavius," she said wryly.

He grinned at her, then looked up at the silent rain and shivered, pulling his cloak around him tightly. "I swear – I am soaked to the very bone. I think you could wring out my limbs and gain a bucketfull of water."

She sighed. "Yes, it is a miserable time at the moment."

Gavius nodded and then lowered his voice. "We must be careful not to let spirits slip too low, though."

She cast a quick glance over her shoulder. The Militis were hunched in their saddles, hoods pulled over their faces, muscles bunching from the cold, and had straggled out in a line a good few hundred yards. She guessed the loss of Erubesco had reminded them they too were not infallible and any mission was a dangerous one in a foreign land, at a time when people were struggling to survive and growing increasingly desperate.

It was very easy to get caught up in one's own misery, she thought, but she remembered the wise words of a previous Dean, long since departed, who had given her much sound advice when she was younger. "Happiness and misery are diseases," he had said to her puzzlement at the time. "They infect us as surely as a head cold, or the pox. When one person contracts either ailment, it spreads quickly to the next person, and before you know it, everyone is contaminated."

She recognised the need to raise the spirits of her fellow travellers, for depression would cause the party to slow and their reflexes to dull, and she needed them all to remain with their wits about them. Without turning round again, she began to sing a traditional Heartwood hymn, one they would have all learned on arriving at the Castellum, and she knew would stir many memories in them.

As she sang, her clear voice carried back to them, and gradually, one by one, they joined in.

The roots of the Tree
Sink deep into the earth,
They ground us, they anchor us,
They lead us down the path,

Our journey is a mystery
But wherever we may roam,
The Arbor leads us onwards
And returns us safely home,

The leaves and branches guide us
And the sap runs through our veins,
We'll dream of you, sweet Arbor
Till you bring us home again.

There were several more verses and they sang them all, each louder than the last, and by the time they had finished they had bunched together in a group and were laughing and talking. Another hymn followed, and another, and thus the rest of the journey was spent in song. The miles seemed to pass more quickly, and before they knew it they were nearing Hicton and the light was beginning to fade.

II

For Grimbeald's party, the journey from Karlgan to Montar was not a picturesque one. The Farmines were so called because the ground was rich in minerals and metals, and the once-green hillsides were pockmarked with quarries and mines, like the face of a beautiful woman who had caught some disfiguring disease. There were no animals, and the villages they passed through looked run-down, the children dirty and thin, the women listless, the men sour and dissatisfied.

Grimbeald saw the looks exchanged between the Heartwood knights. He could only imagine what they might be thinking. Being in the Exercitus, they would be used to the rolling green hills and patchwork fields of Hannon and Barle on the south of the wall, and the tree-crowded Lowlands and windswept fields of the Plains on the north. They would probably never have seen a landscape as bleak and inhospitable as the Farmines, or a people as hopeless and depressed as those who lived there.

Grimbeald didn't like the Farmines, either. Usually, he made the trip to Isenbard's Wall by boat, on rivers that cut across the Highlands and down through the Flatlands, avoiding the Farmines completely. But because he had accompanied Fionnghuala and Bearrach to Karlgan, he had no choice but to take the road this time, although he was already regretting his decision.

Several times as they passed through villages he looked over his shoulder to see the men gathering ominously behind them, their spades and pickaxes hefted menacingly in their hands as their eyes lingered on the weapons and bags the little group carried. None of Grimbeald's party wore expensive clothing or jewellery, but their cloaks were thick and lined, their boots heavy, and their swords – especially the Heartwood ones – well-crafted, with intricate carving on the pommels and hilts. Clearly the party had items worth stealing, and Grimbeald rode all the time with his great cloak thrown back, and his hand resting on his sword, noticing the others did the same.

So far, though, none of the mining Wulfians had done anything but mutter as they passed through, and he began to hope their lethargy was so strong they were unable to bring themselves to rise up against those they saw as having more than themselves. Still, he felt a twinge of sympathy for them as his gaze flicked over the dull eyes of the children, devoid of all hope their lives would consist of anything other than hardship and struggle. These were his countrymen, and yet he felt no kinship to them, no connection with them. They were as alien to him as the far-off Komis.

Suddenly he longed for his home in the Highlands. Although he had spent many days there dreaming of leaving and of investigating the world, the thought now of Calemar and the beautiful view from his bedchamber across the Fallen Isles out to sea made his heart ache. He thought about the lake behind the castle, bordered to the west by the Crest Forest and to the east by a soft green meadow, where he sometimes lingered during the day to compose music, under the shade of a willow that bent gracefully over the water.

"What are you thinking about?" Tenera asked, and he realised she had been watching him. "You look sad."

He smiled. "Home."

"You miss it?"

"More than I thought I would." They rode for a little while and then he said, "Do you miss Heartwood?"

He had thought she would immediately say yes, but to his surprise she thought for a while before answering, "Truthfully? I am not sure. I have spent more years away from it than I did living in it. I used to love it; I could not imagine leaving. Yet now, when I return..." Her brow crinkled. "I find it... constrictive, claustrophobic."

"That makes sense, if you are used to being on the road."

"I suppose so. But it is more than that. It is like... being given a sword, and practising with it and getting used to it and thinking it is the best sword in the world, only one day somebody announces it is just a play-sword, and they give you the real thing, all shiny and heavy, and suddenly you realise how lightweight and insubstantial the original one was."

Grimbeald's eyebrows rose. It was quite a profound thing to say, he thought, and yet he knew what she meant. He had felt the same, going to Heartwood, but had been unable to put his feelings into words. He had composed a song about how he felt, which was the closest he could come to explaining himself. But it still didn't express the strange mixture of emotions he had experienced on staying in the place: unease at the unfamiliar rituals, regular bells and rigid programme of the days; excitement at finally seeing the Arbor; awe at witnessing the Veriditas; and disquiet at the realisation that Heartwood was like a stage, with the Militis carrying out an elaborate and well-rehearsed play. It was not real; it was a fabrication, a parody of real life – although he realised those who went into the Exercitus were probably the only members of Heartwood who realised it.

How strange it must be for those who returned to the Castellum, he thought, for Valens, and Dolosus, after being out in the world. Perhaps that was a better explanation for Valens's restlessness than frustration at his disability; deep inside, he must be aware of the glamour Heartwood cast. Re-entering its walls must have been like watching a magician's performance after he's told you how all his tricks work.

He sighed, looking across at his companions, wondering if they felt the same way about the place they had grown up in. Revoco and Feritas were two typical Wulfians, muscular warriors with thick dark hair and, in spite of their Heartwood upbringing, rather fierce expressions. Born to fight, Grimbeald sensed for them their religion was of secondary importance, although at sunset they joined their companions in the Arbor ritual with the same seriousness and apparent commitment to the tree.

Elatus was slightly different from the other two: Laxonian by birth, he was slender and had an arrogance about him Grimbeald tended to associate with people of the Seven Lands, be they of noble or low birth. He had brown curly hair and sharp blue eyes, and for some reason made Grimbeald feel uneasy, as if he had the ability to look straight into his soul.

Grimbeald watched the three of them and Tenera carrying out their sunset ritual that evening from a distance. Tenera had invited him to join them but he had declined; he felt his was a very different religion, and their complicated rituals unnerved him. He watched them for a moment as they all knelt under a tree and kissed the grass between its roots, then proceeded to sing to it, their left hand clasped around their wooden oak leaf pendant, their right raised in supplication to its branches.

He turned away, staring instead across the pitted landscape, looking up to the stars beginning to twinkle through the dusky sky, the clouds parting momentarily. Up there was the constellation of the Warrior, Animus with his shield and sword, who watched over his people as they lived their lives, reminding them strength was the way, and life is a constant battle, where the winner is always the fittest and the strongest, and the weak fall by the wayside. He had not been brought up to recite long prayers or carry out elaborate rituals, but he did now look up at the stars, close his eyes and send his good wishes to his home town. For the first time he wished he had not left all his followers behind; it would have been nice to have someone from home with him.

It was the fact that he had his eyes closed that stopped him from seeing the armed villagers as they came over the hill. By the time he heard their footsteps he was barely able to leap to his feet and yell the alarm before the first peasant was on him.

Grimbeald was pushed backwards, tripped on a rock and went sprawling, the peasant on top of him. Behind him he heard briefly the exclamations of the Militis as they turned to see the villagers spilling down the hill, and then he had to concentrate simply on saving his own life as a cold blade pressed against his throat. He roared and reared up with his arms and legs, throwing off the peasant, but not before he felt a burning that meant the blade had cut through his skin. Ignoring the pain and the blood gushing down his neck, he got up and released his blood axe from his horse's saddle, then prepared himself as the peasant struggled to his feet.

A brief glance around confirmed there were maybe a dozen villagers who had sprung this surprise attack. They were outnumbered two to one. But of course, these were unskilled peasants, hungry and desperate to steal something they could sell; they had no idea how to wield a sword or defend themselves against an experienced knight. The Militis were coping capably with the attack, and he turned his attention back to his assailant.

Another had joined him now, perhaps assuming the member of the party not wearing the gold Heartwood tunic would be the easier target. Grimbeald gritted his teeth and determined that would not be the case. Planting his feet firmly, his left hand gripped the blood axe near to the blade, the right holding further down the shaft, and he gave a nasty smile to the villagers who crept nearer, eyeing the axe cautiously. One of them lunged towards him clumsily, and he stepped back and swung the axe, his left hand sliding to meet his right so he could put his whole weight behind the swing. He saw the movement as if in slow motion – the startled look on the Wulfian's face, quickly turning to incredulity; the blur of the blade through the air; the low roar of the other villager; the shudder through his body as the movement of the blade came to a sudden halt; the sickening crunch of metal dividing skin and bone as the edge bit into his assailant's upper arm, severing tendons and ligaments until the limb hung by a thread, the peasant clutching it with his other hand and looking up at him in disbelief before sliding to the floor.

The other villager gave a howl and launched himself at Grimbeald, but by then the element of surprise had passed and Grimbeald was ready for him. He neatly sidestepped the clumsy thrust of the Wulfian's old sword, dummied a swing with the axe that caused the villager to turn away from him, then turned the axe in a deft arc to double back and completely cut off the peasant's head.

For a moment he stood and watched the head roll down the hill, bumping over stones and molehills, and then he turned his attention back to the grassy field. The villager whose arm he had severed lay motionless in a huge pool of blood, his face pale as milk, eyes glassy. He turned to look behind him. The grass was littered with the bodies of the raiding party. The Militis moved amongst them, checking for life, pushing the limp torsos with their toes and occasionally crouching down to lift up an eyelid. He looked across at Tenera. She was wiping the blade of her sword on a cloth, removing the sticky residue of blood that had soaked it. She looked up and he saw her face crease with concern.

"Grimbeald?" She sheathed her sword and ran over to him quickly. "You are injured?"

"It is nothing," he said, putting his hand up to his neck. It came away thick and wet with dark red blood. "Oh," he said. Alarm registered in her eyes, and he thought how the dark blue orbs looked like thunderous skies crackling with lightning. Then the world began to turn black, and the ground rushed up to meet him.

III

Beside Beata, Gavius lowered himself into the adjacent tub, and he too let out a long "Aaah" of satisfaction as his body penetrated the hot water. "It is only now I realise how fit the Exercitus are," he said, groaning at his aches and pains. "I hardly ride anywhere at all."

"Me neither," Beata agreed. She soaped herself with a cloth, scrubbing away at the dirt from the journey. When she was finally happy with the cleanliness of her skin, she lay her head back on the tub and let the steam warm her cheeks.

It was a lovely end to what had not been a bad day, she thought. Her bones felt loose, as if she were melting into the water. She rolled her head and looked over at Gavius, who was almost asleep in his tub. "So you are off to the Knife's Edge, then?" she said sleepily.

He looked over at her, peering through the mist arising from their baths. "Yes. The real adventure begins tomorrow."

"Are you looking forward to it?"

He laid his head back and looked up at the ceiling. "Yes and no. It is exciting to be travelling to a place I have never been, or indeed very few people in Heartwood have ever been to. But I must admit to more than a little trepidation about the journey."

"Really?" she said. Gavius was such an enthusiastic, impulsive, uncomplicated character that she was surprised he ever felt nervous at all. "Why so?"

He looked back at her. His blue eyes, usually bright and clear, were shadowed with troubled thoughts. "I... I had a sort of premonition..."

"Oh?"

Heartwood was not a particularly superstitious place. Militis were not brought up to touch objects for luck or to follow a rigorous set of rules about things that could and could not be done to bring good or bad luck. As a general rule, the existence of ghosts was not believed in, and a practical approach to faith and their religion meant fortune tellers and other mystics tended to be scorned rather than revered.

For down-to-earth, practical Gavius to admit to a premonition, it must have been quite convincing, she thought, wondering if what he had seen what a true shadow of things to come, or a figment of his imagination. "What was it?"

He swallowed. "I dreamed of the Giant – the figure in the ground. I was walking over him, and he somehow came to life and clutched me in his fingers. And he crushed me until the breath left my body and my bones crunched in his grip."

"Sounds like a case of too much cheese before bedtime to me," she said lightly, seeing the fear in his eyes was real.

He focussed on her and laughed, and suddenly he was the old Gavius again, cheerful and indomitable, excited and eager for the adventure. "Yes, I am sure that is all it was."

Beata knew his premonitions of disaster were more than likely due to self-doubt, a fear he would fail the Quest and it would be his fault Heartwood fell, as it was a fear of her own. She decided the best plan of action would be to turn his mind to other things.

"Will you miss Gravis?" she asked playfully, surprised when he did not answer with a resounding yes, but instead considered her Question seriously.

"It will be strange not having him around," he said.

Beata looked across at him, her brow furrowing. "Is everything all right between you? Only for a while I have some sensed some friction, although I cannot fathom its cause."

Gavius shrugged. "We have been together a long time. Any such relationship would undoubtedly wear thin after a while, like a favourite garment donned day after day."

Beata said nothing. She knew there was something underlying the tension, but also sensed Gavius did not want to talk about it. Well that was his prerogative. But she also did not want them to make the mistake of parting on anything other than the best terms. These were dangerous Quests, and there was no surety they would all make it through them.

She would speak to them about it in the morning, she thought, before Gavius left for the Knife's Edge.

Getting out of the bath, for the first time that week she did not put on her armour, but went back into the Hall instead in a tunic and breeches, thinking that if Hicton was attacked during the night, she should at least have some warning from the castle guard.

Settling down in front of the fire, she chatted to Sarilo, the steward, for a while about this and that, while the other Militis talked among themselves, or played dice with some of the castle's occupants who had come in for the night..

She asked Sarilo whether he had ever met the Virimage, and was surprised when he told her he had.

"Here?" she asked, her heart thudding at the thought that the magician may have been sitting by the very fire by which she was warming her feet.

"No, no," he said. "This was some time ago, down south, on the Seven Hills. I was visiting my daughter, who had married into the local family, and while I was at the castle, the Virimage arrived."

Beata sat up with interest. Though both Malgara and Kenweard had said they had met him, she had not really had a chance to quiz them. This was the first time she had really spoken to anyone who had seen him.

"What was he like?" she asked, realising she didn't even know what he looked like. "Tall, short? Hairy, bald?"

Sarilo smiled. "You could not miss him. He is from Komis – with that distinctive hair black as evil's shadow, and those entrancing gold eyes. They unnerved me, Beata, I can tell you. A handsome fellow, though. And he had all of his own teeth."

She smiled, clasping her hands around her knees, pulling them up to rest her chin on. "What was he like as a person?" she asked.

"He was pleasant enough. Fast-talking, a real charmer, put on a good show. I do not know what he was *really* like. I never really got to talk to him properly; he put on this persona like a heavy cloak, and it was difficult to tell what was under it."

"And what about the tricks he did?" she asked breathlessly.

He shrugged. "Well, of course I assumed they were just tricks, but they were still impressive. He played the lute and sang tales of romance and adventure, and illustrated them with his 'magic'. For example he made vines grow up the legs of the tables and flowers bloom out of thin air."

Beata frowned. "I do not really understand. Why did everybody think this was just a trick? How could he have made that happen? Why did nobody Question him about it?"

Sarilo shrugged again. "We just all assumed it was part of the act. We had no reason to doubt otherwise. How could it have been anything other than an illusion? I know what you have told me about the Custos of the Arbor, but we are simple folk; we would not think to Question. To us it was a trick – a damn fine one, and for days afterwards people discussed how it might have been done – but a trick nonetheless."

Beata sighed. It was growing late and most of the Militis had wrapped themselves in their blankets and closed their eyes. She said goodnight to Sarilo and did the same, staring into the leaping flames of the fire.

She found herself thinking about the Virimage, and wondering how he could have got away with his gift for so long. She wondered what he himself thought of it. Had he asked heartfelt Questions about it, studied it, puzzled over it for years? Or did he just accept it as part of him, like his hair and nails, like she accepted her gift for dealing with people?

She fell asleep that night dreaming about forests growing up around her, and of a magician with glowing gold eyes.

IV

When Beata awoke the following morning, it was dark and cold, although she knew the sun had risen behind the grey clouds. She dressed in her armour, shivering, and watched Gavius and his party don their mountain clothes. First they put on a tight pair of linen leggings and a-long sleeved vest, then a pair of woollen breeches and a thin woollen tunic. Over this went their usual leather breeches and thick padded hauberk, and finally the mail coat over the top of this, tight against the unusual layers.

"Like a caterpillar in a cocoon," Gavius said wryly when asked how he felt. He shoved his feet into his boots after placing woollen socks over them and accepted a pair of thick, fur-lined leather mittens from Sarilo. They would make holding the reins difficult, Sarilo explained, but they would be glad of them after ten minutes in the freezing cold.

Finally they were encircled by heavy woollen cloaks, which were fastened at the neck, the material voluminous enough to wrap right around them almost twice.

They waddled out to their horses, Gavius complaining that if anybody were to attack them they would be in trouble, as he wouldn't be able to draw his sword, and even if he did, it would be lost in the folds of his cloak.

"I very much doubt there will be anyone living in the mountains at this time of year," said Sarilo. "You should be safe until you exit the pass. Then you will need to be on your guard."

The party mounted their horses. Beata looked around for Gravis, but he was not there. She had seen the twins talking that morning but had not been able to hear what they were saying. She hoped they had not argued and had said their goodbyes peaceably, in case they lived to regret it at a later date.

Beata went up to Gavius and held his hand. He had not yet put on his mittens, and his flesh was warm and dry. "May the Arbor watch over you and keep you safe," she said, putting her hand to her heart.

Gavius did the same, exposing his oak leaf tattoo. He looked suddenly very young and unsure of himself, and she was reminded of his premonition. Was he thinking about it now?

He gave her one last smile. "I hope you find him," he said. Then he turned his mare around and tapped it with his feet, and he led the party out through the gatehouse, disappearing as the road bent around and up to the mountains.

Beata sighed. Already she felt soaked from the rain, and she had a whole day of riding ahead of her. Her spirits were low, but she had to look bright and cheerful for the rest of the Militis, and so she walked around speaking to them and smiling and clapping her hand on their backs, and soon the party was mounted and talking about the day to come. Gravis had come out of the Hall at the last minute and he mounted his horse silently. Beata noted his appearance and made a mental note to talk to him on their journey about how he was feeling.

She clasped Sarilo's hand, then neatly mounted her horse, which was waiting impatiently once again, having been well rubbed-down, fed and rested. She raised her hand in salute and drew the hood of her cloak over her head. Turning the mare, she headed out through the gatehouse and across the drawbridge, and took the road south.

In spite of the fact that they were now well into the Stirring, it was cold and she did not feel the lightness of heart that often accompanied the first few days after the Sleep. As they left Hicton behind and headed south, Beata's heart sank even further at the thought of the long journey ahead. Sarilo had informed her it would take them nearly three days to reach Lornberg, which was where she would turn off for Henton on the coast, leaving Gravis to continue on to the Henge south of the Seven Hills. She was not sure the Virimage would be at Henton, and knew she could in fact end up chasing him around the country, but it was the last place he had been seen, and it was as good a starting place as any.

Sarilo had told her there were a few isolated villages on the way where they might be able to find a barn or an outhouse to bed down in for the night, but she knew it was possible they might have to find shelter on the road, and the thought of sleeping rough in the cold and the wet did not lift her spirits.

She tried singing again as they meandered along the road, but although the Militis joined in with the choruses, it was half-hearted and nobody protested when she eventually lapsed into silence.

She sighed, looking around at the view. The road veered away slightly from the mountains, and the landscape had opened up, the hedges and terracotta-brown crop fields giving way to rolling hills with low fences, the green fields filled with sheep. Occasionally a lake nestled in the valleys like a jewel in the dip of a beautiful woman's throat, and Beata thought that on a sunny day the view would probably be breathtaking. But today, the lakes were grey as beaten metal and the fields dull as unwashed linen, and the trees that occasionally lined the roadside drooped from the weight of the rain.

Gravis chose to ride at the back, next to Fortis, so Beata was unable to speak to him on the road. She wondered whether he had moved there on purpose to avoid talking to her. She checked back over her shoulder occasionally, seeing them talking every now and then, and tried to shake off the uncomfortable paranoia they were plotting against her. Procella trusted Fortis, she told herself. Hopefully, her faith had not been misplaced.

The first night they stopped at a small village – more of a hamlet really, at the conjunction of the main road and a lane leading off over the hills. It consisted of half a dozen small cottages and a variety of sheds and barns, and on talking to the village leaders they were given permission to rest in the barn, although the farmers told them outright they had no food to spare.

"We have brought our own supplies," Beata told them, hoping they still had enough to see them through the night. "But we would be grateful if we could purchase some ale, or some milk to drink." The farmers saw the glint of the Laxonian coin in her hand and agreed yes, they could spare some milk for the travellers, and brought it to them in two large pails, the liquid still warm from the cow's udder.

The two travelling parties split and rested in two separate barns, and Beata curled herself up in her blanket, ate her rations and drank the warm milk, and tried to ignore the scrabbling of the rats in the straw behind her. She felt very homesick, and kept thinking about Heartwood and her bed in the dormitory, and wondered when she would be able to see it again. She was sore from all the riding, and missed the hot bath and hospitality she had received at Cherton and Hicton. Feeling very sorry for herself, she turned her back and eventually fell asleep.

The second day's ride to Lornberg was just as miserable. Beata knew the importance of keeping up the spirits of her party, but it was an impossible job. Though the Exercitus were used to a life on the road, the indomitable weather seemed to be depressing everyone, difficult as it was to remain cheerful when soaked through with rain, and with teeth chattering. To top it all, Caelestis had contracted a cold and, although she did not complain, Beata knew she was suffering from aches and pains, and had a temperature.

Gravis did nothing to help either; he remained morose and silent in the saddle, refusing to talk to anyone, and gradually they all left him alone. Beata knew the Quests relied on everyone working together to support each other, and her skills as Dean meant she should have no problem in pulling everyone together, but truth to tell she was at a loss, and felt out of her depth for the first time in her life.

It did not help matters that she made a couple of wrong decisions on the journey. At a fork in the road that wasn't on the map, she made the decision to go right, but the road twisted and turned and eventually almost doubled back on itself, and in the end they had to retrace their steps and take the other road. Though there was no way she could have known it was the wrong path, it had been her decision to take it, and she knew the others blamed her for losing a good half day's ride.

Secondly, during the afternoon they passed through a village; it was a decent size and had an inn with available rooms, and some of the party asked if they could stop there for the night. Beata made the decision to go on, however; there were a good three or four hours' ride left and time was of the essence, and they needed to travel as far as they could each day. So after stopping for a drink at the tavern, they continued on. However they did not pass another village, and eventually when it grew too dark to keep riding, they had to pull off the side of the road and take shelter in an old deserted barn. There was some hay there for the horses, but nothing else, and though they had bought food and ale from the village, it was a miserable meal, and nothing she could say or do would raise their spirits.

They rubbed the horses down and fed them, and then because there was little else to do and nobody seemed in the mood for singing or playing dice, they rolled themselves in their blankets and went to sleep.

Lying on the ground that night, cold and wet and suffering from saddle sores, Beata knew things were going to come to a head. Feelings and emotions were being suppressed, and it was only a matter of time before someone was going to explode and say something. She wondered whether to initiate the conversation and wake everyone up and force them to talk, but instinct told her it was not the correct time, and she must wait until the moment was right. So she lay there awake, listening to Caelestis cough, and the rain hammering on the roof of the barn.

The next day she got up knowing if anything was going to happen, it would be today. The mood of the party was sullen, seeming to match the weather, which continued to be grey and drizzly. Everyone ate their breakfast rations quietly, then mounted and left the barn with hardly a word.

In the end, nothing was said until they reached Lornberg around midmorning. This was a fairly big town at the junction of the path running to the south lands and the road southwest following the river to Henton on the coast. Here the two parties would split, Gravis heading for the Henge and Beata to try to track down the Virimage on the coast.

They stopped just outside the town and dismounted for a quick talk before they separated. Beata felt butterflies flitting in her stomach, sure something was going to be said. She had still not been able to get Gravis to talk to her, though she had tried several times during the morning to get him to open up about what was bothering him.

She did not have to wait long. It was Fortis who broke the ice, and her heart sank as he began to speak.

"We have been talking," he said, frowning at her, imposing with his sheer size and visage. "We think it would be better if we all stick together and continue on to the Henge before trying to find the Virimage."

"Do you?" Beata said acidly. "Well, I think you know my answer to that."

"And will you not take our opinions into consideration?" he said. "This is a long journey, and we are all in unfamiliar territory, and it makes sense for us to remain as one group, with safety in numbers."

"We do not have the time," she protested, looking around the group, annoyed when nobody would meet her eyes. "Time is of the essence. We must find the Virimage and we must activate the Node; we cannot choose between them." She glared at Fortis, her anger rising. "Somehow, I do not think this is the real problem. Why do you not tell me what is really troubling you?"

Fortis looked at her coolly. "If you insist." He paused and flicked a glance around the group before continuing. "We do not have confidence in your abilities as a leader. We suffered an attack in the forest which should not have occurred; we should have taken extra forces from Ogier when he offered them; we took the wrong road; we should have stopped at the village. These are mistakes a good leader would not make."

"Rubbish," Beata snapped. "Each of those events was just an unfortunate occurrence and they could not have been prevented, whoever was in charge."

Fortis glared at her. "I do not agree. And I will not be going to Henton. I am going to join Gravis's group."

V

Gavius did not look back when his small party left the others behind and headed west for the mountain pass. For a while he said nothing to his companions, lost in his own thoughts, but as the snowy peaks of the mountains began to loom in his view, he looked across and gave them an encouraging smile.

Trained as they were as soldiers to obey and follow an officer's instructions, the members of the Exercitus had said nothing to him about their fears of the journey ahead. Still, he knew they must be feeling the same wariness as he was about entering a country that had for so long been thought of as an enemy of Heartwood's.

They all smiled back at him, however, and he found himself hoping his dreams were unfounded and they would all make it safely to the Green Giant, activate the Node and then return to Heartwood safe and sound. He looked at the two knights riding at that moment on either side of him. Mellis and Niveus were both originally from Hanaire and could almost have been twins like him and Gravis, he thought. Tall and slim, with long blonde hair braided and pinned at the nape of their necks, they were both confident and accomplished female warriors, Mellis probably slightly better with the longbow and Niveus with the sword. But as alike as they were in appearance, they were very unalike in character; Mellis was quiet and determined, while Niveus was energetic and outspoken, and they made interesting companions.

Brevis, riding behind them, was a Wulfian, short and muscular, with long dark hair caught back with an oak leaf clasp, and a beardless but continually stubble-coated face. He wore a permanently fierce expression, which Gavius had thought was affected but he had eventually come to realise it was just the way the knight's features were set.

The last Exercitus warrior in the group was Hodie. He had arrived at Heartwood in the same Allectus as Gavius and Gravis, and they had all grown up together until Hodie had chosen to serve in the Exercitus. Their reunion at Heartwood had been a happy one, and Gavius was glad he had an old friend riding with him into Komis.

The mountain pass was narrow but short and they knew they should reach the other side in a couple of days. However, it was the first time any of them had been in such difficult terrain, and the going was slow. The further into the pass they went, the colder it became, and when the rain turned to sleet and finally to snow, Gavius knew they were in the heart of the mountains.

The horses slipped and stumbled on the snow-covered path, which cut a way through the sheer mountains to their left and right. Gavius kept a tight grip on the reins and pulled the fur-lined cloak closer around him. The path soon became too narrow for them to ride abreast and they fell behind one another, continuing in single file, Gavius in front and Hodie at the back.

It was too difficult to speak over his shoulder through the whirling snowflakes, and Gavius soon felt as if he were in his own private world, all sound muffled by the blanket of snow, and barely able to see more than a few feet ahead of him. He trusted to his mare's careful footsteps and hoped fervently the steed would not slip and send them both plummeting down the mountainside.

Enclosed in a white cocoon, with only himself for company, he soon found his mind wandering. He thought about Gravis and wondered how he would fare on his Quest, knowing his brother would not find the task an easy one. He was well aware he, Gavius, was the stronger twin, the one who had all the ideas, all the intuition, and all the courage. How would Gravis cope without him?

Though they were twins, he had always thought of himself as the older brother. Because of this, he had tried to persuade

Gravis to come with him on his Quest rather than go off on his own. For some reason Gravis had been insulted by his brother's insinuation that he would be unable to complete his own Quest. They had argued, Gavius trying to explain he just thought Gravis would feel more comfortable if they stayed together, but Gravis had been unable to shake off the thought that his brother was sure he would not be able to cope on his own. It had made him even more determined to undertake his own Quest to the Henge. Gavius had been disappointed and confused with both the argument and Gravis's coolness towards him afterwards. They had not parted on good terms, and that saddened him now, as he thought about the journey ahead and considered the fact that he might not return to Heartwood at all.

He pulled his hood low to try to stop the snowflakes touching his face. Why did he have this recurring feeling he was going to fail? It wasn't because he doubted his abilities; he was a confident knight, aware of his intelligence and strength, and he had faith in his companions. He felt he had enough courage for two men! He did not worry they would not reach the Green Giant, nor was he particularly afraid that he would not be able to activate it. But it was something else, something hanging over him like the shadow of a cloud as it passed across the landscape.

Gavius blinked. Ahead of him, through the swirling snow, something moved. He reined in the mare, frowning, squinting and trying to see through the flakes. He could not explain what he had seen. Was it just the snow moving in the wind, a sudden eddy that had whipped it around in a spiral to form a long shape? Or had it been something more, someone standing on the path in front of him, revealed and then hidden by the curtain of white?

"What is it?" Mellis yelled from behind him, suddenly realising Gavius had stopped in front of her.

"I do not know... A shape in the snow," he called back. He turned, seeing the others appearing out of the blizzard, stopping as they reached him and Mellis on the path. Mellis relayed that

Gavius thought he had seen something. He turned to look in front of him once more and held his breath. Yes, there it was again. It was definitely more than just a pattern of snowflakes. There was someone standing there, shrouded in white.

Deftly, he dismounted, dropping soundlessly to the ground. He pushed back his hood, then pulled off his mittens and lay them on the mare's saddle. Silently, he swept back his cloak and unsheathed his sword.

Snowflakes fell onto his face, onto his eyelashes and cheeks, and into his mouth. He brushed them aside impatiently with hands growing colder by the minute. His heart pounded, but he was not afraid. He went forward, feeling as if he wanted to push aside the snow as if it were a curtain. His boots scuffed on rock. He narrowed his eyes against the flakes, trying to peer ahead. There was definitely a shadow there, about his height, dressed in white, camouflaged against the wintry scenery.

Behind him he heard Mellis calling his name. She sounded far away, her voice muffled by the white blanket that had fallen between them. His hair was wet and his face numb with cold. He paused, wondering if he should turn back and get them to follow him. But ahead of him the figure moved, and he found his feet walking towards it. It shifted like a wraith, fading in and out of the white scenery. He had to find out who or what it was.

Mellis called his name again. Her voice sounded distant and echoed around him so for a moment he could not tell whether she was behind or ahead of him. He turned, suddenly disorientated. He could not remember which way was forward and which was back. Everything looked the same in white, like being at a wedding where everyone was dressed as the bride.

He swore softly, realising how foolish he had been. Why had he not taken his horse with him, at least? He listened for Mellis's voice, but she did not call again. Turning, he took a step forwards, hand held out in front of him as if he was blind.

Then, suddenly, he froze. Before him was the snow figure, appearing out of the gloom so suddenly and silently it made Gavius gasp. He stared. The figure stood directly before him in the same pose as himself – hand outstretched, the other clasping the hilt of a sword with numb fingers. He drew in his breath so quickly the cold air stung his throat.

It was Gravis.

The oak leaf tattoo was clear on his right arm, mirroring Gavius's own tattoo on his left. He wore a cloak completely covered in snow, hence Gavius' thinking the figure had been dressed in white. His hair, like Gavius's, was wet, hanging limp around a face white with cold.

Gavius dropped his arm. The figure dropped his. Gavius stared, a sudden realisation dawning on him. Was it Gravis? Or was it just his reflection? There were no mirrors in Heartwood save the few small ones they used for shaving, and Gavius had never looked at himself in a full-length one. The sensation was unsettling, disturbing.

Once again he lifted up a hand and reached out to see if he could touch the person in front of him. But this time something peculiar happened: the figure dissolved, disintegrating as if it had been made of snow. Around him, the wind spun flakes in a whirl of white, and then suddenly, briefly, the snow before him cleared and he could see clearly the view before him.

He gasped. He was standing on the edge of a ravine, his feet inches away from the sheer sides of the chasm. One more step and he would have plummeted to his death.

He stumbled back and fell, landing heavily on his backside, and scrabbled backwards even more until he felt the mountain at his back. His breath clouded before him as his chest heaved. The curtain ahead of him closed, hidden in a whirl of white, so suddenly he wondered if he had dreamed it all.

To his right he heard voices and then Mellis and Brevis appeared, turning to shout to the others they had found him.

Mellis dropped to her knees beside him, taking his sword and stuffing his numb hands into the mittens she had brought with her. Ruffling his hair to dislodge the snow that was beginning to settle there, she raised his hood to cover his ears, which were beginning to ache from the cold.

"What happened?" she said, turning to look over her shoulder. "You are right near the edge of the ravine. Was it someone in the snow? Did you see who it was?"

Gavius shook his head, unable to put his emotions into words. How could he tell her what he had seen? Either a reflection of himself, or his twin brother, neither of which made any sense. Either way it had been some sort of vision, which was unnerving in itself, and not something he really wanted to admit to seeing.

But most disturbing of all was that he did not know whether the vision had appeared to stop him plunging into the ravine, or whether it had led him there to do just that.

CHAPTER EIGHT

I

Gravis stared at Fortis, who had just declared his wish to split from Beata's party and travel with him to the Henge. He felt shocked at Fortis's disobedience. Following orders was one of the first things they were taught when they came to Heartwood, and it was well known the Exercitus were the most obedient of all the Militis. Fortis had spent many years at Procella's side; she trusted him, and had sent him with Beata because she had thought he would be a great support to her. In spite of Beata's being a Dean, Gravis knew she was not used to commanding others. Procella had expected Fortis to be Beata's right hand, to back her up and follow her to the end.

But now? Gravis frowned, kicked his feet free from the stirrups and swung himself to the ground, intending to intervene. However, even as he did so, however, Fortis said to Beata, "May I speak to you privately?"

Beata looked across at the other knights, then sighed and walked a short distance away, Fortis following. They then engaged in conversation, with Beata gesticulating angrily and Fortis speaking calmly, occasionally dropping his eyes to the floor in a deferential manner. Eventually Beata's shoulders sank. She turned and looked straight at Gravis, then looked away. She nodded to Fortis and spoke in a low voice.

Eventually the two of them rejoined the others. Fortis turned his back on them and began to check his horse's saddle, tightening the stirrups, and left it to Beata to reveal what was occurring.

"Fortis has decided he wishes to join Gravis's Quest," she said coolly. "He has explained his reasons to me and I have decided to grant his reQuest. I shall be continuing on to Henton, and I hope Caelestis and Peritus will come with me. But if you wish to change your minds, you are welcome to do so."

Peritus shook his head. "I will stay with you, Beata."

"And I too," said Caelestis, finishing her words with a cough.

"Good." Beata checked her saddle, then came over to the group who were going to be heading for the Henge. "I wish you all the best of luck," she said, shaking hands and clasping the forearm of each of them. Finally, she stood in front of Gravis, and grasped his arm tightly. "May the Arbor look after you, Gravis, and may your Quest be successful."

"And yours too," he said awkwardly. Her eyes were light grey, like an early-morning rainy sky. She looked at him searchingly, a slight frown on her forehead, and he knew she was trying to decipher why he had been so quiet since Hicton. But she said nothing, and eventually just smiled and went over to her horse, mounting it swiftly and finishing with a salute over her heart, showing her oak leaf tattoo.

They all returned the gesture, and then she was gone, heading down the road towards the coast, Peritus and Caelestis following along behind, casting one last look over their shoulder.

Gravis mounted his horse and said curtly, "We had best be on our way. The sooner we can sort out the Henge, the sooner we can return home." He met Fortis's gaze for a moment, then turned his horse and led the way down the road.

He was not foolish. He sensed Fortis's disagreement with Beata's methods was a ruse, and he was accompanying him not because the warrior did not trust Beata's judgement, but because he felt Gravis needed some extra support. The thought that they did not have faith in him made his cheeks burn, and he turned his face up to the rain to cool his skin.

He glanced briefly over his shoulder, seeing the four Militis who had been allocated to the Quest talking quietly amongst themselves. Fortis hung behind, bringing up the rear, his head bowed and covered by the hood of his cloak. Gravis turned in the saddle again, looking at the rain-soaked Seven Hills before him. He did not know the Militis with him very well and he was sure they were discussing Fortis's decision to change parties. They would be Questioning his ability. As angry as he was, he could not complain, because he had severe doubts himself as to whether he could actually fulfil the Quest.

Something had happened to him at Hicton – and maybe even before that. Gavius had tried to get him talk about it, but he had not been able to, mainly because he was not sure what was wrong. Gavius had tried to help by suggesting Gravis accompany him on his Quest. He had clearly thought Gravis would be lost without him, and that had rankled.

For some reason, even though Gravis knew his twin had always been the leader of the two of them, his brother's assumption that he could not cope on his own had stung. He was a Militis himself, was he not? He had passed the Allectus, done the training, taken his vows, proven himself in battle, albeit a small skirmish just south of the Wall. He had every right to be given this task, to be a leader of a Quest.

And yet… His doubts bubbled inside him. All his old fears, the worries he had pushed to the back of his mind for years, came rising to the surface like fat on a cauldron of boiling stew.

Deep inside, he had always wondered whether the Abbatis at the time of his Allectus had allowed him to stay merely because he wanted Gavius so much. The two of them had been inseparable, clutching hands as they were brought into Heartwood and speaking almost as one; it had been clear how close they were, and how difficult it would have been to separate them. Gavius had shone on the day – been the first to go around the exercise circuit; the only one to complete the complicated wooden puzzle they had all been given; received the highest mark in the written tests about history, mathematics and science. In comparison, Gravis's nerves had let him down, and he had fallen at the hurdles, only half-completed the puzzle, and struggled with all aspects of the tests. He had never understood why he had been taken into Heartwood. As a child, those first few nights after they arrived, he had wondered silently if his acceptance had been just to keep Gavius happy.

Gradually, however, the fears had faded as he had relaxed into daily life at the Castellum and begun to excel at the various tasks they had to learn. But now, with the drizzle soaking him to the skin and his spirits plummeting, his childhood uncertainties haunted him, as if they were spirits of relatives come to watch him as he failed in his Quest.

Fortis had obviously spotted his doubts and must have asked Beata if he should change Quests so he could keep an eye on him. He resented the seasoned warrior for his acute observations, but was also glad of his company. The other Militis were all young: Aranea and Justina both female Laxonians, sturdy and proficient warriors but lacking experience in the field; Parco and Letalis both male Wulfians, picked for their size and aggressive fighting ability, but not the sort of friends he would have chosen for confidantes. He hoped Fortis would be a good guide if he fell at the last hurdle.

It was a long and tedious journey that day, and he barely talked to the others, too wrapped up in his own thoughts to converse. They stopped that night at a village halfway to Realberg, enjoying the luxury of a real bed in an inn after their previous night spent on the road, and after a hot bath and a decent meal they turned in for the night, everyone falling into a sound sleep.

Everyone, that is, except Gravis. He was tired, and his body felt heavy with weariness, but he could not get to sleep. He lay there for a long while, listening to his compatriots' steady breathing, and then eventually got up and made his way downstairs, through the darkened inn, and outside into the cool night air.

It was still raining, but very lightly, more like a low mist than rain, and for once it refreshed him rather than bothered him. The clouds had in fact parted to reveal the Light Moon in its first quarter, casting its pink glow over the countryside, though the smaller Dark Moon was hidden behind the clouds. The village was sleeping, the cottages darkened and quiet. Behind him one of the horses whinnied in the stables. Somewhere in the distance, a dog barked.

Gravis had never felt so alone. He shivered, wishing he had brought his travelling cloak with him, but he was only wearing a light tunic and breeches, not even his mail. He felt strangely light without it after wearing it continually for several days now. He walked down the lane, not knowing where he was heading, but feeling the need to get away. It seemed like an eternity since he had left Heartwood, even though it had only been seven days. He remembered his time spent in the Exercitus, and how he and Gavius had comforted each other with tales from their childhood at the Castellum, and stories about Militis both past and present.

He thought about Gavius now, and wondered where his brother was. Somewhere in the Knife's Edge, he guessed, trying to get some sleep in the midst of the cold. Did Gavius miss him? Or was he relieved to be free of the dog-like hanger-on who was continually at his side?

Gravis's feet had led him onto a bridge that crossed a pond. The circle of water looked dull in the watery moonlight, like a beaten but unpolished sheet of steel. He leaned on the bridge, looking down at the water, remembering the way the channel had erupted in the Curia, and how the Darkwater Lords had formed from the liquid into solid warriors. Any form of water left him uneasy now, and he eyed the pond with a frown, uncertain what was making him feel apprehensive.

And then suddenly he realised what it was. The reflection of the Light Moon lay on the surface of the pond like a dead fish, a sliver of pink silver against the grey flatness. This in itself was not disturbing.

It was the fact that he could not see his own reflection that made him catch his breath.

Gravis blinked and looked up. A cloud covered the Moon, and he was cast suddenly into darkness. He gripped hold of the wooden handrail, wishing he had been sensible enough to bring a lantern, but even as his knuckles whitened and his heart rate increased, the cloud passed and the Moon appeared again, and he looked down and there was his reflection, anxious and white, but as real as the wooden bridge on which he leaned.

He breathed deeply, calming his racing heart. He had been mistaken the first time – of course his reflection had been there; how could it have not? It had been a trick of the light, an illusion, like the time one of the Deans at Heartwood had done magic for him and Gavius, making a coin mysteriously appear and disappear beneath a square of cloth.

And yet… Gravis shivered. Deep inside, he knew he was not mistaken, just as he had known as a boy the coin had not really vanished into thin air. For some reason, he had not cast a reflection.

What did that mean for him? And what did that mean for the Quest?

II

Beata pulled the hood of her cloak down over her face to hide her tears. Her stomach felt knotted like a skein of tangled wool.

As Dean, part of her role was to act as mediator and intercede if there were problems between people. However, she was unused to direct confrontation, and her disagreement with Fortis had unsettled her greatly. His direct criticism of her as leader had knocked her confidence and upset her. When he took her to one side she had assumed he was going to continue his diatribe towards her, and had steeled herself for an argument, only to find him apologising and telling her his rebellion was a ploy. He had explained he thought Gravis was going to have trouble with his Quest and wanted to help him.

Beata had got very angry at this and told him he had undermined her authority with the others, but he had been defensive and said he was only doing what he thought was best, which was what Procella had told him to do. Beata told him this was not what Procella had had in mind, and had promised him she would take it up with the Dux when they got back to Heartwood, but he had been unrepentant, saying any other way of changing groups would have seemed like a lack of confidence in Gravis's ability, which would only make the matter worse.

"And what of my confidence?" she had asked him miserably. He had appeared astonished at that comment, and said he thought her confidence was high, and he had complete faith she would fulfil her Quest. Beata had sighed at that point. It seemed pointless to her to force him to stay; it would only lead to further resentment and bad feeling between the two of them. And besides, if he was right and Gravis would need help in activating the Node, it was better Fortis went with him.

Still, she now felt concern for her own party that they were down to three, and she was also disappointed in herself, for she set very high personal goals, and so far on the journey she had failed to meet all of them. There was no way realistically she could have avoided the problems that had beset them, but as Quest Leader she was responsible for the others, and she had not done a good job so far.

Caelestis and Peritus rode behind her in single file because the road was too busy to ride abreast, and for a while they said nothing, each caught up in their own thoughts. They passed through the town centre, busy with trade and bustling with people, but as the shops petered out and the houses gradually grew less numerous, the other two were able to pull up beside Beata and relax as the noise and hubbub of the town died away.

The path matched the course of the river south-west, passing through the Seven Hills which reared before them, the ground too high and poor for crops, home only to sheep and ponies. They hoped to follow the river through the valleys and steer clear of the highest peaks, which although not as troublesome as Gavius's mountains, would be an even colder and more miserable journey than the one they were already undertaking, although at that moment, Beata found that difficult to imagine.

Never had she felt so low. And never had she felt so unable to complete a task given to her. She hardly felt like she could go another yard, let alone the five-day ride to Henton.

Peritus smiled at her. "Everything is going to be all right."

Beata sighed heavily. "It would be nice to think so, although I do not see as yet how that could be the case."

"We are together, are we not? We stand by you, Beata, in spite of what Fortis said."

She smiled back. She wanted to tell them the main reason Fortis had decided to go with Gravis, but did not want to betray his confidence. Instead, she just said, "Well, I hope we have better luck in the second half of our journey."

"So do I," said Caelestis, accompanying her words with a cough. Beata looked at her with concern. The cough was beginning to sound as if it came from her chest rather than her throat, and her face looked drawn, her forehead glittering with sweat.

"You do not look well," she said, reaching over to touch the knight's face. Her skin burned under Beata's fingers. "You have a fever and it sounds like your chest is thickening. When we stop tonight, I will make you a tea from some herbs I have in my saddle bag. And you must keep warm. Do you want a blanket around you?"

Caelestis insisted she was warm enough and Beata said nothing more, but as they followed the road down to the river, she worried about her fellow knight, knowing really she should be in bed resting, but also knowing they had to keep moving, for the journey was long and each minute that passed was another minute the Darkwater Lords could be preparing to invade.

The road continued to follow the river, just above the water, on the right bank. The river was quite wide and fast flowing at this point, and the horses would struggle to ford it. As would she; although she had splashed about in the Flumen during hot summers, she was not a strong swimmer and had never even seen the sea. Her time in the Exercitus had been spent mainly on the central forts where most of the trouble occurred, and her particular year had seen a major uprising of a particularly aggressive raiding party, and therefore she had not had the tour of the full length of the Wall many of the Heartwood army had.

Still, she reasoned, there was no reason she should have to swim the river. Nearer Henton, there would undoubtedly be a bridge. She wouldn't have to go into the water.

She realised her experience with the Darkwater Lords had ruined her pleasure of water forever. Never again would she be able to think of it as just liquid. Always she would picture the way the warriors had leapt into the Curia, forming as if the water had been poured into a vessel, the way she had seen liquid metal poured into moulds to make arrowheads.

But still, the river on this day was pleasant enough, the water higher than normal with the constant rain, but still a foot from the top of its bank, its colour a lush dark green, its surface – where it wasn't broken by rocks – occasionally littered with moorhens and the brilliant flash of a kingfisher.

The day went quickly enough and they camped that night in a small hamlet, paying valuable money for a small room in a farmer's house, but glad of the shelter as the clouds seemed to thicken over the moors, and the rain intensified as the sun slipped beneath the hills.

The farmer's wife sold them some milk from their cow and some bread she had just baked, and – a real treat – some cod from the coast, which she had poached in milk until tender, along with some cooked carrots and leeks. The hot meal warmed their bellies and in spite of the rain that hammered against the roof of the little cottage, Beata felt a sense of well-being that evening which she hoped would last for some time as they continued on their journey.

After they had eaten, she heated some water over the small fire in their room and tipped some herbs into a pan she had borrowed from the farmer's wife, and made an infusion of coltsfoot and elecampe to help Caelestis bring up the phlegm now lying on her chest, then chopped up a raw onion and mixed it with honey and encouraged her to eat the mixture, laughing as the warrior pulled a face and explaining that in spite of its strange taste, it would aid her cold. Soon afterwards, Caelestis fell asleep, and Beata and Peritus talked quietly as the fire gradually burned low, discussing their childhood at Heartwood, and reminding each other of events and incidents from their youth.

Eventually, however, with the fire now only glowing embers, it was too dark to see each other, and so they curled up in their blankets next to each other for warmth, and fell asleep with the sound of the river gushing in the distance, and the rain beating on the roof.

The next morning the rain had lessened, but only slightly. The light mist they had been travelling through was now a thick downpour, and Beata's heart sank as she stepped out of the cottage door and looked up at the heavy grey clouds, which seemed lower than before, as if the sky were gradually descending onto them.

"Can you not stay another day?" said the farmer's wife anxiously, looking across at Caelestis, who was mounting her horse, looking more exhausted than before she had gone to sleep. "She is not well – a day in the cold and wet will do her no good."

Beata hesitated. They were already more than halfway through the Lamb Moon and she had not even yet reached Henton. Animus knew what was happening back at Heartwood. It had only been Nitesco's guess the Darkwater Lords would not attack until the High Moon – what if he was wrong? What if they had already attacked? Or were planning to attack tomorrow? No, she could not waste a day without moving forward. Every moment counted.

"I am sorry," she said to Caelestis, "but we must keep going. But I understand if you would like to stay here – we could always pick you up on the way back."

"No, I am fine," Caelestis insisted, looking anything but as she had a sudden fit of coughing. However, when she finished, she gave them all a grin and sat straight in the seat, and Beata sighed, knowing the knight would feel responsible for the fact that there were now only three of them left, and would be unable to desert her leader.

Beata thanked the farmer's wife and mounted the mare, and then they were off again, hunched in the rain, heading for the coast.

It was harder going now the rain was heavier. The road had turned to mud with large pools of water, and it was difficult to pick up the pace. Sometimes, they met carts coming the other way with goods from the coast, and they had to move aside to let them pass, as the road wasn't wide enough for them all.

To make things worse, the wind blew the rain towards them, so even when they pulled their hoods down low over their faces, they could not avoid getting wet.

Beata felt miserable enough in the cold, wet weather, but she knew Caelestis must be feeling even worse. She kept looking over to check on the warrior, but she was wrapped in the folds of material of her cloak, and kept her face hidden out of the rain.

The first sign she received that Caelestis was really unwell was when she fell off the horse.

III

After leaving Grimbeald at Karlgan, Fionnghuala and her party travelled for another three hours before deciding to stop at one of the lodges placed there long ago by Hanairean traders travelling to the Twelve Lands. The lodges were one-room huts built out of logs, but basic as they were, they did provide protection from the weather. They also contained cooking utensils, as well as firewood, some food, and hay for horses, which was replaced on a regular basis by travellers from Fintaire, Bearrach's town on the other side of the Pass.

Fionnghuala tied up her horse with the others in a space covered by a sloping roof to provide them with some shelter, then spent a while rubbing the steed down and making sure it had access to hay and water before going into the lodge. The three Militis who had travelled with her, as well as Bearrach and their two fellow countrymen, had already started a fire, and someone had placed a pot over it from which a rich, meaty aroma was already emanating.

She pulled her blanket out of her bag and unfurled it near the fire, then sank onto it gratefully. She was not used to spending so long in the saddle, and although her muscles did not burn as they had after the first few days' ride from Hanaire to Heartwood, she still ached. How she wished she could have a hot bath! But that was out of the Question, obviously. It would take about ten refills of the pot hanging over the fire to get an inch of water in a tub, had there been one, and by the time the tenth one had boiled, the other nine would be cold. The thought made her smile and appreciate for the first time the work of her household at her home in Salentaire, who always managed to have a hot bath ready for her whenever she wished it.

"Something funny?" asked Bearrach, coming to spread his blanket beside her. He groaned as he lowered himself onto the floor. "I cannot possibly imagine what you can find amusing after spending so long in the saddle."

"Having such a big thing between one's thighs does make one ache a bit," she admitted, only realising the connotations of what she had said when Bearrach burst out laughing and the others exchanged wry grins.

He patted her knee affectionately. "If you have such high expectations, I guess I should forget about letting you discover what is beneath my breeches!"

She smiled as the others guffawed but made no reply, turning instead to pull her bag towards her and hiding her flushed face by looking inside. She felt confused by his words. Obviously he had been jesting, but still, there had been a ring of truth about them. Had her instincts been right – was he interested in her?

She released her hair from its braids and began to comb the long, blonde locks. She knew he, like her, had never been married. In Hanaire, families took priority over politics, and a married man or woman was expected to spend as much time as possible with their family and thus could not serve on the Council.

She didn't know why Bearrach had never got married. He was a handsome Hanairean, clever, witty, affectionate and kind, and there was no good explanation for his continued single status. Of course he could be wondering the same about her, she thought. But he would never guess her reason for staying unmarried.

The stew was soon ready and ladled into bowls, and the party ate it hungrily, glad of some warmth inside. Their mood was high; they were warm, dry and full, and Fionnghuala soon discovered the Heartwood knights to be good company. Audax was a stocky Wulfian, but had retained none of the traits she disliked so much in that people and instead was outspoken and funny, and teased his companions mercilessly. Mundus was older, a Laxonian, quiet and patient, steadfast and true. Fionnghuala found out as they talked that he had travelled extensively on missions for Heartwood, had been to Hanaire several times, and knew the Twelve Lands well. The final Militis was a female Laxonian, Lalage, who was probably older than she looked at first glance, but had a youthful, bubbly personality, and talked continually, though luckily not in an irritating fashion.

Fionnghuala's companion from Hanaire was a quiet council member called Kinaed, whom she had known for many years.

Bearrach's companion was a tall, rather fierce-looking Hanairean called Ruadh, whom she thought probably had more than a little Wulfian blood in him. And so that was their party, and they knitted together well, and talked for many hours until they finally curled up in their blankets and subsided into sleep.

That night Fionnghuala was tired and, having drunk a little ale too, fell asleep quickly. It was the next day and they were back on their horses heading for Hanaire before she had chance to think again about what Bearrach had said.

Had it been just an idle comment provoked by her unfortunately lewd-sounding remark? Or had it been more than that? Certainly on their trip he had been attentive, caring and thoughtful towards her. But she sensed that was his nature – that was how Hanairean men were brought up to be. Was there anything more to it than that?

She glanced surreptitiously across at him to find him watching her, a small smile on his face. The smile widened as he saw her look over and he gave her a little nod. She smiled back hesitantly, then turned her attention back to the rocky path, now covered with a light dusting of snow. The jollity of the night before slunk away like a cat, and she gazed into the falling snow before them with a sigh, wishing they were nearer to their destination.

The road had climbed steadily higher, shadowing the mountainside, and the snow was beginning to fall more thickly. The party fell quieter as the path became narrower, and they had to travel single file and watch their step. The horses ploughed on solidly but the pace became slower, and the mood of all the companions seemed to darken with the weather.

They spent that night in another lodge but this time there was no jovial atmosphere, no teasing or laughter around the fire. Even Audax was subdued, and Lalage's babble reduced to a trickle of conversation in hushed tones. Fionnghuala said very little as they ate, and afterwards went out to tend to the horses, enjoying the peace of the blanketed world, and the company of the horses who snorted and stamped as she rubbed them down.

It was some time later that she looked up, hot and sweaty from the activity in spite of the cool air, and saw Bearrach standing just outside the makeshift stable, cloakless, his hands in the pockets of his breeches, his blond hair covered with a layer of snow.

Fionnghuala stood and brushed back stray strands of hair, using her cold hands to cool her flushed cheeks. She waited for him to speak but he said nothing. Eventually she said, "Is there a problem?"

"No. I just came to make sure you are all right."

She smiled. "I am fine, thank you."

He did not move, however. He leaned against the side of the lodge and looked out at the snow, falling softly like ash on the road. He opened his mouth to speak.

Fionnghuala, however, came over to him and put her hand on his arm. "Dear friend," she said gently. "Do not."

He looked at her, his green eyes puzzled. "I…"

"I know," she said. "But I am a High Council member, and I do not want to give that up. I will never marry, Bearrach. But I am flattered by your attention, and I thank you for your offer."

He stared at her for a moment, his face unreadable. She felt she had hurt him terribly, and something twisted inside her stomach. But still, it had to be done. She could not allow him to go on thinking she was a suitable wife.

Suddenly his lips twitched and his eyes twinkled. "I only came out here to ask you if you wanted a drink," he said.

She smiled, knowing from the look in his eyes his words were untrue. "In that case, yes, I will join you."

He held out his arm and she took it and went back into the lodge, thankful he had not tried to press her for a reason why she did not wish to commit herself to a relationship.

She had thought turning him down would lift her mood, relieving the pressure she felt had been building, but as they settled down for the night, she felt restless, as if sleep were an animal that had scuttled over the mountain and was refusing to come back when called. The breathing of the others in the room soon became relaxed and light snores filled the air, but still she remained awake, staring into the embers of the dying fire.

It was as her eyelids were beginning to droop that she heard the baby cry. It came far off in the distance; a high, thin wail. Her eyes flew open and she lifted her head, straining her ears. There was a moment's pause and then it came again, the small cry of a newborn, cutting through the air.

She pushed herself up, looking around the room to see if anyone else had heard it, but they were all sleeping, the room almost in darkness save for the fire and the light from two small lanterns. She sat for a moment, puzzled, wondering who on earth would bring such a young baby up through the pass at this time of year. Was it a band of travellers who were spending the night on the mountain? But the nearest lodge was at least half a day's ride, and the baby's cry would not carry from there. Were they out in the cold?

Getting quietly to her feet, she gathered up her cloak and swung it around her shoulders, stuffed her feet into her fur boots, then picked up one of the lanterns and moved silently through the sleeping bodies to the door. Gently she opened it, letting in a brief flurry of snow as she slipped outside, pulling it shut behind her.

Outside, the mountain was in darkness. The light from the lantern spread out from her in a small circle like melted butter at her feet, illuminating the snow which fell in front of her face like a blanket, muffling all sound.

All sound, that was, except the baby's cry. It came again, from somewhere in front of her, high and thin as the reed pipe she had played as a child. Clutching her cloak around her neck with her left hand and holding the lantern aloft with her right, she started to walk along the mountain path towards the child. She wore heavy leather boots that made no sound on the snow-muffled path, and for a moment she felt as if she had no more substance than a wraith, a ghost moving through the spirit world.

The cry continued to come from in front of her, but seemed to be getting no nearer. Her heart thundered in her chest and she began to doubt the wisdom of coming out alone as the lodge disappeared into the darkness behind her. She stopped and turned, finding herself in a well of blackness, the only light coming from the small circle that spread around her as if she herself were the candle. The cry now seemed to come from the north. She hesitated, struggling to get her bearings. That was off the edge of the path. It didn't make sense. She turned again, beginning to lose her sense of direction. Which way was forward and which way back to the lodge? Her breathing came more quickly and her mouth went dry. Snow fluttered down onto her eyes and lay on her lashes, and her ears were numb with cold.

Then something happened which sent her into a blind panic – a sudden gust of wind whipped open the door of the lantern and blew out the candle.

She was plunged into darkness. Her breath caught in her throat and her heart pounded. The baby's cry seemed to echo all around her; she could no longer tell which direction it was coming from. She clutched her cloak with numbed hands, biting her lip, terrified to take a step in any direction in case she plunged off the edge of the path. Her teeth started to chatter with the cold. She was going to freeze right there on the spot, and in the morning she would just be another shape under the snow.

And then suddenly, off to her right, she saw a small light like the flare of a tinderbox. She stood still, not knowing from which direction it was coming, but it gradually began to grow in size and she knew it was coming towards her.

It was Bearrach. She saw his blond hair illuminated in the darkness as he held the other lantern out in front of him, even before his face became clear. Running up to him, she threw herself into his arms, burying her face in his neck as he put his free arm around her.

"It is all right," he soothed, "you are safe now."

"I heard it crying," she sobbed, "but I could not find it."

"I know," he said, taking her hand and beginning to lead her back to the lodge. "Come on, we must get you inside or you will freeze to death."

"But the baby," she said, casting a last look over her shoulder.

He strode out along the path, the lantern held out in front of him, his grip so firm on her hand that for a moment she was not sure which fingers were his and which were hers. "Nothing could survive out here," he said. "That is not the cry of an earthly child."

Fionnghuala stumbled along behind him, his words ringing in her ears. No earthly child...

So what was it she had heard?

IV

Beata saw Caelestis slipping from her horse and thought for a moment she was reaching down for something, so by the time she realised Caelestis was actually falling it was too late to catch her. The knight fell heavily to the ground without making a sound.

Beata called out to Peritus, who was a few feet in front. He turned and, seeing the scene, leapt off his horse and ran to help. Together they turned Caelestis over, smoothing back the hair from her face. Her eyes were closed and her face flushed with fever, and her breathing was harsh, sounding like bellows squeezed to fan a blacksmith's fire.

Peritus cradled her in his arms and looked around wildly. They were over half a day's ride from the place they had stayed the night before, and did not know how long it was until the next hamlet. "What are we going to do? We cannot stay here. She will die in this weather."

"We will have to get her onto my horse and continue until the next stop." Beata hoped it wasn't far. It would be a struggle for the mare to carry both of them, sodden and heavy as they were with rain. Peritus stood with the unconscious knight in his arms and then together they struggled to lift her in front of the saddle. Luckily the mare seemed to understand what was happening and stood patiently, letting the knight lean heavily on her shoulder and neck. Beata mounted behind her and clasped Caelestis around the waist. It was uncomfortable and far from ideal, but it was the best they would be able to do.

Peritus caught the reins of the spare horse and tied them to his saddle, and they set off again.

This time Beata felt every bump in the road, every dip in the ground. She tried to brace herself to keep some of Caelestis's weight off the mare's neck, but soon realised she would not be able to continue like that for very long – she didn't have the strength. She just had to hope the horse could continue to bear the weight, and did not dip her head, or else Caelestis would just roll off.

Luckily, there was not much grass for the mare to nibble at the side of the road. Everything seemed to have turned to mud, and the river rumbled to their left, now a deep brown colour, carrying with it the earth and stones it had picked up coming down from the mountains. It had risen by about six inches, Beata thought, and it would not be long until it reached the top of the bank. They would have to be careful – a flash flood could easily sweep them away.

They plodded along for another hour or two, and then to Beata's relief ahead of them she saw a hamlet straddling the road, grey and quiet in the insistent rain. It was slightly bigger than the one they had left behind and had a small but pleasant inn, which clearly catered for those travelling from the coast to the towns by the mountains.

As soon as the innkeeper heard from Peritus that they had a sick Heartwood knight with them, she came out and lifted her down herself, carrying her into the warmth of the inn and placing her by the fire in one of her rooms.

Beata followed her in, exhausted but knowing she must attend to her fellow knight, but the innkeeper would have none of it. "You will be ill too if you do not take care of yourself," she said crisply. "My name is Ida and you shall do as I say while you stay in my inn. Take your horses around the back – my boy Waldhar will look after them. Then come back in here and get out of those wet clothes. My daughter Gisila will prepare you a bath, which you will get into immediately. After that, you will eat."

"Yes, madam," said Beata meekly, leaving Caelestis in her capable hands and going out to Peritus, who looked as fatigued as she felt. Together they led the horses around the back and found Waldhar, who took the reins and promised to rub the steeds down and feed them well, and then they went back into the inn and up to their room, where Gisila had already started pouring pails of hot water into two large wooden tubs.

Beata looked at Caelestis by the fire but, seeing Ida had already removed her wet clothing and wrapped her in blankets, knew there was little she could do and instead stripped herself, stepping into the hot water and lowering herself with a sigh until she was immersed up to her neck.

Gisila took her wet clothes, wrung them out, then hung them on a rack over the fire to dry. She did the same for Peritus, who also climbed into his hot tub, sighing with pleasure as his aching muscles relaxed in the hot water. Gisila came over and offered them a cup of ale, which they accepted gratefully, taking a long swig before settling back, their heads resting on the edge of the tub.

Beata unpinned her hair and washed it, then spread it over the back of the tub as she soaked, letting it dry. She looked across at the two figures in front of the fire. Ida was dipping a cloth in water into which she had put some herbs, and was sponging Caelestis's face and body.

"Will she be all right?" Beata asked.

Ida looked across at her. She was a big woman with a frank, no-nonsense face, and was clearly not going to sweeten the news. "She is very ill. She has a high temperature and her lungs are thick. How long has she been coughing up blood?"

Beata looked startled. "I did not know she was."

Ida nodded. "I thought as much. She has been hiding it from you – she did not want you to know how ill she was. It is not a good sign. I will do what I can, but... you must prepare yourself for the worst."

Beata sat up in the bath, shocked at the news. Obviously, Caelestis had been ill, but she had not thought she was *that* ill. All pleasure in the bath now dissipating, she got out and dried herself, then put on the loose tunic and breeches Ida had lent her until her own clothes were dry. Coming over to Caelestis, she sat beside her and stroked her face, which was flushed and covered with a sheen of sweat.

"Come downstairs and have something to eat," said Ida.

"I should stay here with her," said Beata hoarsely, awash with emotions as she looked at the ill knight.

"There is nothing you can do, and she needs her rest now. Gisila will empty the tubs and then sit with her for a while. Come on, you need to eat or else you will be ill, too."

Peritus was now out and dressed, so reluctantly they followed Ida down the narrow stairs and into the main room of the inn.

It was a pleasant-enough establishment, thought Beata, and she knew it would probably make a fair amount of money, being on the only real route from the mountains to the coast for many miles. The room had a bar at the end behind which Ida now prepared them some food and drink, and there were four or five tables with chairs dotted around the sawdust-covered floor, and more chairs in front of the open fire at one end. There were a couple of other visitors at the inn, travelling to Lornberg, but they kept themselves to themselves, and Beata and Peritus sat by the fire and stared into the flames, quiet with their own thoughts.

Ida brought them a plate of bread, cheese, cold meats and pickled vegetables, and they ate these slowly and drank their ale, the thought of Caelestis ill upstairs weighing on them like the heavy grey clouds outside in the sky.

Afterwards they stared sleepily into the flames. In spite of the warmth, Peritus shivered, pulling his too-big tunic close around him. "Do you think we will find him?" he asked.

Beata did not have to ask to whom he was referring. There was a time when she would have offered him platitudes, for as a Dean that was her job, to make people feel better, but she did not feel like a Dean now. That life felt like a million miles away, and after the mistakes she had made she wondered how she could ever have felt like she could help other people.

"I do not know," she said honestly, watching the way the flames seemed to dance on the log resting in the grate. "I do not know anything any more."

Peritus said nothing else, and after a while they both fell into an exhausted sleep.

They were awoken some time in the middle of the night by Gisila, who touched them both gently on the arm. "Mother wants you to come upstairs," she said, holding up her lantern to illuminate her worried face. "Your friend... she... well, you had better come and see."

Beata and Peritus got to their feet hurriedly and followed Gisila up the stairs. Going into the room, they saw Ida kneeling by Caelestis, holding her hand. The fire had been kept going and its light illuminated the unconscious warrior. Beata came over and knelt beside her. Caelestis's skin was waxy and pale, her eyes sunken like two stones pressed into dough. She breathed very shallowly, and her chest rasped.

Ida looked up at them. "I have done all I can, but I do not think she will last long. The infection has spread into her lungs."

Peritus sat in a chair and put his head in his hands. Beata took Caelestis's other hand. It was clammy and limp like a fish in her fingers. She began to pray, finding the wooden oak leaf around her neck and clutching it until it bit into her fingers, asking Animus and the Arbor to help Caelestis and make her well, but even as she prayed she knew it was hopeless, that the knight would not be well again. Instead, she changed her prayer and prayed Caelestis would find peace and be welcomed into Animus's arms, where she deserved to be.

Caelestis died just before daybreak, the coldest, darkest hour. Beata and Peritus wept as Ida tried again and again to get a pulse, eventually announcing the knight had finally slipped away.

Ida covered her with a sheet and, taking the arms of the two knights, led them downstairs. She poured them a mug of her strongest ale and made them drink it, then led them in front of the fire. "I will prepare her for burial," she said. "You must get some more sleep."

"I could not sleep now," Beata protested, but it was a feeble argument – her eyelashes felt as if they had horseshoes attached and hung heavily on her cheeks. Peritus was the same, grief and tiredness sapping his energy, and eventually the two of them slept, as the sun crept slowly over the horizon.

When they awoke, Ida was waiting for them. She told them she had said goodbye to her other customers and Caelestis had been bathed and prepared for burial.

"Where shall we bury her?" Beata asked hoarsely, rubbing her face, which felt tight, the skin stretched across her bones.

"We have a small graveyard just down the road, under an oak tree," said Ida. "But before we take her down there, I want to show you something."

She took their heads and led them outside.

Something rather incredible had happened. The sun had come out. They stared up, squinting from behind their upraised hands as the golden rays painted the landscape with beautiful warm tones. Tears formed in Beata's eyes. It was still raining lightly, but that just meant the creation to the south of a stunning rainbow that arced across the hills.

She looked up at the rainbow and blinked as sharp tears stung her eyes. "Poor Caelestis," she whispered. "It is all my fault."

"Nonsense," said Ida firmly. "Sickness is nobody's fault. You cannot be blamed because the girl caught a chill."

"I should have left her behind in Lornberg," said Beata, thinking this was another disastrous situation that could have been avoided if she had thought sensibly.

"Would she have remained there while you continued on?" Ida argued. "I do not think that is the case. She was quite a strong-willed person until the moment she died. It is ego and nothing more to think you can impose your will on another."

Beata frowned, wiping her cheeks. "But surely that is what a leader has to do? Otherwise, everyone would do just what they wanted and never follow orders."

Ida thought about it, wiping her hands on a cloth as she did so. "I suppose so, in a battle situation. But this does not seem like the same thing at all to me. You are a group of knights who banded together to go on this Quest. Each person is accountable for their own actions. You are their guide, Beata, nothing more. You can lead them, but you cannot force them to choose another path than the one on which they were destined to travel."

She walked away, leaving Beata and Peritus looking up at the rainbow, tears still fresh on their faces. Peritus reached down and took her hand, wrapping her fingers in his own. "We will still succeed on this Quest," he said fiercely. "Caelestis will not have died in vain. We will continue on to Henton, and we will find this Virimage, and then we will bring him back to Heartwood and save the day. Do you understand, Beata?" He turned her roughly to face him and grabbed her by the shoulders. "Do you understand?"

"I understand," she said, and he released her, satisfied, wiping his face before going back into the inn. But she stayed there, looking at the rainbow, hoping the journey was not all in vain.

V

The road from Lornberg to Realberg wound through the peaks and dales of the Seven Hills, a picturesque journey, or at least it would have been if it had not rained steadily the whole time. Gravis, riding at the head of the party, barely noticed the twinkling rivers and fascinating variation in the colours of the fields from the terracotta-red of ploughed earth to the shining emerald-green of meadows. He was too caught up in his own thoughts.

He had not mentioned to anyone what had happened at the village that night. It sounded ridiculous when he tried to put it into words; he could imagine their responses: "It must have been a trick of the light," or "Perhaps you were dreaming," or "How many ales have you had to drink?" How could he explain to them the fear that had overtaken him on gazing at the lit pond, only to see no reflection staring back at him? True, it had reappeared after the cloud passed over the Light Moon, but he knew it had not been there before.

Or did he? Huddled in his cloak, in his own private world, Gravis found himself suffused with doubts, which soaked into him like the rain that dampened all sounds around him. Perhaps he had been mistaken. Perhaps he *had* drunk too much ale, or had merely been looking in the wrong place. How could he be sure?

His self-doubt ignited and flamed within him as if his innards were made of paper, and he soon began to think about the Quest and Questioned his ability to complete it. How could Valens have thought him a worthy leader? Even if they made it to the Henge, what was he supposed to do to activate it? He couldn't even grow the tiny flower that Silva had urged him to do. He thought about the way the daisy had blossomed in Gavius's hands, and envy surged through him. He had no doubt whatsoever Gavius would complete his mission. He just *knew* his twin would find his way to the Green Giant easily, would do whatever was needed to be done to open the Node and get the energy flowing, and would return to Heartwood triumphant, probably in time to come down to the Henge and help Gravis out with his own failed Quest.

He lifted his face up to the rain, trying to stem the hot tears threatening to course down his face. What was wrong with him? Why did he feel this heaviness in his stomach, as if it had been lined with lead and was trying to sink to his boots? He had always known Gavius was the clever one, the strong one; he had never been blind to his own failings but had accepted them cheerfully. Why now was it bothering him so much?

He knew the answer even as he formed the Question. It was being apart from his brother that made the difference. Gavius was like a huge sun; he lit every room, and the people within were like planets orbiting around him, caught up in his gravitational pull. Gravis felt he knew what the Light and Dark Moons felt like, circling Anguis in a steady, never-ending cycle, looking down on the world with its plants and people and wishing it could be part of it, but condemned to merely watch from the shadows. While he was with his brother, he did not notice the light that emanated from himself was mere reflection from his twin. But now they were apart, Gravis could see himself for what he truly was: darkness, which is really nothingness, because darkness is just an absence of light, and nothing in itself.

He looked up from his fixed gaze a few feet in front of his horse to see the town of Realberg nestled in the valley between two hills. He looked around, surprised to see the sun setting – it was nearly night-time, and he had spent the whole day in silent gloom, unaware of time or distance passing.

He looked behind him, relieved to see his party of five still trailing there, Fortis bringing up the rear as usual. They looked tired but smiled as his gaze rested on them, and he gave them a small smile back, suddenly guilty he had not spoken to them all day. It was his role as leader to keep his party together, and he had not fulfilled that at all.

But he was tired of berating himself, and so he said now, "Come, let us find ourselves an inn for the night, and have food and ale and forget our dreary journey today."

The others cheered and the horses picked up their hooves, and so they trotted into Realberg, a bustling Laxonian town, on the main road from Amerle and Frennon to the north. Though the hour was getting late, there was still plenty of movement in the town; many shops were open and tradespeople spilled out onto the street, touting their wares. The party stopped to buy some food, an extra cloak or two and other bits and pieces they felt would aid them on their journey, chatting to the vendors and smiling at the children who ran up to stare at these unusual knights.

Gravis watched his compatriots talking to the townspeople but felt strangely separated from them, and light-headed, as though he had not eaten for days, although he had stopped for lunch with the rest of them. He spurred on his horse a little further down the road, stopping when it showed interest in a drinking trough. He sat for a moment, people milling around him, then looked down to see a little girl staring up at him, maybe three or four years old. She had a ragged object tucked under her arm, which could have been a dirty, well-loved doll, and sucked her thumb. He looked at her, thinking how blue her eyes were, how clear and how piercing, as if they were seeing right through him.

As if to confirm his thoughts, someone – presumably her mother – came up to her and took her by the hand and made to walk off with her, scolding her for wandering away, but she resisted, taking her thumb out of her mouth and saying: "That man, Mummy. I can see through him."

"Oh come on," scolded her mother, giving Gravis an apologetic smile before leading her away. Gravis, however, didn't return the smile. The little girl's words had chilled him. *I can see through him*. He held his hand before his face. It looked normal, if somewhat dirty after the day's ride. Not transparent, anyway. And yet, he thought he knew what she meant. He *felt* transparent. As if he were fading away gradually, no more substantial than mist over water.

The others were passing him now, heading down the road, searching for an inn, and so he nudged his horse forwards to follow them, but his heart pounded, and his mouth was dry.

A little further along was a tavern called the Oak Leaf, a common name for an inn in Anguis, and so after enquiring if they had rooms, the party took their horses to the stable around the back to be rubbed down and fed by the owners' sons and then went inside. After a long day's ride, the warmth from the crackling fire was very welcome, and the smell was strangely comforting, thought Gravis: ale mixed with hot meat blended with the rosemary and mint from the rushes on the floor. They sat at two tables, ordered several plates of meat, bread and cheese, and talked quietly about their journey while Gravis stared into the fire.

"Are you all right?"

He looked up to see Aranea looking at him with concern. He studied her for a moment, seeing her properly for the first time. She was average height and quite slender, but with the telltale muscles of a trained knight. She had loosened her dark blonde hair from its braids and it hung in a wavy curtain down her back. She was young, although probably not much younger than him, he thought, with smooth, unlined skin and wide greeny-blue eyes.

"Can you see through me?" he asked, then immediately thought how stupid the Question was.

She didn't laugh, however. She observed him thoughtfully, her eyes running over his face, light frown lines crinkling the space between her eyebrows. "I can see you are in pain," she said.

"I am not hurt."

"I did not mean that kind of pain." She looked up as the innkeeper brought over their food, and accepted a plate, putting it between herself and Gravis. He was not hungry, but took the bread and meat when she handed it to him. Suddenly, he was tired of being alone, of bottling up his fears. He wanted someone to tell him he wasn't going mad, that everything was going to be all right.

He pushed away his plate and said, "Would you like to go for a walk?"

She looked surprised, but said, "All right." Picking up a piece of bread and topping it with cheese and meat, she followed him out of the inn.

The rain had lessened and they threw back the hoods of their cloaks and walked along the muddy streets, which were beginning to quieten as the shops had started to shut.

Aranea nibbled on her bread and cheese, glancing in the shops as they passed, seemingly content to be quiet and just look and walk. Gravis was glad; after asking her to go with him, he immediately regretted the impulse, as the last thing he was in the mood for was an inquisition. But her presence was strangely soothing, and after a few minutes he was pleased she had agreed to accompany him.

They walked down the high street, past a couple of other inns which were gradually getting busier, light spilling out onto the darkening road. At a crossroads Gravis stopped, then turned left as he saw a domed building in the distance. Aranea followed him down to the Temple. He stopped outside. It was not unlike the Temple at Heartwood, but on a much smaller scale, and was nothing like as grand. But he liked the familiarity of the large oak doors, the curving stone walls and high, domed roof, and he went inside, welcoming the echoing sound of his boots on the flagstones, and the recognisable smell of incense.

There were no tiers of seats in this Temple, just rows of chairs surrounding the oak tree that resided in the centre of the room. Like the Arbor and all other temple oaks, it had not shed its leaves during the Darkening, but to his eye the leaves seemed to be hanging on by their fingertips, and the whole tree had a slightly droopy look to it. Still, it was good to see a holy tree, and he went up to it and, putting his arms around the trunk, placed his cheek against the bark. There was no familiar rustle of welcome, but it was good just to feel the rough trunk, and to know this tree, like all in Anguis, was connected to the Arbor.

After a while he turned to find Aranea. She was walking around the Temple, giving him time to carry out his ritual, looking at some of the embroideries hanging on the walls completed by the townsfolk. He walked up to her where she was admiring a picture of a family tree, the names of various generations embroidered in between the branches.

She turned to look at him as he approached and smiled. "Are you feeling better?"

"A little," he said, not knowing whether that was the truth. Feeling suddenly weary, he sank into one of the chairs.

She took a seat beside him and reached out and took his hand. "What is the matter? Can you not tell me about it? Are you missing your brother?"

Gravis gave a wry smile. "Yes. But not in the way you mean."

She frowned. "I do not understand."

"I do not think I can explain. It is like... together we were one person, but now..."

"You feel like half a person?"

He looked up at her. "Sort of. It is like... when he left, he took part of me with him."

To his relief, she didn't laugh, nor did she exclaim how ridiculous his words sounded. She just continued to frown, her hand warm in his. "I think I know what you mean. You have been together a long time. It is natural you would feel odd at being apart..."

"No, that is not what I meant." He stood up in frustration, running a hand through his hair. "When you are with Gavius, you feel alive, you feel witty and clever, as if you could accomplish anything. But now, I just feel empty. It is like we were a wishbone, and when he left, he took the bigger half. I know it sounds ridiculous, but..." He opened his mouth to tell her about the incident by the pond, but his voice faded as he saw her staring at the floor. He looked down and his heart seemed to stop in his chest.

The room was nearly dark now, save for the candles placed on the stand to one side of the tree. Their light cast long shadows from the surrounding objects, the chairs, the pulpit: all were casting shadows like felled trees onto the floor.

All, that was, except Gravis.

CHAPTER NINE

I

The Woods of Brant were pleasant enough to walk through, thought Gavius, except for the fact that he was sure the trees had eyes. He was used to thinking of them as alive, of course, and even to seeing them move, but in these woods he could actually feel them watching him.

Of course he knew it wasn't really the trees; around him, somewhere, were the Komis, high up in the branches, watching his every move. He expected continually to feel an arrow in his back, and he kept the party tight together, swords drawn and resting on their saddles, but after three days' ride there was still no sign of them, and he was growing tired with being constantly on guard, his aching back illustrating how tense he felt. At night they had to take shifts to keep watch, and they were all tired and growing increasingly nervous at the lack of Komis presence.

Out of the blue, his childhood friend Hodie, riding beside him, said, "What's that?"

Gavius followed his pointing finger up into the trees. Ahead of them was the beginning of a walkway lacing through the branches, leading deeper into the wood. They exchanged glances. Gavius began to realise this was not just some outpost in the middle of nowhere. The walkways increased, the branches became filled with houses, and it became clear this must be Brant, the major Komis settlement not far from the Green Giant.

222

His heart pounded and his right hand tightened on the hilt of his sword, but still there was no sign of anyone living there. Where could they all have gone? He wondered if they were all hiding in their houses, but there was absolutely no sign of anyone, not a rustle or a movement, and he found it difficult to believe they managed to keep everyone – even the children – completely quiet and still. Perhaps the place was abandoned. And yet as he rode close to the beginning of a walkway, he could see one of the wooden slats had recently been repaired with fresh green twine, and he knew that was not the case.

Yet again, he had the uncomfortable feeling of being watched. The Komis were there; he knew it. And yet they had not attacked. He wondered why. From his history lessons at Heartwood, he knew all about their invasion of the Twelve Lands over a thousand years before, and had always been taught they were an aggressive nation. Diplomatic parties sent from the Twelve Lands had always met with resistance and had barely been allowed beyond the Knife's Edge Pass. But so little contact had been had with them for so long, he wondered if they had changed their ways. Although a few Komis filtered through occasionally, such as Silva, the Custos of the Arbor, they were usually from families who had lived on the borders and sometimes even had one Hanairean or Laxonian parent, and so were not able to comment on the society deep in Komis.

He looked around at the rest of his party, wondering if they were feeling the same sense of unease that he was. Mellis seemed relaxed, but he noted she rode with her longbow lying across her saddle, an arrow nocked and ready to fire. Niveus's sword was drawn and she looked tense, her eyes darting around the trees. Brevis's grimace had deepened, showing a deep dissatisfaction with the quietness of the wood. And Hodie caught his eye as he looked over and raised his eyebrows, the small shake of his head evidence of his worry. Clearly, they were all as nervous as he, which didn't really make him feel any better.

However, gradually they made their way through the wood; nobody appeared and nothing happened to stop them. The walkways began to grow smaller, the houses fewer in number, and then the settlement was behind them, and Gavius realised they had made it through.

He let out a long sigh. The others heard it and nervous laughter ensued.

"I cannot believe we made it through that," said Niveus, casting a quick glance over her shoulder to make sure she wasn't speaking too soon.

"I cannot, either," said Gavius, "but let us stay alert. We may still have a while to go before we clear the wood."

He tried to think about the map rolled up in his bag. Komis was uncharted territory, the area put together from rumours and speculation, and the best he could estimate was they had another three or fours hours before they left the trees and saw the hills where the Green Giant resided.

As the horse plodded along, he found himself thinking about his brother, and wondered how he was faring on his Quest. Had he reached the Henge yet? He made a quick calculation in his head. Probably not. They would most likely reach their destinations at around the same time.

He wondered if Gravis was feeling as strange as he was, being apart. He thought about what had happened up at the Knife's Edge. Had that merely been a reflection of himself he had seen, or was it truly some image of Gravis? And if the latter was the case, had his brother saved his life by appearing at the edge of the abyss, or had he been leading him to his death?

Surely it must be the first option? For why would Gravis want to harm him? Gavius loved his brother deeply. Gravis and Gavius. Which is which? It doesn't matter! To him that witticism was more than a joke. They were one person, divided into two. Which made it all the more difficult to be apart.

And yet... He had discussed this with no one, but lately he felt as if part of his brother was with him, inside him. He had first noticed the sensation up at the Knife's Edge, and he could feel it now too. He held his hand up a little way in front of him and moved it from side to side. It was still there – that silvery-grey shadow, moving a little after his hand in a blur. He could not explain it. And although he felt it was something to do with his twin, whom he loved, it sent a shiver down his spine.

The light was beginning to fail, and so they called camp, deciding the next day they would make it their target to reach the hills. They cleared a spot in a ring of oaks and rubbed their horses down, tying them loosely and letting them graze on the grass around the copse. They spread their blankets, made a fire and ate some of the food from their packs. Then, as it grew gradually darker, they curled up in their blankets and dozed, Brevis keeping first watch.

Gavius had no trouble in getting to sleep. The days were long and he was unused to riding such long distances; his muscles still ached and he felt weary after the day. He lapsed into sleep, for many hours being unaware of anything, too deep into slumber to dream.

But gradually, as the hours went by, the dreams began to come. Gavius was not a fanciful knight; he could rarely remember his dreams and never had nightmares. But that night he twitched and tossed as his dream came for him like an animal on the prowl.

He was back at Heartwood. Only this was not his Heartwood – it was a Heartwood of the future, where the Darkwater Lords had returned to smash through their defences and kill all the knights within.

All except himself. He was standing in the middle of the Baillium, facing the Porta, or what used to be the Porta. It was now just a collection of crumbling blocks, the magnificent gatehouse reduced to a pile of rubble. Turning, his heart in his mouth, he looked at the Castellum.

Even in his sleep, he felt the pain in his heart as he looked on what had been in his eyes the most beautiful building in the whole of Anguis. The Castellum was in ruins. There were great holes in the sides of its walls, and the top floor of the Domus had gone completely. Birds nested in the nooks and crevices of the broken walls, and grass grew in the cracks. The building was like a mighty warrior who had been bested in battle, and now sat there broken and forlorn, with no further energy to fight.

Slowly, he began to walk towards the Temple. The domed roof had gone, and the walls were haphazard, some still standing tall and proud, others just blocks of chipped stone. One of the large doors had gone completely; the other sagged on its hinges, the beautiful oak clawed and split.

He stood in the doorway and stared at the scene within. Without its roof the Temple looked smaller. Its interior was a shambles. It looked similar to how it had after the invasion of the Darkwater Lords, only this time the chairs and candles had been smashed to pieces and littered the ground in a carpet of splinters and wax. The windows were gone, the beautiful paintings and embroideries hanging in tatters.

It was all heartbreaking. But what he could not take his eyes off was the Arbor.

Or what was left of it. In the middle of the Temple, where once the beautiful oak had stood tall and proud, was just a dead stump, ending about a foot high off the ground. He walked over to it with horror in his heart. The stump was slightly hollow, and he sensed here, in the middle, was where the Pectoris had resided. But the tree's heart was long gone, its energy depleted, the only thing left a shell of broken wood.

Inside him, something clicked. A phrase repeated itself in its brain. Heartwood. The dead wood of the tree. For a moment he felt a swell of understanding, a clearing of his mind, as if the sun had suddenly come out after all the days of rain. But then something happened and he forgot about his revelation.

From the middle of the tree, smoke began to curl upwards, rising like a snake, coiling towards the open sky. And in the smoke a figure began to form. Gavius stood and watched, finding that his feet would not move in either direction. He seemed frozen, his gaze fixed on the tree. He watched the figure harden like molten iron setting in the mould, and before long he could see who it was. It was Gravis.

Or was it himself? Once again, as on the Knife's Edge, he felt the confusion of being confronted with a figure that looked so like him, and yet he was sure was not him. The oak leaf tattoo was on the right hand, like Gravis's. He stared at his twin, and suddenly he could feel his heart, his own Pectoris, thudding in his chest. Gravis's gaze dropped until it rested on Gavius's ribcage. Then, slowly, he reached out a hand.

Gavius watched the ghostly hand come towards him, stop at his ribs, and then pass into him. Exruciating pain filled him, but still he could not move. He felt the hand close around his heart, then slowly begin to extricate it from its rightful place behind his ribs. In horror, he watched his brother pull it out of his body until he stood there with it in his hand, blood dripping onto his floor. Gavius looked down at his chest, seeing the gaping, ragged hole in the middle. And then he looked up to see his brother start to laugh as, gradually, Gavius sank to his knees and collapsed onto the floor.

II

After the incident in the Temple in Realberg, Gravis and Aranea hardly exchanged two words. This was not necessarily her fault, although there was no doubt she had been extremely shocked by what she had seen. She had attempted – as he had at first – to try and explain the absence of his shadow with logical reasoning – it was a trick of the light, or something to do with the angle of the setting sun, or tiredness, or a hundred other reasons that eventually petered out as she came to terms with the fact that she knew there was no logical explanation for it – he had had no shadow, it was clear and obvious to see, and she could not explain it away.

Gravis had walked out of the Temple and back to the inn, not stopping to see if she followed him. On reaching the inn, he had gone straight to the bedchamber and lay down to sleep, turning on his side away from the door so when they entered, the others assumed he was sleeping and did not try and disturb him. And the next morning, he arose and pretended nothing had happened, and after a few failed attempts to engage him in conversation, Aranea joined in with the pretence.

He could tell she was thinking about it, from the way she kept glancing over to him as they rode, and the thoughtful expression on her face. But he did not want to hear her ponderings on what the reasons were for these strange occurrences. Truth to tell, he was frightened, and the foolish, illogical part of him that resides in us all hoped that by ignoring it, it would go away.

But of course it didn't. In fact, it only seemed to be getting worse. Several times on the last leg of the journey to the Henge, he found himself glancing into the still surface of ponds, or watching the ground as he stood in the light of a lantern, only to see the absence of a reflection or shadow, sometimes briefly, sometimes for half a minute or more before it flickered back to life like a lit candle. But in those thirty seconds, his heart seemed to stop, and he knew something was seriously wrong.

As if sensing his increasing weakness, Fortis began to ride next to Gravis, forsaking his usual place at the rear, and although he did not say much, and his very visage was somewhat intimidating, Gravis did find some comfort in the older man's calm presence, as if he provided the aura of self-confidence Gravis himself was lacking.

As they journeyed across the ridges and dales of the Seven Hills, with villages growing sparser and the Highlands bleaker, dotted only with sheep, Gravis sometimes thought they were never going to reach their destination.

But the miles were eaten away, and the sun rose and set through the gloom of the persistent rain, and one day they topped a hill and suddenly, in the distance, they could see the Henge on the skyline, propped up like a child's pile of blocks, silhouetted against the darkening sky.

"You made it," said Fortis with an uncharacteristic smile. Gravis returned it falteringly, noting the choice of "you" instead of "we", confirming his original thoughts that the veteran had chosen to come with him because he thought Gravis needed extra support. And don't I, he thought miserably, surprised by the lack of enthusiasm inside him as his destination neared? Indeed, a feeling of dread enveloped him, as if he had been dropped into a barrel of honey and were sinking slowly to the bottom.

They camped that night in an old barn and Gravis dreamed about the Henge, feeling its presence as if it were an animal stalking him, waiting in the shadows for a sign of weakness before it pounced. Strangely, though, in his dreams it was daylight, the sun shone, and he felt brave and held his head high, a reversal of the usual situation, where dreams carry the shadows and things in the dark, which disappear when you open your eyes.

The next day dawned with rain continuing to fall steadily, turning the ground to mush. In the Quest party, however, there was a rising sense of excitement as they all breakfasted and dressed ready for the day's journey. They knew they would be at their destination before the day was out and that was cause enough for celebration. But they also felt a sense of destiny, a feeling they were playing their part in the rescue of Anguis.

Gravis, however, just felt an impending sense of doom. Part of him felt exasperated at his continuing depression, as if he were watching himself from above, confused by this gloom weighing him down as if he were smothered in a heavy blanket. But he could not fight it off, and it only grew heavier and heavier as he neared the Henge, and they began the slow climb up the hillside towards the monument.

The path curled around the hill, and it was only as they began to go around the east side they found something surprising. There was a village there.

They reined in and stared at the array of houses in surprise. It wasn't really a village, more of a hamlet, just a row of five or six little cottages, and a tiny wooden temple around a solitary oak.

As they watched, a figure came out of one of the cottages. He was tall and thin, and dressed in a long green woollen tunic with thick brown leggings. He had a heavy, shaggy brown beard and piercing blue eyes. He stared up at the travellers, then turned and called over his shoulder. Immediately, the doors of the other cottages opened and another five people came out – two men and three women.

If it were possible, Gravis's heart sank even further. Was he going to have to fight his way to the top? He didn't think he had the stomach for a battle, especially against unarmoured peasants. However, the people wore broad smiles and came up to the Heartwood party, with no sign of weapons.

"Welcome, weary travellers," said the first villager. "My name is Thancred. We are the Guardians of the Henge, and we welcome you to this holy place."

Gravis dismounted and the others joined him. He walked up to the smiling Thancred and laid his hand across his chest, so his Heartwood tattoo was evident. "Greetings," he said. "As you can see, we are from Heartwood. We have journeyed a long way to be here today."

The Guardians' eyes widened as they realised where the travellers had come from.

"We are honoured to have Militis come to visit us," said Thancred sincerely. "It is the first time in… well, a long time!"

Gravis looked up at their little settlement, then back at the small group standing before him. "I did not realise the Henge had Guardians." He wondered what they did. They were obviously not like the guardians of the Arbor – they appeared to have no military background.

"The holy site has always had keepers, since it was created," said Thancred. "Come. If you will join us, I will be glad to tell you more of our history." He gestured towards their horses. "We do not allow horses up onto the Henge, but you are welcome to keep them in our stables. There is plentiful hay and water available." He gestured around the back of the cottages.

Gravis let a Guardian lead away his horse. He noticed Fortis's reluctance to relinquish his horse and wondered if he was foolish to trust these people, but his instincts told him they were safe, and somehow he knew they would not bring him trouble. He followed Thancred and the other three Guardians through one of the doors of the cottages.

It was only as he entered that he realised the dwellings were not in fact individual cottages, but actually one long house divided at the front into small bedrooms, while the back was one large area with several tables, a kitchen area and looms for them to make their own clothing. At one end, he saw a door through to the Temple beyond – to allow easy access, he thought, for prayers and rituals. It all looked very comfortable and welcoming, and he felt immediately at home.

"We have several spare bedrooms for guests," said Thancred, "so you are welcome to stay for as long as you like."

"Do you have many visitors?" Fortis asked, taking a seat with the others at one of the tables.

"The occasional pilgrim, but they are few and far between now." Thancred joined them while the other Guardians busied themselves pouring drinks and bringing food for the visitors. "The secret of the Henge has gradually been forgotten by all except the Guardians." He fixed his bright blue gaze on Gravis. "But more of that later. Why do you not start by telling me why you are here?"

"It is rather an incredible story," Gravis began, not wanting to go into detail about Nitesco's ideas on elementals. But then he thought about Thancred's words: *the secret of the Henge has gradually been forgotten*... Perhaps these Guardians knew about

the Nodes and could help him to activate this one. He sighed
and began telling them all the story of how they had come to
be there, so far from home. He told them about the Darkwater
attack on Heartwood, and about Nitesco's discovery in the Cavus,
of the *Quercetum* and its story. He explained how they had all
undertaken to go on the Quests and reactivate the Nodes. "Only,
I am not sure how to," he finished lamely. "I do not think I have
much of the power of the Veriditas. Actually, I was beginning
to wonder if one of the others should not take on the role of
Leader."

He said the words almost before he thought them and saw the
astonished looks of the members of his party around the table.
But of course, it made perfect sense; why had he not thought of
it before? There was bound to be someone else there who would
be better at it than he. The responsibility would be lifted.

But even as his hopes began to rise, Thancred shook his head
and dashed them back down. "Once it is set in motion, we cannot
change the course of Fate. We are bound by its laws, and have
to see our tasks through to completion. The Quest is yours and
yours alone to complete, my friend. But do not worry. Though
we cannot carry the burden for you, we may be able to make its
weight a bit more bearable." He smiled and gestured to the table,
where the Guardians had laid a loaf of bread, a bowl of butter,
sliced meat and jugs of ale. "Please, help yourself. It is not much,
but you are welcome to it. Once you have eaten, we will make
you hot baths to rest your bones. And then," he said to Gravis,
"we will take you up to the Henge."

The others started eating, tucking into the hearty fare and
chatting to the other Guardians as they did so. Gravis, however,
had no appetite and arose from the table, walked out of the
cottage and stood looking up the hill at the Henge, which towered
over them majestically on the summit. The stones looked cold
and haughty, forbidding as ghostly sentries preventing him from
reaching the precious Node.

Beside him, he felt a presence, and turned to see Thancred standing there, also looking up at the Henge. "I know it looks daunting," the Guardian said. "But the Henge is there to help you, Gravis."

"I do not know if anyone can help me."

Thancred turned his bright blue eyes on him. Then his gaze moved across to the window. Gravis followed it, and his breath caught in his throat. Thancred's reflection stood alone in the window, staring back at them both.

Gravis's mouth went dry. Now the Guardian would see him for what he truly was. He would step back in horror, shout to the others they had a coward on their hands. They would not let them go up to the Henge. He had failed.

But Thancred did none of those things. He stared thoughtfully at the window, then turned his gaze back on Gravis. His blue eyes were like stars in his face, burning white-hot.

"Ah," he said meaningfully. "I see."

III

It was a long ride from their last camp in the Neck Pass to Fintaire, but Fionnghuala pressed the others to move on, eager to reach a Hanaire town and leave the drama of the snow-filled night behind her. It was well into the Stirring now, and almost the Bud Moon, and the lowlands around Bearrach's home town were showing signs of emerging from their long sleep. The continual rain meant the ground underfoot was soft and marshy in places, but still she preferred it to the hard white surface of the mountain pass.

She had not spoken again to Bearrach about what had happened the previous night, and nobody else had noticed her absence, so she was left to ponder on the baby's cry – and Bearrach's strange choice of words – alone. *That is not the cry of an earthly child*, he had said. She had known what he meant; how on earth could any young thing survive out in that weather? But still, the memory of his words sent fingers of ice running up her spine.

Fionnghuala shivered again, pulling her cloak close around her as the horses splashed through the marshy ground, the hills of the Snout Range on their right. Of course, it could just have been a family of travellers lost in the snow. There may have been no more complicated reason than that. And yet, deep down, she knew it had not been a real baby. The cry had changed direction too many times for it to have come from one source. Bearrach was right – nothing could have survived outside in those temperatures for long, let alone a defenceless baby. It had not been the cry of an earthly child.

So what was it? The ghost of a baby who had died? Or the flicker of a moment in time, a memory, playing back on the wind?

She shook her head as if she could shake the memory out of her ears. She didn't want to think about it any more.

Luckily, the town of Fintaire was just visible in the distance, so she had other things to distract her. This was where Bearrach and Ruadh would leave them, so it was nearly time to say goodbye.

She had mixed feelings about this. The memory of flying into his arms the night before when she was so frightened left a bittersweet flavour in her mouth. His body had been warm, his firm grip reassuring, and she had welcomed his commanding manner as he led her back to the lodge, and the way he had settled her beside the fire, and wrapped her in blankets. He had been so comforting, and comfort was not an emotion that occurred often in Fionnghuala's life.

Still, she knew comfort was like fire – beautiful and yet dangerous and, like a moth to a flame, she would be drawn to it until she burned. She could not allow herself to fall in love with him. Love was dangerous and secret and, like a rose, full of thorns. That was why she had not mentioned the incident again, and had not told him how she felt when he held her in his arms.

As they got closer to Fintaire, the roadside gradually became dotted with cottages and traffic increased. Fionnghuala felt so relieved to be back in her homeland. Going to Heartwood had been an experience she had been looking forward to and had generally enjoyed, and there had been so much going on she had not had time to feel homesick. But the journey through Wulfengar had been long and irksome, with its dull, flat plains and pitted hills, and she had been eager to leave it. Now she looked on the high wooded hills of the Snout Range with tired relief, glad to be amongst her own people.

She had been to Fintaire many times and knew it almost as well as she knew her home town of Salentaire. It was a large town that had begun as a trading post on the main route from Hanaire to Wulfengar, and gradually developed into a settlement in its own right, its roads created in a haphazard fashion that lent the place a cosy rabbit-warren feel, with elegant buildings and a close-knit community. They wound their way through the streets to the large villa on the northern edge belonging to Bearrach. The Hanaireans had little need to fortify their dwellings, as theirs was a peaceful nation, and so far they had suffered few raiders from either the south or east, so Bearrach's home was surrounded only by a low wall, the amber stone of the sprawling villa clear to see.

"You must come and stay the night," Bearrach told them all, and as it was nearly dark and they were tired, Fionnghuala agreed, trying to ignore the little warning voice inside her that told her she should not stop, but carry on and find an inn. But she *was* tired and, truth to tell, she did want to see Bearrach for a little longer.

They left their horses with the stable lads at the side of the house, and went inside. The place was light and airy, with fresh rushes on the floors that smelled of lavender, large, open rooms and a wonderful smell of baking bread. Servants led them through to the guest rooms, and before long Fionnghuala found herself soaking away the day's aches in a hot bath.

Afterwards, she joined the others in the main dining room for a wonderful evening meal. After their meagre fare for the past few days, it was lovely to have hot food served to them, and the mood around the table was quite jovial. Fionnghuala had a taste of all the dishes brought out – the vegetable stew, freshly baked bread, cooked meats and cheeses, and a wonderful pie made with seasonal fruit. Bearrach also served wine instead of ale in the Hanairean way, and Fionnghuala drank freely, relieved to not have to drink the loathsome beer.

The result was that by the end of the evening, she felt deliciously full and slightly drunk, though she had taken plenty of water with her wine. The company had been good, with Audax in fine form and Lalage keeping the conversation bubbling, and Fionnghuala found she had no wish to go to bed. Neither had anyone else, it seemed, and so the party stayed up for several hours, discussing all manner of things from the Darkwater Lords to the Nodes and their likelihood of success.

Eventually, however, eyelids drooped and it was time to retire, and so Fionnghuala stood to leave the room. Glancing over at Bearrach, she caught his eye unintentionally, and gave a little smile before looking away. It had been a good evening, but she must not get sidetracked. She still had a long journey ahead of her, and she must remain focussed.

She went to her room and changed for bed, slid under the furs and curled up on her side. Through the small windows at the top of the wall, she could see the stars, and she traced the Horseshoe constellation with her finger, the sign of luck. She could do with a bit of that now, she thought, aware she was on the last leg of her journey, and before long would be facing the Portal and attempting to activate it. As yet, she had no idea what was required of her and was plagued by doubts.

Why had she offered to be the Quest Leader? Why had she assumed she was suitable for this role above all others? Suddenly, the task seemed impossible. They had spoken all evening about the importance of the Nodes, and what would happen to Anguis if they failed at their Quest, and now, lying in the dark, hugging the blankets to her chest, Fionnghuala felt weighted down by the pressure of her responsibilities. True, the others were members of the party and had agreed to help, but she felt the activation of the Node was something she had to achieve alone, and as yet she had no idea how to go about it.

She felt a sudden surge of homesickness for Salentaire and wished she were at home in her own bed. She had lived there all her life, knew every inch of every street, and the name of nearly every person living there. As High Councillor, she was responsible for the welfare of a great many people, and she wore that responsibility well, like a comfortable cloak, not afraid to immerse herself in it.

But the responsibility of the Quest was something different. She was certain the activation of the Node was not something that could be dealt with by mediation, or planning, or even by battle. It required something else – something she didn't even know about yet, talents she wasn't even sure she had. She was a person who coped by being organised, and how could you organise something so unknown?

Her stomach churned, and suddenly she wished she had not eaten or drunk so much. She sat up in bed, thinking maybe of taking a walk to let her stomach settle, and then felt her heart leap as she saw someone standing in the doorway.

"I am sorry," he said, coming forward into the light of the candle that had nearly burned down to its wick. It was Bearrach. "I did not mean to startle you."

"Well, you did," she said breathlessly, clutching the covers to her. "What do you want?"

He came over and sat on the side of her bed. He shrugged. "Just to be near you. I missed you."

She shook her head. "I have a long journey still to do. I do not want to be distracted from my purpose."

He tipped his head, studying her. "What are you so afraid of? What has happened in your past to make you so wary of men?"

It was her turn to shrug. "I am High Councillor. I cannot afford to get embroiled in a relationship. I love my job and I do not want to lose it."

He smiled. "There is nothing in the rules that says we cannot be friends."

"Friends?" Her eyes misted over suddenly. "You want to just be friends?"

He laughed. "Of course I would like more! But I am in the same position as you – as High Councillor I do not want to lose my job any more than you do. But I like you; I want to be with you, spend time with you. Is that such a bad thing?"

A tear ran down her face. In her job, it was difficult to have friends. She had colleagues, and acquaintances, and she was not short of a social life. But time spent dining with others members of the Council or visiting dignitaries or members of the various Guilds around the town was not the same as walking or talking with someone just because you *liked* them.

"I feel lost," she said suddenly. "I have this important job to do, and I feel like I am standing at the edge of a maze, and the path ahead of me twists and turns, and I do not know which branch to take. I am usually so in control of my life, and yet now I am not sure what to do or where to go. I do not like the feeling."

He smiled again. "Then let me be there to walk with you. I would like to continue on with you, to the Portal. And once we are there, perhaps we can work it out together."

Emotion rushed through her, and tears began to pour down her cheeks. Shushing her softly, Bearrach took her in his arms, and together they lay on the bed until she quieted, as he stroked her hair and back with light fingers. Eventually she fell asleep, curled around him, safe and secure in his warm arms.

But Bearrach lay awake for a long time, listening to the sound of a baby crying in the distance, and wondering why it haunted the woman he loved.

••••

IV

Gavius was awoken from his dream by Hodie's firm hand shaking his shoulder.

"Wake up," Hodie urged in a low voice. "You are having a bad dream, Gavius, wake up!"

Gavius came to as if climbing out of the bottom of a deep well. His heart was pounding, and he felt light-headed with panic. Gradually, however, as he realised it had just been a dream, his breathing slowed and he lay back on the ground in relief.

"That must have been some nightmare," said Hodie, sitting beside him. It was still dark, and the only light came from the embers of their fire, barely enough to illuminate the knight's face, which was creased with concern.

"It was," said Gavius. Already the fear and panic that had engulfed him were dying down, but he could still remember the disbelief and utter horror he had felt when his brother had reached into his chest and pulled out his heart. What did it mean? Did he fear deep down that Gravis was going to turn on him, or was it just a nightmare brought on by the pressures and tribulations of the Quest?

"What was it about?" asked Hodie.

Gavius remembered the broken walls of the place he loved more than anything in the world. "Heartwood," he said, his voice catching. "I dreamed we were too late. The Darkwater Lords had won. Heartwood had fallen and the Arbor was… gone."

Hodie shook his head. "I think the same thought is in all our minds. But we can only do our best. We cannot save the world alone, Gavius; we have to trust everyone else is doing their part. And just maybe we can all pull together to save Heartwood."

Gavius gave a wry smile. "Bit of a long shot, though, is it not?"

Hodie just shrugged.

Gavius sighed. "Look, I might as well take over the watch now. Why don't you get some sleep? There are a couple more hours yet before sun-up."

Hodie nodded and rolled himself up in his blanket, his face to the fire, catching the last tiny bit of warmth. Gavius took out another blanket from his pack and wrapped it around him. They were always the coldest hours, the ones before dawn.

Lost in his thoughts, his eyes continually searching the darkness for signs of the Komis, he barely noticed the time passing, and before long the horizon had turned milky and the others were rousing, packing their bags and preparing for the day's ride. Their mood was buoyant, as they knew they would reach the Green Giant that day. Mounting their horses, they set off, leaving behind them little trace of their presence and, Gavius hoped, his bad dreams.

Within a couple of hours, they were clear of the woods and emerged onto a hilly landscape scattered with sheep. Clearly, although the Komis lived in the woods, they also kept sheep either for meat or fleeces, although there was no sign of crop cultivation. But the hills were mostly clear of trees, and even from several miles away, the figure of the Green Giant that was cut into the chalky hillside stood out against the green of the grass.

The party stopped and stared at the figure. It must have been a couple of hundred feet high, thought Gavius in surprise, and depicted a naked figure – obviously male – who held a longbow in one hand and an arrow in the other.

"Arbor's leaves," exclaimed Brevis. "He is huge!"

"You can say that again," said Niveus in an impressed voice, and they all laughed.

"Come on," said Gavius. "Let us get going. We have still got a few miles to cross before we get there."

The ground, although slightly marshy in the valleys from the continual rain, gradually grew higher, and by the time they reached the foot of the Giant's hill, the horses were sweating. It was only as the group looked around, however, that they saw what a great view it was, in spite of the misty rain. They could see over the hills and down onto the forests in the distance; no doubt the Green Giant would be visible from the top of the tree houses the Komis built, watching over them all as they lived their lives in the forest.

Gavius dismounted and walked up to the Giant's foot. Of course, from this close, it wasn't easy to make out its shape, but he knew he was at the base of the figure, and he knelt down to touch the chalk with his fingers. He was surprised to feel a tremor in his fingertips as they touched the soil – a tremor which quickly disappeared. Had he imagined it? He was sure he had not. The Node was there, he knew it, ready for him to activate. He felt suddenly alive, elated, buzzing with energy. He was ready to do it, but he knew instinctively he was not in the right place.

"Well?" asked Hodie as Gavius stood up. "How do you feel?"

Gavius grinned. "Ready to go! Let us make camp at the bottom of the hill and go up on foot."

At the base of the hill was a small copse of trees with a river running through it. They took off their packs, tied the horses up loosely, rubbed them down and left them to feed on the lush grass around the water's edge. They had a quick meal, then, rejuvenated, they began to make their way up the hill.

Instinctively, the other four kept a few feet behind Gavius, who walked with his head down and his brow furrowed in concentration. He knew they had realised he could sense something, and they wanted to give him room and time to read the ground as best he could.

Gavius walked steadily, unable to explain to the others what he was feeling. He felt so alive, literally buzzing with energy. It coursed through him, beginning at his toes, which tingled as if he had been sitting on his legs for too long, and moved up through his calves and thighs and body.

Still, he knew he was not at the right place. He walked up the hill, following the line of the Giant's right leg. Behind him, he could hear the others talking in quiet voices, and he heard Niveus joking that the Node was almost certainly going to be beneath the Giant's erection. But although he smiled, Gavius knew she was wrong. Instinctively, he knew where the centre was.

Passing over the Giant's groin and walking more quickly now, he went up the torso until he met the ribs. He felt a rising sense of euphoria. This was it. He walked until he was over the place where the Giant's heart would be.

Then he stopped.

The ground trembled under his feet. Gavius looked around. The rain was still falling steadily, but he did not feel it. He sank to the floor and sat cross-legged upon the earth. Around him, the others fell quiet and sat in a ring around him. He was hardly aware they were there. His head buzzed.

He put his hands on the ground, clutching the grass with his fingers. He closed his eyes and tried to slow his breathing.

For a moment, nothing happened.

Around him, the others shifted, murmuring to each other. His fingers tingled where they clutched the earth, and his limbs trembled, but he wondered in his head: is this it? How would he know if it had worked? Would there be some noticeable change?

He forced himself to concentrate on the ground beneath him. In his head, he thought of the daisy he had held back in Heartwood, and the way he had made the flower grow. Love, he thought, it was all about love. He had let love flow through his body, his heart, into the tiny weed. Now, he fixed his inner attention on his heart, imagining it burgeoning, swelling with love. He thought about all those in his life he had loved – his mother, father, his first Dean, Dulcis, Valens, Procella, Beata, Hodie, Gravis.

Gravis.

As soon as he thought of his brother, something changed. Something flooded through him – energy? Or was it his own blood rushing in his ears? Pain spiked his nerve endings and he opened his mouth to cry, but nothing came out. He tried to call to the others to help but his voice would not speak. He felt a rush, as if he were falling from a great height, and he clutched the earth to steady himself, his breath coming in a sudden gasp. Then, just as suddenly, everything stopped.

For a second he panted, his eyes closed, trying to steady himself. Then, slowly, he opened his eyes.

He was still sitting in the middle of the Green Giant. But everything had changed. For a start, it wasn't raining. The sun shone hot and high in the middle of a bright blue sky, and the grass was emerald-green and lush. The hill on which the Giant was carved seem higher than it had previously; he felt he could see for miles around over Komis, or was it just that the day was clear and there was no rain to fog his vision? He was alone; the other members of his party had vanished.

He was not surprised, however. This was not the same hill as the one on which he and the Militis had arrived. The change in the weather; the way he seemed higher than he had before; were factors that told him he was somehow in a different place – a dreamworld, perhaps, a world between worlds.

And therefore he was not really surprised, either, when he stood and turned around and saw Gravis standing before him. Or was it Gravis? Yet again, as in his dream in the woods and the vision at the Knife's Edge, he felt the disjointed uncertainty of not knowing whether he was looking at his own reflection or at his twin brother. They were dressed in the same mail armour, the same brown breeches and leather boots; their hair had the same ruffled curls, the same fringe flopping over their forehead; there was the same amount of stubble on their chins. As Gavius raised his left hand, the one with the tattoo, so the other raised his right. And yet when he spoke, the other did not, but waited his turn.

"Are you me, or are you Gravis?" said Gavius.

"It doesn't matter," said his twin, and smiled.

Gavius looked around them, studying the landscape. There was nothing for miles, no sign of any movement. He looked back at Gravis. "Are you really here?"

"You can see me, can you not?"

"I mean is it really you? Or are you just an illusion?"

Gravis studied him. "What do you think?"

Gavius lapsed into silence. It was clear the figure – whoever it was – was not going to give him a straight answer. Instinct told him it was not really Gravis; his twin was somewhere in Laxony, trying to complete his own Quest. It made no sense for him to be here. The person before him was therefore some reflection either of himself brought on by the power of the Green Giant, or an image conjured by someone else playing with his mind.

He wondered what to say next. Was this all part of the activation process? He was reluctant to play the game if this was indeed someone playing with his mind, but perhaps he would have to, if it meant in the long run the Node could be opened.

"What do you want me to do?" he asked eventually, simply.

Gravis smiled, but it was not a nice smile, a brotherly smile. It was a nasty smile, and hatred hovered behind his eyes. "I want you to explain to me why you have sent me to my death."

V

Chonrad hefted his sword in his right hand, wiping away the sweat from his eyes with his left. In spite of the continuing rain, it was a warm day, and his whole body felt superheated underneath the thick jerkin and the heavy mail. But he could see Procella had not yet burned off her anger, and he was determined to continue the fight until she was too exhausted to shout at him any longer.

It had been a fretful few weeks for those left behind at Heartwood. After the tension of the Darkwater attack and the frenzy of preparation for the Quests, everyone had felt decidedly flat when the last party left. It had taken Valens a considerable amount of encouragement, manoeuvring and sometimes downright bullying to get the Militis back up and running and improving the defences of the site.

Everyone dealt with their frustration in different ways. Valens threw himself into the defence preparation, organising the remaining Militis into teams and drawing up rotas to make sure work continued until daylight faded. He spent hours limping around the site from both inside and out, testing areas of the wall, measuring distances and drawing up plans for further improvements. He was perhaps grumpier and testier than usual, his impatience at being forced to stay in one place compounded by the increasing possibility of another Darkwater attack, but he worked methodically and logically, and slowly the defences began to strengthen and grow.

Dolosus found solace in manual work. Though his one arm meant he could not join the bands of those who lugged around heavy rocks all day, he was able to lift the heavy pails of mortar, and he spent much of his time helping to steady the rocks while they were put in place. Keeping busy stopped him from thinking, which in turn kept him calm, and it also left him exhausted by the end of the day, so he fell into a deep and dreamless sleep, a fate which was not shared by everyone in Heartwood – there were many who had nightmares about the Darkwater attacks.

With many of the Militis dead or on Quests, Chonrad took over the Exerceo training, working the rest of the knights who were not involved in other tasks through strengthening and skill exercises to keep them battle-ready and fit to fight at any moment. Though he was not one of them, the Militis respected his obvious expertise and experience in the field, and he found it a rewarding task to keep them busy to stop them worrying about the coming invasion.

Nitesco spent all his waking hours – and most of his sleeping ones – in the Cavus, reading through the old texts hidden down there, desperately searching for a way to transform the Darkwater Quest party into water elementals. As days went by, he was hardly seen at all, and although Valens had visited him several times and told him nobody would think less of him for admitting he couldn't find an answer, the young Militis refused to come out, certain he would eventually find what he was looking for in the books, although his increasingly haggard face and the nervous tic at the corner of his eye spoke otherwise.

Procella was the one person who seemed unable to find a role to occupy her during this waiting time. For a while, she joined Dolosus in the manual work but found she was the opposite of him – engaging her muscles but not her body gave her too much time to think, which made her irritable and aggressive. Dolosus reached the end of his tether one day when she snapped at him for the umpteenth time for dropping something, and when he told her to go away, she did not argue with him; if nothing else, she was honest with herself and knew she needed to do something to keep her mind busy.

She tried to help Valens organise the planning of the defences but kept interfering with his ideas, and eventually in no uncertain terms he told her to find something else to occupy her time. Finally, she joined Chonrad in the training area, but a few hours before he had told her he didn't want her there either, as she was too aggressive and fought too hard, as if the battles were real and not just for the purpose of keeping fit.

She had responded angrily, shouting at him in front of the other Militis. He had responded by telling her she was being an idiot and she wasn't the only one who was frustrated, but by then she was past the point of listening and her frustration turned to violence, and she had drawn a sword on him.

Chonrad did not find her an easy opponent. She was a trained knight, Dux of the Exercitus, and it was certainly not a case of just fending her off – there were moments when he found himself fighting for his life. But her anger and frustration made her clumsy, and there were moments when he was sure he could have ended the fight.

But he let her continue to vent her anger, as he did not blame her for it. She was used to a life on the road; every day a different fort, constantly riding up and down the Wall, checking the garrisons, organising defences, managing thousands of knights. It was a busy, sometimes frantic life with constantly changing scenery, and to be bottled up like this was, he knew, perhaps the worst thing that could happen to her. Like a wild bird forced to live in a cage, she had been flying at the bars, and he had known it was only a matter of time until she crashed into them.

They had been fighting now for what felt like hour, solid hand-to-hand combat, and Chonrad was starting to get tired. He knew he wasn't as fit as Procella, but even so, he was sure she must be feeling the strain, too. Thought her attacks were not any less violent, she was taking longer between them, and her hair was flattened to her head with sweat.

He knew it was annoying her she couldn't take him, and he realised it probably didn't happen to her very often. And she knew her failure to win was due to her own frustration getting the better of her, rather than his superior fighting ability, and that only angered her more.

They had gathered quite a crowd now; the training Militis had all stayed to watch them fight and many more had come over from work on the defences to see what was going on. Chonrad knew they were putting on a fine display of swordmanship. He had been a knight long enough to put up a good fight, and although on her best day he suspected she could take him, today they were even, which was why the fight had taken so long.

But now he was getting tired and bored, and although she was obviously starting to feel the strain, her stubbornness was stopping her from calling an end to the fight until one of them could physically no longer hold up his or her weapon.

He locked swords with her and thrust her away, putting all his strength into the push so she stumbled back several yards. As she did so, he lowered his sword and raised his left hand. "Enough of this," he said. "We should not be wasting our energies on fighting each other. We need to save our strength for the Darkwater attack, when it comes."

She approached him slowly, her sword still held aloft, her eyes glittering. "Are you finally admitting you cannot best me, Lord Barle? Do you finally admit I am the better knight?"

The crowd murmured. Chonrad gave a little smile. "Trying to taunt me into making a mistake, Procella? You know that will not work. You are the one making mistakes today."

"I am not," she snarled, wiping the sweat off her brow with the back of her left hand.

He backed off a little as she advanced. "Come now, we both know you are the more seasoned warrior. That is not in dispute. But you are still obviously unable to separate your emotions from your fighting. Until you can do that, you will not be the wonderful knight you know in your heart you can be."

"Stop being such a coward and fight me!" she yelled, taking a wild swing at him.

He sidestepped it easily but felt his ire rising. "We must stop this now, before one of us gets hurt."

"Fight me!" she yelled, swinging at him again.

He stepped back again. He was tempted to put down his sword, but was afraid he might literally lose his head if he did that. She swung again, this time more neatly, coming forward and ending on a thrust, and he parried clumsily, so their swords rang throughout the courtyard, causing the onlookers to gasp and cheer. She pushed him back with brute force, hilt locked on hilt, and his boots slipped on the wet sand. Digging in his heels, he leaned into her, and she finally stumbled back, cursing. It was time to end this foolishness, he thought.

For the first time since they had begun fighting, he went on the offensive, fighting to disarm her, but now he really began to realise just what a skilled warrior she was. She parried his every move, matched his every swing, knocked away each thrust, her eyes gleaming, and he realised this was what she had wanted – a real fight. She wanted to test his strength. Was this more than just an explosion of temper, then? Was she testing his ability, finding his strengths and weaknesses, making sure he was up to scratch before they went on their Quest?

The sheer arrogance! For the first time in the fight Chonrad lost his temper. Now intending to knock her off her feet, he swung too hard and too far, and she came up under his guard. Her glancing blow knocked him off balance, and before he knew it she was pushing forward with her weight and he was falling backwards heavily onto the sand. The fall knocked all the breath out of him, and she took the opportunity to sit astride him, her sword tossed aside and her dagger drawn, blade across his neck. The crowd cheered.

"Now do you accept I am the better warrior?" she asked silkily.

His eyes met hers. For one, hot moment, he saw her true feelings there, like spotting a fish in the depths of a pool. He'd impressed her, and she desired him. His blood, already hot from battle, surged through him. He grinned. "Never!"

Thrusting up with his arms, he took her by surprise and knocked the dagger, sending it sprawling across the grass. The crowd whooped. Grasping her arms, he twisted her body and they rolled on the ground until she lay under him. He took her wrists and pinned them to the floor. He was heavier than her, and although she struggled beneath him, she couldn't move.

Her eyes blazed, but Chonrad could think of nothing but how much he wanted her, and he crushed his lips to hers, aware of nothing but the womanly feel of her body beneath him. For a very brief moment, she returned the kiss – long enough to convince him he'd been correct, and she did desire him.

And then she gave a muffled protest. He raised his head, only then becoming aware the crowd around them were cheering. He'd kissed a holy knight of the Arbor in plain view of everyone – and not just any holy knight, but the Dux, the leader of Heartwood's Exercitus. Suddenly, he wished he hadn't done it. He had forgotten they were being watched. She would not forgive him for proving he was stronger than her, especially in front of everyone.

He released her wrists and moved off her, and it was only then he realised Valens stood to one side, watching them with an unreadable expression on his face. "When you have quite finished," he said quietly, "Nitesco has something he would like to tell you."

They stood, perspiring and panting, freezing on the spot as they saw the look on the young Militis' face. He beamed at them, seemingly unaware of the frosty atmosphere. "I have done it," he announced with glee. "I have found out how to get you into Darkwater!"

CHAPTER TEN

I

Grimbeald opened his eyes with a gasp. The room was almost dark, lit only by a few candles, and he felt completely disorientated. The last thing he remembered was standing on the hill looking down at the wound in his shoulder, and then gazing into Tenera's eyes, and then everything had gone black. Where was he? And how had he got there?

"Grimbeald?" Tenera's voice came from behind him and her face appeared, pale as the moon on a dark night. She looked tired and drawn, but lit up as she saw him. "You are alive!"

"Of course I am alive," he said gruffly, coughing a little and wincing at the pain in his shoulder.

"It is a miracle," she breathed.

"Hardly." He coughed again and looked around him. He was in some sort of underground cave. The ceiling was low, only a few feet above Tenera's head, and the room was long and narrow. He was lying on a makeshift bed in the centre of the floor. To one side he could see shelves lining the wall, each filled with objects. His eyes were blurry and he could not make them out. "Where am I?"

She glanced around the room and he thought she gave a little shudder. Then she looked down at him and smiled. "Do you remember being injured on the hill in the Farmines?"

"Yes. That is the last thing I do remember." Apart from your eyes, he thought.

"You lost a lot of blood. We could not bring you round. It was clear we had to get you out of the rain. So we bought a cart from one of the villages and, as it was not far, brought you here."

He looked around again. Where was "here"? He squinted at the objects on the shelves, barely illuminated in the light of the scattered candles. They were white and all different shapes, some round, some long and slender, laid together in piles. Wait a minute. Were they… bones?

"You are in the Tumulus," said Tenera softly.

A chill ran through him. "The Tumulus? Why have you brought me here?" Panic rose within him at the truth in her eyes. "You thought I was going to die?"

"Grimbeald… I do not think you understand. You had lost a lot of blood. You needed to be somewhere warm, and we were not far from the Tumulus. When we got here, we realised there was a room underneath the mound, and it was out of the rain. We did not take you here because you were dying. But just now, I swear to you, you stopped breathing. I truly thought you *had* died."

"Is that why you said 'it is a miracle'?"

She nodded, then hesitated, as if she was afraid to admit something. Finally, she said, "One reason we decided to bring you here was that we thought the energy from the Node might help you to recover. It was a long shot – I do not know if any of us truly believed it. But just now, when your chest ceased to rise and fall, a light appeared above your heart, I swear it, and it glowed like a lantern, and then suddenly you gave a great gasp, and you were breathing again."

Grimbeald remembered the gasp, and the feeling of life flooding through his veins. He looked around, seeing now his vision was clearing that the wall to his right was laced with tree roots that clearly strengthened the hollow earthen mound. So this was it – the Node, the centre of energy he was to activate.

He managed to raise himself on an elbow, wincing at the sharp stab in his shoulder, and looked at the ground. It was made of hard-packed earth. There was no sign of any energy centre, no indication of where any light could have sprung from.

"I had assumed there was just one person buried here," he said, sitting up with Tenera's help. "I had thought it was the grave of some long-forgotten king or ancient war leader. I did not realise it would be the last resting place of so many souls."

She glanced around at the bones lying on the shelves. "I do not know there are souls here. Remnants of bodies, yes. To one side of the Tumulus, there is an area with a scattering of tiny bones that has led us to believe it is an excarnation place – where bodies were left for the elements and the wildlife to strip the flesh. Afterwards, we think the bones were then brought down here. The souls were gone long before the bones were clean."

Grimbeald shivered. Her words did not make him feel any easier.

Although Wulfians, Laxonians and Hanaireans all followed different forms of Animism, their basic beliefs regarding death and the afterlife were the same. When you died, your life energy was absorbed by the earth and the flowers and trees that grew in it, including the Arbor, and thus in a way you continued to exist by giving your lifeforce to other living things.

Whether a person had a soul as such was a matter of debate in the universities and amongst those who liked philosophical discussions. Was one aware of an afterlife – of existing in a sentient form after the body had expired? The general consensus was that one was not; the process of awareness occurred through the living brain, and this ceased to exist upon death. However, many others liked to think that when the life energy was absorbed by the earth, awareness continued – a person's lifeforce retained its oneness, its completeness, in some form or other. Thus, the concept of reincarnation was a popular theory, with the belief that this complete lifeforce, or "soul", was reborn into another living thing, be it a plant, a tree or a person.

Grimbeald could tell from Tenera's comment that she was one of the latter, and she believed in the existence of a soul after death. He was not sure. When young he had scorned the idea of reincarnation, thinking death was death – the end, a crumbling into dust, like falling into a deep void, with the darkness and silence of a deep, deep sleep. But now?

He thought of the figure he had seen at the edge of the Forest of Wings, and shuddered. Even those who believed in souls rarely believed in ghosts – in the presence of a soul outside a living body. But his romantic heart was unable to push the idea completely out of mind. As he had grown older, his thoughts had naturally turned more to what happened after death, and he had found if he accepted the presence of a soul, he could not dismiss the idea of ghosts. That thought was something that haunted him more than any spirit.

There was a clattering of stones at the entrance to the Tumulus, and then the three male Militis appeared, sliding down through the loose, wet soil into the cave below. They stopped for a moment, startled to see Grimbeald sitting up and talking, then came forward with exclamations to clap him on the back and shake his hand.

"We thought you were gone," said Feritas with relief, looking even fiercer in the candlelight, his bushy brows like caterpillars crawling across his forehead. Revoco was the same, his Wulfengar heritage evident in his wild hair and the angry expression that seemed to reside on his face permanently, even when smiling. Even Elatus looked pleased to see him, the young Laxonian's arrogant face creased with a smile.

"It takes more than a fatal wound to get rid of me," Grimbeald joked, and accepted Elatus's hand to pull him to his feet. His neck and shoulder felt stiff and sore, but he could tell he was on the mend. He was puzzled at that – it had been a deep dagger wound, and the blade had not been clean. The wound should have been infected and swollen, but when he looked, he found it flat and clean, as if someone had drawn a line upon his skin with red ink.

"You can put that down to Tenera's skill with herbs," said Elatus as they helped him up the slippery slope to the outside. "She studied with the Head Gardener at Heartwood for a year or two, and then with the Medica."

"Thank goodness," Grimbeald said, but although he acknowledged her healing skills, he was not sure his recovery was entirely to do with her talents. He had been treated before for injuries by skilled physicians and had never recovered this quickly. And he must not forget Tenera had thought him dead at one point. Had the Node really healed him with its energy?

Grimbeald pulled himself up into the daylight. He was not surprised to see it was still raining. They were right on the edge of his beloved Highlands. To the north the hills rose and fell into the distance, their slopes filled with forests, the valleys with rivers and lush green grass. He could see carpets of bluebells, as if the trees had spread cloaks on the floor on which to rest, and grazing goats and wild ponies on the cleared hilltops.

The Tumulus had been built on a small, flat-topped hill on the edge of the Highlands, almost as if guarding the entrance to them. He walked down and then around the mound. At the bottom of the hill were two oak trees standing like brothers guarding the tomb, their roots obviously those he had seen below, holding up the side of the cave. They masked the tomb from the south side, making it invisible to those travelling to the Highlands. Grimbeald had known it was there, but had never investigated it in any detail; he had always been in too much of a hurry to pay any attention to it.

Now he wondered who had built it, and who had been buried in it. As he had said to Tenera, he had always assumed it was the burial site of some rich lord, a final resting place where the inhabitant had been surrounded by his or her earthly belongings, which had almost certainly been robbed out long ago. However, now he doubted there had ever been anything inside the Tumulus except bones.

Walking around to the side, he saw the area Tenera had told him about; it was about fifteen feet square, and when he looked closely he could see scatters of tiny bones in the soil. There was a stone table at one side, and he guessed that was where bodies had been placed in the past to decompose; skin, flesh and muscle stripped by birds and wild animals and the cold, bitter wind.

Tenera walked up to him. "We have been working on cleaning up the area. There was not a lot to do, thankfully, but we have tidied up the grass, removed loose rocks and dead branches from the trees, just as Nitesco said to do."

Grimbeald shivered. Was it his imagination, or could he feel a slight vibration beneath his feet, as if a herd of cattle stampeded in the distance? Cold droplets of sweat formed on his back. Was he coming down with a fever?

He looked over at Tenera, intending to ask her if she could feel anything, but to his surprise, she stared past him at something on the top of the mound, her mouth open and astonishment on her face.

He turned and gasped. Standing there was the figure of a Wulfengar knight in full armour, his face set in the usual Wulfian grimace, which wasn't particularly surprising in itself. What was surprising, however, was the way Grimbeald could see through the figure to the hills beyond, and the way the knight dissipated suddenly, as if he had dissolved in the drizzling rain.

II

For Beata, the journey to Henton was long and unrelenting. Caelestis's death had been a huge blow, and she could not shake off her feelings of guilt and sorrow. It was a momentous task to even get up in the morning, let alone get on her horse and continue each day with the aim of completing her Quest. Many times she felt like giving up, and would have rolled over in her blankets and buried her head beneath them, refusing to get on with the day. Luckily, however, Peritus was a rock at her side, postponing his own grief and worries and supporting her continually throughout the last leg of their trip. He planned where they would stop, organised lodgings and food for both them and their horses, and generally tried to keep her thinking positive, though it was a difficult task.

He finally managed to perk her up with the news he obtained from an inn in a little village where they stopped just a day's ride from Henton on the coast, having finally found a bridge across the river. Beata had taken to bed, claiming tiredness, but Peritus had gone down to the bar and joined some of the locals in a pint of ale to pass the time. He had returned to their tiny room excitedly, and had dropped to his knees before Beata where she lay listlessly on the bed, taking her hand and pulling her upright before telling her the news.

"I am tired," she had protested. "Leave me be."

"You are always tired lately," he replied impatiently. "Look, I have news. They told me downstairs the Virimage is still in Henton."

This made Beata sit up properly, and for the first time since Caelestis's death a spark of interest flared inside her. "Are they certain?"

"Two of them saw him last night, up at the... what did they call it? The 'Castle on the Rock'. Apparently, his name is Teague. He entertains there every night. In return, they give him board and lodging. He has been here quite a while, it seems."

"Teague..." She rolled the name around her tongue. "It sounds like a Komis name."

"Oh, he is definitely Komis all right. Black hair, light brown skin, gold eyes; they were full of it downstairs."

Beata sat back against her pillows. "Well, I suppose it makes sense. Just look at Silva. The Komis have always been said to have a strong connection with the land. Did they say what he was like?"

Peritus hesitated. "They called him 'a bit of a lad'. That is about as much as I could get out of them. Not a talkative bunch, these fishermen."

A bit of a lad? Beata couldn't begin to think what that meant. She had had very little experience with people outside of the Exercitus, and nearly all Militis were serious warriors committed to their work. She had never had such a thing as a social life, had never been to court, or had an admirer. It just wasn't part of her life. That didn't mean she wasn't aware it happened, but it was like trying to imagine the sea when you've always lived in the mountains; no matter how much someone tries to explain it to you, it's very difficult to conceive exactly what it's like until you experience it.

In spite of her naïveté, however, she was not stupid. The description of this Teague gave her the impression he was very young and still finding his way in the world. Well, that wasn't necessarily a bad thing, she thought. Young probably meant impressionable, and that was not a problem considering what she had to persuade him to do.

She found it difficult to sleep that night, and when she eventually dozed off her dreams were filled with the Virimage and his strong brown hands casting spells in the sky and making flowers fall onto the ground and scattering her in petals.

The next day dawned much as the previous few weeks, but Beata finally felt in a better mood. Achieving their Quest would not bring Caelestis back, she knew, but still it would go some way to making her death have meaning; she would not have died in vain if they found Teague and brought him back to Heartwood.

It was the last day of the Lamb Moon, and it had been raining almost continually for the whole of its fifteen days. The second Moon of the Stirring, the Bud Moon, was usually a joyous time at Heartwood, Beata thought as they mounted their horses and set off from the village. It was a celebration of the renewal of life, when everything began to show signs of recovering from the Sleep, when the whole of Anguis began to awake. But the world as yet did not seem to show signs of awakening. The continual rain had drowned a lot of the early seeds, and the oaks she had passed so far had been bare of buds.

The river they had followed all the way from Lornberg had widened considerably as they got nearer to the coast, and Beata was shocked by the sheer amount of water thundering along its course, its colour an unhealthy brown, a clear indicator of the earth it had churned up along the way. Everywhere, the ground was waterlogged, the horses having to plough through thick mud as they plodded their way along the road.

Still, it was good to feel lighter of mood, and Beata almost felt like singing as they began to see houses peppering the sides of the road, a sure sign the town wasn't far away. They went on for a mile or two in that manner, the houses becoming larger and closer together, and then rounded a hill to see in the distance a high ridge topped by a large, long defensive wall. Leading up the slope towards it, streets began to leave the main road and weave across each other like threads in a blanket. Beata's heart beat a little faster as the amount of traffic increased and the roads became harder to negotiate. They made their way up the slope and passed under the massive portcullis that hung suspended from the gatehouse. As they got to the opposite side and the road began to go downhill once again, she stopped her horse to stare at the view, and gasped.

The ridge curved in a ring around the town of Henton, which lay sheltered amongst the hills like a stone inside a peach. Atop the westernmost edge of the ridge, overlooking the sea, perched the "Castle on the Rock", a huge stone edifice consisting of a mish-mash of turrets, crenellations and walls that surveyed the goings-on in the busy town like a stern fighting instructor watching the practice moves of its students. If it had been a person, she thought with amusement, it would have had its arms crossed and a frown on its face.

The town spilled down from the wall right to the topmost edge of the beach, which curved from one end of the ridge to the other like the silvery strip of the crescent moon that would soon appear in the night sky. It was a bustling community, the roads filled with carts and people, easily the biggest settlement she had ever seen.

But the thing that won her attention most of all was the sea. She had never seen it, and although she had often heard others speak about it, she had never been able to truly picture it in her mind. Now she just stood stunned at the sheer amount of water in one place, watching the grey waves crash onto the shore like angry warriors beating on each other's shields.

"Get a move on!" yelled someone behind her, and she realised she was blocking the road. She nudged her horse along the ring road at the top of the hill leading to the castle, thinking that was obviously the best place to start, as the villagers Peritus had spoken to had mentioned Teague had performed at the castle.

"Isn't it amazing?" Peritus said now, moving his horse alongside hers. "I have imagined often about how the sea would look, but had never dreamed it would be like this."

"It is a truly stunning view," Beata admitted, but already her mind had moved on to other things. "Peritus, there is something bothering me. I had planned to go straight to the castle, explain our plight and ask to see Teague directly, but I am now not sure that is the right way to approach him. I wonder whether we ought to go in disguise and assess the situation."

"Disguise?" He stared at her. "You mean a false moustache or something?"

"Not quite," she said with amusement. "But we are quite conspicuous wearing our Heartwood armour. Perhaps we should... dress down a little."

He took some convincing to go into the castle without his armour, but they took a detour via a group of shops and she showed him what she had in mind, and eventually he agreed. They walked the horses to a cluster of trees a short distance from the castle and she took off her armour and changed into her new outfit as quickly as she could without drawing attention.

She had bought herself two tunics, of the kind and quality, she hoped, a lady of a countryside estate might wear when visiting family on the coast. The first tunic was a deep green and long-sleeved, and reached to the ground, just covering her new small leather slippers that felt decidedly strange after her heavy leather boots. Over the top she wore a thigh-length short-sleeved tunic of a lighter green. She uncurled her hair from its usual tight bun at the nape of her neck and let it fall around her shoulders in light brown curls.

She came out from behind the tree hesitantly. She had lived almost her entire life in some form of armour or other, and had no idea whether she could even pass as a real lady. As soon as she saw Peritus's face, however, she knew it had worked. His mouth fell open, and he found himself completely speechless, even though she glared at him and told him to close his mouth before flies flew in it.

She made him take off his armour, and they rolled up the mail and jerkins and attached them to the back of their horses. In just his breeches and leather tunic, he could easily pass for her manservant.

They rode up to the castle and left their horses in the front courtyard with the stable hands, and were shown by the steward into the Great Hall, which was much bigger than the ones at Cherton and Hicton. The Hall was pretty much empty, as the servants had not yet started preparing for the early evening meal, and everyone else was out on errands or business around the town. They were then left to have a look around while the steward went to fetch refreshments for them.

Beata let out a long breath as he left the room, relieved her disguise had worked. Peritus sat himself at one of the long wooden tables, but she still felt too nervous to sit, so she began to walk down the Hall, looking up at the banners that hung limply at right angles from the wall, depicting the coats of arms of various members of the Lord of Henton's family.

Looking up as she was, she did not notice a figure asleep in the shadows and stumbled over him, causing him to awake with a curse and sit up and glare at her.

"Watch where you are walking..." he began, but his words ground to a halt as he saw who had just trodden on him. "My lady..." He got hurriedly to his feet – a task obviously not easy for him, thought Beata wryly, for he was clearly drunk as a man on his wedding night. He swayed slightly as he stared at her, his eyes wandering lewdly around her body before they finally focussed on her breasts. "Arbor's roots," he exclaimed. "What a great pair of pillows."

Behind her Peritus snorted with laughter, but she ignored it and glared at the drunken lout before her. "Excuse me," she said icily. "I think you should mind your manners."

He blinked. Then, in an affected attempt to act in a lordly fashion, he gave a drunken, lopsided bow. "My dearest lady, please accept my humblest apologies." It would have been a gallant gesture, except for the fact that as he arose he let out a deep, rumbling belch. To her amazement, as he did so a cloud of rose petals emitted from his mouth and floated delicately to the ground in front of them.

She stared. He stared back and then grinned. "Did that surprise you? Well that's nothing. You should see what happens when I fart!" And then he collapsed in guffaws of laughter to the ground before quickly falling back into a drunken sleep.

Beata stared at him. She wouldn't have believed it if she hadn't witnessed it herself. But realisation gradually sank in that it was clear from the rose petals – and his brilliant golden eyes – that this drunken idiot was the magical Virimage who was supposed to save the world.

III

Gavius stared at the person before him who looked just like his twin brother, although he was certain it could not possibly be him. However, he had no answer for who this person really was and, until they revealed their true self, he had to go along with the game.

I want you to explain to me why you have sent me to my death, Gravis had said. Gavius's brow furrowed. "I do not understand," he said. "Why have I sent you to your death? You agreed to take on the Quest as I did. I did not force you into anything."

Gravis nodded. "A true Gavius answer. You could not possibly have done anything wrong. I do not think the words 'I was wrong' are even in your vocabulary."

Gavius said nothing for a moment, struggling with his irritation and anger. His success at this game depended on his ability to keep calm. "Tell me why I am wrong," he demanded. "How exactly did I force you to go on the Quest?"

Gravis stared at him directly, his dark blue eyes sorrowful. "You know what I am like. You know how you influence me. I have always stood in your shadow, followed along behind you. I could not bear to admit I am not strong enough for this role. You could have stopped me – argued you needed me with you. But you let me go, knowing I could not cope on my own."

Gavius did not reply, outwardly calm. Inside, however, his stomach churned. He could not deny the truth of some of Gravis's words, and it singed his cheeks with shame. But not all he said was true. "I did not think you could not cope on your own," he said honestly. "I know I have always been the strong one. But I had no doubt in your abilities, or else I would not have let you go."

"Would you not?" Gravis taunted. "Or were you secretly just glad to get me out of your way? Are you not relieved you do not have to think about me now?"

Again truth twisted like a blade within him. How could this person – whoever they were – know about his most private and personal feelings?

"I..." He was loath to admit the truth, but on top of this most powerful energy centre, he was somehow being tested, and the truth mattered. "I admit there have been times I wished you were not always hanging on my every word. I have often hoped you would spread your wings more and follow your own path in life, rather than shadowing mine. But that stems as much from a desire for you to be true to yourself as from a longing to be on my own."

Gravis took a step forward, and his eyes blazed like a storm in a hot Harvest sky. "Liar."

"I am not!"

"Search your feelings, brother, and search deep. Falsehood has wormed its way within you like a maggot in an apple. You are rotten to the core."

Gavius felt sick. In all their years together, Gravis had not spoken to him thus. His brother was a kind and gentle knight in spite of his warrior upbringing; Gavius had not thought he had a ruthless bone in his body. And still his brother had not finished.

"You believe I was only taken into Heartwood because of you. All this time, you think I owe my place there to you."

"That is not true," Gavius protested weakly, but this person could see into his heart and knew the truth before he uttered the words.

"Of course it is true. Why else would you have been so patronising all my life? Treated me like your pet dog, sniffing at your heels?"

Gavius finally exploded. "Well, what else would I think? You did appallingly badly at the Allectus; failed practically every test we took there. And yet they still took you on, in spite of there being many other better candidates."

Gravis gave him a nasty smile. "Well, I have news for you. Before I left Heartwood, Valens let me into a little secret. Actually it was the other way around."

Gavius's heart seemed to stop. He didn't want to ask, but he had no choice. "What do you mean?"

"He told me Abbatis Aquila chose me first, and decided to take you on only because he knew I would miss you so."

Gavius's teeth clenched. "That is not true. I came top in the tests. I beat every single one of those children."

"And it made you exceedingly arrogant. What is one of the main attributes of a Heartwood Militis? Humility. Well, I am afraid you were at the back of the line when that was given out. The Abbatis thought you overbearing and conceited for a seven year-old. They wanted children they could mould to their own image. It was not actually about doing well in the tests; it was about proving you had a suitable character for the job. The Abbatis told Dulcis before he died that he wanted to send you back. He thought me a far more worthy candidate. But one of the Deans said I would find it difficult to stay without you, because I loved you so. So they kept you – because they wanted to keep me."

Gavius felt cold inside as if he had swallowed an icicle. The sharp piece of ice travelled down his throat and into his stomach, piercing his heart along the way. Was this the truth? How was he to know? There was nothing stopping this person making up whatever "truth" he wanted.

And yet something about it rang true. Deep down, wasn't it what he had feared all along? It was true he had always believed Gravis to be a favourite of Dulcis; they had often taken long walks together in the evenings, whereas he had always felt her to be somewhat cool towards him. He had put it down to imagination, but now it made him wonder. Gravis the chosen one…

Gavius felt someone had scooped out his insides with a spoon, then scoured them with a rough brush. He felt raw as an open wound. He looked up at the figure before him, seeing his twin smiling as he observed his brother's pain. Was he wrong? Perhaps this *was* Gravis, or at least a projection of him. Perhaps this *was* Gravis talking, and he actually did feel this way.

"I am sorry if I hurt you, brother," he said. "I never meant to." He turned his face up to the sun. Suddenly, he thought the weather was all wrong; though he had missed the sun, he wished it was raining again, echoing his mood.

"We never mean to step on ants," said Gravis, "but we do it all the time."

Gavius knew he spoke the truth. He had never given much thought to Gravis's feelings. But he had never wished him harm. He had always striven to protect him, and although perhaps he was at fault for thinking himself superior to his twin, he had done everything out of love.

"You do not love me," sneered Gravis, reading his mind. "You love nobody but yourself."

Gavius frowned. He again doubted this was his brother. Though Gravis may have had suspicions about his brother's feelings of superiority, he would have known Gavius loved him. That could not be contested. That was fact.

"I do not think you are my brother," he said quietly.

"Who am I, then?" jeered the figure.

"I do not know. But I think this is a test. Maybe you are just a projection of myself, a fabrication to force me to confront my deepest fears." Suddenly, he knew he was on the right track. "Yes, that is it. The Node has forced me to examine myself and my motivations for coming on this Quest."

"Very clever," said the figure. But he no longer sneered. "So tell me, what answer do you have to the accusation of your superiority over your brother?"

"I acknowledge its truth," said Gavius. "I have always assumed I was chosen first, and I am still not sure it was the other way around – if you are a projection of my fears, then you are merely expressing my deepest worries. But even if that were the case, I do not feel it actually changes anything. I have served Heartwood well; I am a good knight, and I have never broken my vows. I pledged to defend the Arbor until my death, and that is why I am here, on this Quest. I do not feel I could have done more with my life. I do not feel any guilt. I love my brother and I have tried to care for him and do my best for him. And I honestly felt sending him on his own Quest might make him realise he can cope without me, and stretch his wings."

The figure nodded, then suddenly smiled. "You are correct – I am not your brother. But I must tell you – you do carry a piece of him inside you. A piece he needs back if he is to complete his Quest."

"What... how..."

The figure held up his hand. "But for now, your Quest is done." He dropped his hand.

Gavius stepped forward. "Do you mean that...?" But he stopped as the figure stepped forward too. He raised his own hand; the figure raised his. The image in front of him truly was a reflection of himself.

The ground began to tremble beneath him. As it did so, his reflection vanished. He looked around, startled to see the whole landscape flickering, as if clouds were passing rapidly over the sun. He saw the scene he had left come into focus – the other Militis seated around him, now staring at him with wide eyes – then it flicked back to the sunny hillside. What was happening? He planted his feet more firmly as the ground trembled again, threatening to throw him to the floor. Was it an earthquake? He had heard of such things in other lands, although he had never experienced one himself.

But it was only as he looked up the hillside he realised exactly what was causing the tremors in the ground.

The Green Giant was literally ripping himself out of the grass and rising up above him.

He stepped back, fear firing arrows into his stomach as he looked up at the enormous figure. The Giant tore himself out of the hillside, clods of earth flying around him as he sat up, towering over the tiny knight who trembled in the grass. Gavius slid down the Giant's chest as he rose up, and he rolled down the bank and fell off to the side as the monster heaved himself upright. Gradually, the figure pushed himself up to his knees, and then to his feet, until he was standing upright, tall as a mountain, blocking out the sun.

And then he spoke.

"Who has awakened me?" he bellowed, his voice rolling like thunder around the countryside.

Gavius had never known such fear, but he stood his ground and called, "I am the one."

The Giant looked down. His eyes were vast hollows in his grassy face, his nose a ridge of hills, his mouth a chasm of ripped grass and torn earth. "Why are you here?"

Gavius swallowed and said, "I have come to activate the Node. We are under attack from the water elementals and the Arbor is dying. We need to get energy flowing through Anguis again."

The Giant let out a deep, booming laugh. "At last!" he said, his hands on the peaks of his hips. "I have slept long enough."

He raised his arms up to the sky. His deep voice began calling in words Gavius could not understand. The clouds in the sky roiled and churned, like great fists bunching and clenching, and thunder echoed in his ears. Then the Giant did something that completely took him by surprise; he bent down and placed his gigantic hand over the top of Gavius's head. Clods of earth rained down on him, and he cowered beneath the vast shadow, but he was not crushed. Instead, he began to feel a heat emanating from the Giant's hand. Gavius stood once again, realising he was not going to be flattened like a fly, and turned his face up to the energy.

Around him the scenery was flickering again. He could feel the energy rushing through him. The Node was activating! He felt it open up beneath him like an enormous whirlpool, spinning beneath the earth. He tipped back his head and opened himself up to it. Light flooded through him, and he knew he was shining like a beacon. But it did not hurt – instead he felt exultant, as light as a snowflake, radiant as the sun.

And then, just as suddenly, everything vanished. The Giant, the heat, the light, the thunder, the rumbling in the ground. He fell to his knees, exhausted.

For a moment, he could do nothing but sit there, gasping, too tired to even open his eyes. But gradually, as he realised the others had not spoken to him or come up to him, he opened his eyes, hoping his friends hadn't been hurt in the activation process.

They had not.

They had, however, been captured.

Gavius stared in astonishment at the group of Komis warriors who stood in a circle around him and the Militis, spears pointed at their throats. One of them, presumably their leader, stepped forward to stand in front of him. He was tall, slim, long of limb; his skin was the colour of polished oak, his hair black and elaborately braided. He wore a tunic and breeches in a dark green and brown, which would camouflage him perfectly in the forest. His eyes were the colour of molten gold. And when he spoke, he spoke in perfect Heartwood.

"Hmm," he said, eyeing Gavius curiously. "Very interesting."

IV

Bearrach awoke to find Fionnghuala's bed empty. At some point he had dozed off, although it had taken him quite a while; the sound of the crying baby had lasted long into the night. She had already been asleep by then, but he had heard it clearly, and had lain awake staring at the stars, wondering what ghostly child this was who had followed them all the way from the Neck Pass.

That morning, he could hear nothing except the sounds of people getting ready for breakfast, however, and so he arose and went to his own bedroom, washed and dressed, putting on his light jerkin only, deciding to leave his mail behind. Now he was in Hanaire he should have little need of it, and it was a relief to get rid of the weight.

He was not used to wearing mail on a regular basis and found himself walking with a lighter step than he had for the past few weeks. As Head of the Council in Fintaire, his day was filled with meetings and audiences rather than battles, and although he travelled widely and always dressed cautiously when he went into the Twelve Lands, most of the time he left his battle armour at home.

He walked through to the dining room, which had been cleared of the meal from the night before, and the tables were now laid for breakfast. Bread, butter, steaming bowls of porridge and a variety of fruit lay on the table, along with jugs of cold water from the well. Audax, Lalage and Mundus were already there, and so were Fionnguala's companion Kinaed and his own compatriot Ruadh, who had left with him from Fintaire. Fionnghuala herself, however, was not.

"Where is she?" he asked, helping himself to a large bowl of porridge and ladling strawberries into it. They were early strawberries, from his hothouse at the back of his villa, but they were soft and sweet.

"She went out for a walk," said Kinaed in his quiet voice. "She said she needed some air."

Taking his bowl with him, Bearrach walked out into his gardens. The place was quiet and peaceful, being some way from town. He walked through the gardens under a covered walkway that protected him from the worst of the rain still falling, and saw with sadness the lawns had been flooded in several places, and the flowerbeds pooled with water. It would be difficult to get things to grow if the rain did not stop soon.

At the end of the garden, still under the covered walkway but looking out onto the marsh meadow, he finally saw her. She was dressed and wore her mail coat, but still she looked small and delicate, like a white flower, easily crushed beneath one's boot. He wandered over to her, eating his breakfast.

"No sign of it easing," he said as he approached, trying not to make her jump.

She turned, looked at him and smiled, and then glanced up at the heavy clouds. "I cannot believe it has rained for so long," she said. "I feel that there is something supernatural about this continual weather. And that makes me fear even more for Anguis, should we not be successful."

Bearrach nodded. He looked at his bowl, suddenly losing his appetite. "Are you coming in?" he asked, shivering a little in the early-morning coolness. "You ought to eat before we leave."

"We?" she repeated. "Are you still sure you want to go with me? This is my Quest, and I know I am the only one who can complete it. I feel it. I cannot explain how."

He shrugged. "I am not looking for glory. I just want to go with you."

"To protect me?" Her eyes twinkled.

He laughed. "I just think... you could do with the company."

She smiled then, raising a hand to touch his cheek softly. "I cannot believe there is a person in this world as genuine as you, Bearrach."

He sighed. "Aye. I am a hero."

She laughed and joined him as he began to walk back to the villa. For a while she said nothing, and he sensed she was thinking, so he remained quiet, content to just be in her company.

Eventually, however, she said, "Can I ask you a Question?"

"Of course."

"Why have you never married?" She looked around the gardens. "I understand you are committed to the Council – no one could understand better than I. And yet... you have a lot of love in your heart. I find it strange you have remained alone for so long."

Bearrach thought about the time he had first seen her, many years ago, on a visit to Salentaire when he was a young Councillor. She, too, had been young, and he had walked into the town's Council Chambers to see her giving a speech on the rights of women to inherit a Guildship if their husband died, as under the law at that time the Guild passed to other male kin such as a brother. She had been outspoken, brilliant, beautiful, her long blonde hair hanging down her back like a waterfall, her eyes blazing with passion, and he had fallen in love with her at first sight.

It was only afterwards he had learned she was completely committed to her position in the Council, and had stated she would never marry. But by then his heart was captured, and he knew he would never get it back.

"I suppose I have just never met the right person," he said with a smile, opening the door to the villa and standing back to let her through. "Or she has been... otherwise engaged."

She stopped to look up at him. She was barely inches away, her beautiful green eyes wide and dark with concern, her mouth looking so soft he longed to kiss it.

"Do not fall for me, Bearrach," she said in a low voice. "I do not want to break your heart."

Too late, he thought. Outwardly, however, he just smiled. "I understand. Now, we had better prepare for our journey."

Later, back on the road and heading towards Fionnghuala's home town of Salentaire, Bearrach turned to thinking about the phantom baby, crying into the night. He wondered why they kept hearing it. She had clearly not heard it before the night on the Knife's Edge. Why had it started then? Was it something to do with the Quest?

He mused on the reasons behind it as his horse picked its way along the muddy road. To their right ran the Snout Range, a ridge of mountains eventually petering out into high hills, which they had to cross to reach the Portal. From Salentaire, there was a pass through to Crossnaire, which lay in the Lakes: still technically part of Hanaire, but with a vastly different landscape from that through which they were travelling now.

Had she lost a child when young? It seemed to be the most plausible explanation, although he was sure he would have found out about such a devastating event by now. Children were revered in Hanaire and a child's death was a phenomenal event, prompting elaborate funerals and weeks of mourning.

Nor had he ever heard her name connected with anyone else. At some point in a Councillor's life, there was a choice to make – Council or family? And someone always came along to make that choice more difficult. But he had never heard of her having a love affair, and he was certain she had never been married. It was one reason for her rising so high in the Council: her complete commitment to her town and its people.

Of course, that didn't mean she had never fallen in love. Maybe she had had a child secretly, and it had died. But it was very difficult in Hanaire to do anything secretly, and he was sure he would have heard if she had left Salentaire to go away – a long absence would have been most conspicuous.

He sighed. He supposed he would have to wait until she confided in him. And that would probably be quite a while, he thought. He looked at her where she sat in the saddle, lost in daydreams: a tall, proud figure, her hair still loose down her back as it had been when she was young. She was not one to open up easily to others. But then, he was in no hurry, either, he supposed.

The journey to Salentaire was uneventful; they stopped one night at an inn in a small village that catered regularly for travellers to and from the towns. Bearrach lay awake for several hours waiting for the baby to cry, but this time he heard nothing, and eventually slept soundly in his bed.

They arrived at Fionnghuala's home town late on the second day. They sun had set and they were cast in a grim world of mist and shadow as they rode through the town gates. Salentaire was laid out in a similar fashion to Fintaire: created haphazardly, roads criss-crossing each other like strings in a spider's web, the houses displaying a wide range of styles. Fionnghuala took them to her home – an elegant stone-built house in the very centre of town, quite different from his quiet villa in Fintaire. Her house was on the edge of the central town square, opposite the Council chambers; it was several storeys high and very homely, he thought, filled with knick-knacks and treasures she had gathered from her travels, with embroidered cushions and wall hangings and even a few books, carefully treasured.

She showed them all to their rooms, and he placed his bag beside his bed, but although she had told them they had an hour or so before dinner, he did not feel the need to lie down. He was not a moody man, and was usually even-tempered and calm, but that evening he felt restless, even a touch irritable, although he could not put his finger on why.

He went down the stairs to the ground floor. He could hear Fionnghuala talking to the servants in the kitchen about dinner, but for once, it was not her he wished to see. He walked by the door, then along the hallway, and let himself quietly out of the front door.

Outside, it was cool and quiet, the rain pattering gently on the grass lawn in the centre of the square. The shops had shut for the night; it was nearly dark and the square was empty of all save a few going to the tavern for the evening. Bearrach walked along the edge of the square. Although he had only been to Salentaire half a dozen times, he knew the location of the Temple, and besides, its domed roof was visible above the low houses on the south side of the square.

When he got there, the evening service had just ended. He sat on a bench by a little fountain and waited patiently for the place to empty and the priest to finish tidying up the chairs. When the priest left, Bearrach made his way inside.

The Temple was cool, quiet and dark. Through the glass roof he could see only blackness, the stars covered by the rainclouds refusing to depart. The only light came from the stand of candles in the centre by the oak tree, whose spindly branches cast spidery shadows on the floor. He saw with dismay the oak had dropped its leaves – a sure sign the energy problem caused by the Arbor was spreading.

He picked up a candle and began to walk around the Temple.

He knew Fionnghuala's family would have an area devoted to family inscriptions somewhere. There were no such things as tombs, of course; the dead were taken by the tree. But all families had inscriptions; it was just a matter of searching until he found them.

It did not take him long. The small cluster of plaques was on the east wall, in shadow, only highlighted when he held up his candle.

He read them swiftly. There were dedications to people long gone, as well as more recent family members that had died. He passed over most of them, his eye going for the elaborately carved ones that illustrated a child's death. He read them all. There was nothing that indicated a child Fionnghuala had lost.

Then, however, his eyes went to a very small plaque, almost at floor level. It had the intricate carving that spoke of the death of a child. It did not have any detail of whom the child belonged to, or any details about the child itself, or even a date. However, instinctively, Bearrach knew it was Fionnghuala's. Something inside him just knew.

It held just one word.

Buairt. Sorrow.

V

The Henge of stone loomed forbiddingly on the high hill where Thancred and Gravis were climbing. As they walked up, Thancred told Gravis what the Guardians knew of the stones.

"They were built several thousands of years ago, before even the first Heartwood temple," he said, walking easily up the steep path to the top, though Gravis found himself puffing. "We do not know a huge amount about the builders. They lived off the land, as we do, and they studied the sky and were very knowledgeable about the stars and the seasons. I will show you more about that in a minute. I think they were simple people, but by that I do not mean simple-minded; I mean they lived simply, with little complication to their lives."

"And you try to emulate them," stated Gravis, recognising the description as almost being that of the Guardians' little village.

Thancred smiled. "Yes."

About a hundred feet or so before the summit, there was a small hut, with a wooden bench covered by a sloping roof. Not yet ready to enter the Node, Gravis took a seat out of the pattering rain and Thancred joined him. They sat there for a moment looking down over the Laxonian countryside. Gravis glanced across to the coast and wondered how Beata was faring at Henton. Had she found the Virimage? And Gavius, how was he doing? Had he reached the Green Giant yet?

With no answers forthcoming, Gravis turned to look at Thancred. "Did you know what had happened in Heartwood? Have you been able to tell from the Henge?"

Thancred seemed suddenly hesitant, even embarrassed. "There have been Guardians here for a very long time. We have old knowledge, back beyond the Great Quake and the founding of Heartwood. But there are gaps in what we know. Though we understand the Henge is a great centre of energy, we do not know how to activate it. We can feel the energy flowing – or not, as the case may be – but we cannot affect it. We have been able to do little more than keep the Henge tidy and protect it from raiders." He looked very sad. "We know something has happened to the Arbor – we can feel it in the energy flow. But we have been unable to help."

Gravis reached out and touched his arm. "From what I understand, the upkeep of the physical site is as important as keeping the energy flowing. I was worried the stones may have fallen – for how would we be able to erect them again?"

He went on to tell the Guardian more about what had happened at Heartwood. When he explained about the Darkwater Lords,

Thancred's brow creased, but the Guardian did not interrupt as the Heartwood knight told him how they had risen from the water and returned to it afterwards. He explained about the *Quercetum* and what Nitesco had found out. And he explained he was there to activate the Node. When he had finished, he asked – like a small child – "Do you believe me?"

Thancred nodded, looking out over the hills and valleys. "We have many stories about the elementals, and I think we have all come to the independent realisation that our physical presence on this earth is not everything there is. What you have described makes perfect sense to me." He turned and gave Gravis his full attention. "And so here you are to undertake your Quest. Are you ready?" .

Gravis shivered and looked away. "You saw in the reflection of the window there is something wrong with me," he said quietly. "I do not know what it is."

"When did you start feeling it?"

Gravis thought about it. "I started feeling strange before I left Heartwood, but I put down to the nerves about the journey. It was after I parted from Gavius that I really began to feel odd."

"Gavius?"

"My twin. He is on his own Quest, to activate the Green Giant Node in Komis."

"Ah." Thancred nodded.

"Do you know why I have been casting no reflection, and no shadow? Is it something to do with him?"

"Maybe," said Thancred. "We will talk more about that later. Now, I think we can put it off no longer. It is time to see the Henge."

Gravis's heart thumped. Together they rose and climbed the last hundred yards to the summit.

It was still raining, but he tipped back the hood from his cloak as they crested the rise. There, they stood and surveyed the site.

The top of the hill was flat and about a hundred feet across. In the middle stood the henge, about half that distance from side to side. It consisted of a horseshoe shape of five trilithons – each trilithon made from two standing stones with a third resting on the top. The stones were massive, at least twenty feet tall. Gravis stared up, and up, and up at them, speechless with awe.

"Impressive, are they not?" said Thancred, somewhat smugly. "They go at least eight feet below the ground, too, you know."

"How on earth were they erected?" Gravis could not conceive of how something so big and so heavy could ever be hauled up the hill and turned upright.

"We think maybe a pulley system was used – they would use slaves and/or animals to get one stone up, then lower it carefully down the hill again, using its weight to lever the next up, and so on. But we do not really know. It would be a hugely difficult task today, let alone two thousand years ago when they did not have the building technology that we have."

"Can I walk through them?"

"Of course. Visitors are free to do as they wish while they are here, as long as it does not mean defacing or damaging the stones."

Gravis walked towards them. His fingers tingled. The air was thick and oppressive, as if a storm were coming. Suddenly, it felt difficult to breathe. He tried to ignore the feeling and began to walk around the stones. He could not explain to either Thancred or himself how imposing the stones were. It was as if they had more than a mere physical presence; as if somehow his subconscious were aware of a brooding aura they exuded. Such thoughts did not come easily to his mind and even as they entered his head, his conscious no-nonsense brain wanted to discount them.

But he made himself think about them as he walked around the site. Things were different now; he knew he was not a mere physical being, and there was a world beneath the physical. He could not discount theories just because he did not understand them, or because they did not fit in with his straightforward thinking. He must learn to consider other possibilities; only then would he find a way to activate the Node.

He thought about the effect different people had on a room when they walked into it. Some people could enter – could even sit there for an hour – and you would never know they had come in, and would look at them in surprise when you finally realised they were there. Others, however, made the room glow as soon as they walked in. It was not necessarily because they were noisy, or extrovert; some people just had an inner quality that made others turn and look at them. Gavius was one such person; when he smiled, he shone, and others shone too as a mere reflection of his glow. Chonrad, too, had a personality that exuded warmth and friendship, and Beata would have been beautiful even if she hadn't had the face of an angel.

Other people, however, could darken a room by their mere presence. He had found Dolosus to be one of these; the knight emitted an aura of doom and darkness, even on a sunny day.

And somehow, Gravis knew the stones to be like this. They had a presence in addition to the physical one – he could feel it as surely as he could feel the cold stone under his fingertips. He sensed them watching him, glowering, frowning. They did not approve of him being there. They thought him insufficient, inadequate, weak. They wanted to be activated, and were certain he couldn't do it.

"Are you all right?" Thancred came to stand next to him, and Gravis was suddenly aware he had been motionless for several minutes, his hands on one of the massive standing stones.

"They do not want me here," he whispered hoarsely, his heart pounding. "They know I cannot do it."

"You can hear them?"

"I can *feel* them…"

Thancred took Gravis's hands and turned the knight to face him. "If you can feel them, then you are the one, my friend. Only those connected to the stones can feel their desires. But they do not see you as a failure; they only sense your indecision and your feelings of inadequacy."

"I do not know how to change that," said Gravis hoarsely. "I want very much to be different, but I know I cannot..."

Thancred led him to the centre of the circle. There was a stone slab on the ground there and, in spite of the rain, he spread out his cloak and pulled Gravis down to sit cross-legged opposite him.

"I have a theory," he said. "Life is all about energy. Our relationships are about the exchange of energy. Energy flows, like water, in everything; in channels underneath the ground, and between each other. Sometimes, when we are feeling particularly emotional and vulnerable, it can happen that the energy exchange can be unequal. Someone takes more than they should, and because you are feeling weak you are unable to stop that exchange. I think this is what has happened to you."

Gravis hardly felt the rain falling on his face; all his attention was focussed on the Guardian who sat before him. "You think Gavius did this?"

"I do not think it was a conscious act. But yes, I think he has 'stolen' something from you. If you cannot think of it as energy, then think of it as something more visible. Your shadow perhaps – your reflection, for that is how you are projecting the loss."

A sense of relief flowed over Gravis, as if someone had emptied a bucket of water over his head. "So this is not my fault?"

Thancred shrugged. "It is useless trying to working out who is responsible. It happened. We need to deal with the consequences rather than waste time apportioning blame."

"What can we do?"

"It may take a few days, but I think we can build up your energy levels again. But for now, let us try and see if we can make that connection with your brother. Maybe if we achieve that, he will release the energy he holds."

He took Gravis's hands. "Close your eyes," he said.

Gravis did so. Even though he could see nothing, he immediately felt the presence of the stones around him, towering over him, forbidding, resentful. He tried to shut the image out and concentrate on what Thancred was doing.

The Guardian did not speak, and for a while nothing happened. Gravis tried to relax. He could hear the rain pattering on the ground and feel the cold and hardness of the stone beneath him through the blanket. He tried to stop thinking of the stones as his enemy. If they wanted to be activated, then he was their friend. He tried to send out feelings of love towards them, but it was like trying to show love to a harsh and violent teacher; it just didn't feel right. Still, he persevered.

And then something happened.

In his mind's eye, he saw Gavius. Excitement and happiness surged through him, quickly followed by a frisson of shock. His twin sat on a horse, riding through a forest, which wasn't in itself a surprise. What was shocking, however, was the fact that his brother's hands were bound behind his back, and there was a cloth tied across his mouth.

CHAPTER ELEVEN

I

Gavius watched the blood drip from his bruised mouth onto the wooden platform. He had to look through his right eye, as his left was swollen until it was almost shut. His touched his teeth tenderly with his tongue; one was loose. His whole body hurt.

He raised his head slowly. He could see from the limp figures around the platform that the others had fared little better than he. Hodie wasn't there – he was currently in a hut with the Komis leader, suffering Animus knew what horrors. His cries occasionally cut through the darkness, like sharp knives slicing through silk. Brevis was on his front and looked unconscious; at least Gavius hoped he was – that way he wouldn't feel any pain from his arm, which was quite clearly broken and lay at an odd angle. He looked across at Mellis and Niveus. Uncharacteristically, his eyes filled with tears. Mellis was curled in a ball, and although he couldn't hear her, he knew she was crying. Niveus sat upright, her back against a tree trunk, her whole body rigid with anger. Her face, too, was bloodied and swollen where she had fought her assailants. Her mouth was set in a firm line, as if gritting her teeth. She met his gaze briefly, then looked away.

He thought it had been harder for the two women. Pain was always easier to bear than shame, he thought. Although they had experienced a great deal of pain, too. Fury rose inside him again as he thought of what had happened to them, but he clamped it down, knowing it would do him no good. He had already rubbed his wrists raw trying to get out of the shackles; he was bound too tightly to wriggle free. He had the impression the Komis were quite skilled in the art of keeping captives.

It was nearly dark. He looked across the wooden platform at the treetop houses and saw minor movements, and he knew Komis were there, watching him. He thought that was the worst thing about what they had all undergone so far; not only had they been beaten and, in the women's case, sexually abused, but mostly it had all been carried out publicly, in the middle of a large platform elevated in the trees in the centre of Brant.

He had to admit the treetop settlement was an amazingly innovative construction. Long walkways had been laced from tree to tree, connecting all parts of the town. Houses hung like apples from the branches, and he now knew the Komis had been hiding there when they passed through on the way to the Green Giant.

He looked across at the hut where they had taken Hodie. Firstly, they had tried to extract information by beating them. All three Heartwood men were made of stern stuff and had refused to cave. However, when the leader took Hodie off into the hut, Gavius knew they probably had a more refined torture in store for him, and his stomach began to turn to jelly inside him.

The screaming started again, and Gavius broke out in a sweat. The cries were cut off suddenly, as if someone had put a hand over Hodie's mouth. A few moments of silence followed, and then suddenly the cloth over the doorway moved and out came one of the Komis guards, dragging Hodie by his shackles. He dumped him some yards from Gavius and went back into the hut.

Gavius looked down at his old friend, and his heart twisted inside him. Hodie's hands were a mass of blood and gore. It looked as if they had pulled all his fingernails out.

Slowly, the broken knight opened his eyes. He looked up and saw Gavius, and his eyes filled with tears. "I told them," he whispered, shame making him look away. "I am sorry, Gavius; I could not hold it in. They... they were going to pull out my teeth."

Gavius shuddered. "What knight would not do the same in that situation?" he said, but he knew his attempts to comfort Hodie were futile. The knight would not forgive himself for divulging any information. He wasn't quite sure what the Komis wanted to know, but he sensed it was something to do with Heartwood. Were they planning another attack?

The cloth door shivered again, and a figure came out onto the platform. Gavius now recognised him as some kind of leader – the lord or king of Brant, maybe. His long black hair had been braided elaborately with brightly coloured fabric. He wore a finely woven shirt and dark breeches, and his clothing was covered in delicate embroidery. The guards who had brought them from the Giant called him Aukaneck. He strode across to the captives and looked them over. He kicked Brevis with his toe, but the Militis did not move. Gavius wondered if he were dead. He had heard of people who died from shock after an injury. Aukaneck turned his back on him and walked over to the two women.

Mellis looked up, saw him standing over her and screamed, scrabbling away to the edge of the platform. He grinned and walked towards her. "No!" she cried, her sobs heart-wrenchingly pleading. "Please... no..." Aukaneck reached down to take her by the hand. Gavius gritted his teeth. She was already broken; she would not stand another assault, he was sure. The Komis warrior pulled her to her feet, holding her by the top of her tunic. Mellis's eyes were wide. She looked over at Gavius and in them he could read her thoughts: she knew she could not stand another assault; would beg and tell them everything they wanted to know if they promised not to rape her again, following which they would probably do it anyway.

With one last spark of the resilience she had shown throughout their journey, a decision flared in her eyes. He opened his mouth to protest, seeing what she was going to do, but it was already too late; she wrenched herself free of Aukaneck's grasp and flung herself over the edge of the platform.

Gavius gasped and Niveus cried out. Aukaneck peered over the edge. There was no sound from below. Gavius closed his eyes briefly. She would not have been able to survive the fall from that height. He opened them again and saw Aukaneck shrug. Then the Komis turned to face Niveus and grinned.

"No!" yelled Gavius. But Aukaneck ignored him. Niveus met his gaze and shook her head slightly. Tears ran down his face. She looked away. The first time she had fought them, she had ended bloodied and beaten, and they had still raped her at the end. This time, she had obviously decided to let them do what they want. Her jaw set, she let the Komis king turn her over and, knuckles white where her hands were clenched tightly on the wooden bar before her, she let herself be violated. Gavius looked over to where the others had come out of the hut to watch and stared at them with hatred pooling in his stomach like acid. But their attention was focussed on the grunting, sweating Aukaneck.

Gavius wrestled with his shackles again. They were so tight; he could feel they had cut through his flesh. He wriggled until blood ran over his hands, but still he could not free them. Eventually he sank back, the pain from his wrists making him shake, and he turned away, unable to watch his friend being hurt in such a way.

Eventually, Aukaneck finished, and Gavius looked over to see Niveus curl up on her side, feebly pulling up her breeches to cover her naked form. She glanced at him, though, and he saw the spark of defiance in her eyes and was glad of it. Clearly, she was attempting to treat the defiling of her body as a physical thing only, and was determined to try and remain aloof from it. He wondered what good it would do her. Were they all doomed to die in this Animus-forsaken place?

Aukaneck turned, tightening up his own clothing, and stared at Gavius. The Militis met his gaze boldly, although his heartbeat grew faster. The king came over and unceremoniously grabbed him by his tunic and hauled him to his feet. They had removed all the knights' mail – Gavius guessed that would be the last he'd see of that – and left them with only their tunic and breeches, which wasn't really enough cover for the cool night.

But the cold was the last of his worries at that moment as he was pushed towards the hut. He baulked at the door, smelling blood, but hands grabbed him and he was pulled inside. He fell heavily onto the floor and lay for a moment, winded, then gradually struggled to a sitting position.

It was dark inside. As far as he was able to establish, candles were not used, presumably because of the fire hazard. However, the room was lit by half a dozen or so strange creatures the size of his finger, presumably some sort of worm, which glowed with a blue phosphorescent light. It gave the occupants an eerie cast to their faces, and Gavius had to concentrate hard to keep a tight hold on his fear.

He considered himself a brave knight; he had fought in several battles during his time in the Exercitus, and had thrown himself into the attacks fearlessly, with little thought to his own danger. But now, watching the curiously metallic eyes of Aukaneck lighting up at the thought of the torture to come, panic stirred within him like a coiled snake.

"What is it you want?" He asked the Question calmly, trying to give the impression he was not afraid. The more he could keep them talking, he figured, the longer it would be before they started to torture him.

"The other one told me everything I need to know about why you are here," said Aukaneck. He spoke in the language of Heartwood, his accent strange but his words perfect. He pulled a small knife out of a sheath on his hip and examined the blade carefully. "He told me about the Darkwater attack, and Heartwood's plan to activate the Nodes. He told me about the Virimage and Beata's journey to find him. And he told me about the Quest to Darkwater to retrieve the Arbor's Pectoris."

Hodie had held nothing back, Gavius thought, but even though his friend had divulged information which could be dangerous to Heartwood, Gavius could not blame him. What knight was strong enough to withstand hours and hours of painful torture?

"What else do you need to know?" he asked coolly. "It sounds as if you have all the information you need."

Aukaneck came towards him stealthily, like cat about to pounce. "I would torture you purely for the fun of it," he admitted, turning Gavius's blood cold. "But there is one thing your friend could not tell me. I want to know the secret entrance to Heartwood."

Gavius's mouth went dry. He had not been aware anyone knew of that. Before he had embarked on the Quest, he had not known about it, either. Valens had told him of it on the day they left so if Heartwood was under siege when they returned, they would still be able to get into the Castellum. The Imperator had made him swear not to tell anybody about the secret entrance, not even anyone who was on the Quest with him. Nor had he. So how did the Komis know about it?

It hardly mattered, he thought wearily. The fact was that they did know, and they were obviously sure he knew, and they would therefore do their utmost to get the information out of him.

Well, they weren't going to get it easily, he told himself furiously. Every second he could withhold it from them meant another second of safety for Heartwood.

"What secret entrance?" he said.

Aukaneck smiled. "I was hoping you would say that," he said silkily, and brought forward his knife.

II

By the time of the evening meal, Teague appeared to have sobered up. Beata studied him as she took her place at the high table as the guest of the Lord of Henton, sending Peritus an apologetic smile at the fact that he had to wait on her, but he just smiled back and shook his head slightly, saying he didn't mind.

They had spoken for several hours after the earlier debacle in the Hall. Beata had been all for leaving then and there, convinced this Virimage or whatever he called himself was an idiot, and there was no hope in asking him to help. Peritus had managed to calm her down, however, suggesting when he sobered up he might be of a better disposition, and more inclined to accept their entreaty of help.

So far, she thought wryly, she had seen no evidence of that. True, he did not appear as drunk as he had earlier, and was conversing easily with a number of people around the Hall, but he still acted the fool, being very theatrical in his gestures and obviously keen to be the centre of attention.

She thought about the way rose petals had fluttered out of his mouth when he had belched. Had that been a trick? Or was that real, an indication – however small – of a power he might possess? She watched him now, talking animatedly to a small group of women, who giggled behind their hands and looked up at him under lowered eyelashes with false modesty. What did they find so attractive about him? She felt genuinely confused. He was surrounded by admirers, holding court as if he was the lord and not the fat, bumbling fellow who sat a little down the table, busy tucking into a whole chicken. She looked over her shoulder at Peritus, who shrugged. Clearly, he was as nonplussed as she was.

He was not uncomely, she thought. He had changed into a bright green tunic and had braided his black hair with golden cord that matched his eyes. But still, the memory of their first conversation rankled, and she knew that would stay with her, however charming he now appeared.

The meal was pleasant enough, but seemed to go on forever. Course followed course, and she was soon too full to eat any more. The plates of fish, meat, vegetables, bread and fruit passed her by, making her wonder if the people in the town had anything to eat at all – weren't they on the cusp of a famine? She wished desperately she had a bedchamber she could retire to. As a guest, however, and not a very well-known one at that, she would be sleeping in the Hall that night on the floor, and although she was not bothered by the discomfort, it did mean she would have to wait until the tables were cleared and everyone else was ready for bed. She began to wish again she had not listened to Peritus's advice and had decided to return to Heartwood. But then the Arbor would be lost, she thought sadly, and what would happen to them all?

"Virimage! It is time for some entertainment," called the lord, waving a half-eaten toffee apple in the air. "What will you sing for us tonight?"

"Whatever my generous lord desires," said Teague, coming forwards into the space in front of the lord's table and giving him a bow. "Would you like a tale you have heard before? Or something new?"

"Something new, something new!" chanted the diners.

Teague nodded. "I have been working on a new tale. It is about a fair princess who has been locked in a tower in a castle, and a brave and handsome knight who has to rescue her. Would you like to hear that?"

The crowd cried that they would. Teague laughed and took a small lute that had been leaning against the table, and began to strum a tune.

The story was not a particularly innovative one; how many tales have been sung about fair princesses and handsome knights? But nevertheless, Beata sat entranced. She would not have guessed the idiot who had discoursed with her so drunkenly earlier that day could be the same person who was singing now. His voice was not deep, but it was rich and mellow, and sent shivers down her spine.

However, it was not his voice that made her catch her breath and watch too scared to blink in case she missed something. It was the magic he performed with his hands.

He illustrated his tale with clever movements and tricks which he carried out in between strums of the lute. When he sang of the beauty of the princess's golden hair, he waved his hand palm down over the ground and up rose a tall sheaf of yellow corn that seemed to sway in the wind as if it was still in the field. When he told of the storm the knight had to ride through to get to the castle, he swirled his hand gently in the air and tiny silver petals fluttered down on the crowd to their cries of delight. As the knight reached a dark and dangerous forest, the crowd screamed to find green vines climbing up their legs and lacing themselves around the table. And when he spoke of the joy the knight felt when finally seeing the maiden lying in her chamber, blue and yellow flowers bloomed in front of all the ladies, causing several to swoon.

Walking among the guests, he finished his song with a verse about the knight singing to the princess about how much he had longed to be with her, and how glad he was that he had found her. The knight produced a rose for his beautiful lady, which he gave to her as he kissed her.

Teague was standing almost directly behind Beata as he sang the last words. She had to turn slightly in her chair to see him, but was close enough to him to see that, as he produced the rose in his hands, there was nothing up his sleeve, and no secret hiding place for him to produce it. The flower grew from his palm, as if an invisible hand had quickly drawn it there with red and green ink. He looked at her, and she felt a shock go through her at the warmth in his beautiful golden eyes. "I am sorry," he mouthed, and then before she could react, bent forward and pressed his lips briefly to hers.

The crowd cheered. Teague turned away, strumming his lute and laughing as they all cheered for him to play more, but waved his hand, complaining his throat was dry and he needed a drink.

Beata sat still as a rock, her cheeks scorching, her fingers resting on her mouth where he had kissed her. Had he apologised for being rude to her earlier? Or had he apologised for the fact that he was about to kiss her? She looked over at Peritus, who just raised an eyebrow, and she looked away again, her head spinning. Why had Teague chosen her as his princess? And why had he kissed her?

She glanced up, looking around the room for him, but to her surprise, he had vanished. And for the rest of the evening, he did not appear. Eventually, the tables were cleared and pushed back against the walls, the blankets and pillows were brought down into the Hall, everyone began to prepare for bed, and still he did not appear. Beata found a place not far from the door and curled up on her little pallet, wondering about where he had gone, and what he was doing.

She thought about the tricks he had done there that evening, and knew in her heart he had some form of the Veriditas within him, some ability to control nature that maybe existed in all of them, but he clearly knew how to use his. And eventually she fell asleep, thinking about him, and remembering the soft touch of his lips on hers.

When she opened her eyes in the morning, at first she thought she was still dreaming, because the first thing she saw was those golden eyes fixed on her, watching her. Then she blinked and realised it really was Teague, and he was sitting beside her, cross-legged on the floor, waiting for her to wake up.

She sat up, the knight's natural ability to wake immediately springing into life. "You!" she said, half-alarmed, half-intrigued.

"Me," he replied, amused. He studied her carefully. "Who are you?"

She said nothing for a moment but was aware she would eventually have to tell him if she wanted him to go to Heartwood, but for the moment decided she would keep things simple. "My name is Beata," was all she said. "Why?"

He frowned at her name and she realised she should have given herself a Laxonian pseudonym, but he did not comment on it. Instead he said, "Because I had a very strange dream about you last night."

"You did?" Now it was her turn to be amused. "Dare I ask?"

He did not smile but continued to frown. "It was actually about a Heartwood knight. I saw his tattoo. He had light brown hair that curled on his forehead, like this." He drew the shape above his eyebrows.

"Oh?" She kept her voice neutral, but inside her heart was beating quickly. It sounded like one of the twins. "What happened?"

He blinked, his unnerving gold eyes fixed on her. "He was being tortured. I saw a knife carving patterns on his skin. But he did not cry out. Instead he looked up at me and said, 'Follow her'. And then I saw you."

His words made her heart miss a beat. Was it Gravis or Gavius he had seen? And was it actually a vision of something that was happening, or just a glimpse of a possible future? "Which arm was his tattoo on?" she asked.

Teague tipped his head, studying her curiously. His eyes looked above her as he pictured the knight in his head, trying to remember. "His left, since you ask. Why should that matter?"

Beata said nothing. So it was Gavius. What was happening to him? Was he really being tortured? "Did he say anything else?" she whispered. She fought back the tears at the image of poor young Gavius being cut with a knife.

"No. I woke up."

"Do you get these visions often?"

He watched her, suddenly wary. "Maybe."

She realised he was afraid of acknowledging his true gift. He had obviously spent so long marketing his magic as tricks that he was reluctant to admit he really could control nature. "I know what you can do," she said simply. "The Veriditas. The Greening."

He went still at those words. His gold eyes looked suddenly beyond her again, as if he was seeing something in another time.

Eventually, however, they dropped back to her. "Sometimes Anguis speaks to me," he said. "She sends me glimpses of things that have happened, or are yet to pass."

She nodded. For a moment, they were both quiet.

Eventually, however, Teague spoke. "So, are you going to tell me what this is all about?"

Beata smiled at him. "How would you like to come with me and save the world?"

III

The baby was crying again.

The high, painful wail followed Fionnghuala across the Snout Range, all the way to the Portal. It wasn't always there; when they were riding, she didn't hear it, and it was more obvious during the night than the day. But – and here was the strangest thing – she and Bearrach were the only ones aware of it; the others didn't seem to hear it at all.

That fact puzzled her more than the actual noise itself. She still wasn't sure why she was hearing the noise – well, she knew *why*, it was more the *how* she was confused about. And, if it was indeed a slip through time or a message from the otherworld, she understood why the others couldn't hear it. But that didn't explain why Bearrach could. But she knew he was aware of it. At night, when she covered herself with blankets and lay in the half-dark, and the crying began, she would look over at him and he would be watching her, his green eyes dark with pity, and she knew he could hear it, too.

There was no point in looking for the baby; she had established that fact quickly enough. No, the baby was definitely not of this world, and when its crying increased as they crossed the Snout Range, she knew it was something to do with the Portal.

Her Quest now began to press in on her as they traversed the last of the hills. The weight of the world seemed to be on her shoulders. The weather probably wasn't helping; it was raining particularly hard that morning, and although her cloak had been treated to make it waterproof, it still felt sodden, and her face was continually cold and wet. The rivers had continued to rise, and she noticed as she looked down into the valley they were inches from breaking their banks. Every flower they passed, every leaf and every blade of grass bowed beneath the pressure of the rain. The whole of Anguis seemed to be depressed by the imminent arrival of the Darkwater Lords.

They started to crest the hill, and Fionnghuala held her breath as they topped the rise and brought the horses to a halt. There in front of them, halfway up the crest of the next hill, with a splendid view over the lowlands of north Hanaire, was the Portal. A huge trilithon consisting of two standing stones topped by a third, the Portal looked like a magical gateway to another place, although she had been there several times and walked through it, and had never found herself anywhere but on the other side.

They began to make their way down the hill. Bearrach manoeuvred his horse until it was beside hers but didn't say anything, and she realised he felt she needed moral support. She smiled to think he had read her thoughts and had felt her growing hesitation.

How strange it was to have lived so close to him for so long and never to have known him better. She had known him since she was young; he had been there at her first speech in the Council, and she remembered seeing him watching her as she spoke. But until now, he had never pushed a relationship with her; she wasn't sure why. Perhaps he had realised how important her role in the Council was to her and understood she didn't want to have to make the choice between family and her job.

And now? Now he had realised she was struggling, and had realised she needed a friend.

She was saved further contemplation by their arrival. They dismounted at the bottom of the hill, where there was a small copse of trees with a large pool. They tied up their horses and let them graze before walking up the hill to the Portal. The stones stood about halfway up on a flat shelf, looking rather like a giant figure that stood imposingly watching over the land, hands on hips. Fionnghuala walked up to them. They looked much the same as the last time she had come; pitted and weathered, but strong and solid and clearly not going anywhere any time soon.

She watched the others admiring them, especially the Militis, who had not been there before, and she saw them wandering through the gap between the stones to the other side without a second thought.

For a moment, however, she could not follow them through. The thought of her Quest and what she had been sent there to do was suddenly so prominent that she felt if she walked through the Portal, a door might open to another place – a place she did not want to be, or from where she could not return. Her feet felt frozen to the floor and she stood, petrified, her heart pounding.

"Have you seen the flowers over there?" asked Bearrach gently, taking her hand. He indicated a small cluster of wilting blooms that lay on the hill, visible through the Portal. "Come and look at them with me."

Initially, she baulked – why could they not walk round the Portal to look at the flowers? Why did they have to walk through? But she knew he was trying to get her to go through with him, and so eventually, she let him lead her into the shadow of the stones, and under them, and her heart hammered, and her mouth was dry as sun-bleached rock. They reared above her head, and then suddenly she was through, and Bearrach was still holding her hand, and nothing had happened. She could have cried with relief, but instead she just smiled at him shakily, and he squeezed her hand and wandered off to talk to the others. Clearly, the Node was not ready to talk to her, she thought. The day of reckoning had not yet arrived.

They spent the rest of the day making camp. There was no real shelter anywhere near the Portal, and so eventually, they decided to erect a tent-like structure under the copse of trees at the base of the hill. They had several waterproof sheets with them, which they strung around the trunks so one made a large, sloping roof to let the rain run off, and two others formed walls to keep out the worst of the rain that drove in from the east. They quickly made a fire, and Audax, Mundus and Lalage went off to catch them some tea, returning after an hour or so with several rabbits, a pheasant and a bowl of berries and edible plants. They had brought one fairly large cooking pot with them and made a stew, eating it sitting under the shelter on their blankets, watching the rain and talking quietly about the Portal and what it was they were expected to do.

"Nitesco told us we should first of all tidy the site," said Fionnghuala, keen to do anything that put off the business of actually activating the Node. "There are lots of boulders around, and grass on the stones; we should start with that."

They all agreed. Lalage looked up at the Portal, which watched over them like a mother observing her children as they played near water. "I wonder what you actually have to do, though," she said. "How do you activate the Node?"

"I was hoping it would become clear once we were ready," said Fionnghuala. She gave the young Militis a smile. Lalage had been exceptionally quiet the last day or so, considering her near-constant chatter on the rest of the journey, and Fionnghuala was beginning to wonder if she was sickening for something. "I do not know how, but I have the feeling the way will become clear when the time comes."

"That is probably just wishful thinking," said Audax wryly. "Let us face the facts: we have no idea whatsoever what we are supposed to do."

"Maybe not," said Bearrach, "but I agree with Fionnghuala. It is pointless to worry about things that have not yet come to pass. Let us clear the site, and then we will consider the next step in the process."

Fionnghuala smiled at him gratefully. She did not want a long conversation or an argument about the activation, and once again Bearrach had sensed her feelings.

It was growing dark, so they decided to turn in for the night. Fionnghuala was tired from the day's ride and dozed off quickly. She slept soundly and dreamlessly, and was surprised when she roused and sat up to see it was some hours later; the rain had eased and for once, the Light Moon had come out. It should have comforted her, for it had been days since they had last seen it, and in Salentaire she often passed time after Council matters had finished watching the evening skies. But tonight, it made her shiver, its pink crescent like the blade of a scythe cutting through the blackness of the night.

Then she realised what had awoken her. The baby was crying again. She clasped her arms around her knees and leaned her chin on them, puzzling over the sound. She looked across at Bearrach, wondering if, as usual, he was awake, but for once, he was not watching her but was sleeping quietly, facing away from her, and she did not want to disturb him.

Then she saw the small pile of blankets where Lalage had been lying. The Militis had left the shelter, which was unusual in itself because she of all of them usually slept the most soundly, and snored and talked in her sleep, and had to be woken in the morning. Fionnghuala slid out of her blankets and wrapped her cloak around her shoulders. Suddenly, the ceasing of the rain seemed menacing – why had the clouds now, of all times, chosen to part and reveal the icy moon? She rose and ducked under the roof covering and stood in the cool night. Everything glistened with the droplets of rain that still lay on plants and rocks alike. She scanned the countryside. There was no sign of Lalage.

She looked up the hill at the Portal, the stones of which shone almost white in the light of the moon. It looked ethereal, and she shuddered as she thought about the task that lay ahead. But she must not think about that; she must think about Lalage. Her instincts told her the knight had not just gone out for a stroll under the stars.

She frowned, her stomach stirring agitatedly. Should she wake the others? But that would be silly if indeed her instincts were wrong and Lalage *had* just gone out for a moonlit stroll.

She turned to walk down the valley, but then she heard the baby crying again. It seemed to come from behind her this time, and she turned instinctively to find the child, although she knew it to be only a phantom. And then she saw the sight that turned her blood to iced water in her veins.

For in the small pool in front of the horses' shelter floated the body of the Militis knight, face down, her hair spreading out from her head like the pad of a lily, her pale limbs like white branches on the surface.

IV

"No, thank you," said Teague in reply to Beata's plea for him to help her save Anguis. He laughed and got to his feet. "I am no hero. I cannot save myself, let alone the world."

Beata got up hurriedly and caught his arm. "You do not understand the power that you have. We need you, Teague. We are desperate."

"Well, thanks," he said with wry amusement. His gaze ran up and down her and his grin deepened.

She realised she must look quite a sight, hair all wild around her face and clad only in a thin linen tunic. She glared at him fiercely, unabashed by his open lechery, which was plainly trying to embarrass her. How could she be shy after years of undressing in communal barracks? "You do not understand. I have come halfway across Anguis to find you."

"Me?" He frowned now. "Why me?"

"Because of your special abilities."

"These tricks?" He laughed and threw his hands up, and a scattering of tiny petals floated down through the air. "How can such illusions save the world?"

"Because they are not illusions," she said quietly, giving him a warning glance. "I told you, I know your real power. I have seen another with it; albeit not quite so strong as yours."

"You have?" His eyes were suddenly wary. "Where?"

"In Heartwood."

He stared at her, realisation suddenly dawning in his eyes. "You are a Militis?!"

"I am." She showed him the oak leaf tattoo on her wrist. "They have heard about you in Heartwood, Teague. And they sent me to find you."

She had thought flattery might persuade him, that the thought that the holiest knights in Anguis were searching for him would inflate his ego and make him agree to go back with her. But his face darkened like a cloud passing over the sun, and she realised it wasn't going to be that easy.

"You are mistaken," he snapped. "I do not have the ability to do anything more than entertain people while they dine, and to delight bored children. I am happy here; I do not want to go traipsing across Anguis saving damsels in distress."

She frowned. "It is so much more than that! The whole world is at stake here; do you not think you should do your utmost to help save it?"

"Why? What has it ever done for me?" he said fiercely. "I have been given nothing in life; cast out from my homeland, left for dead, a stranger in a strange land; I have had to hang on to my life with my fingernails and claw myself back up to a decent survival. Why should I suddenly declare that I wish to save this world that has abandoned me time and again?"

"It was not Anguis that abandoned you," said Beata softly. "Nor Animus. Only people."

"Animus!" he snorted. "Do not start talking to me about religion. I have had enough of this conversation." And with that, he turned on his heel and marched out of the Hall.

Beata sighed and watched him go. She could see she had a battle on her hands. But she was not ready to give up yet.

For the rest of the morning, he disappeared, presumably down to the town, she thought, but eventually, he returned as the midday meal was served, and she wandered over to sit beside him at the table as the bread and meat were laid out before them.

He sighed as he looked up to see her. "I am having lunch," he stated firmly, ruling out any Question of a discussion.

"So am I," she stated back, filling her plate and proceeding to eat. He did the same, but she could see him repeatedly casting glances at her, and eventually he put down his knife with exasperation.

"I cannot sit here and eat with you waiting like a hungry wolf at my side."

She stared at him innocently. "I do not know what you mean."

He snorted. "You are not as innocent as you make out, so you can drop that act."

Beata said nothing. Eventually, he sighed. "I am sorry; I did not mean to be rude."

"I am getting used to it."

To her surprise, he grinned. "I know it takes a while, but most people come around to liking me eventually."

Her lips twitched. "You do not make it easy. But I am determined that you will listen to my plea."

He studied her with his golden eyes. They unnerved her; there was clearly nothing wrong with his vision, but she couldn't shake the feeling that he was blind, and she was certain she was going to do something foolish under the impression he could not see her.

He sighed. "I give in. Explain why my returning to Heartwood is so important to you."

She did not have to be told twice to convince him. She told him all about the Darkwater attack, explaining what had happened in detail so he really understood how the water lords had faded away into the channel at the end. Then she told him about the information that Nitesco had discovered, about the Nodes, and how the Veriditas was supposed to make the Arbor grow. "But none of us has the gift," she said. "Well, except for Silva, and even her power is not enough to give the tree back its life." She watched his brow furrow as he thought over what she had said. "Do you think you could help?"

For a while he said nothing. Then, eventually, he said, "I will think about it."

"I can ask for nothing more."

They did not speak about it for the rest of the afternoon. Teague spent some time preparing his entertainment that night, practicing his songs on his lyre, while Beata and Peritus went into Henton to get some supplies ready for the return journey. By the time they got back, the court was preparing for the evening meal, and the day was darkening, although there was still no sign of the sun.

Beata purposefully sat away from Teague for the first part of the meal, hoping her words would gradually sink into his brain like stones into a vat of honey. Sure enough, as the evening wore on, he glanced over at her more and more, and she knew he was thinking about what she had said earlier.

Convinced he was coming round to the idea of accompanying her back to Heartwood, for the first time in days her spirits began to brighten, and she finally relaxed, enjoying the food and drink and the company around her. Her tankard was filled with ale repeatedly, and as it was warm in the Hall she kept drinking, only realising when her vision began to blur that she was on the way to being drunk.

Part of her was also aware that she should be angry with herself for becoming drunk, but somehow she wasn't, and somehow it didn't seem to matter. All there was in the world were Teague's fascinating gold eyes like two bright buttons fixed on her no matter where she was, or who she was talking to.

She watched him as he did his evening performance, and caught her breath when he glanced over at her, his hands casting strange patterns in the air, causing petals to float from the ceiling and land on her hair like jewels threaded through her braids.

When he had finished, he lingered for a while talking to the lord and some of the visitors to the court, but he kept casting glances over at her, and each time he did, her stomach fluttered. She was excited about the thought of him returning to Heartwood, she told herself. Of course that was the reason.

Eventually he came over and dropped to her side on the bench.

"Did you enjoy the performance?" he said, pulling a tankard of ale towards him and drinking it down thirstily.

"It was very good," she said primly, unwilling to give him too much encouragement, aware that his ego was probably big enough already.

He laughed. "Now I know you are jesting. I was on *fire* tonight!"

She smiled, unable to resist his infectious good spirits. "Yes, you were. Now do you believe in the importance of your gift?"

He gave her a look that said, Oh, not that again, and poured himself another tankard of ale. Looking at her empty cup, he poured her one too.

"No more," she protested, her vision succumbing to the effects of the drink.

"Go on," he said, and to encourage her, he traced a ring around the top of the cup, and a flourish of flowers appeared, the same colour as her dress.

Beata sighed. Who could resist such an extravagant gesture?

"Tell me more about your life at Heartwood," he said, speaking softly and moving closer to her, as he knew she didn't want anyone else in the castle to know her true identity. "How long have you been there?"

"I was chosen for the Allectus at seven," she said.

"Were you an only child?"

"Yes. It cost my parents dearly to send me away from them. Emotionally, you understand, not in coin. I was much loved, and they could not have any other children. But they said that from an early age, I had stated that I wished to go to Heartwood, and where I come from, it is a very great honour to be a Militis, and so they decided to send me, in spite of the loss they would feel."

"And did you miss your parents?" he said. She smiled, and he sighed. "Stupid Question. I shall rephrase it. Are you glad that the decision to send you was made?"

"Oh, very. I cannot imagine myself to be anything else."

He considered her thoughtfully. "You would have made a good actress."

She laughed heartily at that, thinking of the absurdity of such a profession and how meaningless her life would have been had she trod the boards and not served the Arbor. "I do not think so," she said, sipping her ale. "I was born to be a knight, and nothing else would have been right."

He cocked his head at her, studying her carefully. "Can you tell me about your vows?"

She shrugged. "They are sacred. We are not supposed to discuss them outside Heartwood."

He chewed thoughtfully on a wooden toothpick. "I think I am a little envious."

"Envious?"

"Yes, of your conviction, your dedication, your passion. I have none of those things."

She tried to think how her life would be without the qualities he had mentioned, and failed. "But then, you have had a difficult life. You have shown different qualities in order to come through the hard times – resolution, courage and the ability to depend on yourself where others learn only to depend on each other."

He smiled at her. "You are kind and thoughtful as well as brave. You have a beautiful spirit, as well as a beautiful face."

Against her wishes, Beata flushed. Beauty was not a quality considered important, or even desirable, at Heartwood, and it was not a word she would ever use to describe herself. Courageous, yes. Determined, yes. But beautiful?

Still, there was some small part of her that was flattered by his compliment.

"Shall we take a walk outside?" Teague asked suddenly, surprising her.

"It is still raining," she said wryly, comfortable and warm and unwilling to go out into the darkness and the wet."

"I know, but the arcade is covered, and there is a lovely view of the town from the gardens to the west. I am hot in here, and bored, and I want you to myself."

Beata smiled. Perhaps if she was alone with him, she might have another chance to persuade him to come with her.

V

As he passed under the huge gates of the Porta, Chonrad looked up at the Heartwood seal on the front wall and wondered whether he would ever see it again. He was not sure if he wanted to or not. He still did not feel comfortable within its walls. He glanced across at Fulco, who made the simple gesture: *home*. Chonrad smiled. Yes, it was nice to be going home again, and it would be good to see his children.

He glanced across at Procella, stiff-backed on her horse. She raised her hand in a formal salute to Valens before kicking her heels into her horse and sending him over the wooden drawbridge towards Laxony. She did not look back. Of course, she would have spent more time on the Wall than in Heartwood itself, but still, he could tell from her rigidity that it was taking all her self control not to turn around and cast a longing glance at the place.

The others with them, Nitesco, Solum, Terreo and Hora, all cast fleeting glances back before also setting their heels to their steeds, and Nitesco looked plainly terrified.

Strangely, however, thought Chonrad, it was the last member of their party who seemed the most affected by their departing.

Dolosus, late to Heartwood, misfit and outcast, had tears in his eyes as he grasped Valens's right hand with his own. Valens's jaw was set and he just nodded as the Dean mounted his horse and galloped past Chonrad, his face a strange mixture of fear, regret, anger and possibly even hatred, although of what Chonrad wasn't sure.

Following Nitesco's announcement that he had finally discovered a way to change them into water elementals, Valens had called a meeting for that Quest party and there had followed a heated debate, during which people's real feelings had become evident: none of them truly believed that Nitesco could do what he was claiming. In spite of the fact that they had all seen the Darkwater Lords emerge from the river, it all just seemed too fantastical. Their bodies were far too real for them to believe that they could magically transpose into water, just like that.

To be fair to the young Libraris, Nitesco had been exceedingly patient with them. Time and again, he had stated he was certain he could do it, that he trusted the ancient texts and felt Animus had guided him to the place where he had found the answer.

They had had a discussion about whether they should try the transforming spell before they left, but it was generally decided it was too dangerous.

It was only then that Chonrad began to realise how dangerous their Quest was. Even if Nitesco was successful in transforming them, they had no idea what would happen in that instance. Nitesco insisted that they would be in control of the water spirits inside them, but Chonrad knew he could not be a hundred percent certain. There was a great chance that they might be engulfed by the water spirits and either killed immediately or lose their identities forever. Or if that didn't happen, and they managed to control the water elementals, the very spell that Nitesco would cast could alert the Darkwater Lords to their plan, meaning that they would be dead the moment they arrived at Darkwater.

Chonrad's knuckles were white where his hands were clenched so tightly on the reins, and he loosened his grip, taking deep breaths. One thing at a time, he promised himself. It was no good getting ahead of himself and worrying about things yet to come. Concentrate on the problem in hand, he thought.

He lifted his hood a little and looked around him. They were travelling on the eastbound road that ran a few miles south of the Wall. It was good to be back in Laxony, he decided, looking south towards the hills. It was also good to be riding towards his home town. He had spent a lot of time away from home, travelling the Seven Lands, but he never tired of returning to his castle and his family. He glanced at Fulco, who gave a wry smile. Chonrad knew he would be glad to be going home, too. Though he couldn't voice his feelings, his companion had a deep love of his homeland, and would be relieved to see his wife and five children.

They rode all day, passing the occasional traffic on the road, and by nightfall had reached Lothgar's Fort, a small settlement that served as part trading post, part army camp for those travelling from one side of the Wall to the other.

As the majority of the Exercitus in this region had been withdrawn to Heartwood, most of the barracks were empty, save for the small group of Laxonians who had been sent from Setbourg to try to protect the area from raiders in Heartwood's absence. The Quest party rubbed down their horses and fed them, and then retired to their lodgings. There were no hot baths, but there were cauldrons of hot water and plenty of food, and they went to bed with full stomachs and clean bodies.

Chonrad lay on his back on his pallet and stared up at the rafters as the others gradually sank into sleep. His brain would not seem to stop, and although he repeatedly shut his eyes, they kept floating open as thoughts and images filtered through his mind.

What was to be their fate, he pondered, in spite of his oath to himself that he would not worry about the future? He found himself contemplating the fact that Nitesco could do as he said, and turn them into water elementals. What would that actually involve? Nitesco had been miserly with the details, saying he thought it best to keep the spell to himself in case the Darkwater Lords somehow got wind of it, but Chonrad was not so sure. He had a sneaky feeling it was going to be painful and horrific, and the Libraris just didn't want to panic them.

Irritable with himself for not being able to sleep, he turned over on his pallet. As he did so, there came a muffled clonk. His whole body tensed. The noise had sounded at the exact moment he turned over. Had his movement caused it? Or had it come from outside? He held his breath, and slowly his hand moved to the hilt of his sword. For a moment there was nothing.

Then, out of the corner of his eye, he saw the door open slowly.

Chonrad tightened his grip around the hilt. Sweat beaded on his brow. Was it someone returning to the room after slipping outside to relieve themselves? Or was it a foe?

Outside, the light shone through briefly, illuminating the figure in the doorway. Chonrad saw clearly the wild hair, the blade of the raised axe, and the other figures crowded behind him.

"Raid!" he yelled and, thrusting his covers back, swung his sword across his body.

Trained from an early age to be ready to fight from the moment they opened their eyes, the knights in the room awakened instantly and reached for their own weapons. Dashing sleep from their eyes, they kicked aside their beds and fanned out to meet the marauders who were bursting through the doors now their surprise attack had been thwarted.

Back-to-back with Procella, Fulco only feet away, Chonrad swung and parried with his blade against the Wulfian raiders, cursing loudly at the lack of space. All around him came the grunts and gasps of battle. At one point he glanced over and saw with shock that Dolosus had been cornered by two raiders and was currently struggling to defend himself against their repeated blows, his one arm a blur of movement, feet plantly widely apart to keep the balance that his other arm would have afforded him. He was clearly a strong and able fighter, but Chonrad could see instantly that he was struggling. Still, he could not help until he had beaten his own opponent. So he focussed on his assailant, and tried to think of nothing else as he concentrated on finding a weakness in his foe's guard.

The raider he was fighting was skilled enough with the sword, but he was no match for the powerful and experienced Lord of Barle. Chonrad spotted that the Wulfian was favouring his left side and concentrated there until the raider dropped his guard, leaving his upper torso exposed, and in went the blade, cutting him under the armpit and severing muscle and sinew so the raider screamed, dropping his blade and clutching his cut shoulder with his other hand. Leaving nothing to chance, Chonrad pulled out his dagger, put the point to the gap in the raider's armour at the neck and leaned his weight onto the hilt until the blade slid slowly in. The raider jerked, blood bubbled out of his mouth and he collapsed onto the floor.

Chonrad turned to aid Procella, smiling briefly to see she quite clearly needed no help, judging by the ashen shade of her assailant's face as he fell to one knee, driven there by the sheer force of her blows.

Turning, Chonrad saw they were gaining predominance in the battle. Several of the raiders were already on the floor, unmoving, and the others would not survive much longer. Even Nitesco stood victorious over his victim, blood dripping from his sword.

Only Dolosus was still struggling. He crouched in the corner; one raider was dead, but the other sensed victory, and this had given him added strength. Dolosus's sword was now only being used in defence, trying to shield his body from repeated blows. Chonrad had seen enough battle to realise his defeat was imminent. He strode over and, grasping the Wulfian by the collar of his mail shirt, hauled him off the cowering Militis. Throwing him to the floor, he finished him off quickly.

Dolosus struggled to his feet. Chonrad put a hand under his armpit to help him up, but the knight threw him off. His face was screwed in a ball of anger, fury and shame. He pushed past Chonrad and went out into the night.

Chonrad shrugged and, cleaning his sword on some straw, turned to survey the damage. The raiders were all dead. There didn't seem to be many injuries among his party; Nitesco had a graze on his cheek and Hora had blood on her right forearm, but it clearly wasn't bothering her and seemed to be superficial. Fulco was unharmed, and Procella didn't look as if she had even broken into a sweat.

The Dux now walked quickly to the door, making sure that there weren't more raiders waiting outside, and came back in shaking her head. "The Laxonians have finished off the others," she said. "The raid is over." She looked at Chonrad. "Where did Dolosus go?"

"Out" was all he could offer. He walked closer to her so that only she could hear his soft words. "He was nearly bested in that fight. I helped him out, and I do not think he will thank me for it."

"Better pride wounded than body," said Procella matter-of-factly, but as she walked away to check on the dead raiders, her words echoed in Chonrad's head, and something inside him knew that, in Dolosus's case, her statement simply might not be true.

CHAPTER TWELVE

I

Beata pushed herself to her feet. She held onto the table for a moment, slightly unsteady, then accepted Teague's hand and let him hold it tightly as he guided her along the tables past the guests. She was aware of the women watching her curiously, and saw many envious looks. It was so strange and foreign, this world of court and manners and correct procedures and lords and ladies, and she didn't understand it at all. Suddenly, she missed Heartwood desperately, her emotions bobbing to the surface like a piece of wood on the river, and she stumbled as tears flooded her eyes.

"Careful," said Teague, steadying her before leading her out through the large oak door to the courtyard. "Are you all right?"

"Better now," she admitted, taking deep breaths in the fresh air. She was out of her depth, she thought, in such company; give her an army and a sword in her hand any day!

He pulled her arm through his as they walked, and looked down at her dress curiously. "I suppose you do not ordinarily go around dressed like that? What is your normal attire?"

"Padded tunic and leggings, and a coat of mail on most occasions," she admitted.

He laughed. "I cannot imagine you dressed so – you are such a lady."

She smiled wryly. How strange, when she felt anything but.

The oak door opened and shut again, and she cast a quick glance over her shoulder. She saw a glimpse of red tunic as someone slid behind a tree, and knew it was Peritus. He would shadow them quietly, and she felt comforted by his presence.

The covered walkway from the courtyard towards the gardens was relatively free from the misty rain that continued to fall, and she enjoyed the freshness of the sea air as they walked slowly along. Teague didn't release her hand, and Beata didn't ask for it back, content to continue the pleasant atmosphere while it lasted, hoping it would make him congenial to her demands.

Eventually, they came to the gardens, and he led her along the narrow walkways meandering through the herbs and flowers which filled the air with an intoxicating aroma. At the end of the gardens, a sheltered viewing platform with a long bench looked across the city, a pearl that nestled in the oyster shell of the bay. Through the rain, she could see the lights that glowed from hundreds of houses and inns like fireflies, roads linking them in an intricate latticework of threads strung from one side of the bay to the other.

In spite of the beauty of the scene, however, to the east the waves tumbled and turned on the long line of the shore, like great grey creatures rolling onto the sand. The thought made her shiver as the memory of the Darkwater Lords rising from the channel in the Curia filled her head.

"Are you cold?" Teague asked, offering her his coat.

"No," she said truthfully. But she appreciated his gesture. "Why do you not live with your own people?"

He turned to look at her, the circles of his eyes like gold torches in the night. He shrugged. "In Komis I am just ordinary. In the Twelve Lands, I am a curiosity. I like that."

She smiled. "I know that is not why you left."

He looked away. "No. But I would rather not talk about that."

"Okay. But can we talk about your gift?"

"I would rather not."

She sighed with frustration. "I do not understand your reluctance. It is such an amazing gift. I wish I could do it!"

He smiled. "Actually, I believe anyone can; it is just a matter of knowing how."

"That is what Silva says; she tried to get us all to grow this daisy before we left for the Quests, but I could not manage anything."

"But it is so easy," he protested.

"Show me," she asked breathlessly.

For a moment, she thought he would refuse. His eyes dropped to the ground. But then he leaned forward and picked up a seed lying on the path. He lifted his hand, palm upward, and held it out towards her, the seed in the middle. He closed his eyes. She watched the seed, holding her breath, feeling a jolt inside her as it sprouted green shoots and swiftly grew into a seedling, then a plant, and finally flowered into a beautiful yellow bloom, which he handed to her with a smile.

"How do you do it?" she asked wondrously, turning the flower around in her hands.

"Our energy and Anguis's is the same," he shrugged. "I cannot explain it. It is just a natural thing to me. Anyway," – he made a flicking movement with his hand – "I am bored with talking about myself. Tell me about Heartwood."

"What do you want to know?"

"I know nearly nothing about it. What it is like?"

So for a while, she talked about Heartwood and her life as a Militis. She talked enthusiastically, and it was only when she saw him smiling that she realised she must have been talking too long. "I am sorry," she said, "I have said too much."

"Not at all. I am just so impressed with your passion. You make it sound very attractive."

"Are you tempted?" she teased.

"Not in the least," he said vehemently. "I do not think I could be celibate all my life."

She shrugged. "I am so busy, there is little time to think about copulating."

He grinned. "That very description shows how little you know about it. You make it sound so bland and functional."

"Sex is required for the making of children, is it not? That seems pretty functional to me." She knew she was goading him but could not help herself.

He just smiled, his gold eyes studying her. "You are so beautiful. I cannot believe you remove yourself from this world. It is a sin to deny us all your beauty."

She laughed. "Now I know you are teasing me."

His smile gradually faded and his hand came up to touch her face gently. "You really do not know how beautiful you are, do you?" he whispered.

"I..." She was suddenly speechless.

Teague's face was not far from hers, and those golden eyes were like magnets, so attractive she could not move her own gaze away. He leaned even closer, and suddenly, more than anything, she wanted to feel his lips on hers. He hesitated for a second, just millimetres away from touching her, and before she could think twice about it, she moved the final distance and they were kissing.

It was the first time she had ever kissed anyone, and Beata's face flamed and her heart thudded. The world spun, and she didn't know if it was from the kiss or the ale or whether there was an earthquake.

She melted into his embrace and did not protest when he lowered her gently onto the seat so she was underneath him. There was a small part of her that knew she would probably regret this in the morning, and which counselled her to stop now before she went any further, but there was a greater part of her that was curious about love, and its voice was so strong it drowned out the rest.

He unlaced her dress and began to kiss her skin, and all thoughts went out of her mind. She forgot about Heartwood, forgot about Peritus hiding somewhere in the gardens, forgot about her vows.

The only thing in the world was Teague and his soft lips and tongue, and as his kiss traced down over her stomach, and then lower, she even forgot about breathing.

He made love to her slowly, thoughtfully, blissfully, and afterwards Beata fell asleep in his arms, content and without a care in the world.

When she awoke, some hours later, it was completely dark, the only light from the small lantern they had brought to guide their way, the candle burned almost to the base. She pushed herself to a sitting position awkwardly. She was stiff, cold and sore and had a throbbing headache. Instantly, the memory of what she had done rang in her head like a bell and she groaned. She was still in the garden, lying on the seat, but she was alone. Teague had gone.

As she got to her feet, a spark of anger flared in her chest at the realisation her lover had abandoned her. What on Anguis had possessed her to give herself to a complete stranger, and such an important one at that? She should have known she couldn't trust him!

He had left his cloak, however. She wrapped it around her and began to walk slowly back through the gardens. Why on earth hadn't he woken her? Clearly, he had used the opportunity to sleep with her as a ruse, maybe to show her he wasn't to be told what to do, and to give him the opportunity to get away while she slept.

What was she going to say to him when she got back to the castle? Well, she was certainly going to give him a piece of her mind. If he was still there. She went cold at the thought that he might have fled the town to get away from her. Obviously, he was not to be trusted; he enjoyed his freedom and his lifestyle and had made it plain he wanted nothing to do with her Quest. How could she have been so stupid?

And then she saw the figure lying face down on the ground in the flowerbeds. Beata gasped. She recognised instantly by his clothing it was Peritus. She ran up to him and, gathering him in her arms, turned him over. Immediately, she could see he was dead. His eyes were open, unseeing, and there was a deep knife wound in his chest. His tunic was soaked in blood.

How had Teague – a musician and magician with no fighting skills whatsoever – managed to best a Heartwood Militis? He must have taken Peritus by surprise, she realised numbly. The knight must have stayed in the gardens, close but far enough away to give them some privacy, expecting a threat to come from the castle, not from behind him. She wondered if he had managed to wound Teague and, before she could stop, felt a stab of hope that her lover had escaped unharmed. Then guilt washed over her, and with it came a large measure of anger.

Her lover had taken her, and then abandoned her, in the process killing the last colleague and friend she had with her. With her foolish act, she had done what every knight was taught not to do – surrender to her emotions, and with that act, she had sacrificed the last chance to mend the Arbor. Heartwood was lost.

Horrified, broken, Beata sat there with Peritus in her arms and wept.

II

Grimbeald hunched himself into his blankets, huddling beneath the makeshift tent the Militis had erected to keep off the worst of the rain. He had refused to stay underground in the Tumulus, finding it too unsettling after the event of the night before, when the ghost of his father had appeared on the top of the mound.

Now he looked over at Tenera, and found her eyes on him, the deep blue orbs warm, a hint of a smile hiding with them. She had not been as frightened as he on seeing the figure on the Tumulus. In fact, she had comforted him when – startled as a deer – he had fled the mound, shaken to his core at seeing the apparition.

He gave her a half-hearted smile and turned over, somewhat unnerved by her steady gaze. Unfortunately, however, it meant he was facing the Tumulus, and his stomach clenched as he saw through the gap in the tent the shadow of the mound rising before him.

Why was he so afraid? Grimbeald could not understand his fear. He was not a coward, and in spite of the fact that he did not consider himself a natural warrior, he had proven himself fearless in battle, and did not dread handling a sword. Just one glimpse of that ephemeral figure, however, outlined against the darkness on the top of the mound, struck terror into his heart.

His eyes wandered to where the figure had appeared and his breath froze in his throat as, in the midst of the gloom, a dark shape materialised. His heart seemed to stop. It was his father; he knew it, even though he could not see its face or its dress clearly. But something inside him just knew it was him.

Grimbeald gritted his teeth, fighting the urge to flee. It was ridiculous! He was a grown man, and his father had been in the earth these past ten years. Maegenheard, the once-lord of the Highlands, no longer had a hold over him; he was lord in his own right, and no longer subject to the whims and wishes of his father.

But as the thought entered his head, he knew it was untrue. Even now, from the grave, Maegenheard still had control over him, like an animal that has clamped its jaws around a victim and refuses to let go, even after death.

Anger rose within him like a tide, sweeping through his veins. He wanted to be free of his father's unyielding grip. Turning, he looked over his shoulder at Tenera. Her eyes had finally shut, and she seemed to be sleeping. Quietly, with a warrior's stealth, he pushed back his cover and got to his feet.

He ducked under the tent flap and went out into the cool night. The rain fell lightly, fresh on his face. He looked up at the ghostly figure. It stood arms akimbo, and although he couldn't see its face, he felt it was glaring at him. He tightened his grip on his axe, even though the metal blade would be useless against the insubstantial spirit. Still, he felt comforted by the feel of the wooden shaft in his hand, its weight almost a part of him.

Carrying a lantern in his left hand, he stepped forward, walking towards the Tumulus. His heart pounded in his chest and his mouth was dry, but he walked forwards. Some small part of him knew the only way to rid himself of the spectre that haunted him was to confront it, even though to do so caused his insides to melt with terror.

As he neared the mound, however, the figure disappeared. Grimbeald stopped, breathing heavily. He looked to the right, to the entrance of the mound. The figure now stood there, flickering in the dim light from his lantern as if it were a candle guttering in the wind. It seemed to want him to go down into the mound. Grimbeald shivered, his feet frozen to the spot. He did not want to go into the Tumulus again. The thought of all those bones... He shuddered. But still, he knew he had to go. The figure drew him there as surely as if it had called out his name.

He walked forwards to the entrance. As he drew nearer, the figure disappeared again. Grimbeald paused at the doorway. Rectangular in shape, supported by huge wooden beams that held up the weight of the earth mound atop it, the doorway led down several steps to the sunken burial chamber. He paused on the top step, feeling as if he were about to descend into the belly of some giant beast. The wind soughed through the Tumulus, and for a moment it seemed as if the mound groaned – or was it himself? His palms were clammy, his hair damp with sweat and rain.

Taking a deep breath, he stepped down into the burial chamber.

Immediately, his lantern went out, whether from a rush of air or something more sinister, he couldn't tell. He stopped on the bottom step, his heart hammering. His brain screamed at him to turn and run, but with iron willpower he kept his feet still, drawing from his inner depths of courage, waiting for whatever was in there to make itself known.

Gradually, he became aware the room was lightening.

Eventually, he saw the light was emanating from a small sphere that seemed to hover above the floor of the chamber. It must have been something similar to this that Tenera had seen above him, which had brought him back to life. He gasped, entranced by the glowing object. What was it, he wondered? Was it the Node?

The light illuminated the white bones lying on the shelves, and it was only as his eyes were drawn to them that he saw the figure standing to one side of the room. He could not help but give a small exclamation, which he stifled swiftly as he brought his axe up protectively across his chest.

"That will not do you much good down here," sneered the figure, coming forward into the light. "Not that it ever did you much good on the battlefield, either."

Grimbeald's hands tightened on the wooden shaft as the face of his father loomed in the light. "Is that all you are here for?" he returned. "To mock me from beyond the grave?"

Maegenheard shrugged. "No. It is an added bonus."

Grimbeald clenched his jaw, the familiar flush of hurt rising within him. He said nothing, however. Clearly, this was some sort of test, and he wanted to see how the game was played before he reacted. "What do you want?" he asked, watching the ghostly figure walk around the glowing light to stand a few feet in front of him. Maegenheard's form was almost transparent, and he could see through his body to the shelves and bones behind him.

"For ten years I have watched you sit in my seat, in the Highlands," said Maegenheard. "I have observed you as you carried out your lordly duties, hoping beyond hope you would show yourself to be the son I had always prayed you would be. But time and again, you have failed me. And now I use the power from this ancient site to manifest and to beg you to remove yourself from the land, so a better Highlander may take your place."

Grimbeald digested this news with an ache in his gut. He had hoped his father's appearance was a test, part of the process of opening the Node, but his heart began to sink as he realised that was not the case. Clearly, the energy in the Tumulus allowed Maegenheard to materialise, and he had merely seized the opportunity to do so. It was no test, no answer to his problems. It was just his father being his usual angry self, trying to control everything he said and did.

"I have done my best to be lord of our people," Grimbeald said quietly, the axe lowering in his hand until it touched the floor. "I have tried to be just and fair, and treat all folk the same..."

"That is not the true measure of a lord!" snarled Maegenheard. "A lord governs by being harsh and firm with his decisions, by being aggressive, not defensive. How much have you expanded your lands? How many towns have fallen beneath your axe?"

"We are at war with Laxony," argued Grimbeald, "not with each other. Wulfengar's five lands should live in harmony."

"Harmony!" Maegenheard gave a booming laugh. "That is not the Wulfian way, my lad."

"No, but it is my way," Grimbeald said miserably. His axe fell to the floor.

"That is true, and how I regret your weak stomach. I knew from your early years you were doomed to be a failure as a warrior."

"That is not fair," Grimbeald protested. "I have fought in many battles; I am a skilled knight."

"You have the heart of a dove, boy; you are a foolish romantic. You dream of peace and accord between the lands. Bah! You cannot change Wulfian minds. Just because you have a diseased brain does not mean it has to spread to the rest of our kind."

Grimbeald bowed his head. He felt strangely weak and heavy, as if his father were draining strength from him. The light in the middle of the chamber seemed to be growing dim, emphasising the darkness he felt spreading through him. "I have never pleased you. I have tried and tried to be a different person, but I do not think I could ever be the sort of knight you wanted me to be, however much I trained for battle."

"Your weakness grows within you like mistletoe in an apple tree," said his father. "It has invaded all parts of you, and has wrapped tendrils around your heart. You are a failure as a lord and a failure as a Wulfian."

"I do not know how to be different," Grimbeald said, and a hot tear coursed down his cheek. How he longed for his father's approval. Just one smile, one word of encouragement. But it had never been that way, and certainly never would be now.

"You can still change," Maegenheard urged. He came forward and his ghostly hands gripped Grimbeald's arms. "Put aside your foolish, romantic thoughts; your paintings and music; your singing and carving. Your dreams of peace. Turn instead to the true Wulfian path: battle, war, blood and pain. Turn the Highlands into the force it should be. Raise your army. Reconquer the five lands."

Could he? Was it not too late? Hope surged within him. Could he still lay his ghosts to rest by changing his ways? Perhaps it was true, and he could obtain the heart of a wolf instead of a dove. Put aside his hopes, his dreams for a peaceful future for his land. "But what about Heartwood?" he asked suddenly, remembering his reason for travelling to the Tumulus.

"Heartwood?" Maegenheard spat invisible mucus onto the floor. "Those preening knights and their fancy tree? Who needs them? Who needs religion and prayers and speeches of 'energy' and 'Nodes' and 'saving the world'? The Highlands are all that matter. Leave all that behind you, son, and turn to the true Wulfian way."

And with that Maegenheard smiled at his son; the first smile Grimbeald could ever remember him giving that was directed at himself. And it made him so warm inside that suddenly he knew he would do as his father said: forget Heartwood, forget his Quest. It was time he became the son his father had always wanted.

••••

III

Beata sat on the grass by Peritus's grave. He had been buried that afternoon, and the earth was still loose, covering his wooden coffin in a small mound.

The funeral had been brief, attended only by herself and the two servants who had dug the grave, and they had soon left her to her grief, though they puzzled at the depth of her emotion and the amount of tears she had let fall for a mere serf.

She had been allowed to bury him under an oak tree in the cemetery just outside the castle grounds, and for this she had been grateful, distraught as she was that she could not take him back to Heartwood to give him to the Arbor. It would be a peaceful resting place, she thought, looking across the cliffs to the sea beyond, and eventually he would be absorbed by the oak and thus by Anguis, thought she knew it would take longer for him to become one with the earth than it would have done at Heartwood.

Under the relatively dry shelter of the tree, Beata's final energy reserves drained out of her, and she lay down on the grass, her head on her arm, her misery sliding from her like an animal that had been coiled around her body. Never had she felt this low, not even when Caelestis died. And she knew she had to be honest with herself. It was not just the fact that Peritus had been killed that was causing her such misery. True, he was a childhood friend and a good companion, and she would mourn his passing for a long time. But it was more than that.

The whole journey had been a disaster, right from the moment Erubesco had taken the arrow in the forest. She should have done as Fortis said, turned around then and gone straight back to Heartwood, and given her Quest to someone who would have done it right. But what had she done? Lost all her companions, who had trusted her to lead them and keep them safe. And not only that – and here her breath caught in her throat and her heart almost stopped – she had lost the Virimage, the one possible saviour of the Arbor, because she had been lonely and flattered by his compliments, and curious to know about the sexual act. She thought of the way Teague had touched her, his fingers soft, his lips gentle, and cried, aching for him in spite of what he had done, and hating herself for it.

Several times, she tried to wrench herself up from this pool of misery, but each time she felt herself sucked back down, as if she stood in quicksand. She tried to persuade herself that Peritus would forgive her, that he would have understood her feelings for Teague, and that he was enough of a friend to realise she would never have wished him harm in a million years. But deep down, she knew her actions had been unforgivable, and she had surrendered to her emotions without taking the care that should have been second nature to a knight. In doing so, she had sacrificed him – and who would forgive a friend for that?

She attempted to think of Valens's face, and hoped he would understand why she had made the decisions she had; he was fair and just and would not blame her for the way things had turned out. But she was fooling herself; Valens would be bitterly disappointed with the turn of events.

She tried to convince herself Teague's actions towards her meant his heart was black, and therefore he would not have been able to heal the Arbor. For how could such an evil person heal the most precious thing in the universe? But then she thought of the way the yellow flowers had grown on her palm, and she knew in spite of what he had done, this was not the case, and he would almost certainly have been able to do something to help the tree, even if it was against his will.

She had lost the Arbor's only hope; because of her, Heartwood and eventually the rest of Anguis would fall to the Darkwater Lords. The water elementals' reign would be supreme. Everything would crumble, everything would fall to ruin, and it was all her fault.

Lost in despair, as unable to see the way out as if she were in the depths of a dark forest, Beata wept.

It was some time before she realised something was happening around her. She wasn't sure what first alerted her to the fact that the tree was moving; maybe it was the sound of the roots crawling through the grass, or maybe it was a movement out of the corner of her eye, but she wiped away her tears to find the roots snaking towards her slowly, and she gasped, not having seen this done by any other tree except the Arbor.

Was it malevolent? Instinctively, she drew up her legs to escape the thick tendrils. The roots stopped as she withdrew, and above her the tree shook gently, as if rustled by the wind, although there was no breeze. Beata's heart thudded. Part of her wanted to flee, but another part of her, perhaps the child within, remembered the gentle caress of the Arbor, the thing she loved more than anything in the world, and the slow heartbeat beneath its trunk. As a seven year-old, when she had felt lonely and was missing her parents and home, she had crept to the tree in the dark and put her arms around it; its warmth had never failed to comfort her. Something told her to trust this oak. Slowly, she straightened her legs. Just as slowly, the roots moved towards her.

The soft tendrils crept gradually up her legs and over her body. Her breathing quick, she lay on the grass and let the roots slide over her torso and then up, into her hair. The feel of the soft, fibrous plant against her skin was both repulsive and strangely seductive, and she shuddered, although whether from disgust or desire she could not tell.

The roots tightened their grip, and eventually she felt as if she had been tied to the floor by chains. She couldn't have moved, even if she had wanted to. But strangely, she found she didn't want to. As if they contained some kind of narcotic, sleep quickly came upon her, and her eyelids descended like curtains at the end of an act.

And as she slept, she dreamed.

There were six figures on horseback, riding through the Dorle countryside. It was as if she rode, too, beside them, and when she looked across to the right she could see the Henge in the distance, rising up on top of a hill, a dark shadow through the misty rain. Briefly, she thought of Gravis and his Quest, and wondered how he was faring and whether he had been able to activate the Node. But then her attention was drawn to the companions she rode with.

She looked back at the figures and saw in shock that one of them was Teague. He wore a cloak, the hood pulled low over his face, but it was definitely him. She glanced around at the other riders and saw with surprise they, too, were Komis, distinguishable by their jet-black hair, their swarthy skins and their strange gold eyes. So, he was with his countrymen, she thought, and judging by the direction they were travelling, they were headed for Komis.

She gave a little start, and opened her eyes.

She was still lying on the floor beside Peritus's grave, and the tendrils were still covering her body, but they were now slowly pulling away, and she watched open-mouthed as the tree withdrew until its roots were once again just hard ridges, firm in the earth.

Was it the Arbor, she thought breathlessly, wondering if the tree had somehow managed to reach out to her across the lands, to give her the vision? Perhaps it was, perhaps it wasn't. Whatever the cause, the point was that *something* had given her the vision, and that meant *something* wanted her to know where Teague was heading.

She looked down at Peritus's grave, at the little wooden plaque pushed into the ground at the head of the mound, with just his name on it. Reaching into her tunic, she took out the oak leaf pendant hanging on a chain around her neck and pulled it over her head, leaning across the grave to hang it on the corner of the plaque. Perhaps it had been Peritus who had given his last energy to help her.

Whatever, or whoever, had helped her, the fact was that the Virimage was still alive and on his way back to Komis. Teague, who had taken her without a second thought, then killed her friend before abandoning her. He could still help the Arbor recover, she thought, even if he were forced. If she could find him, she could make him come back with her to Heartwood, and then let Valens deal with him as he saw fit.

She had been given one more chance to save the world, and she could not pass on it.

Beata pushed herself to her feet. She stretched her arms above her head, feeling the branches of the oak tree tickle her fingers. She smiled. It was time to let the knight back out, she thought with some amusement, looking down at her soft tunic and smiling wryly. Tearing it from her body, she stood there naked for a moment, feeling the gentle rain wash away the misery and hopelessness that had threatened to drown her barely an hour ago.

Then she turned to the horse that had been waiting patiently, tethered to the tree, and pulled her breeches and padded tunic out of her saddlebag and dressed swiftly. It was not an easy job, dressing herself with the heavy mail, but she did it eventually, welcoming the weight of the metal rings on her shoulders. Taking pins from another bag, she twisted her hair into a tight knot at the base of her neck and secured it firmly.

The lady had gone, probably forever, she thought, with not an ounce of regret. The knight was back. She looked down for the last time at Peritus's grave. *Rest easily, my friend*, she thought. *I will avenge you, and in doing so, I will save Anguis from her foes.*

Turning, she mounted the horse nimbly and guided it onto the track leading south-west across the hills without a backwards glance.

IV

The Darkwater Quest party arrived at Vichton in the late afternoon. At the head of the party, Chonrad led the way along the main road shadowing the Wall the whole way across Laxony, and through the large city gates into the city proper. It had been a long and difficult journey and, in spite of his tiredness, his heart swelled at the thought of being home.

Vichton was a large city but well-fortified and protected, and he had the advantage of knowing the guards manning the city wall were well-trained, as he personally oversaw his army's training whenever he had the chance. For the first time since leaving Heartwood, he relaxed.

He had been shocked at the state of Isenbard's Wall and its forts on their journey. In the short time he had travelled to Heartwood, the Wall had noticeably missed the departure of the Exercitus, and despite a physical presence by countrymen of both Hannon and Barle, the Wulfian raiders had clearly observed the Wall's weakened state, and were taking the opportunity to carry out deeper and more devastating raids. All of the party had been aghast at the devastation wrought to the town of Setbourg, which had seen many of its buildings burned to the ground, and shortly before their arrival, a large raid had seen many of the women raped and the men killed. Chonrad was pleased to see that Esberg, in his homeland, had fared better; with a city wall manned by trained guards, it had managed to keep out the raiders, but the guards had told him of the repeated and increasingly violent raids, and it was clear matters were escalating.

However, there was little he could do for the moment; things were only going to get a lot worse if the Darkwater Lords were successful in their invasion attempts, so he just tried to reassure them and tell them he had a plan in mind and was working on it at that very moment.

In Vichton, however, things seemed little changed. His Chief of the Guard assured him raids had been few and far between, and even the sea traffic had remained steady, with few coastal raids. The city certainly seemed as bustling and alive as ever. As they wound their way through the streets to the castle on the cliffs, he stopped occasionally to talk to the shopkeepers and traders, who greeted him with pleasure, keen to speak to their lord, and clearly fond of him. Procella looked over at him several times, whether amused or puzzled at his popularity, he couldn't tell, but he didn't return her glance; his people were his first priority, and he had to satisfy himself they were relaxed and happy before he finally went home.

They found themselves at the castle gates and he led the party through, dismounting in the courtyard and letting the stablehands take the horses off to be rubbed down and fed. He had just lifted his bags down from the packhorse when there were screams of "Father, Father" from the castle, and then two figures came flying down the steps, running up to leap into his arms to cover his face with kisses.

"Careful," he laughed, picking them both up easily and squeezing them tightly, "you nearly knocked me over."

"We have missed you," said Rosamunda, burying her head in his neck.

"Have you been fighting?" said Varin, pushing himself away from his father and brandishing a wooden sword. "I have been practicing, Father, look!" and he leapt about, swinging the sword around him fiercely.

"Careful, young man, you nearly had my head off with that." Procella smiled, clearly touched by the children's affection for their father.

Chonrad came over, pleased she seemed to like them. "Rosamunda, Varin... This is Procella," he said, bringing them over to her. "She is Dux of the Exercitus. The leader of Heartwood's army."

Their little mouths fell open. Varin, eyes wide, said: "You must be so brave and strong."

Procella tipped her head, her cheeks pinkening a little. "Not as much as your father," she told them. "He fights like a great bear."

"My father is the best," said Rosamunda defensively, but her eyes watched Procella eagerly, and she was clearly impressed.

Chonrad raised an eyebrow at the Dux as he led her up the steps to his Great Hall. "A bear?" he asked dubiously. "I am not sure if that is a compliment or not."

"I just meant you like honey and have big hands," she said mischievously.

Chonrad laughed and swung open the doors to the Hall. "Come in," he said. "For one night, at least, we shall eat like kings."

One of his men had ridden on ahead while Chonrad stopped briefly in Esberg, and thus the household were prepared for their visitors and had laid on a splendid spread. The party were taken first to the baths, of which Chonrad was most proud: huge stone sunken baths with underfloor heating, and they all stripped and sank into the hot water with a sigh, feeling the aches of the journey gradually melt away.

After this, they dressed in fresh clothes and had dinner in the Hall. He watched his servants bring in the food with satisfaction – his staff had done him proud. Huge plates of cut meats and various types of fish, loaves of fresh bread, bowls of stew full of crisp, fresh vegetables, and plenty of flagons of ale to wash it all down. Though food was scarce, still his pride made him want to look like a good host.

The party ate hungrily, complimenting him on the spread. Chonrad made a mental note to go down to the kitchens later and thank the staff. He looked up to see Procella watching him, smiling. "What?" he asked, pulling a face.

"You are proud of your home," she said, "and rightly so."

"I am surprised you have not been here more," he said.

"I tend to stay away from the towns. Too many distractions for the knights. We stay on the Wall road, and in the forts." She smiled. "It is my loss."

Pleased she liked his home, he came to sit beside her, pulling his seat closer to the fire that danced in the central grate. "How do you feel about our journey tomorrow?" he asked. Nitesco had suggested they get started at first light.

Procella shrugged. "What will be, will be, regardless of my feelings towards it."

He smiled. "Very neatly sidestepped."

She sighed. "Truly? I cannot imagine it is going to work. I saw with my own eyes the Darkwater Lords rising from the river, but still I cannot believe I, myself, can be turned into a water elemental."

"I know what you mean," he said, opening his arms with a smile as his children came towards him for a cuddle before going to bed. He placed a kiss on one head and then another, giving them a squeeze before they retired. "Sleep well," he called after them as their nurse led them up the steps to the bedchambers at the far end of the Hall.

"They are beautiful children," Procella commented. "Clearly, they do not take after you."

He laughed. "No, obviously they look like their mother."

Procella turned her tankard in her hands, looking into the depths of the ale. "Do you miss her?"

"Minna?" Chonrad thought of his dead wife and sipped his own drink. "Would I be a cruel man if I said no?" Procella just raised an eyebrow. He sighed. "She was the daughter of a local magnate. It was a good match. She gave me two healthy children before she died. We... tolerated each other. I think I was more upset because I was not more upset when she died, if you understand me."

Procella gave a wry smile. "I think so." She sipped her ale. "I do not understand, though, her lack of enthusiasm towards you. If I were not a Militis, I would have been grateful for such a match."

Chonrad met her gaze directly and smiled. "Why, thank you."

"You are welcome." Her dark brown eyes were very warm. Once again, he felt a surge of desire towards her. She was strong, fierce and striking, and he wondered how her body would feel pressed against his own without the hindrance of armour.

Of course he had seen her without her clothes in the baths, but bathing was such a natural, unsexual thing for all of them that he had done little more than glance at her body to note it was as firm and slim as he had thought it would be. Now, however, he pictured her in his arms, and he realised he wanted her very much.

His desire must have shown in his eyes, because her pupils widened. She hesitated, and he told himself not to expect anything; she was Dux, for Animus's sake, and not likely to jeopardise her position and her place in the Militis for a quick roll in the hay. Neither would he want her to hate him in the morning. However, the next day was a monumental one for both of them – they were about to risk their lives in an act that may well see them die on the spot, and this quite possibly could be their last chance, as clichéd as the fact might be.

Suddenly she stood, and said, "Come, Chonrad. Let us not spend our last night alone."

He looked around the room, surprised at her directness. But the children were abed, the Militis were either asleep or talking quietly by the fire, and none of them even looked up as he took her hand and led her along the Hall to the bedchambers. Only Fulco caught his eye where he lay by the fire, his wife wrapped in his arms, and the knight's lazy wink was enough to tell him that his bodyguard knew perfectly well where they were going.

Chonrad took her up to his bedchamber, wondering as he did so if she would think about the fact that this may be the place where he had bedded Minna, but she said nothing as she entered the room, and he sensed she was past worrying about what had been, and past considering her future. It was comfort that she wanted most of all, and Chonrad could not bring himself to refuse her, as he wanted her more than anything.

She unbuckled her sword and laid it carefully on the top of the oak coffer by the wall. She looked down at it for a moment, and he had the feeling she was mentally leaving her Militis status there too, removing the vows, laying down the restraint and the denial she had carried for so long.

She turned and walked over to him slowly, then reached out and took his hands in her own. Her thumbs rubbed the centre of his palms and she stepped even closer, until her mailed chest met his with a soft clink of metal on metal.

She was tall for a woman, but still several inches shorter than he, and she had to tip up her head to look into his eyes. Her own were dark with passion, and her lips parted a little as she read the desire in his gaze.

Slowly, afraid she might bolt, Chonrad lowered his head. Their lips met gently.

He kissed her softly, then, as he realised she was not going to pull away, more passionately, and his hands rose to cradle her head and the small of her back, his heart thudding against his ribs as she pressed herself against him.

"Help me out of this," she breathed, gesturing to her armour. He lifted the mail shirt over her head, trying not to catch her hair with the links. When she was free, she stretched luxuriously, enjoying the freedom of being without its weight. He watched her remove her leather tunic, and then she stood before him in her linen shift. She released her hair from its tight knot at the nape of her head, and he smiled as she spread the dark brown locks across her shoulders. She looked suddenly much younger and uncertain, and he reminded himself she had not had many – if any – lovers before.

"Your turn to help me," he said, and she took hold of his mail shirt and helped him struggle out of it, laughing as it snagged on his hair. When he was free, he caught her up in his arms, promising she would pay for laughing at him, and began to cover her face and neck with kisses. The play soon turned serious as she began to sigh with pleasure, and it was not long before they removed the rest of their clothes and found their way under the furs on the bed.

And then they made love, and it was as sweet, and as fierce, and as gentle as he had thought it would be. And afterwards she

lay in his arms, and together they dozed as the rain rattled the
shutters and the candle guttered in the midnight breeze.

When he awoke the next morning, the sky was just lightening,
and he turned over in the bed and sighed as he saw she had gone.
With a groan, he stood and dressed, wondering if she would
refuse to meet his eye when he saw her, but when he descended
to the Hall he found her with her knights at the table, and when
he passed her, she gave him a smile and squeezed his hand, and
his heart gladdened that she did not regret what they had done.

The atmosphere was generally subdued, however, and
his memories of the night before began to be blanketed by a
deepening fear of what lay ahead. Within the hour, they were
gathered in the courtyard and, mounting their horses, they made
their way out of the castle and down the coast road to the beaches
beyond. None of them spoke as they rode. Procella was quiet,
and although she smiled at him once or twice, she did not speak
to him, and he continued to wonder whether she was regretting
her act. No matter now, he thought, somewhat bitterly. Life as
they knew it was about to cease.

He had said goodbye to his children in the castle and found
it difficult to think soon he might be dead. Of course, he faced
death whenever he was in battle, but he had grown used to that
foe, who he thought of as a large animal, bristled and growling,
but real and physical and something that, with training, he could
learn to avoid. Now, however, death had become insidious, like a
snake or an insect that slipped into your clothing and, in spite of
its size, brought an end to your life with a simple bite or sting. He
could do nothing to avoid the consequences of what was about to
happen, and that did not sit lightly on his shoulders.

V

Gavius was in a world of light and shadows. He lay down, his
body suspended by some unseen hand, light as a leaf caught on

an Awakening breeze. He was quite happy to be there, and felt no panic or distress, even though he couldn't put his finger on exactly where he was. Gradually, however, he became aware he wasn't floating in air; he was in water. He was deep in a pool of thick, dark water, and above him a hand was reaching in, trying to pull him to the surface. He fought the hand, but it would not let go, and gradually he got nearer and nearer to the light...

He opened his eyes with a gasp. He was not in water, he realised, but merely unconscious, and the hand that had been trying to bring him back to consciousness belonged to the Komis leader, Aukaneck.

"You shall not sleep!" Aukaneck snarled, slapping him sharply on the cheek. Gavius's head snapped back, then fell forward, his muscles too tired to hold him upright. Through his beaten, pulpy face he looked at his body, but could not make out any skin – he was too covered in blood. He felt as if he were on fire. The many cuts Aukaneck had made on his skin stung as his sweat dripped into them.

One of the Komis raised Gavius's chin with his hand and poured water over his face. Gavius gasped, taking in some of the water and swallowing it thankfully, spluttering a little and trying to turn his head to let the liquid clear his face, which he could feel was also covered in blood.

When he was done, he looked across at the figure slumped on the ground opposite him. Thankfully, Brevis was dead, although his screams still rang in Gavius's ears, like a bell whose echo goes on long after it has been struck. Having no luck with torturing Gavius, Aukaneck had turned to Brevis. Although the knight had no idea where the secret entrance to Heartwood was, Aukaneck hoped the torture of his friend would lead Gavius to reveal its whereabouts.

The Komis leader had not counted on the knights' loyalty to Heartwood, however. Greater even than their loyalty to each other – which was very strong – their need to defend the Temple and the tree it guarded inside it was overwhelming, and though it nearly killed him in the process, Gavius said nothing as Brevis was sliced and stuck like a pig, until eventually the shock killed him.

To his surprise, they had not brought in Niveus. Surely she would have been a more obvious candidate to get him to talk? The Komis would have thought this anyway; women had particularly low standing in their society and men saw it as their role to protect them. Such was not the case in Heartwood; there men and women were treated equally and he would not have thought to give a woman preferential treatment. He could just imagine Procella's face if he had suggested he carry something for her! The thought made him smile, in spite of his cracked lips.

Aukaneck saw the smile and snarled, bringing the back of his hand across Gavius's face with a crack. "Do you find something funny?" he snapped.

Gavius said nothing, but hung his head and watched the blood drop down onto the floor. His thoughts, however, were on Niveus. Why hadn't they brought her to him? Had they already killed her? Surely if that was the case, they would have taunted him with her death? Aukaneck certainly knew every trick there was and would not have turned down an opportunity to lower his confidence and spirits by telling him his last companion had died. Was it possible, therefore, she had managed to escape?

Hope surged within him like the wash caused on a river by a fast boat. Of course, it might be a ridiculous thought, and it was possible she was at that moment either dead or waiting outside to be brought in and tortured, but something in Gavius told him he was right.

He pondered on that as Aukaneck and the guards discussed something among themselves. His certainty that Niveus had escaped was not the only odd feeling he had had since he opened the Node. Something had happened to him there, something profound, he knew, that had changed him – and not just in a mental or emotional sense. He felt something within him had metamorphosed the way water changes to steam when heated. He was still the same person, but he *felt* different, and things were happening to him he could not explain. Only the day before, he had had a vision of a person with dark-hair and distinctive Komis eyes, but he had only realised it was not one of the Komis who had taken him hostage when, behind him, the distinct visage of Beata swam into view. Immediately, he realised this must be the Virimage Beata had been sent to find. Gavius froze, thinking, "Follow her!" But before he could say anything, the vision had faded and he was back in Brant.

Other things had occurred since then; he had had other visions, flashes of people and places, some of whom he knew, some he didn't, and he couldn't always make sense of them, as he had not been allowed to sleep and tiredness had made his brain fuzzy.

Now, he accepted he just *knew* for a fact that Niveus was free, and that cheered him more than anything else could do, except maybe being told he was free himself.

Which wasn't going to happen, he thought wryly as the Komis, who had been talking in lowered tones to each other, now broke up and walked menacingly towards him.

Aukaneck, the leader, his dark brown skin slick with sweat and his eyes harder than the metal they reflected, sat before him. Nodding to one of the guards, he waited as they untied Gavius's left hand and pulled it round towards their king. His arms had been tied so tightly that Gavius groaned as the blood rushed through it. Aukaneck smiled as the guard put the prisoner's hand on the table. The king brandished a pair of pliers.

"Now then, where were we?" he said, lowering the pliers until they gripped the edge of one of Gavius's fingernails.

Gavius closed his eyes. "Animus, protect me," he prayed.

Something touched his foot.

He looked down and saw a long, green vine curled around his boot. He had not noticed it before. His eyes followed the vine along the floor of the hut. It vanished into the darkness of the corner where he could not see. He blinked, trying to clear his eyes. The vine was moving. He looked down again to see it crawling up his leg, curling in a helix around his calf, then up his thigh. He shuddered and tried to kick it off, but he could not move.

He looked up at Aukaneck to see the king's attention focussed on his hand, and he was shocked to see one of his fingernails had already been extracted. He had not felt a thing. Blood flowed over his hand, but he could not relate the injury to his own body as he felt not a twinge of pain.

No longer trying to fight it, Gavius watched the vine crawl up him. It surrounded his midriff, curled around his shoulders and finally slid through his hair and over his head.

Feeling as if he was slipping into a dark chasm, he closed his eyes.

When he opened them again, he was standing before a pair of huge wooden doors. He recognised them instantly; he was in Heartwood, standing at the entrance to the Temple. Valens was there, talking to some of the Militis, the huge Imperator striking a commanding figure as he directed the knights where to strengthen the fortifications. Gavius looked around, his heart swelling at being back in the place he loved more than anywhere else in the world. Though it was still raining, the Temple seemed to shine in the darkness, like a beacon on a rocky coast, radiating warmth and light and keeping everyone safe.

Nobody reacted to his appearance, and Gavius guessed they could not see him. He was there in spirit, not in body, as insubstantial as the breeze blowing across the Baillium. Did that mean his body was still in Brant? He suspected so, remembering his hand covered in blood but pain-free. Something had called him out of his body, and for the moment, he wasn't unhappy with that.

He walked up to the oak doors, wondering how to open them if he had no form, but as he approached them they swung open silently, and so he walked forwards into the Temple.

He waited for a moment to let his eyes adjust to the darkness. Gradually, the interior of the Temple became clear. The rows of seating had been removed so the outer circle was bare, presumably in preparation for a possible invasion. He walked forwards slowly, past the occasional Militis, over the bridge crossing the river channel, and then across the Sepulchrum and into the inner circle.

The Arbor stood before him, and Gavius walked up and ducked to stand under its branches. He could see the enormous cleft in its trunk where the Darkwater Lords had opened it up to steal its Pectoris. The tree was, quite clearly, dying. Its branches drooped so much they draped on the floor, and to his shock most of the leaves had already fallen, the last few hanging brown and curled on the twigs, ready to drop at any moment. Still, the tree rustled as he neared, and he caught his breath. Was the Arbor aware of his presence?

He walked up to the trunk and, putting his arms around it, pressed his cheek to the bark. The tree felt solid, rough beneath his skin. If he was spirit, he thought, then so was the Arbor. Beneath the bark, he could still feel a slow but steady pulse, in spite of the fact that its heart had gone. It was not yet dead, he consoled himself. It wasn't far off, clearly, but it wasn't yet completely gone.

The branches and twigs rustled above his head and touched his hair. He remembered the way the energy had surged through him on the Green Giant, and how he had felt when the Node finally opened. That had been the Arbor, he realised now – Animus reaching out to him through the beloved tree. They were all one and the same: one energy, complete and connected, whole even when they were apart.

Understanding now, he closed his eyes. Summoning his strength, he sent a surge of energy, a bolt of his love, through the tree and down its roots into Anguis, to all the Quest leaders. In his mind's eye he saw them all; Fionnghuala, lonely and forlorn by the Portal; Grimbeald, lost in the Tumulus; Beata, heartbroken but determined to hunt down the Virimage; Procella and Chonrad, frightened in spite of their warriors' hearts. To them all he sent his love and his courage, which he didn't need any more, his final gift to them all.

And finally he saw Gravis, his twin brother, the person he knew better than anyone else in the world, seated in the middle of the Henge, swirled in a thick mist, which Gavius in his spiritual state could sense was both physical and emotional. He moved forward until it was as if he stood before his twin, and he looked down and between them he could see a thin silvery line, like a cord binding them both together. And suddenly, he understood.

He closed his eyes, the realisation of what he had done to Gravis more painful than the torture his physical body was undergoing. *I am sorry*, he whispered, bending down to look straight into Gravis's face. *I am sorry; I did not understand what I was doing.* All this time, he had not understood. But at least now he could make up for it.

He put out his hand and placed it on top of Gravis's head. Concentrating, he felt his strength flow out of him and into his brother. As he did so, before him, the image of Gravis gradually began to fade.

As the last piece of energy flowed out of him, Gavius opened his eyes and looked into Aukaneck's. The Komis leader was smiling and Gavius wondered if he had spoken the secret in his dreamlike state. But it was of no matter, he thought. He had done all he could and his time was done.

"You will not succeed," he said. "Long live the Arbor."

Void of energy, of life, very quietly, Gavius died.

CHAPTER THIRTEEN

I

Nitesco dismounted from his horse and tied the reins around the nearest tree. They had no servants with them; only the Quest party was there, in an attempt to keep their plan as quiet as possible.

Nitesco sat himself on the sand and watched the other members of his party as they rode along the beach, dismounting as they neared him and seeing to their horses. Each of them, he knew, was battling with his or her fears and worries.

Chonrad, the mighty lord of Barle, had been his usual practical self that morning, seeing it as his role as host to keep everyone's spirits up, to get them rested and fed, and to organise them for their ride down to the beach. Nitesco knew something had gone on between him and Procella that night; he had seen them leave the Hall together, and their smiles to each other that morning. He had also seen Chonrad watch the Dux when he thought no one was looking. It was clear the lord was enamoured with her.

Nitesco wasn't sure how he felt about that. Procella was his Dux, the leader of the Exercitus army, and should have known better than to involve herself with a knight, especially during a time when they needed to be completely focussed. And as much as he liked Chonrad – and it was impossible really not to like him – Nitesco wasn't sure about his motives. Clearly, the Laxonian held some sort of grudge against Heartwood, and Nitesco had seen the look on his face during the Veriditas. Chonrad quite obviously had issues with Animus and the Arbor. Whether he was suitable for such an important Quest was a matter open for discussion.

Still, Nitesco thought wryly as Chonrad dismounted near him and busied himself with his horse, there was no denying the fellow was an amazing knight; tall and strong and fearless, his skill and power had surprised Nitesco when the raiders attacked them in the barn. And perhaps his feelings for Procella were no bad thing; at least, it might mean he would make an extra effort to keep her safe.

Not that she needed a bodyguard, Nitesco thought wryly as he watched her dismount. Tall, lithe, athletic and fearless, she would not be pleased to think she needed looking after! Nitesco had always found the Dux a little daunting. He knew she was not overly impressed with him, either; only military prowess won her admiration, and he was hardly endowed with that. He also knew she didn't think he could truly turn her into a water elemental. But Nitesco couldn't blame her, really. He wasn't completely sure he could do it himself.

Dolosus was particularly sullen. Never good friends with the knight, Nitesco had kept well out of his way since the incident at the fort, when Chonrad had saved Dolosus's life. Since then, the dour Dean had been resentful and moody, clearly struggling with the fact that he had nearly been bested. Privately, Nitesco thought sending the knight on such an important Quest was ridiculous. When so much was at stake, the last thing they needed was someone so obviously unstable.

However, everyone seemed on edge now the moment of truth was approaching. Fulco, of course, never spoke, although even he seemed more reluctant to communicate than usual. And the other three knights were equally as subdued. Hora, the female Laxonian, was pale as a ghost and paced the sand nervously, desperate to begin, waiting being the one thing she clearly had trouble with. Terreo, the huge male Wulfian, constantly checked his weapons and armour, which Nitesco knew was pointless, as he would not be able to use them after the transformation. Solum, the male Laxonian, was the only relatively calm one and sat cross-legged on the beach sharpening his dagger, more from a need of something to do, Nitesco thought, than because he thought he would need it.

He sighed. It was no good putting it off any longer. It was time he readied for the ritual and got it over and done with, and then at least if it didn't work, they could go back to Heartwood and get on with defending the temple.

Nitesco caught himself mid-thought. Already he was thinking in terms of failure, and that was no good during such an important ritual. At times of crisis, one needed to rely on one's confidence. How good would Procella or Chonrad be in battle if they went in thinking they were going to die?

Casting aside his doubts, he ignored the others and busied himself with the preparations. He lowered the boxes that had weighed down his packhorse and, unpacking them, laid the contents on the sand. Most important was the cauldron where the ritual itself would be carried out. He took it to just a few feet from the sea's edge, along with the metal stand, placing that firmly in the sand where it could not fall over and putting the cauldron on top. Underneath he put some dry driftwood, and proceeded to light a fire.

Then he brought down the other implements that would aid him in the ritual. Herbs, bowls, knives and cloths were all laid out on the sand. He carefully pushed some poles into the ground around the tools and fashioned a makeshift tent over it, to keep the rain off. And then he sat down underneath, beckoning the others to join him.

The seven knights sat cross-legged, forming a circle around him. From inside his tunic, he carefully pulled out the most important piece of equipment – the document he had found in the Cavus telling him how to transform a person into a water elemental.

He could see the knights casting nervous glances at each other, and Hora even giggled a little, but he ignored them. The ritual would demand his utmost concentration, and he was not going to let himself be distracted by the others just because they did not believe he could do it.

Passing a bowl to Solum, who was nearest the water's edge, Nitesco instructed him to fill it with water, which he then poured into the cauldron. Reading the text carefully, he then added the items listed there: rosemary, for concentration; frankincense, to mystify the mind; a piece of gold, to symbolise the transformation of solid to liquid; a bottle, to show that water can be contained; a handful of salt, which dissolved as the water began to warm. Other objects went in, each to show or symbolise something about the transformation that was about to take place. Eventually, he was ready.

"I am now going to begin the incantation," he told the others. "The first part is to separate the water spirits from the liquid; the second part is to transplant them into your bodies. Now, remember what I told you at Heartwood. The earth elemental will still be there inside you, imprisoned in the water elemental, but you will still be in control. This control will, however, weaken with time. Eventually, the water spirit will become strong enough to overpower you. Obviously try to return before this happens!"

"Can you estimate how long it will take?" asked Chonrad.

Nitesco shook his head. "More than a week, less than a month; I cannot be sure. But you should feel it beginning to happen; you will probably feel listless and tired, and sense the water spirit trying to overpower you. If that happens, you must return, whether you have found the Pectoris or not, or you will lose all sense of self, and the earth elemental inside of you will disappear forever…"

The knights around him nodded solemnly. Nitesco sighed. "I wish you all the best of luck. Now, let us get started."

He spread the document on his lap and began to speak the words. The language was vaguely that of Heartwood, but the knights would not recognise the words; it was only he as a student of language who saw the words' origins. He had no way of knowing if he was pronouncing everything right. Even as he spoke, he had to quash a feeling of helplessness that rose up inside of him. *Help me, Animus*, he thought as he continued to speak. *Let me not fail these brave and noble knights.*

The words spoke of water and the spirits within, teasing them from the links that held them in place inside the liquid. Nitesco read the passage and then repeated the words that formed the final spell. He closed his eyes, saying them over and over again. And thus it was only when he heard the gasps from those around him that he realised it had worked.

He opened his eyes. Some of the knights had instinctively drawn back from the cauldron; others leaned closer to get a better look. All of their faces held awe and fear.

Nitesco swallowed and looked into the cauldron. The surface of the seawater, warmed by the fire beneath the stand, swirled as if stirred by an unseen hand. Within it, he could see faces. He gasped. Sucked to the surface, they hung imprisoned in what looked like a silver web, their features constantly distorting and lengthening as they strained to get free.

He counted them – he had commanded seven to rise out of the water, and there were seven caught in the web. "Quickly," he urged the knights, "before they break free. Stand by the water's edge."

The knights did as he asked, which surprised him. He had expected at least one to baulk once they realised he actually knew what he was doing and was truly going to carry it through. But of course, five of them were Militis, trained to obey on command, and picked for their bravery. Fulco would do whatever his master commanded. So perhaps Chonrad was the most admirable, he thought; neither Militis nor servant, he nevertheless did immediately as Nitesco said, and although his quick breathing showed his tension, on the surface he was calm and seemed prepared for what lay ahead.

Nitesco stood and held out his hands towards the cauldron. He began to speak the words he had memorised, the incantation commanding the water spirits to bind themselves to the earth ones before them, using a language as ancient as Animus and imbued with his power. The cauldron swirled before Nitesco, the faces contorting with rage and pain as their bonds were broken from the water around them.

Finally, he paused. The water pooled greasily as if a layer of oil lay on top of it, lit with rainbow colours. It was time.

"Ready?" he asked the knights.

Reluctantly, they all nodded. Nitesco took a deep breath. What if this didn't work? What would he do? For a moment, he didn't think he could bring himself to finish the incantation.

And then, unbelievably, he saw something completely unexpected. A Laxonian face appeared on the surface of the water, a face he knew very well. It was Gavius. He gasped involuntarily. Gavius's brown eyes seemed to look deeply into his own, and the trust hidden deep within them gave him the sudden courage to do what he needed to do.

"Aqua fugit," he yelled, spreading his arms wide.

Although what happened next must have taken merely seconds, Nitesco saw it all as if in slow motion. The water spirits in the cauldron churned and boiled, and for a moment a silvery thread reached out to attach itself to each of the knights. They all went rigid, and for a very brief second he thought it was going to work. A light emitted from the cauldron, momentarily blinding him. Something was happening! But before he could shout out his glee, the thread thinned and broke, and the knights were released and fell to their knees exhausted.

Nitesco cursed and slammed his hands on the cauldron. He had been so certain something had happened.

And then it suddenly struck him. There were six knights kneeling on the sand in front of him being soaked by the rain, not seven.

Dolosus was gone.

With a shout Nitesco, rushed to the edge of the sea and looked into its depths. He could see nothing, however, only the swirl of the seawater, stirring up the sand with its deep blue fingers.

"What happened?" Chonrad staggered to his feet and looked around. "Where is Dolosus?"

"Gone," said Nitesco, returning to the cauldron.

Procella stared at him, pushing herself upright. "It worked?"

He looked down into the cauldron and then got his final shock of the morning. "No. It cannot be..."

"What?" Procella demanded, coming to look in the pot with him.

"There are still seven elementals within," said Nitesco. He looked up at Procella, his mouth open. "Dolosus transformed into a water elemental without having to ingest one."

"What does that mean?" she snapped.

"I do not know." His eyes met Chonrad's, and he saw the other knight's wariness mirrored within them. "But somehow I do not think it is a good thing."

II

There was a sound from behind Grimbeald in the entrance to the Tumulus, and he turned to see Tenera's slim shape in the semi-darkness of the doorway. She was silent, and made no move to come down the steps.

"How long have you been there?" he asked hoarsely.

"Long enough." Her voice was so quiet he almost missed the words.

He tried to think what he had said to his father that she might have overheard. Maegenheard had been trying to persuade him to change his ways, and he had asked: what about the Arbor? And Maegenheard had told him to forget about the tree, and the Highlands were all that mattered. Had Tenera overheard that?

"So you are going to abandon us?" she asked softly.

Clearly, she *had* heard him.

Grimbeald hesitated. Behind him, however, he felt the strong, forceful energy of his father. He remembered his father's smile, the warmth that had flooded through him when he realised he finally had Maegenheard's approval. "My first loyalty must be to my homeland," he began.

He didn't have time to finish the sentence, however, because before he could utter another word, she had closed the distance between them and had thrown herself at him, knocking him to the ground with sheer momentum. Instinctively, he rolled to pin her beneath him, but she threw him off with surprising strength, and before he could draw his sword, her dagger pricked against the vein in his neck. He stilled immediately, and his eyes rose to meet hers. He gasped at the anger blazing in their depths.

"I trusted you," she seethed. "You promised me you would help us to activate the Node. You promised."

Grimbeald said nothing as, behind her, he saw the form of his father standing watching him. There was a sneer on his face, and Grimbeald's cheeks flamed at the thought that a woman currently held a knife to his throat. It made no difference to him, as he was well aware of the prowess of Heartwood women, but his father would see it as a dishonourable thing.

"Get off me," he scowled, pushing out with his legs so he thrust her away. He twisted and shoved himself upright, drawing his own dagger and holding it before him, and they circled each other like animals.

Tenera spat at him. He would not have thought she was capable of some vitriolic anger. "You are like a puppy dog," she taunted. "Waiting for the scraps he deigns to throw you." With a thrust of her head she indicated the hovering shade, which pulsed malevolently.

Grimbeald's insides rumbled with anger. "Why is it such a terrible thing to be loyal to one's homeland?" he snapped. "Surely a Heartwood knight can understand that?"

"Our knights are loyal to Animus and the Arbor, not Heartwood itself," she replied.

"Truly? And what of the Castellum? The Temple and the Domus? You have no loyalty to them?"

"That is different," she said. "They are there for the protection of the Arbor."

"That is a glib response. You will never convince me Heartwood knights do not feel a need to protect their homeland. It is more than a religious need; it is a physical thing; a knight belongs to his castle and to his land, to the grass growing under his feet. In that sense, it is a religious need, too – we are all part of the same energy, are we not? Therefore, we are part of the land, one and the same, adjoined. You cannot tell me land does not matter."

Tenera said nothing, but he sensed his words were getting to her. They continued to circle each other warily. Eventually, she continued, "Even if I were to agree with you, that does not excuse your abandonment of us. We trusted you, Grimbeald. I thought you were an honourable man."

He felt as if she had plunged her dagger into his stomach and twisted it. To the Wulfians, honour was the most important thing in the world, and he could not bear for her to think he was dishonourable.

"I understand how you feel," he said, ignoring her sarcastic huff. "I do. But my responsibility is to my land and to my people. As overlord of the Highlands, I cannot ignore that."

"You are a good lord, Grimbeald. You are fair and kind and just."

"That is not the definition of a Wulfian leader."

"No, because Wulfian leaders have always been cruel and heartless and violent. I understand this is the Wulfian way, but that does not make it right."

"Neither is Heartwood right all the time," he snapped back. "Who are you to tell me how to run my own country? Wulfengar is a nation built on strength; it is what its citizens understand and what they expect."

She threw her hands up in the air. "I cannot believe this is truly you talking! I know you do not believe this, and yet I hear the words coming out of your mouth." She pointed to the hovering shade with her dagger. "That thing has planted these thoughts in your head and it spews from your lips like poison."

"That is my father you are talking about," he said angrily.

"Are you sure?"

Her words made him stop in his tracks uneasily. "What do you mean? You think I do not recognise my own father?"

"Just because he resemblances his appearance, it does not mean it is actually part of the person you knew. A cloud can form the shape of a goat – it doesn't mean it *is* a goat."

Grimbeald looked across at the spectre. It glared at him in exactly the same way his father used to, but suddenly he was not certain.

Maegenheard saw his indecision and his face darkened with anger. "Do not listen to what this *pawes* tells you," he thundered, his form seeming to increase with size until it towered over Grimbeald. "There is one way to rule Wulfengar and one way only. You must learn to be a true Wulfian."

Grimbeald opened his mouth but no words came out. Because as he did so, something happened. Before him and Tenera, and between them and Maegenheard, a ball of light appeared. The two knights watched, shocked, staring as it increased until in the centre it was too bright to look at, like a small sun. Maegenheard brought his arms up to cover his face, letting out a yell of anguish. In spite of the brightness, Grimbeald stared at the centre. He could make out the shape of a person. It was one of the twins from Heartwood – he would recognise that curl they had on their foreheads anywhere. As Grimbeald stared at him, he opened his eyes. Raising his arm, he held out his sword towards Grimbeald, as if offering him the blade. Before Grimbeald could say anything, the light brightened and then suddenly vanished.

Grimbeald gasped. "What was that?"

Tenera turned to face him. Tears streamed down her face, but she brushed them away. "It was a symbol," she said. Her weapon lay on the floor, and she seemed to have forgotten it, her anger having dissipated with the light. "A sword means truth. Gavius was telling you to be true to yourself."

"I... do not understand..."

She came up to him, ignoring the glowering form of Maegenheard, and grasped Grimbeald's hands in her own. "It is time to let the past go," she said urgently. "Grimbeald – you were never able to please your father, because you broke the mould – you are a new Wulfian, a new leader, one who realises violence is not the answer to everything. Times change, and we have to change with them, and maybe you are the light that is to guide Wulfengar into a new age."

Grimbeald could not tear his gaze away from the spectre who resembled his father. "Even if this is so," he said softly, "and this is not my father... I still cannot bear the thought that I failed him. I was never the son he wanted me to be."

"It is not our place to tell our children who they should be," said Tenera. "It is their role to find out for themselves. You found your place in the world – you are a musician, a painter, a creator of things, not a destroyer. And it is time you accepted who you truly are, and put the shade of your father behind you once and for all."

Grimbeald finally looked down at the knight who had travelled at his side since leaving Heartwood. The anger had faded from her deep blue eyes, leaving them soft as a twilight sky. He could not help himself, but bent his head and kissed her lips. He did not know why he did it; it wasn't a kiss of passion, although he did have feelings towards her. It was a kiss of beauty, of thanks, like the nuzzling of two animals looking for nothing more than the comfort one gets from the closeness of a friend.

Behind them, Maegenheard roared, but this time, Grimbeald did not tremble at the sound. For the first time, maybe in his life, he felt as you feel when you have been carrying a heavy weight, and someone offers to take it from you: so light he could almost drift off into space. The disapproval of his father had been hanging around his neck like a physical thing, dragging him down through the years, and although he had thought temporarily that doing as his father wanted might alleviate the weight, in actual fact all it would have done was turned the weight into a yoke, for he would have been little more than his father's pet, trained to do his bidding.

For the first time ever, he felt free. Letting go of Tenera's hands, he stood in the centre of the Tumulus where the light had appeared. Before him, Maegenheard spat and twisted, but Grimbeald was not afraid. Now he saw the spectre for what it really was – a shadow of his own fear, sent to test him, to make him discover what was truly important to him, and to make him realise what sort of person he was meant to be.

"You are not my father," he said.

Immediately, the figure before him vanished. The ghostly shape remained, however, a grey shadow, writhing like smoke. "You are partly correct," the shadow said. "I exist because of the thousands of Wulfians who have died and who lie in this tomb. Each of them gave a little bit of themselves to form me. They guard this land and all who pass through it. And they will answer only to the one true lord – he who is true to himself and who will rule over his people with a just and fair hand."

Something moved out of the corner of his eye. Grimbeald turned as Tenera gasped, and saw with shock the bones that had been piled on the shelves on either side of the chamber were moving. Gradually, they tipped off the shelves and onto the floor, piling themselves up and slowly forming skeletal shapes that sent shivers down his spine. Slowly, however, the figures fleshed themselves out, and soon he was surrounded by lines of people dressed in the same dull brown burial shrouds, who all watched him with the same dark, serious eyes.

He could not see Tenera, and wondered if she had fled outside. He could not blame her if she had; he was tempted to run himself. But he held his ground and watched as the figures all raised their arms, touching the fingers of those standing opposite and forming a long alleyway of people down which he was obviously expected to walk.

Closing his eyes so he could not see the dull flesh of the living dead beside him, Grimbeald walked forwards and into the alleyway. He felt the presence of those around him, felt their hopes and dreams, wishes and desires, the people of Wulfengar – the spirit of Wulfengar itself.

In the middle, he stopped and raised his hands to join with those above him. His fingers touched those of his ancestors, and immediately he felt himself spiralling, his head spinning. He could see back into the past, his parents, his grandparents, great-grandparents and so on, back and back, each linked by invisible threads that joined them all together, and soon he began to see Wulfians linked with Laxonians, linked with Hanaireans, linked with Komis; they were all one people, one element, and finally he understood why there was no need for separatism, and why everyone was the same.

And then suddenly the only thing that existed was light, and the ground shuddered beneath him, and with joy he realised the Node was activating, energy shooting in rivulets through the land. It shot through him, too, like lightning, and he could feel it sparking out of his fingertips and the ends of his hair, and he was a part of it, pure energy. He held the whole of Anguis in the palm of his hand.

Then, just as suddenly, the light vanished, and he stood back in the Tumulus. All was dark, the bodies just a pile of bones lining the shelves, the ground packed earth beneath his feet. Thunder rumbled in the distance.

And the crumpled form of Tenera lay motionless on the ground.

••••

III

Fionnghuala stood on one side of the Portal, looking through to the quiet hillside beyond. It was growing dark, the deepening gloom intensified by the still-falling rain.

It had been a busy couple of days. Following Lalage's mysterious death, the Quest party had withdrawn into grief, tinged with no small amount of fear. It was the first time, she thought, they all realised the seriousness of the task they had been set; the mystical powers they were dealing with had the ability to influence life and death, and if the light-hearted Lalage could be driven to take her own life, then none of them was safe.

Privately, Fionnghuala wondered whether it was the crying baby that had lured the knight to her death. Though she had been quieter over the previous few days, she had not seemed particularly depressed, and certainly not badly enough to end it all. But Fionnghuala didn't share this with the rest of the group, because if she did so, she would have to explain the presence of the phantom child, and she didn't think she could bear that.

Of course Bearrach knew, but he too remained silent, more than a little disturbed, she thought, by the presence of the floating body in the pool. She had not spoken to him much since she woke the others to inform them of what she had found. True, they had been busy, first with burying Lalage and second with continuing to clean the Portal site, but she also felt he had withdrawn from her. Whether that was because he thought her somehow responsible for the knight's death, or whether because he wanted to give her some time to think, she didn't know. Not that it mattered, anyway, she thought miserably. Not even Bearrach could give her comfort now.

They had finally finished clearing the site that afternoon, and no longer could she put off her final task – the activation of the Node. Which was why at that moment she was standing just to one side of the Portal, soaked to the skin, and feeling as if she could quite possibly go and drown herself in the lake, too.

What exactly did she fear? She hesitated on the edge of the huge stone trilithon, her feet freezing to the floor. Just the unknown. It had never been made clear to her what to expect when she tried to activate the Node, because Nitesco himself hadn't known. Each of the Quest leaders had realised they would have to find out for themselves. How were the others doing? Had they activated their Nodes already? Had anyone had any success?

Behind her, one of the others shifted. They were growing impatient. They had been standing there for over half an hour now, waiting for her to begin the process, and she still didn't know what to do. She had hoped it would miraculously come to her, that the answer would reveal itself in a flash of light, but so far there had been nothing.

Still, didn't she really know how to start the process? Fionnghuala turned her face up to the rain and let it fall on her skin, closing her eyes. Of course she did. She had just been putting it off until now.

She looked through the Portal to the hillside. Cast in the same gloom as this side of the hill, there was nothing suspicious about it, nothing unusual. Still, she knew the answer lay this way.

Taking a breath, she stepped through the doorway.

Nothing changed. She looked around, disappointed, having half-expected to step into another dimension, another world. But the rain was still falling, the grass sodden. She turned to look back through the Portal to her companions, a shrug already on her shoulders.

Instead of finding Bearrach and the Heartwood knights, however, there was only one person waiting patiently for her. A little girl sat on the boulder Mundus had been resting on, the knight nowhere to be seen. Fionnghuala stared at her. She was about seven years old, with long fair hair hanging to her waist in braids. She was staring back at Fionnghuala, her face expressionless.

Fionnghuala stepped back through the Portal, half-expecting the girl to disappear as she did so. But she remained, watching as the Hanairean Council Leader walked up to her.

"Who are you?" Fionnghuala asked softly.

The girl stuck out her chin and looked her directly in the eye. "Can you not guess? *Mother?*"

Fionnghuala's heart missed a beat. As soon as she had calculated the girl's age, she had guessed who the girl might be, but it was so incredible that she had discounted the idea immediately. However, at the girl's words, she looked at her more closely, seeing the familiar upturned nose, the wide blue eyes with a hint of gold, the kink in her beautiful hair. All characteristics she herself shared.

"You are the child I lost?" she asked, her voice almost non-existent.

The girl glared at her. Her antagonism was evident, and she perceptibly drew back when Fionnghuala took a step forward. Fionnghuala's stomach clenched. How was this possible? Could it be the spirit of the child she had lost had continued to grow, to age, in whatever place it went after she died?

"Not the child you lost," said the girl. "The child you *murdered.*"

The blood drained from her face. "I…" She fell silent. How could she possibly defend what was quite clearly a just and honest statement about what she had done?

The girl eyed her curiously. "You do not deny it, then?"

"No." Fionnghuala's eyes filled with tears. "I have never denied the act. That is why I have suffered so long."

"Suffered, hah!" The girl was openly scornful. "You have barely given it a thought these past few years."

"That is not true," Fionnghuala protested.

"I know it to be true. You put me out of your mind mentally as well as physically."

Fionnghuala bit her lip. The girl's words were like a sword cutting through her, slicing open her emotions and leaving them fresh and raw. She took a deep breath. "It is true I have tried not to dwell on what I did. I saw no point in that. The deed was done. So I tried to move on with my life."

"Tried to forget me?" For the first time the little girl looked upset rather than angry.

Fionnghuala fell to her knees in front of her. "No, not forget you. Never."

"Do you regret getting rid of me?" asked the girl hoarsely.

Fionnghuala hesitated. She could lie, but somehow she understood the girl would know. "I regret I never got to know you," she said. "I hope one day you can learn to forgive me."

Tears poured down the girl's face. "Forgive you? For taking away my one chance at life? How I could ever forgive you for that?"

Fionnghuala felt as if her heart were breaking. She pressed her trembling hands against her lips but could not stop her own tears. They fell down her face, and soon she could not tell which were tears and which were rain.

It was in the midst of her despair that something strange happened. There was an odd noise, a mixture of a low rumble of thunder and a crackling of static electricity, and then suddenly a gap appeared in the clouds above their heads. Fionnghuala got to her feet hurriedly, looking up in awe as the grey clouds ripped, and through them the late sun shone down, illuminating the two figures on the hillside, the Portal casting a giant shadow across the grass behind them. Fionnghuala felt the sudden warmth of the sun on her face and closed her eyes, filled with an emotion she could not explain, a strange blend of love, happiness and contentment that swept through her leaving her breathless. "Gavius," she said, only realising as she said the word that his was the face that had appeared in her mind's eye.

The whole thing lasted less than a minute, and then the sun faded, the clouds pulled back together and the rain began to pepper her face once more. She opened her eyes, stunned and confused, and then saw she and the girl were not alone. Bearrach stood in the Portal, his face creased with concern. "He let me through," he said.

Fionnghuala did not have to ask who he meant. She wiped her face. "I am glad you came."

He looked down at the ground. "I cannot move. I do not think I have long."

She nodded. "I understand."

He looked across at the girl, who was now standing, her face a mixture of resentment and fury. His eyes narrowed. "Who is this?"

Fionnghuala did not want to answer him, but she knew this was no time to be cautious. "It is my daughter. Seven years ago, I got with child. He was an older Council member... He..."

"You do not have to tell me," he said softly. "It is of no matter now."

She swallowed. "But there is something you must know... I... I aborted it." She bit her lip. It was the most terrible crime you could commit in Hanaire. Children were sacred, and to deny a child its chance of life was the ultimate sin.

However, to her surprise, Bearrach just nodded. "I know."

"How...?"

"The stone in Salentaire. It had no name. I guessed what had occurred."

"Oh." She felt confused. He had known all this time and had not accused her?

He looked across at the girl. "Are you sure this is your daughter?"

"She looks like me."

"That does not make her your daughter."

"I know..." She did not know what to say. "She knows things about me, Bearrach; she can read my mind. She knew what I had done; she called me a murderer..." More tears fell down her cheeks.

Bearrach clenched his fists but could not move. "Do you really think your own child would say such a thing?"

"It is a just accusation," she said, trying to wipe her face clear and failing, "for I did indeed cause her death."

"You were very young. You must have been about to be nominated for the High Council?"

"That does not excuse what I did," she said softly.

He smiled at her. "Is it your daughter who cannot forgive you, or you who cannot forgive yourself?"

The Portal flickered. Bearrach vanished like a rainbow.

Fionnghuala stared after him. His words rang in her head. *Can you not forgive yourself...?* "It is true," she whispered. She turned back to face the little girl. "I must be able to forgive myself before I ask forgiveness from others."

The girl nodded. All resentment and anger had gone from her face, and suddenly, she looked much older and wiser than her seven years. "Come here," she said, and Fionnghuala knelt on the floor, and the girl put her arms around her. "Guilt comes with the milk," said the girl. "All mothers have it, even those who bear their children happy and healthy."

Fionnghuala looked up at the girl's face. "You are not her, are you?"

She shook her head. "But I have seen her. She forgives you, and now maybe you can learn to forgive yourself."

Fionnghuala's lips trembled. "Then who are you?"

"I am all mothers, and all daughters. I am present when you are giving birth, and I dig the grave when you die. I am birth, and death, and the life that comes in between." She put her hand on Fionnghuala's head. "Be at peace. Be open."

There was a huge crack of thunder above them. Fionnghuala gasped. The Portal trembled, the earth carrying the movement beneath her knees. In her mind's eye, she saw a picture – herself giving birth, holding a child in her arms, watching the girl grow up, seeing her daughter marry and have children of her own.

The baby she had lost or one yet to come? She could not fathom; time span like a web, and there was no beginning and no end. "Bearrach," she gasped.

And then, suddenly, all was quiet. She was alone on one side of the hillside, and through the Portal were her companions, their faces filled with fear and awe at what they had witnessed. The Node was open, and instinctively, she knew she would hear the baby cry no more.

IV

On the hill where the Henge stood proudly overlooking its landscape, it was cool and quiet, the dull gloom of the day fading to the grey fog of twilight covering the world like a blanket, muffling all sound.

Gravis sat in the centre of the Henge under a small canopy which just about kept off the rain, as long as the wind didn't blow too hard. He sat still and quiet, although inside his heart pounded, and he had to take deep breaths to calm himself. Around him reared the tall towers of the megaliths that made up the Henge, and at their bases sat the Guardians, who like him were silent in contemplation.

The rest of his party were also there, sitting in between the Guardians, completing the ring around him. He half-wished they had stayed down in the houses. He had not grown close to any of them on the journey, save maybe Aranea initially, but she had not said two words to him since the incident in the Temple, and the others had maintained a respectful but clear distance. Even Fortis, who had wanted to stay with him to protect him, seemed withdrawn and distant.

He was beginning to feel somehow separate from the world, as if he inhabited another dimension. Sometimes he wondered if he were invisible, a shadow that people saw out of the corner of their eye. It was almost as if someone was rubbing him out, he thought, as if he were slowly fading, like a rainbow after the mist.

Gravis looked around the Henge, feeling claustrophobic with the tall stones towering over him. His eyesight was beginning to blur. The drugs the Guardians had given him had started to work.

He had spent some time talking to Thancred, the leader of the Guardians, about his life and the Quest, and the problems he had experienced on the journey. To his relief, Thancred had believed every word he said, listening seriously and nodding intently as Gravis tried to describe the deep misery he felt, although he could not truly give an answer as to why.

"I am so lucky, I do realise," the knight had told the Guardian. "I was chosen in the Allectus, which many are not, and I have had the privilege to serve the Arbor all my life. I know I have led an honourable and worthwhile life. And yet still I cannot shake off this feeling of... being less than whole."

Thancred had nodded, his face solemn. "There is something unseen at work here," he said. "And the only way to find out what is to loosen the bounds of consciousness."

Which was why Gravis was starting to see the stones move, having drunk a full tankard of the herb concoction the Guardians had brewed to instigate visions.

It was the first time he had ever been under the influence of a mind-altering substance, and for a while he sat in wonder as the world around him danced. The stones seemed to sway rhythmically, their tall forms filled with light. Gradually, the background faded into darkness, the forms of the Guardians and his Quest companions vanishing, but the stones remained bright as full moons, until they were all that existed, shining like beacons in the night.

Gravis closed his eyes. Very faintly, he could hear a low, throbbing hum. It pulsed like a heartbeat. No, he was more than hearing it; he was feeling it, through the ground, vibrating up through his bones, echoing in the cavity of his chest.

It was the stones.

Gravis's heart thudded, but he kept his eyes closed. And in his mind's eye, he began to see a picture.

It was a room in a small cottage, lit by candles and a fire dancing in the tiny grate. A woman lay on the large bed that took up most of the room. She was in the process of giving birth. Two women stood by her side, one holding her hand and stroking her brow while the other busied herself preparing for the imminent arrival.

The scene itself was not particularly strange; after all, births happened most years in nearly every cottage in Anguis. But what was most odd was that Gravis felt he was not just seeing the physical side of things; each person had around their bodies a hazy glow that pulsed and blurred as they moved. He had never seen the likes of it before and wasn't sure what it was, but it was clearly something to do with the individuals' energies: all the women's auras interacted with one another, blending and mixing like wet paint as they touched or spoke to one another.

Gravis stood in the corner of the room in awe. He had recognised the place instantly. It was the cottage where he had lived for the first seven years of his life. The place where he had been born.

He looked at the woman straining on the bed, her dark brown hair damp and her face flushed. It was his mother. Was it possible...? Could it be he was witnessing his own birth? It could not be anything else; he and Gavius had been the last of a large family, and she would now be past childbearing age.

As a contraction took hold of her, his mother pushed, and Gravis watched as the midwife guided the head of the baby down the birth canal and out into the waiting world. His mother panted, her face creased with pain, as the midwife turned the child and eased first one shoulder and then the other out, and then the rest of the baby slid quickly into her waiting hands.

The other woman took the baby and cleaned it. Gravis watched, his throat tight with emotion. He did not know whether it was himself or Gavius – his mother had never told them who came first.

The baby was encased in a fine silvery light, as if carried in a web, which turned almost to gold at the crown. A thin trail of the light followed the baby's umbilical cord back into his mother.

Gravis watched as her contractions began again, and she began to push out the second baby. It was not long before the twin followed his brother into the world, wailing a little at being separated from his mother.

Gravis frowned and leaned forward to peer intently at the twins. A silvery trail also led from the second twin to his mother. However, as the midwife cut the cord and he was taken to the other side of the room to join his brother, something happened. The umbilical cord now ended at the babies' navels in a tied stump; however, the silvery trail, severed from its source, continued to hang like a piece of thread from their bodies. And as Gravis watched, and the second baby was laid next to his brother, the two threads suddenly linked around each other, joining to make one thread from the first twin to the second.

He gasped. At that moment, the babies were inextricably linked. Was it always the way with twins? Of course, he had no answer to that, but it was certainly clear from what he was being shown that he and Gavius shared a distinct connection.

The scene before him faded as if a heavy mist had come down, and then it cleared and he was looking at another view. This time it was a sloping field leading down to the river. He recognised it as being a meadow to the south of his village, where he and other children who lived around his house used to play when they were young, before he and Gavius went to Heartwood.

And indeed, here were the six year-old children now, barging through the gate at the bottom of the field, yelling as they ran across the buttercup-covered grass and down to the water. There were half a dozen children, and he could spot the twins instantly: tall, wiry and with the same shock of brown hair, they could have been a mirror image of one another. Once again, he could see the blurred colours of an aura around each child. The other children had greens and pinks and yellows merging like butter left too long in the sun. The twins' aura, however, was a bright gold, and they were clearly still joined by a thin trail that led from one twin's solar plexus to the other. For a moment, he thought their auras identical; however, as he looked more closely, he could see one brother's aura was brighter than the other's. Again, he was not sure which twin was which; they were completely identical, and even Gravis could not pick himself out between the two.

He followed them down to the river and watched as they stopped to drag down a flat piece of wood that appeared to have come off an old cart. They were obviously going to try and sail it to the other side. The boys began to discuss who should get on the raft and who should swim and push. One of the twins said to the other; "Go on. Why don't you go on the raft?" to his brother, in a spirit of generosity.

However, the other twin bristled. "Why? I can swim as good as you!"

"I know you can. I thought you would like to go on the raft."

The brother shook his head. "You go. I shall push."

The first twin shrugged and promptly climbed on the raft. But Gravis watched the second brother. His face showed resentment, jealousy and even a little hatred before it became carefully blank as he slid into the water.

Gravis's face flamed. Could the other Quest companions see these images? He hoped not. He was ashamed to watch the scene, which he remembered. Although, of course, they would not know he was the twin who refused to go on the raft.

Watching the brother before he slipped into the water, he saw the golden aura around him dim a little, Gavius's brightening almost imperceptibly. And at last he began to understand.

"So you are beginning to get it now?" The voice came from right in front of him, and Gravis blinked as the scene dissipated and he was back on the Henge hillside, the darkness hiding those seated around the stones, the only person visible the one standing directly before him. His twin, Gavius.

How could this be? Was this truly his brother, brought there by some incredible magic? Or was it just a shadow projected from his head, yet more fabrication conjured by his paranoid brain?

"I am beginning to understand," he said hoarsely.

"So you thought it was I who stole things from you?" said Gavius mockingly. "You blamed your misfortune on me?"

Gravis said nothing. Already miserable, his shame only compounded his depression.

"It is always easier to blame someone else than to admit you were at fault," said his twin.

Gravis nodded sadly. "It is true. I did think I was the worse student, the least popular knight, because of you. I did not consider it was my doing."

"So many times you have wished me dead," Gavius said bitterly. "And only now you realise you are to blame for your own misfortunes."

"I never wished you dead!" gasped Gravis, but his twin just stared at him, and eventually he dropped his gaze. He put his head in his hands. "I never truly wanted to be rid of you. I love you, brother. My own failings were not your fault. I realise now."

Sunk in the quagmire of despair, for a moment Gravis did not realise something around him had changed. Then, suddenly, he felt warmth surround him, and he looked up, his eyes widening. The figure of Gavius was still standing a short distance away, but suddenly right before him, Gravis saw his brother's face, and instantly he knew this truly was his brother, whereas the figure in the background was some sort of copy, like pretending to be in love in a play, and then experiencing the real thing.

The real Gavius looked into his eyes, and a sob build in Gravis's throat at the love that was buried deep within his brother's own orbs. "I am sorry," said Gavius. "I am sorry for what has happened between us."

Gravis closed his eyes and felt a touch like the warm tongue of a dog on his forehead. Instantly, something flooded through him, as when you have a hot drink and you feel it spread throughout your body. He felt a flush right down to the ends of his toes, and he gasped, an incomprehensible mixture of emotions spilling through him.

Instantly, he realised everything was going to be all right. Gavius loved him and forgave him for the mistakes he had made for all these years, and for the thoughts he had had towards his brother. And the small part of himself he had given to his twin without realising it, through his jealousy and his insecurity, was returned to him.

Gravis stood, the ground shifting beneath him. The very stones themselves seemed to be trembling. They cast their great shadows over him, almost as if they were claiming him, like giant hands trying to cup him in their palms. Against the darkness, the stones seemed to grow even brighter, and finally he realised he could see what looked like water running up them – not down – but as he looked closer he realised it was lines of energy, not liquid. And the energy erupted from the top of the stones and arced over his head to meet in a single point, the energy bands then combining to form one single channel which thundered down to him, and before he could shout or move, the energy channel struck him through the top of his head, passing through him to the ground.

Gravis felt as if he had been cast into a billion small pieces and scattered across Anguis. He could see everything – he could see into every house and every castle, and every person's heart. He saw all his friends on their Quests, he saw Heartwood and the Arbor, he saw to all four corners of the land.

And then, gradually, as the energy flowed back into Anguis, he became Gravis again, and as the light began to dull, he fell to his knees on the ground. The Node, he realised, was opened. He had completed his Quest.

But at what price? Because one thing he had seen when he looked across the world was the death of his brother, alone, in an Animus-forsaken hut in the middle of Komis.

V

When Dolosus transformed from earth elemental to water elemental, he had thought he was dying. If he had known exactly what was involved in transforming, he thought afterwards, he would not have volunteered to join the Quest. It was clear to him that Nitesco had not given him any more information than had been strictly necessary, and for that, at least, he part wanted to thank him and part wanted to strangle him.

When Nitesco had said the final words of the incantation, Dolosus had felt something shudder inside him, as if someone had plunged a hand down his throat and was trying to pull his stomach out of his mouth. Instantly, his body had gone rigid. Though he did not see it enter his body, he immediately felt the elemental inside him, burning in his guts. The pain was excruciating. His fingers curled and his back arched as he tried to scream, but no sound came out. He felt as if he was dissolving, every fibre of his being melting, shrinking down. He knew he was going to die – how could you not when such a thing was happening to your body?

But he didn't die. Gradually, his earth elemental form collapsed, his essence hidden within the water spirit like a pearl inside an oyster. As he was gradually swallowed by the liquid, Dolosus felt as if he were a giant caterpillar, encased in a glass cocoon. He was still there – he was still Dolosus, and he was in control of the form he had assumed, as if he had slipped on a watery suit. Yet he could still feel the water elemental that encased him. It raged and itched, desperate to get away from his earthly form. But, for the moment at least, he was in control.

He turned around, the air feeing thick and viscous, slowing his movements. It was only then he realised he was in the sea, part of and yet removed from the ocean around him. He had not thought there could be anything that would be a greater shock than this, but when he looked down he was startled to see he had two hands at the end of two arms – the water elemental's form had both limbs intact. He moved the limb around in the water, delighted to have it back again, even if it were a false truth. Both hands were almost invisible, just a silvery shadow in the ocean green. Looking down, he was even more amazed to see he no longer had legs but instead his lower body ended in a long fish's tail, which, although transparent like the rest of him, had the same silver sheen.

He circled in the water, delighting in the ease with which he moved. No longer did he feel disabled, frustrated by his missing limb. He was whole again, and he felt amazingly at ease and comfortable in his new skin.

He glanced around him but could not see any of the other knights. He looked up at the surface of the water and was startled to see Nitesco's face peering down at him, and behind him the forms of the others, but clearly they could not see him, and they soon turned and moved away from the water's edge. He realised that for some reason, Nitesco's spell had worked on him, but not on the others. The rescue of the Pectoris was up to him.

He turned in the water. Instinctively, he knew which direction to go. He appeared to be able to access the elementals' thought processes. Hopefully, they would lead him all the way there. Turning away from the shore, casting one last glance back at the golden beach and the backs of his companions, he began to swim east, towards the city of Darkwater he knew lurked beneath the waves.

For a while he swam fairly near the surface, where the water was a light cerulean. Although he could sense that water elementals were more comfortable travelling in the darker waters – and indeed he would have to go deeper at some point to reach Darkwater – for the moment, he felt more comfortable where he could still see the clouds bubbling in the sky, up above the surface, where he belonged.

He flexed his muscles as he swam. He felt strong, unbelievably strong, and now the strange sensation of wearing a suit of water was wearing off, he felt confident in his new skin.

Clearly, the water elemental had amazing stamina, he thought as the hours began to roll past and still he felt no tiredness, though he had not dropped the pace. As a knight, he was no stranger to the necessity of keeping fit. Even after his injury, he trained every day: wrestling, carrying out exercises in the combat arena, practising with his sword, jousting, running and weight-lifting. At thirty-four, he would be the first to admit he was probably past his peak, but he was hardly unfit, and could easily spend hours in the saddle, and fight in battle for long stages without losing his breath. But still, he had never felt as vibrant or as healthy before. He felt as if he could take on anyone, or anything.

He wasn't sure how long he swam, but gradually his thoughts began to turn towards Darkwater, and he knew it was time to start swimming down into the ocean depths. A dark shape swam by him and he blinked, turning in the water and narrowly avoiding the shark which, although small, snarled to show several rows of sharp white teeth. He froze for a moment, afraid it would follow him, but it disappeared into the darkness. He wasn't sure if it hadn't sensed he was there, or if it was aware of him but knew better than to get into an altercation with a water elemental.

He tried to concentrate now, aware the danger was escalating the farther he descended into the sea. All was darkness, and he was swimming purely on instinct, hoping the water elemental wasn't leading him astray. But, even as the thought passed through his head, he saw ahead of him, deep in the heart of the ocean, a silver glow.

He slowed his pace, trying to peer through the gloom to see where the light came from. Gradually, the scene before him became clearer. Eventually, he stopped to take in the fantastic view that lay spread out before him.

Beneath what he realised must be one of the Gantlos islands, an enormous cavern had been hollowed out of the rock. It was within this cavern the majestic city of Darkwater existed. At the front of the cavern, hanging down from the topmost fringes of the island's coast almost to the bottom of the seabed, was a long fringe of seaweed, the sides of which were pulled back like curtains to reveal the jewel inside.

Darkwater glowed like a pearl. Constructed from some kind of lustrous stone, the numerous buildings were clustered on the sea bed and the sides of the cavern, the roads and streets all leading towards a huge palace in the centre, its roof a mass of pinnacles and spires that glittered through the water. Presumably, he thought, that was where the Pectoris would be.

If Dolosus had been impressed with the size of Heartwood when he first arrived there, he was flabbergasted at the scale and beauty of Darkwater. To think this city had existed underneath the Gantlos Islands all this time! The thought made him both shudder and tremble with awe.

Turning, he headed for the weed curtain, the water billowing around his silent form like a sail. He swam slowly, knowing the most important thing was to ensure he didn't draw attention to himself. There was no point in trying to go under cover of night because clearly there was no such thing here; the city was partly lit by strange pearly lamps which, when he swam close to one, were actually like large fish bowls on poles, each containing handfuls of a strange coral that emitted luminescent light. Clearly, this level of light remained the same all the time.

As he swam, he kept his eye out for guards, but there didn't seem to be anyone on watch. He began to feel confused, for surely the Darkwater Lords would be expecting some sort of invasion and a rescue attempt of the Pectoris? But then again, maybe not, he thought with rising excitement. Perhaps they were arrogant and presumed the earth elementals would never find a way to transform into water. And who could hold their breath long enough to dive to the bottom of the sea? Even if a swimmer got deep enough to glimpse the lights of Darkwater, there was no way they would survive the water pressure enough to get into the city and swim around and find the Pectoris. So they left the city unguarded – and maybe that meant the Pectoris was left unguarded too.

That thought gave him hope as nothing else had done since the invasion. He did not realise until that moment how convinced he had been they were doomed to failure. He had doubted every step of the way; well, perhaps now it was time he started to believe they could really be successful. He swam through the heavy curtain into the mysterious city.

From a distance he had thought the layout of the settlement was similar to one on Anguis, with houses and shops fronting a regular pattern of streets. However, as he swam closer, he began to see the houses weren't individual dwellings like they were in Anguis cities. With surprise, he realised the whole place had been formed naturally out of some sort of coral and consisted of a maze of tunnels, nooks and crannies.

He swam slowly through the coral loops. More and more water people appeared, making their way about the city, but thankfully they took no notice of him, and gradually he relaxed as he realised he did not stand out as an invader.

He swam past shops and houses, past many other water elementals, but nobody spoke to him, and nobody stopped him. He began to feel as if he were invisible, but occasionally people moved aside for him, so he knew they could see him.

He headed towards the centre of the city and eventually found himself in a large courtyard that fronted what could only be described as a palace. It was formed from the same pearly coral but was absolutely huge, rising above him a good halfway towards the top of the cavern. Topped with turrets, spires and more intricate coral loops and twists, it put their shabby stone castles to shame, he thought, wishing he could take some of the luminescent building material back with him.

He swam slowly up the front steps towards the palace. There was still no sign of guards, and nobody seemed to be taking any interest in what he was doing. He hesitated at the top, then decided he might as well take the risk and entered the main front doors.

The entrance room was huge. The ceiling towered above him, hung with the same pearly lamps that were outside. The coral walls were carved with intricate geometric patterns and swirls, some of which had been painted in startling blues and golds. There were a few elementals swimming around, going about their daily business, but nobody stopped him or even seemed to notice him. He swam across the entrance hall, then up the next flight of steps.

A wide passageway led to another room, and then another, each seemingly more elaborate than the last. Dolosus proceeded cautiously, every sense twitching that something wasn't right, but still nobody stopped or Questioned him.

Finally, he entered a wide, open room, with only one piece of furniture in the middle. It was a low table, on which rested one lone object. Dolosus swam slowly up to it. The object sat on a shallow silver tray, and as he neared, he realised it was moving. He stopped in front of it, hardly able to believe his eyes. It was the Pectoris. He knew it immediately, even though he had never seen it before. It looked like the heart of a person, but much bigger, and was the colour of polished oak, although clearly formed from something other than dead wood. It beat slowly as he watched it, still alive, still hanging onto the dream of the Arbor, where it had resided for so long.

Mouth open, Dolosus reached out a hand to touch it.

Then he stopped. Slowly, he turned his head. Silently, twenty or so water elementals dressed in some kind of military uniform had entered the room and now blocked all the exits. And hovering before him was an elemental who was clearly some sort of leader. He was a striking figure. Fully armoured, he was huge, his shoulders broad under the sleeveless tunic woven from some kind of dried weed, the thick, fibrous strands knitted together to form a thick padding. Over this, his upper body was protected by a breastplate of small shells, linked together so they moved with his body while still providing protection to his watery skin. A golden sash proclaimed his role as leader. A short sword hung in the scabbard from his hips, the large pommel inlaid with gold and pearls glinting in the light from the lamps. His face was just a silver shadow in the water, but his eyes were bright green jewels.

The leader did not speak, but Dolosus heard his words in his head. "Welcome, Dolosus, mighty warrior of Heartwood." The leader held out his hands. "Welcome, my son."

CHAPTER FOURTEEN

I

Teague lay on his side in front of the fire. The flames were dying low, and he longed to get up and poke the embers and make the fire flare, but his shackles were pinned into the earth, and he knew from experience he could not get close enough to touch it.

He shifted awkwardly, stones and twigs digging into his hips, and sighed. He was not made to lie on the hard ground, he decided. His body was meant for soft beds, for mattresses and blankets and deep feather pillows. Not for him, the beautiful cruelty of nature!

He shifted again, then froze as he thought he heard a rustle in the trees. He had seen several animals in the forest fringes; a couple of wild boar and a fox or two, to name a few, but he would not be surprised if there was a wolf or even a bear in there. Such was the wildness of Harlton Forest, which bordered the even wilder Komis lands.

He sighed again as his golden eyes searched the dark depths of the trees for some sign of life. Not that it would matter if there was a bear in there – he could hardly defend himself, his hands bound behind his back, and tied to the ground. He would be a nice, easy meal for whatever fanged monster was waiting.

He looked across the fire at his captors, who all seemed to be sleeping peacefully, save for the man on watch, who sat eating, his eyes occasionally resting on Teague. In spite of the fact that they were countrymen, Teague hated them. Hated them for what they had done to him, and the manner in which they had done it.

He thought back to the evening he had spent in the gardens with Beata. Passionate Beata, with her long hair and her wide, innocent gaze. Although he had seen her oak leaf tattoo, he had a hard job accepting she was a Heartwood knight. She seemed too gentle, too beautiful to be confined to mail and sword, to be celibate for her whole life. A citizen of the world, Teague had seduced her with some measure of mischievousness, unable to resist the challenge of leading a holy knight astray. Afterwards, however, as she had lain in his arms in that arbour overlooking Henton Bay, he had half-regretted his actions; not because he wished he hadn't slept with her – quite the opposite: she had surprised him with her passion, and it had shocked him how appealing her naivety and innocence had been. But he wished he had not seduced her so quickly. He was certain she would regret it in the morning, and he could not bear to see a look of resentment or shame on her face.

Now, however, he was sure she would be feeling a damn sight more than resentment at what she found when she awoke. The Komis had come on him in the night while he slept, and even Peritus, that brave knight who had tried to defend him, could not stand up to the ruthlessness of the Komis warriors who had slaughtered the Heartwood Militis and left him to bleed to death in the dirt as they bound Teague's hands and led him away. He had tried to call to Beata, who – suffused with ale – had slept soundly, and so they had knocked him out, and by the time he had come to, his head throbbing in time with the horse's hooves, he had been far from Henton, Beata already awake and discovering her childhood friend was dead.

He wondered if she hated him, and immediately knew that to be the case. He was surprised at how much that saddened him. It was not the first time a woman had wished him dead, by any means. But somehow, the thought of her sweet face turning hard and bitter made him ache inside. He just hoped she recovered quickly and learned from her lesson.

Something rustled in the trees, and he froze as the Komis guard turned in the direction of the noise, confirming it was not his imagination. But the leaves stilled and eventually, the guard leaned back, chewing contentedly on some piece of meat he had pulled from his saddlebag.

Sleep refusing to come, Teague thought for a while about Heartwood and the things Beata had described to him, about the Darkwater Lords and the Arbor, and the Veriditas ceremony. He wondered if he would have been able to help. Would he have gone with Beata? Maybe when she had awakened, she would not have wanted him to go, he thought sadly. Trust him to ruin the one good thing that had come into his life in ages.

He looked again at the sleeping Komis. Was his kidnap something to do with Heartwood? Had they got wind of Beata's plan to use him to resurrect the Arbor, or was their attack on him something completely unconnected? He couldn't think why else they would come all the way across Laxony to find him. What was so important about him? Komis left their own land so rarely; they must want him very badly, he thought. The idea did not please him.

In the trees, a rustling sounded again, and Teague frowned and pushed himself up onto his elbow, which was difficult with his arms behind his back. There was definitely something in the fringes of the forest. Closing his eyes, he felt with his senses along the forest floor. As clearly as if his hand was brushing the grassy glade, he felt with his mind along to the trees, touching Anguis like a lover, reaching out. His fingers became leaves that danced and brushed the air around the place where he had seen movement, and then they found the culprit.

There was a person crouching in the bushes. Shocked, Teague withdrew his senses and stared at the trees. The leaves rustled and very slowly the person crept forwards. Teague frowned to try and make him out. He was slim, dressed in mail and breeches with short dark hair. Teague watched him creep forward and then something caught in the fire and the flames flared a little, lighting up the intruder's face.

It was Beata. Teague gasped, and the noise made the guard's head snap round to look at him. Following Teague's gaze, the guard turned to look into the forest. Teague watched, cursing himself for his explosion, as Beata, realising all hope of surprise had gone, sprang from the forest edge and sprinted towards the guard.

She bowled straight into him, knocking him flying, and was on top of him before he could draw his sword. Teague watched, shocked, as she calmly slit her assailant's throat, leaning hard on the blade so it cut deeply into the sinew and muscle of his neck. Blood flowed thick and dark red from the wound, and she quickly wiped her dagger on the grass before pushing herself to her feet.

She risked one quick glance over at him. He tried to smile, but his face felt frozen with the shock of what he had just seen. He could not equate the knight in front of him with the passionate woman who had lain in his arms. Could they really be one and the same? In the dull firelight, he saw the oak leaf tattoo on her arm, however, and knew it was she. He had been foolish to underestimate her before. She was not a lady, simpering and flustered, who had been seduced by his masterful embrace. She was a powerful and passionate knight who had merely put aside her years of training to find comfort in love. He was the innocent, not she.

The rest of the camp had begun to realise what was going on, and there were shouts as everyone roused and began to look for weapons. Teague watched in horror as the remaining five Komis got to their feet. She was vastly outnumbered, and he was in no position to help her – not that he would have been any good to her, he thought painfully, well aware his battle skills were virtually non-existent.

However, she seemed to be holding her own. He watched her, stunned to see how agilely she fought, finally able to accept she truly was a knight of Heartwood. Her moves were clearly instinctive, and she cut, thrust and parried expertly, easily deflecting most of the Komis blows.

The first warrior she knocked to the floor with one blow and finished off with a sword thrust to the neck above the collarbone, pushing the blade in deeply, then pressing her foot down on his body and using her weight to withdraw the weapon. This was done in seconds, and she spun in a circle to avoid a swinging sword from behind her, bringing up her own blade to meet it with a ringing clash. She twisted her sword so the hilts locked together, and while he struggled to free his weapon, she kicked up with a booted foot into his groin, causing him to suck in his breath and bend instinctively. As he did, so she cut deeply into his right arm, severing it just above the elbow. He fell to the ground, and from the amount of blood and noise emanating from him, he wasn't going to last long.

The third was more difficult, especially as the fourth and fifth began to circle her too, and for a moment, Teague thought it was going to be too much for her. He watched for some sign of panic, a realisation that she was defeated. But it did not come. She remained calm and silent, her eyes watching and assessing the skills of her assailants. She struck out several times, making no real impact on them, and for a moment, he thought she was backing off, afraid to take them on, but finally he realised she was testing them, finding out their weaknesses.

Eventually, she picked one of them and attacked, her sword cutting a swathe through the air and then twisting cleverly to turn aside the other's blade so she could continue her cut down into the scarcely protected upper leg. The weapon sliced through the large artery in his thigh, and he fell to the ground, groaning and clutching it as he bled into the earth.

The last two Komis were stronger, and Beata fought these for some time. First one and then the other would attack her, trying to tire her, and then both would mount an assault at once, trying to prise open her defence from both sides, but each time she sprang away from them, forcing them to turn around and follow her, guarding her back and probing continually to try and find a spot she could weaken.

Eventually, one of them stumbled over a fallen log, and she immediately took the opportunity while he was distracted and flicked aside his sword. Grabbing her dagger by the blade, she flung it at his head. The point hit the centre of his right eye and pierced through to the brain, and he fell to the ground, motionless.

The remaining Komis warrior let out a great roar and doubled his effort to attack her. For a while, Teague held his breath, certain this time she would be beaten; clearly, she was tiring – her face was red with exertion, and her movements were slower. Still, she moved like a blur, and he found himself mesmerised by her expertise, fascinated by the way she reacted so instinctively, parrying and thrusting, sidestepping and turning without thinking.

And eventually, the last Komis made the mistake of being distracted; Teague heaved himself to his knees as Beata stumbled, and he let out a shout of fear; the Komis glanced over at him, and she wasted no time in swinging the blade around with all the force she could manage. His head rolled on the floor, severed with the one swing.

Immediately, she turned to check behind her, then quickly ran over to the other Komis. She finished off the two who were wounded without a second thought, showing them no mercy but making their deaths quick. Then she knelt and wiped her blade on the grass.

Teague sat back, his heart starting to hammer in his chest. Until that moment, he had been thrilled to see her, certain she had come to rescue him, flattered and encouraged by her appearance. As he watched her pull the dagger out of the dead

Komis's eye, however, suddenly the thought occurred to him she wasn't actually there to rescue him at all; what if she were so angry with him she wanted the opportunity to kill him herself? He had seen her be brutal, fearless and bloodthirsty – would she stoop to torture, just to pay him back?

He watched her now slide the sword into her scabbard, but the dagger remained in her hand, blade pointing towards him. She came towards him slowly, stealthily, and knelt down on one knee in front of him. Up close, he could see the sweat beading on her forehead, her hair curling around her temples from the warmth, and distractedly, he thought she had never looked so beautiful.

"Hello, my lover," she said softly. Her grey-blue eyes were cold as a glacier. She turned the blade in her hand. It caught the last dregs of the firelight, glinting, blinding him. Fear crusted inside him, and his mouth went completely dry.

She smiled. "Now, where were we?"

II

The journey back from Henton to Heartwood seemed a long and laborious one after the events on the beach. Chonrad's spirits were very low, and he sensed from the lack of conversation the others felt the same. Of course, it was possible Dolosus had transformed into a water elemental and was at that very moment on his way down to Darkwater, about to rescue the Pectoris from the clutches of the Darkwater Lords. But he doubted it. Chonrad had not liked Dolosus from the beginning, and the suspicious way he had transformed while the others had failed made him think there was something suspect behind Dolosus's transformation, something that had nothing to do with Nitesco.

He also recognised that his own guilt and resentment at his failure to transform might have something to do with his suspicions. Although he had told himself he did not believe it was possible, it wasn't until the spell had failed that he realised deep down he had placed his faith in Nitesco and had in fact been sure it would work.

He looked across at the Libraris, knowing Nitesco, too, was fretting at his failure. Following Dolosus's disappearance, Nitesco had tried several times to get the spell to work but was unable to do so, and eventually, they realised it was time to call it a day. Procella had told them that in the morning, they would be returning to Heartwood, and Nitesco had not argued with her but had hung his head, clearly dejected at his failure.

Now the hood of Nitesco's cloak was pulled well over his face, and Chonrad could not see his features. He wondered whether to call out to him, to reassure him, but he knew it would be a waste of time. Nitesco would blame himself when Heartwood fell, convinced that had he been successful in transforming the other knights, Heartwood would have survived, and nothing Chonrad nor anyone else could say would convince him otherwise.

Chonrad caught himself with that thought. Was he already so sure Heartwood could not be saved? He could not think how it could be, when the Arbor's Pectoris was gone forever. Was it possible to save Heartwood, and indeed Anguis, without the Arbor? He was not a theologian and did not understand exactly Animus's connection with the Arbor, but even he knew the tree was the key to the energy that flowed through the land, and without it, the land would die. There would be no food to feed the people, and eventually they would cease to exist, whether the Darkwater Lords invaded or not.

He looked down at where his knuckles were white on the reins of his horse. Like the burgeoning waters, panic threatened to rise up and overwhelm him. All was not lost, he told himself, trying to breathe deeply and slow his pounding heart. Surely not even the most educated theologian could say for certain they were doomed. They did not know yet how the other Quests had gone; if they had been successful, then maybe they could buy some time to sort out how to get the Pectoris back. He must not lose all hope. Not yet.

He turned in his seat to call to Procella, intending to convey his thoughts and try to lift her spirits too. However, as he looked over his shoulder, he saw with shock that about a dozen raiders on horseback were riding towards them at a furious rate; what with the roaring sound of the river and the fact that he had been so lost in his thoughts, he had not heard them approaching.

Cursing himself for his lack of attention, he pulled back on his rains sharply, and the palfrey reared and twisted in the air, turning to face the other way. "Attack!" he yelled, drawing his sword from the scabbard at his side as the others turned, startled, taking out their own weapons as they saw the approaching party.

Chonrad ripped at the fastenings of his cloak, undoing it and throwing it to the ground, knowing the heavy, sodden wool would hamper his movements. Immediately, the coldness of the heavy rain soaked through his mail into his jerkin. With alarm, he saw the raiding party were carrying spears. It was a weapon he used in battle, and could be extremely dangerous in experienced hands. He cursed that he hadn't thought to bring one with him, but truth was he hadn't expected to encounter so many Wulfians so far south of the border, and it was a cumbersome weapon, especially when riding long distances. Clearly, the retreat of the Exercitus was proving fatal to the Laxonian patrolling of the Wall, he thought, steadying himself in the saddle, sword lowered at his side.

Beside him, he saw Solum and Terreo stand in their stirrups, crossbows in hand, and both fired a shot, each bringing down one of the party. That left about ten compared to the seven of them, he thought. Normally, he would have fancied those odds; although the Wulfians rode well and had spears, five Heartwood knights and two trained Laxonians should have been more than enough to best them easily. However, they were all tired and dispirited, and he knew that the worst thing for a soldier to experience before going into battle was low morale.

Procella yelled at everyone to fan out, and automatically they did so, Hora, Fulco, Chonrad, Solum, Procella, Terreo and Nitesco forming a line, forcing the raiders to do the same. The raiders yelled, raising themselves up and throwing their spears, which came whistling towards them through the rain. Chonrad tensed in the saddle, then bent hurriedly to the right, feeling the whoosh of metal and wood by his ear. To his left, he saw someone fall from the saddle, but he did not know who it was. There was no time to look – the raiders were on them.

He raised his sword and met his opponent's with a clash as the horse thundered into him, and his own palfrey reared, hooves flying. Dropping down, the horse spun around, and he met his assailant's weapon with a parry, feeling the weight of the blow all the way up to his shoulder. He hammered blows onto the Wulfian, the warrior's parries weakening. His years of training and experience were beginning to show through. Seeing the raider lean back in the saddle on the verge of losing his balance, Chonrad whipped his sword around and it cut deeply into the raider's upper arm. The Wulfian screamed and dropped his sword to clutch the wounded limb. Chonrad kicked him from the saddle, then pulled hard on the palfrey's reins, causing him to rear again. The horse's hooves dropped down onto the grounded raider with a sickening crunch, and his screams ended abruptly.

Chonrad dashed the rain from his face and scanned the scene quickly. The first thing he saw was Procella; she had dismounted and was finishing off one of the raiders, who was clearly no match for her in her current mood. Chonrad could see clearly the anger on her face, and she was obviously taking out her frustration on the warrior. Chonrad felt almost sorry for him. However, as he looked across, he saw behind her another raider who had spotted she had her back turned, and evidently thought it an easy target; he was riding towards her, sword raised. Intent on defeating her victim, Procella had not seen him.

Beside him, out of the corner of his eye, Chonrad saw Fulco move to stop him, anticipating what he was going to do, but Chonrad ignored him and kicked his heels into his palfrey's sides. The horse leapt forward and covered the distance in a flash, flanks bunching and heaving, shiny with rain. But it was going to be too late, too late...

Chonrad saw the raider start to bring down his sword; he could picture it biting into Procella's skull, cleaving skin from bone. He let out a roar and swung his legs up behind him and over the saddle, holding tight to the front and bringing his body up, feet first, between the raider and the oblivious Dux. The raider's sword came down and glanced off his body armour, cutting instead into his thigh. Then they clashed; Chonrad's weight slammed into the Wulfian, and together they crashed to the ground. Pain lanced through his leg as if it had been seared with a hot rod of iron, but he ignored it and rolled to his feet. He could put his weight on the leg, so he knew it couldn't be too bad.

Next to him, Procella had spun at the crash and now fell on the raider, pinning him to the ground. Smoothly, she drew her dagger and pushed it up under his chin. The raider shuddered, blood spilled from his mouth and he went limp.

She got to her feet, wiping the blade on the dead raider and sheathing it at her side. Then she turned to Chonrad. If he had expected to see a thank-you on her lips, he was to be disappointed. She glared at him. "What are you doing? You idiot!"

He gave a quick glance around to confirm there was no more immediate threat and then stared at her, confused at her anger. "I saved your life!" he snapped.

"And what is the point of that when it nearly cost you yours?" she yelled.

Chonrad said nothing. He knew he had transgressed the unwritten law of battle that you were never to risk your own life to save another's, but still, he had expected some small display of gratitude for the fact that his act meant she lived to see another day. The rain hammered down between them, cold in the gash in his leg. He knew what the problem was. He had saved her, and now she was in his debt. And she would never forgive him for that.

She glanced past him, and her expression changed. He turned and cold rose up to engulf him. All the raiders were dead – but two of their own were on the ground. Hora lay motionless, the spear that had killed her still sticking out of her ribcage at an angle. She had been an honourable knight, and he felt sad she would no longer fight another battle.

But it was the sight of Fulco lying in the mud, and the huge sword wound in his stomach, that made his blood turn truly cold.

He ran over to his bodyguard and knelt by his side. His thigh throbbed, but he hardly noticed it. Solum had already pulled up Fulco's jerkin so he could see the wound, and Chonrad saw now it was irreparable, a gaping hole that could not be mended even by the most skilled surgeon in the land. Solum had tears in his eyes, and when he spoke his voice was hoarse. "He saved you, Lord Barle. You did not see the raider coming at you from the side, and he got in his way and took the sword for you."

So Chonrad had saved Procella's life, and Fulco had saved Chonrad's. Chonrad gripped his friend's hand tightly. Fulco's face had taken on the greenish-grey shade of near-death, but he still managed a small smile. *Last battle*, he signed weakly. *Waste*.

"There is nothing ignominious about this death," said Chonrad fiercely. "Your name shall be remembered, my friend. You fought bravely and with honour. I shall see your family does not suffer."

Fulco coughed, and blood flecked his lips. His head fell back. His eyes met Chonrad's, and it seemed to Chonrad their light was slowly fading, like the sun setting after a brilliant day. *Arbor*, Fulco signed. *You are the key*. Then his eyes dulled, his hand fell to his side and his body went limp.

••••

III

Teague's insides turned to water as he looked at the sharp end of Beata's dagger. Even if his hands hadn't been shackled and pinned to the ground, after watching her make short shrift of the other Komis, he knew he would never have been able to match her in combat.

"I did not do it," he said immediately, knowing he had to convince her he was not responsible for Peritus's death.

She turned the knife in her hand, kneeling down before him, far enough away so he couldn't touch her, but close enough for him to see the sheen of sweat lying on her forehead after her battle. "Do what?"

"Kill Peritus." He did not miss the flinch she gave at the mention of her dead companion. "They took me by surprise; you have got to believe me."

"Have I?" For the first time she showed emotion: her blue-grey eyes blazed like lightning flashing across a stormy sky. "And how can I believe anything you say after what you did to me?"

He tried to push himself to a sitting position, fell, and tried again. He felt weak lying beneath her, and although he was no fighter, he didn't want to make her think he was totally at her mercy. "I did nothing to you except love you," he said imploringly.

Beata laughed, although there was no humour in it. "Love me? Love me! I do not think you know the meaning of the word!"

He gazed into her eyes, trying to see inside them some of the woman he had slept with that night, but there was no sign of her. All that was left was this bitter knight. He gestured angrily to his shackles. "Would I be bound like this if I had left voluntarily?"

She looked at the shackles as if seeing them for the first time. She shrugged. "So your friends turned on you? What a surprise!"

"They are not my friends!" he insisted furiously. "I have never seen them before. I was sleeping with you that night, looking out over Henton Bay, and the next thing I knew, someone had put their hand over my mouth. I struggled, and I saw Peritus in the distance, fighting furiously, and I tried to fight back, but someone knocked me on the head and I blacked out. When I came to, I was tied to the back of a horse somewhere in the hills of Dorle."

For a moment, she said nothing. The knife turned again and again in her hands. The fire had almost died and she was completely in shadow except for the slight glint of the dying glow on the blade. "Even if what you say is true," she said eventually, "I was still a fool to trust you and let you make love to me."

"Yes," he said honestly. "You were. You are a Heartwood knight, who revealed her emotions and slept with someone you had only just met. It was irrational and foolish." The blade turned, glinted. He continued hurriedly, "But you cannot deny there is – was – an attraction between us."

"You took advantage of me," she said flatly.

"Maybe, maybe not. I do not recall you pushing me away."

Suddenly, she stood, walking off and disappearing into the darkness. Teague tried to peer through the blackness to see where she had gone. She had completely vanished. He moved his hands around in the shackles tiredly, wondering if she had left him to be eaten by whatever animals roamed in the forest. Closing his eyes, he stretched out with his senses again, feeling for her. No, she was still there, somewhere in the bushes. Thinking. He wondered if she were planning how to kill him.

He sighed and lay down. He was tired and fed up with playing her game. If she was going to kill him, there was nothing he could do about it. He might as well get some sleep before it happened.

It was still raining, but the trees provided a little protection, and the ground wasn't too wet. He dozed off quickly, and when he awoke, he was surprised to see the sky was beginning to lighten. He pushed himself upright, his arms stiff where they were still bound, and looked around the glade. The dead Komis had all been removed. Beata was there, sitting on a fallen tree, watching him. He wondered if she had stayed awake all night.

"You have not killed me, then," he said.

She said nothing. Her eyes were still slices of frozen blue, her face expressionless.

He sighed. "If you are still going to kill me, please get on with it. I am tired of waiting, and I am stiff as a plank of wood. And not in a good way."

She pushed herself off the tree and came to kneel beside him. Then, bending, she pulled out the hook that had bound his shackles to the ground. "I am not going to kill you," she said calmly.

He looked up at her face, unnerved by being so close to her. He could remember the soft touch of her lips beneath his own, and the feel of her hair under his hands. She had looked so different in the dress, with her hair down. He could not reconcile the two Beatas: the sensual, passionate woman and the hardened, accomplished knight.

"Are you going to let me go?" he asked hoarsely.

She smiled. "No. You are going to return to Heartwood with me."

His heart sank. "Heartwood?"

"That is why I was originally sent to find you."

"I thought you were sent to *ask* me if I would return with you."

She tipped her head, and for the first time there was real humour in her eyes. "Actually, the Imperator told me to get you back any way I could – even if I had to drag you there."

Teague sighed. He knew she meant what she said. He flexed his fingers, the shackles tight on his wrists. "Can you at least take these things off?"

She studied him for a moment, then pulled out a small iron key. "I found it on one of the Komis guards. I will undo them. But be assured, if you try to escape, I will come after you. And I will not be as forgiving the next time." She unlocked the iron links around his hands.

He rubbed his arms, which throbbed painfully as the blood coursed through them. "Thank you."

"No need to thank me," she said briskly. "It is in my best interests to keep you well for our journey. It is not done out of the kindness of my heart."

"Of course not," he said, accepting some bread and cheese from her, and eating hungrily. He felt surprisingly cheerful, in spite of her words. He was still alive, and at last, the dreaded shackles were off. Of course, she would be watching him like a cat. But she had to sleep sometime, he thought. And he had made a living out of blending in with nature. When he disappeared, he would make sure she would never find him.

They left Harlton Forest and started to bear east to avoid the Tail Ridge of the Spina Mountains. Amerle was a beautiful land, Teague thought: a softly rolling landscape of hills and dales, covered with sheep like specks of fluff on a green blanket. However, he began to realise how much the rain was starting to affect Anguis; although not heavy, the continual drizzle had caused the rivers to rise and there was flooding in some fields, the crops drooping miserably and animals huddling under trees to escape the non-stop downpour. They passed over a river and stopped on the bridge to look down at the water gushing below; though it had not yet burst its banks, the river was a deep brown colour, thick and heavy as a too-long-boiled stew, and turbulent as if filled with nervous energy. It would not be long before the rivers started rising too far to be contained, and that would mean disaster to this already-suffering land.

He noticed that after seeing the river, Beata picked up the pace a little, not pushing the horses too hard but no longer travelling at the slow walk they had been. She was obviously as aware as he was that Anguis's time was running out.

They spent the first night in a small inn, in a settlement little bigger than a hamlet, mainly used for travellers passing from Harlton to Cuddington, as they were. There was only one room available, and so he spent the night sleeping next to Beata, but every time he turned to look at her, he saw her deep blue eyes shining and knew she was watching him. When she slept, he did not know, but it was quickly becoming clear to him he was going to have to take a risk if he really meant to escape.

His opportunity came when they stopped at Prampton. He had passed through it before and remembered it as a bustling trading post, full of people travelling across Laxony, its inns packed with merchants and messengers on the business of local dignitaries. As they rode into it now, however, he found it quiet and empty, as if the rain had washed away all the people and all the life in it. The roads were ankle-deep with mud, and their horses splashed through the water lying in rapidly growing pools around the houses.

For the first time, Teague was frightened. He had seen flooding before, of course, but he could sense this was something different. He thought about what Beata had said, that he could help fight back against the Darkwater Lords, but he could not see how. Deep down, he knew he had a power others did not seem to have, but it was an instinctive thing, and he had no idea how he could be of help to anyone. If he left, then Beata would return to Heartwood, and they would forget about him, and he could hide away in the forests somewhere, and nobody would ever find him.

Beata led him to an inn, and they rented a room for the night. It was almost dark, and they were both sodden from the continual rain. They left the horses in the inn's stable with the stablehand and made their way inside. There was a roaring log fire, and she ordered food and ale, which he consumed with relish, knowing it might be a while before he got any more.

Beata ate little and did not engage him in conversation. He was content to sit in silence and ate looking into the fire, planning his escape.

After they had eaten, they went up to their room. There was a small fire there, and Beata stripped and hung her wet clothes over the clothing stand and placed it near the flames. Teague tried not to look at her but found his eyes drawn to her slim, pale body shining in the darkness of the room like the rising Light Moon. She ignored him, and he remembered what she had said about living a communal life, that she was used to undressing and even bathing in front of both men and women. She certainly had no sense of embarrassment or self-consciousness, which he found strange, as women usually undressed coyly, shy as they revealed themselves to him. Yet again, it drew attention to the fact that she was so different from all the other women he had ever met. He watched her pull on a set of clothes from her bag and dress, then come over to lie beside him on the pallet. He lay on his left side, facing her, and closed his eyes.

For a while he stayed still. She moved restlessly beside him, then after a while, she relaxed. He waited as long as he could, then slowly opened his eyes. He was startled to see her blue ones open, fixed on him. He blinked and lowered his eyelids again, feigning sleepiness. Irritation burned inside him. Did she never sleep?

This time, he left it a long while before he opened his eyes again. He listened to her breathing slow, and for a while he dozed too, warmed by the fire and the food in his belly. Some time later, he roused. He opened his eyes slowly. At last, she was asleep.

Like a cat, he got to his feet, hardly making a sound. He was helped by the rain, which pounded mercilessly on the shutters, dampening any sound he might have made. He was already dressed, and he did not stop to take anything. Quietly, he let himself out the door, then quickly descended the stairs.

The inn was quiet, and he met no one on the way to the front door. He lifted the latch as carefully as he could; it squeaked a little, and he grimaced but did not stop, sliding out of the gap and closing the door behind him. Swiftly, he made his way around to the stables. The stable door was closed, and when he tested it, he found it bolted from the inside.

He cursed under his breath. The rain seemed to be coming down even heavier, running down his face, blinding him, his clothing completely soaked. The rain ran out of his boots in rivulets. He would have to leave the horse and try to steal another on the way, he thought. He could not waste more time before leaving the town.

He turned – and immediately felt as if he had walked into a solid wall. Beata's fist met his nose with an audible crunch, and blood spurted immediately down his face, into his mouth and all down his clothing. His knees wobbled and he fell backwards, landing in the mud with a resounding squelch.

He looked up at the knight standing over him. There was a little light coming from the house across the road and she was silhouetted against this, a towering figure wielding a heavy sword. He didn't have to see her face to know it would be thunderous.

She moved before he could blink, delivering a blow between his legs with her foot that made him curl up in pain. "What was that for?" he said in a hoarse voice. "I was already on the ground."

"That was for ruining my only dry set of clothes," she yelled. With a final blow, she knocked him across the head, and then the mud and the rain melded into the darkness and everything went black.

IV

Chonrad stood atop the Porta, the sodden canopy above him dripping sporadically on his head, and looked down at the Flumen that flowed to the north of Isenbard's Wall. It was within inches of bursting its banks, and from the increasingly dark colour of the clouds above his head, he knew it would not be long before that happened.

Behind him, he could hear Valens and Procella arguing with half a dozen Laxonian officials. They had arrived at Heartwood with a plea to send the Exercitus back to man the Wall against the Wulfians. As Chonrad knew too well, their reQuest was highly justified, and he had no doubt the towns south of the Wall were suffering greatly from the Wulfian raids. However, he also knew Valens had no intention of letting the Exercitus out of his sight, and he understood why. The Exercitus was needed for the imminent raid on Heartwood, and nothing was going to make Valens send it away and leave Heartwood vulnerable. The Wall was still manned with local troops, Valens was arguing; they would have to do for now.

Chonrad sighed, feeling strangely lonely. He had not realised how much he had grown used to having Fulco around him until he was there no longer. Though of course his bodyguard had been unable to talk, and his constant presence had meant Chonrad forgot he was there more often than not, it was now very strange not to see him at all. Chonrad folded his arms, not sure if it was his eyes misting or merely the low cloud that seemed to be settling over the Baillium. He felt humbled to think Fulco had died saving his life. It was very odd how it had happened; Fulco saving his life so he could save Procella's. It was almost as if it were meant to be…

Fulco's last message to him rang around his head: *Arbor… You are the key…* Procella had asked him what Fulco had signed and Chonrad had said it was nothing, just the nonsensical ramblings of a dying man. But he had pondered on the words ever since. You are the key? What could he have meant? Was he just saying he had an important part to play in the saving of the Arbor, as they all had? Or was it something more mysterious, a message he was supposed to convey…?

Chonrad shook his head. It was just fanciful talk. The man had been in incredible pain, aware of the fact that within minutes he would be dead – he had just been trying to convey his feelings for his overlord, to somehow express his emotions towards the man who had been his companion for thirty or so years. It was nothing more than that.

The conversation was growing increasingly heated, and he sighed again, wishing he had chosen to remain in the Castellum. But truth was the presence of the dying Arbor depressed him, and he had been glad to get out of there.

His mood had lifted a little when on arrival at Heartwood, his party discovered both Grimbeald and Niveus had returned from their Quests, and also both Quest parties had been successful, and the Nodes had been opened. This news had filled everyone with hope, but the price that had been paid soon sobered everyone's mood. Tenera had been seriously injured, brought back to Heartwood on a pallet, stricken with some sort of sickness, and Grimbeald had been beside himself with worry about her. And Niveus's description of the suffering her party had endured had filled everyone with anger. Chonrad had felt an immense sadness at the thought of poor Gavius and his companions and what they had been made to go through. Hopefully, the price was worth it, he thought fiercely.

After the returning people had rested, the Militis had held a ceremony for the death of Gavius, Mellis, Brevis, Hodie, Hora and Fulco. Valens had refused to include Dolosus in the list of the dead, unable to accept he had gone for good, and Procella had not argued with him. But the Imperator had been shaken by their news that Dolosus had vanished. It was clear to Chonrad that Valens thought of Dolosus as more than just a Dean, and his disappearance was a real blow to his morale.

Chonrad wondered how Dolosus was faring. Had he been killed outright during Nitesco's attempt to transform them? Or had it actually been successful, and was he at that moment somewhere deep at the bottom of the sea? He couldn't bring himself to believe that was true. But then, he had witnessed many odd things over the past few weeks; he had to keep an open mind to all possibilities.

Avoiding the arguing party to one side of the battlements, Chonrad walked across to look out over Heartwood. The Baillium was busy, seething with the Exercitus who occupied themselves preparing weapons and reinforcing the already formidable fortifications. He wondered whether the Darkwater Lords would find it easy to breach the walls. If it were any ordinary army, he would have said no, but who knew what tricks these strange elementals had up their watery sleeves?

The mist was definitely getting worse, he thought, as if the very clouds were descending and perching on top of Heartwood. He shivered, the cold biting deep into his bones. He was not a fanciful man, but through the greyness, the Castellum seemed menacing, like a giant insect waiting for unsuspecting prey. He thought about the Arbor inside, a symbol of the decay spreading throughout the land. Resentment surged through him that he was here, in Heartwood, about to risk his life to defend it, when he should be at home in Vichton with his family. What would happen when Heartwood finally fell? For fall it would, he was sure of it. Would it, in fact, make any difference to the rest of Anguis? Or would everyone carry on with their lives, oblivious to what had happened?

Across the Baillium, there was a sudden surge of movement accompanied by loud shouts, and he frowned, watching as a group of Exercitus spilled out from the Custodes Barracks onto the grass. Behind them, a group of figures in dark armour followed them, and immediately hand-to-hand fighting broke out across the grass. Chonrad yelled, and Procella and Valens turned to see what was happening. Chonrad clenched the stone parapet – was it happening early? Had Darkwater invaded? But even as the thought went through his head, Valens snarled, "Komis!"

"Komis?" Chonrad's head whirled. "But how did they get in?"

Valens and Procella exchanged a look as they all hurriedly began to descend the stairs, leaving the Laxonian officials behind to argue amongst themselves what to do now. Procella looked over her shoulder at Chonrad and said, "There is a secret passageway beneath the Barracks into the forest to the south. We informed the Quest Leaders of it in case a siege was underway when they returned. The Komis must have extracted that information from Gavius."

Chonrad gritted his teeth. Were they all to die before the Darkwater Lords even got there?

They ran down the stairs, through the weapons room and then along to the main entrance, Procella barking orders all the while to the Custodes they passed. The main drawbridge was up and the portcullis lowered, as it had been since the Darkwater Lords first invaded, but she placed extra guards there anyway, just in case the Komis decided to try a two-pronged attack.

They ran out into the Baillium and down the centre road, ankle-deep in thick mud. The rain was close to torrential, coming down in sheets, and visibility was poor. Still, Chonrad could see the dark-armoured Komis warriors spilling out onto the grass, more and more of them, and already there were dead on the ground, the wounded crying in agony as the fight continued around them.

Without stopping, the three of them ran straight into the battle, Valens limping as best as he could. Chonrad had the brief thought that he should have told Valens to stay behind in the Porta, before all thoughts fled his head and instinct took over. Almost immediately, he found himself face-to-face with a Komis warrior, and he began to swing his sword, cut, thrust and parry, his superior strength and experience showing quickly as he beat his opponent to his knees, ending his life with a thrust in the gap between his arm and chest armour.

Even as the warrior fell, Procella grabbed his arm, saying urgently, "We must get to the entrance – we have to close the doorway and cut off their reinforcements."

He nodded, following her as she fought her way through the melee towards the Barracks. In the background, someone had started to ring the Castellum's bell, and its loud peal cut through the cries and shouts of battle as if sounding the deaths of all those yet to fall. He ignored it and hacked his way through, following the slim form of the Dux as she forged a passage through the warring bodies.

Finding themselves at the Barracks, they were unable to push any further, the surge of Komis too great to get past. Fighting back to back, they kept trying, however, and when suddenly there was a lull in the influx of invaders, they took the opportunity to push through the doorway into the ground floor of the building.

Immediately, Chonrad could see where the secret entranceway was; a huge hole in the floor had opened up, and through it more Komis were spilling like ants out of an anthill. He looked at their black hair, their eerie golden eyes, and thought of Gavius and his friends being tortured by these people, and anger overwhelmed him. With a roar, he hacked his way forward, Procella at his side, warriors falling around them as if they were merely cutting their way through a field of corn. His superior strength and their combined experience made them more than a match for the Komis who, disorientated by their long walk in the dark, were an easy target.

Reaching the hole in the floor, Chonrad saw a large iron handle emerging from the stones at the side. Procella nodded as she saw him looking at it. "Push it." He did so, leaning on it with all his weight, and suddenly, the handle shifted and the stones grated, and the steps that had led downwards into the dark lifted to close up the tunnel. Once the entrance was closed, he sat on the handle as Procella dragged a heavy oak chest across the floor. Together, they lifted the chest and heaved it onto the handle at an angle.

"They will have trouble opening that again," said Chonrad with feeling.

Procella nodded, hair plastered to her head with rain and sweat. She was breathing heavily, but her eyes were bright as stars and suddenly he felt a surge of desire for her. Before he could think twice about it, he leaned forward and kissed her on the lips, cupping the back of her head with a hand. She did not pull away, and when he drew back he saw amusement on her face.

"What was that for?" she asked.

"You are the most accomplished knight I have ever met," he said. "You are brave, strong and beautiful with it."

Her face flushed, and he wondered if she had ever been told she was beautiful before. She met his gaze openly as she said, "You should have been a Militis. It was a great, great loss to us, when we turned you away."

It was probably the highest accolade she could have given him, he thought. "Thank you," he said with a smile.

"And thank you for saving my life before," she said. She shook her head so drops of water fell onto the floor. "I know I was ungracious. I am just not used to being saved."

He opened his mouth to reply but, at that moment, someone appeared at the door. They looked over, seeing Solum leaning heavily against the doorpost. They could see immediately by the look on his face something was wrong.

"What is it?" Procella demanded. "Is it the Castellum? Is the Arbor all right?"

"It is Valens," he said.

V

Dolosus froze on the spot and looked around him warily, assessing his situation. It was clear to him immediately there was no way he could escape from the room. All the exits had been barred, and the guards that lined the walls did not look like half-trained commoners dragged in from the streets; they were well-armoured, muscular, alert soldiers, comfortable and able in their own environment, whereas he had no weapons and was still getting used to the way his body moved under the water.

The way out of this situation was not to fight, he realised. He was going to have to think of another solution.

He turned his attention back to the leader, who was waiting patiently for some reaction to his words. Dolosus looked him up and down, noting the strength in his arms and back, the noble way he held his head.

Gradually, the leader's words sank in.

"Your what?" said Dolosus, thinking he must have misheard.

"My son," confirmed the large warrior, his green eyes burning into Dolosus's. He held out a hand to a doorway on the back wall through which Dolosus could see a small anteroom. "Come with me, and we can sit and talk a while."

"I am going nowhere until you explain what you meant by that statement," demanded Dolosus. His heart pounded inside his watery skin. He knew the leader was talking nonsense, but still…

The warrior nodded. "I am Thalassinus, High Lord of Darkwater. And you, whom Heartwood calls Dolosus, were born Damaris, the product of my union with a female of Anguis some thirty-five years ago."

Dolosus stared at him. The use of the name he had borne until he was twenty-four years old shocked him; only Valens knew it and had changed it when he welcomed him into the Exercitus.

He had heard the stories all his life about the water warriors who came ashore to mate with the women, but had always thought it just that, stories; even after Nitesco's speech about the origin of the Darkwater Lords, he had never suspected it to be true.

And he had never suspected he would be the product of such a relationship.

"I do not believe you," he said instinctively. "How do I know if what you say is true? You could be saying this just to distract me from my goal. You think because I came late to Heartwood, I will be easily swayed; you know I am dissatisfied there and think that means I will turn traitor. You are wrong."

Thalassinus nodded. "You are wise to be cautious. I would not expect anything less from my son." He motioned once again to the antechamber. "Let us go and sit and talk about this properly. You are probably hungry, too, and there is food in there."

He walked away, disappearing through the door into the chamber. Dolosus cursed but knew he could do nothing but follow him. Though he had scorned the High Lord's words, deep inside he was curious and wanted to hear more.

He followed Thalassinus across the floor, feeling the eyes of the guards upon him as he swam. He looked over, wondering if their gazes would be mocking, or scornful, but in them he read only respect. Shivering, he swam through the loop in the coral that served for a doorway, and entered the antechamber beyond.

Unlike a room in Anguis, the chamber did not have furniture as such. The seats were made from more coral, as was the table, and there were no cupboards or chests with ornate crockery and ornaments. However, the walls were intricately carved and decorated, painted with gold and silver and blue, work that must have taken several artists years to complete. Dolosus marvelled at the workmanship as he swam up to join Thalassinus, who was reclining on a couch, nibbling at a skewer of sea vegetables. "Please," said the High Lord, indicating Dolosus should join him. There was nobody else in the room apart from a couple of quiet servants, who did not look up as Dolosus entered.

Dolosus let his body sink onto the couch next to Thalassinus, but did not eat. Although he was hungry, he was afraid the food might be poisoned, or laced with a sedative at the very least, and he wanted to keep alert and ready to flee at any moment.

"You do not believe me," said Thalassinus, finishing the skewer and throwing it over his shoulder, where it floated gently until one of the waiting servants caught it. "How can I convince you?"

"I do not know," said Dolosus. "What proof do you have?"

Thalassinus beckoned to one of the servants, who brought forward a flat silver mirror. The High Lord placed it on the couch between them and indicated for Dolosus to gaze into it. "Look," he said, and passed his hand over the glassy surface.

Dolosus looked. For a moment, he saw nothing but the reflection of his own face. Then his features blurred, as if he was actually looking into a pool of water and someone had dropped a stone into it. Slowly, the surface stilled once again, but this time it was not his reflection he was seeing, but a scene featuring people he recognised. He gasped. He could see Nitesco, Procella,

Chonrad, Fulco, Solum, Terreo and Hora, and behind them the golden sand of the beach from which he had vanished into the water. Procella was talking, and in his mind he heard her words: "Why did it work for Dolosus and not the rest of us?"

And Nitesco's reply: "I do not know, but there are seven elementals still in the cauldron; Dolosus made the transition of his own accord."

The picture swam again, and then there was only his reflection staring back at him, the confusion evident on his face. He looked up at Thalassinus. "I do not understand. How could I make the transition without the water elemental?"

"Because you already had one within you," said the High Lord, his green eyes gleaming in the pearly light from the lamps. "I planted the seed of one within your mother, and it has remained inside you ever since, waiting for its chance to return to its origins."

For a moment, Dolosus could think of nothing to say. The thought of a water elemental lying dormant within him all his life was abhorrent to him. And yet... somehow, hadn't he always known there was something wrong with him? That a seed of evil lurked inside him, and there was nothing he could do about it? At least now it made sense.

Thalassinus was frowning. "There is nothing 'wrong' with you," he corrected, leaning forwards intently. "And it is not 'evil'. This is who you are, Damaris; you cannot deny your heritage. I know you have always felt misplaced, as if you do not belong up there. This is why: you were destined to be at my side. My son. My rightful heir."

Dolosus pushed himself away from the table and swam agitatedly in front of the High Lord. "This does not make sense! How do I know the vision you just showed me is the truth? How do I know the elemental within me has been there all this time – that it wasn't just placed within me on the water's edge?"

Thalassinus just smiled. "You know, Damaris. You know the truth. You have always known. You have never fitted in and have always felt yourself to be an outcast, different from everyone else."

That, at least, was true. He swam around the edge of the room, trying to think, then suddenly realised what he was doing. Was it a coincidence he had felt so comfortable in his watery skin? That he had adapted so easily to the form of a water elemental? Obviously, part of that must be due to the fact that he had regained the use of his arm, but even if he took that into account... Had he slipped into the role too quickly, too easily?

He looked at the Darkwater Lord, who was watching him with a small smile on his face. He could not think of him as "father". "Why have you not informed me of this before now? Why have you chosen this moment to reveal the secret?"

Thalassinus shrugged. "It was out of my hands. Once I went back into the sea, I had to wait until Darkwater called you."

Dolosus frowned. "You must be able to breed amongst your own people. You must have other sons."

"Yes, many."

"Then why me? Why am I so important?"

For the first time Thalassinus showed impatience, pushing himself upright and swimming over to face Dolosus. "Because you have a foot in both worlds, of course. You understand the ways of the earth elementals. You, Damaris, are the key to Heartwood!"

"I see," said Dolosus quietly. "You want me to betray Heartwood; open its doors for you."

Thalassinus smiled. "We will take Heartwood with or without you, my son. The tides are rising; in three days' time, they will be at their peak, and we will invade. If you wish to help us, that will be a bonus. If not, I understand. But your rightful place is still beside me. My other sons have always known this city will one day be yours. And I know you were unhappy on land. You felt weak with your arm removed and hated the fact that people took pity on you. You felt alienated and frustrated with your life. Here, you can be whole once more."

"How do you know what I felt on Anguis?" said Dolosus hoarsely.

"I have been watching you, of course. We are in every sea, every river. You just cannot see us." He smiled at Dolosus. "Come with me; let me show you what I mean."

He swam out of the door and Dolosus followed him, not knowing whether or not he wanted to see what Thalassinus wanted to show him. They swam along a passageway and up through a series of highly decorated coral loops. Passageways led off to the left and right, but Thalassinus ignored them, taking him instead straight to the top.

When they reached the summit, they swam out of the final loop onto a small platform. Above them, the ceiling of the cavern – the underside of one of the Gantlos Islands – shimmered with stones and gems set into the rock like stars. Thalassinus swam to the back edge of the platform and held his hand out to Dolosus. "Look."

Slowly, Dolosus moved to the edge and looked down. He gasped. There, as far as the eye could see, were Darkwater soldiers readying for war; some drilling, some practising with swords and other weapons, too numerous to count.

Thalassinus nodded. "And one day, my son, they will all be under your control. You will be High Lord of Darkwater."

Dolosus couldn't believe what he was seeing. Suddenly, he realised what Valens and Procella and the others had not – the invasion was not just going to come at Heartwood; it was going to come across the whole of Anguis. Darkwater warriors were going to rise out of every natural piece of water throughout the land. All the people, the defenseless peasants, all the innocents were going to die.

He was horrified, and yet some small part of him admired the Darkwater Lords and the height of their ambition. If, truly, he was half water elemental, he thought, then it was natural he sympathised also with the Darkwater Lords, that he felt this strange attraction for this mysterious underwater world, wasn't it?

Was Thalassinus speaking the truth? Did he really mean to make Dolosus High Lord after him? Was it really possible one day he could be in control of everything he could see from the top of this palace?

He turned and looked down on the glittering settlement that sprawled on the ocean floor. Darkwater glowed like a beacon in the dark, drawing him, changing him. Dolosus flexed the fingers on his right hand, felt the strength within him he had missed for so long. Could he really go back to being the one-armed Dean at Heartwood? The place where he had been so unhappy. Was that really his destiny?

He looked across at Thalassinus, the High Lord of Darkwater. His father.

And he smiled.

CHAPTER FIFTEEN

I

Chonrad stood in the atrium of the Temple, quietly watching the ceremony being carried out in front of him. He had looked all over Heartwood for the Imperator and his Dux, and had not found them in the Baillium, nor investigating the defences, nor in the Barracks. His final option had been the Castellum, and on slipping through the great oak doors held open for him by the waiting Custodes, Chonrad had realised that Valens and Procella were taking the opportunity to carry out a quick ritual before the furore of the coming, inevitable battle.

Valens had been badly wounded in the fight against the Komis warriors. One foe had obviously spotted the weakness he had in one leg, and had concentrated his attentions there, and eventually Valens had received a sword thrust to the muscle above the damaged knee. Solum had only just saved him from the Komis warrior's final blow, and when Valens went to stand he could not put his weight on the leg.

Now, he could just walk by leaning heavily on a cane, but it was clear the knight's battle days were completely over. Chonrad thought they had probably been over before that, but it was only now that Valens fully accepted it. Chonrad had thought this realisation would make the Imperator angry and resentful, but if anything Valens seemed calmer, more resigned to the fact that he must completely hand over his physical as well as mental role of Dux to Procella.

Chonrad waited reluctantly in the shadows as Procella and Valens paid homage to the great tree. Silva was there, too, and several Militis also watched from just outside the inner circle, their attention focussed on the Arbor and those doing the ritual within.

Valens sipped Acerbitas from a cup, then passed it to Procella. He approached the Arbor, limping heavily, with Procella at his side. Procella knelt, and Valens sat in a chair, holding their oak leaf pendants in their right hands. Heads bowed, they murmured their prayers as Silva chanted quietly, her hands raised in supplication to the tree.

Unseen, and as yet unnoticed, Chonrad did not move. They would have welcomed him in the inner circle – in fact, would have been thrilled if he had joined them in their ritual, but he had no wish to do so. He looked up at the dying oak tree and felt tightness in his chest and the taste of bile at the back of his throat. The Arbor was now completely void of leaves. Its branches hung towards the ground instead of reaching up to the dome of the Temple. The great tear down the middle of the trunk had caused the tree to sag to either side. Silva insisted the tree was still alive, but now Chonrad wondered whether that was just wishful thinking. It looked dead, and like the decaying corpse of a creature on the side of a road, it disgusted him.

His feelings would have greatly upset the holy knights, which was why he had so far kept them to himself. And it was also why he now kept in the shadows. He did not want them to see the look he could not keep from his face, the look of disgust that played upon his features. From the beginning, he had found the tree abhorrent, and now, in its present state, he could not bear to be near it.

Were it not for the fact that Valens had called for him, Chonrad would have gone back outside, albeit into the rain – anything to get out of the oppressive and depressive atmosphere of the Temple. But in the inner circle, Procella was pushing herself to her feet and Valens was rising stiffly, so Chonrad sighed and waited.

Watching Valens limp towards him made Chonrad think of his own retirement one day. How would he feel when the time came when he could no longer ride for too long in the saddle and his own reactions grew too slow, making him a hindrance in the battlefield? For a knight who had known no other life, such a verdict would be a slow death, he thought.

They turned, and Procella saw Chonrad immediately as he stepped forward into the light. She smiled and beckoned for him to come closer. He did so reluctantly, but stopped at the gate to the Sepulchrum, even though it was open.

She beckoned him closer, but he shook his head. "I would rather remain here," he said.

Procella's eyebrows rose, but she said nothing. She and Valens crossed the inner circle to stand next to him.

"You wanted to see me?" Chonrad asked.

Valens nodded. "How goes the morale around Heartwood?" He had given Chonrad the task of speaking to the visitors in Heartwood to find out how their spirits were holding up. Valens liked to think he could judge the mood of his Militis. The Wulfians had mainly returned to their land, but there were still lots of knights from Laxony and some Wulfians and Hanaireans present, and he wanted to find out how they were faring.

"As is to be expected," said Chonrad, turning his back on the lifeless tree. "They are missing their families. There is some resentment that they are here when they feel they should be at home, protecting their kin." He did not say this was how he felt, but Procella's forehead furrowed, and he sensed she understood.

Valens nodded. "And are they hopeful of a positive outcome?"

Chonrad said nothing. Valens nodded sadly. "I thought as much."

"And yet they are steadfast," said Chonrad, feeling he had to carry on at the hopeless look in their eyes. "Though they miss their

homes, they are adamant that they will not let Heartwood fall easily
to the invaders. They are prepared to die in the defence of it."

Valens nodded. He turned away, and Chonrad sensed the
Imperator could not trust himself to speak. Procella met
Chonrad's gaze. Her face was solemn, her deep brown eyes filled
with concern. Chonrad wished he could console her, tell her she
mustn't worry, that everything was going to be all right. But he
found he couldn't do that, because he didn't believe it, and he
didn't think she would want empty platitudes.

Valens cleared his throat. "I had a dream last night," he
declared. "Of Dolosus."

Chonrad's eyebrows rose. "Oh?"

Valens turned to look at him. "I dreamed I awoke in my bed
and he was standing before me, looking down at me. I smiled and
spoke to him, but before I could move, he leaned over me, and
suddenly I saw he was holding a dagger. He plunged it straight
into my heart. The blade pierced my skin and muscle; I swear
I felt it go right through to the bone. He leaned over me as I
looked up at him with horror, and he laughed. He laughed at me.
Then… I awoke."

Chonrad blinked, looking from the Imperator to Procella and
back. "It must have been quite chilling. But still, it was only a
dream…"

Valens shook his head. "It was a portent. An omen. Dolosus
has turned traitor on us. I can feel it. The Pectoris is lost. The
Arbor will not regain its life."

Confused, Chonrad looked back at Procella. Was Valens
serious? Did he truly believe in this night vision? Immediately,
however, he could tell from the look on her face that not only
did Valens feel he was speaking the truth, but Procella believed
it, too.

"Then all is lost?" she asked quietly.

Chonrad glared at them. "Of course all is not lost! It was just
a dream."

"We believe Animus speaks to us through our dreams," said Procella sharply. "We believe they can be visions of what is to come. Do not mock our beliefs."

Chonrad bit his tongue. He must not pour scorn on their religion, especially when standing in front of the Arbor. Briefly, he thought of Dulcis's words; that there were Militis they had taken on that she regretted. Had she been referring to Dolosus?

Still, it didn't mean the knight would definitely defect, he thought. "Even if that were so," he said as patiently as he could, "it does not mean there is no hope. Beata may yet return with the Virimage. Or Nitesco might find the fifth Node. The future has not yet come to pass – a vision can only be one possibility of what might happen."

He could see from their faces they did not understand. To them, Valens's dream was a truth, as set in stone as the oak leaf carving above the Porta. And who was he to argue with them?

There was a movement behind them – the creak of the old oak doors and a draught around their ankles, and they turned to see Solum standing in the doorway. As was commonplace now, he was soaking wet, his hair plastered to his head and the tunic beneath his mail skintight on his arms, but it was the look upon his face that drew their attention.

"It is the Flumen," he gasped, his chest heaving, clearly having run all the way from the Porta. "It has finally burst its banks."

Chonrad pulled the hood of his cloak over his head and followed the others out of the Temple and down the central road to the walls. If it were possible, his spirits felt even lower than before. If the river truly had finally broken free, it could only mean the Darkwater Lords were on their way, and their annihilation was just a matter of time.

Reaching the Porta, he and Procella ran up the curving staircase to the top. Valens followed them very slowly, his leg clearly painful and stiff. Chonrad ran on ahead, his powerful legs pushing him just a few steps above Procella.

Reaching the top, he paused before exiting the stairwell, letting himself be identified by the guard. The guard motioned him forward, and so he crept up the final steps then moved quickly to stand behind one of the battlements. Procella did the same. Slowly, carefully, they peered around the stone wall.

The vista was a grim one. The low clouds gave the countryside a greyish, dull hue as if the rain had washed away all the strong colours, leaving only shades of black and white. To the south, the fields and roads of Laxony lay sodden and dripping, a landscape of marshes and quagmires through which people were increasingly scared to travel, made doubly dangerous now by the Komis army, which had spread itself like a disease across the surrounding land. Beata would have no hope of returning now, Chonrad realised, if she was indeed on her way; there simply was not a clear passageway through to Heartwood.

He wondered, however, how long the Komis would be able to hold out under these conditions. Their tents had been placed on the few areas of higher land but the flooded areas were increasing rapidly, and Chonrad knew from experience there was nothing more depressing for a soldier than an inability to keep oneself dry.

It was a fairly large army, maybe ten or twelve thousand, from what he could make out from the amount of tents and horses, enough to make a sally from within the grounds a foolish notion.

He wondered how the tree-faring folk were feeling in such alien territory. There were few trees immediately surrounding Heartwood, as the land had been cleared in previous centuries to make roads for easy access for transport for the Exercitus to other places, and for supplies into Heartwood itself.

However, looking round, Chonrad realised it was possible that it was not the Komis who was the most immediate threat. Directly to the east, Isenbard's Wall stretched away into the distance, a heavy grey line cutting across the land. To the north of the Wall, the Flumen – swollen from weeks of rain flowing down from the mountains – had finally overflowed its banks, like a person whose overeating stretches his stomach until his trouser button bursts. Water had spilled across the plain flanking the Wall, and the Wall itself had diverted the flow, causing a torrent to spill down past Heartwood itself. The moat level was rising, and eventually, he knew, it would overflow, and then the waters would be pressing at the walls, and Heartwood itself would be in jeopardy.

Behind him, he felt Valens finally press up against the wall, and the Imperator peered over his shoulder to look at the view. "So, it has happened," the older man breathed. Chonrad turned and was startled to see there were tears in Valens's eyes. "The end is nigh. The Darkwater Lords are massing, and soon, we shall be like the sand at the bottom of the ocean, and there will be none left to stand in their way."

II

Damaris, the water elemental who now had control of Dolosus, stared at himself in the silver mirror hung on the wall of his chamber. Thalassinus had showed him to his rooms, claiming he had recently had them decorated in honour of the imminent arrival of his son. They were certainly impressive, grander than any place Dolosus had ever stayed. They consisted of a series of five hollow coral spheres around a central larger sphere, which was his main living chamber. The walls were carved intricately with patterns and scenes from Darkwater legends, which had been painted with iridescent colours of blue, purple, silver and gold that stood out in the blue-green seawater like stars in the night sky. His furniture was made from large seashells and woven reeds, anchored to the coral floor with gold hoops. When he thought of the dormitory in Heartwood, the large room he shared with the rest of the Militis who worked in the Castellum, he laughed. Talk about progress!

Staring at himself in the mirror, he strapped on a breastplate of iron-hard shells over a thick reed jerkin, surprised to feel it move as he moved, although he had been told that, in spite of its flexibility, it would repel any sword or spear. Standing beside him, his father handed him the golden sash, which announced his birthright. Damaris lowered it over his head and buttoned it at his waist.

He stared at himself in the mirror. The part of him that was Dolosus, the earth elemental, was buried deep within the water elemental's form, sinking deeper every second. And yet although he had two spirits, he was still one person, with access to the thoughts of both water and earth elemental.

Somehow, he felt his watery spirit had always been stronger than his earth one; he was sure that was why he had felt so out of place and had struggled so on Anguis. Damaris and Dolosus had been fighting for superiority ever since he was born, and finally, Damaris had won.

He closed his eyes. Around him, he could feel the gentle but insistent pull of the ocean. It had been growing stronger since his arrival at Darkwater, and at first, he had thought it was because he was adjusting to life under the sea. He had only just connected the feeling with the fact that the High Moon was approaching. Now, he felt the presence of the satellite in the sky, even though he was miles below the surface of the ocean, as if she were urging him to rise, as if he were attached to her with watery threads and she was trying to pull him out of the sea. Above him, he knew the tides would be at their highest, the waters gnawing at the cliffs on the coast and rivers straining at their banks. With the continual rain, the time was ripe for invasion.

Inside him, Dolosus squirmed. Damaris smiled. He could feel his alter ego's torn loyalties.

Then, inside his head, he saw a flash of the face of Valens. His smile faltered.

His relationship with the Imperator was a long and complicated one. He was well aware Valens saw in him the son he had never had, and that had always puzzled him, for it was hardly as if he was the epitome of the Heartwood knight, a shining example of a Militis. But he knew little of Valens's past and had come to the conclusion the older man had had some similar problem when he was young; perhaps he had rebelled against his upbringing, or had been resentful or impatient in his youth. Dolosus had tolerated Valens's subtle attentions, thinking it was nothing to do with him, and if it in any way granted him a quieter or easier life, then he might as well cultivate the relationship.

However, as time had gone by, he had come to admire the quiet but steadfast knight. The Imperator demanded nothing from his Militis he was not capable of himself; he expected them to be physically strong, devout and honest, brave, unflinching in the face of danger, resolute in the presence of evil. And gradually, Dolosus's feelings for him had deepened.

He could not bring himself to say he loved the old knight. Dolosus did not consider himself capable of that emotion. But he did admire him and until now had considered himself loyal, and suddenly, the thought of advancing on Heartwood with a thousand Darkwater Lords in tow struck a chord within him that resonated through both earth and water elemental.

He had always thought Heartwood in no way meant the same to him as it did to the other Militis. He had not been chosen in the Allectus, had not grown up there, and did not seem to feel the same draw to the building the others did. He carried out the rituals with the others because it was required he do so, but they meant little to him, and he was not a deeply religious person.

The Arbor... He thought of the tree, and his insides twisted. He did not know what he thought of the Arbor. If asked, he would have said it meant nothing to him; it was just a tree, a symbol for the Militis to focus on. But inside, he knew it was more than that. He had touched the tree and felt its heart beating; he had drunk the tea made from its leaves; he had watched the Veriditas and seen the Arbor grow, and it had changed him without his knowing.

In the mirror, his eyes met those of his father. The huge water elemental's face was impassive. Damaris looked at his impressive physique, at his hard features, and shivered. Heartwood did not stand a chance against an army of elementals like this. He wondered if Thalassinus could read what he was thinking, and whether he would be angry, but the High Lord just smiled.

Damaris looked at himself in the mirror again. He wished he could expel Dolosus from him, split himself into two, although he knew that was impossible: Dolosus could not be extracted without killing them both.

"What will happen when we arrive at Heartwood and leave the water?" he asked. "Will my water spirit will once again be engulfed by my earth one?"

"Yes."

"Is that what happens to you?"

"Yes. We ingest an earth elemental and take its form."

Damaris wondered who the earth elementals were the Darkwater Lords captured, but did not ask. He thought they were probably from the Gantlos Islands; after all, hadn't Nitesco spoken about the mysterious disappearances of people from there?

"What will happen when my earth spirit takes over again?" he asked. "Will it not keep me out? Follow its own course?"

Thalassinus turned to look at him. His eyes were like emeralds in the glitter of his face. "No, not now. Damaris has been awakened, is in the ascendant. Dolosus's sun is setting. He will no longer have a hold on you."

Damaris thought of Heartwood, and of Valens, and wondered if that were true.

Thalassinus swam around him in a circle. "You look tired, my son," he observed. "And I have chores to carry out. Why don't you rest for a while, gather your strength? You are still getting used to your new form; it will take time to adjust. In the meantime, you should rest as much as you can. You will need every ounce of strength when we advance on Heartwood."

Damaris nodded and watched his father swim out of his chambers. He went over to his bed and curled up on the mattress of soft ferns. Lying on his back, he held his two arms up before him, seeing the shimmering, almost-translucent hands before his face. He was whole again, complete. And in this world, he was the son of a king and heir to a whole kingdom – what did he have on Anguis? An adopted father, too old and injured now to be a warrior on the battlefield, and a dormitory he shared with twenty of his brothers and sisters. And just the one arm, his missing limb on his mind from the moment he awoke until he closed his eyes at night.

Did he really want to give up a whole kingdom, and a whole body, for that?

Exhausted, he closed his eyes and was soon fast asleep.

Dolosus dreamed. He was back in Heartwood. He saw himself walking through the door from the Temple into the Domus. Although he knew he must be dreaming, he felt as if he were actually there; he could hear the scuff of his boots on the flagstones; he could smell the loam from around the Arbor, and taste the bitter Acerbitas drink in his mouth.

He entered the corridor behind the Temple, but instead of walking through to the Domus, he found himself climbing the stairs to the upper level. It was dark, and he met no one on the stairs. When he got to the top, he walked silently through the dormitory. The beds were full of sleeping forms, but he could not distinguish between them.

He walked along the row of beds to the one at the furthest end. He knew whose bed this was without looking; this was where Valens slept. He walked over to the bed and looked down. The Imperator's face was graceful in repose, his harsh features softened in sleep. Dolosus stared at the man he had thought of as his father until he met Thalassinus. He bent over. Valens stirred, then opened his eyes and looked at him. A smile appeared on his lips.

Dolosus stared at him for a moment, then raised his good right hand. To his shock, he saw it held a knife. His heart pounding, he tried to drop it, but he wasn't in control of his body. He raised his hand and brought it down hard. He watched with horror as the blade punged into Valens's body. Valens jerked, his eyes startled, filled with shock, disappointment and agony. Dolosus heard himself laugh.

Then his eyes flew open, and he realised he was still in Darkwater. It had just been a dream... Or had it? Maybe it was more than that: it was a portent, or a symbol, of what he had done. In defecting to Darkwater, he had caused Valens's death as surely as if he had plunged the dagger in his heart.

Dolosus stood and swam over to the mirror. And suddenly, he realised he was thinking of himself as Dolosus – not Damaris. In sleep, the earth elemental had somehow gained control of the water elemental again.

Dolosus raised his hands in front of his face. He turned them backwards and forwards, then flexed his left arm. Yes, it was wonderful to be whole once again. His arm dropped to his side. But it wasn't worth the price he had to pay. Being whole was more than physically having all your limbs. Whatever he thought of Heartwood and the Arbor and the rest of the Militis, he wouldn't be able to live with himself if he caused Valens's death.

He turned in the water, thinking he heard movement in the doorway, but there was nobody there. Suddenly, everything seemed alien and threatening. He thought of the Pectoris sitting on the display stand in the ceremonial room and knew what he had to do.

Quietly, Dolosus swam out of his chamber and along the tunnel that led deeper into the palace. He twisted and turned through the passageways, swimming silently, ducking behind walls and entrances each time he thought he heard someone coming the other way. Although there was no such thing as day or night in Darkwater, there were rest times, and many in the palace would be sleeping. And somehow, he didn't think Thalassinus suspected he might give up being the heir to a vast city such as Darkwater. Dolosus almost laughed then. What was he doing? But his mind was made up.

As he approached the ceremonial room, he saw a guard standing sentry outside. He swam up to him slowly. The guard saw him and straightened, eyes ahead. Dolosus nodded and swam past him, then turned in the water. Drawing the dagger the High Lord had given him only hours before, he drew the blade swiftly across the sentry's neck. The sentry went limp and floated to the floor slowly, dark green blood leaking from the jagged hole in his neck.

Dolosus entered the ceremonial room. To his relief, it was empty. He swam straight up to the Pectoris, which lay on its cushion, beating very slowly. He stared at it for a moment, then, carefully, he lifted the large object from its resting place. The Pectoris in his hands, he held his breath. Nothing happened. No alarms went off, and no one came running. The Darkwater Lords had not anticipated this at all; they clearly thought there was no way anyone could come down from Heartwood to rescue it, and they obviously thought there was no way he would turn his back on what they had offered him.

Ignoring the little voice inside him that screamed What are you doing? Dolosus reached for the bag he had slung across his back and placed the Pectoris in it. He pulled the handle of the bag over his head. It was heavy, heavier than he had anticipated. It would slow him down in the water, and he wasn't as fast as the Darkwater Lords to begin with. Still, it was pointless for him to return to Heartwood without it.

Leaving the display room, he swam silently out of the door and past the sentry he had put out of action. Nobody had raised the alarm yet. He went along the corridors, keeping his head down when he passed the occasional servant still working, and then suddenly, he was outside the Palace and swimming through the loops and tunnels towards the cavern entrance.

The large green curtain that covered the entrance to
Darkwater was in sight when he heard the first alarm – a giant
bell ringing from somewhere deep in the palace, although how
they could ring a bell underwater he didn't know, but the clapper
reverberated through the water, and he felt rather than heard the
peals echoing throughout the city.

Well, this is it, he thought. He had got farther than he had
hoped before the alarm was raised. There was no point in keeping
quiet and trying not to be noticed now.

Dolosus increased his speed and shot towards the cavern
entrance like an arrow released from a bow.

III

Down in the depths of the Cavum, the young Libraris, Nitesco,
was oblivious to everything going on in the Castellum above
his head. Since his return to Heartwood, following his failure to
transform the knights into water elementals, Nitesco had not left
the Cavum, spending the time with his head buried in the books
and parchments, and even sleeping down there. Some small
part of him felt if he discovered the location of the fifth Node,
it might make him feel better about his failure to complete the
transformation spell.

He had been determined he would not leave until he found
some clue as to its whereabouts. Both Valens and Chonrad had
visited him at various times to try to persuade him to return and
help out with the fortifications, but Nitesco had refused, insisting
he could be of more help in his searches. However, even he was
beginning to feel it was useless, and his time would be better
spent doing something with at least some guarantee of a result,
such as helping to carry stones from one place to another.

He turned over the last page of a heavy book and, sighing,
picked it up and put it to one side. He had already been through
all the books in the room; this was his second search and so
far was proving as fruitless as the first. But inside, he knew the

answer was in the Cavum; he didn't know how, but he just *knew* it.

He rubbed his eyes tiredly. The constant reading of such small writing in such bad lighting conditions had long been giving him a bad headache, but he had refused to give in – until now. He sighed again. Reaching to a bottle at his side, he took a long swig of the water that had been there since the morning and was now covered in a fine layer of dust. He coughed, then swigged again. He must remember to drink more often. He just forgot when he got lost in the books…

It was no good; he was too tired to read any more. Knowing it would be useless to continue reading because he wouldn't be able to process the words, Nitesco curled up on the pallet he had brought down there and pulled the thin blanket over his legs. A short doze might refresh him enough to find something new, he thought.

Within seconds he was asleep.

For a while, he slept undisturbed, his tired young body resting and regenerating, his mind resting, too, with no thought to the work he had carried out in his waking hours. He was not aware of his surroundings; in fact, the whole Komis army could have run down the Cavum stairs and trampled over the books, and he probably wouldn't have awoken.

Gradually, however, something roused him from the depths of slumber, as if he were a fish at the bottom of a deep pool, and someone had hooked him and was reeling him in. Slowly, he climbed to the light of consciousness, and as he came to, he opened his eyes and realised he was not alone in the room.

Someone was sitting on the lid of a chest, over in the shadows. The last mists of sleep still clouding his senses, Nitesco blinked several times and pushed himself upright. No warning signals sounded in his head – after all, if it had been an enemy, surely they wouldn't be waiting for him to awake before they attacked him? The person sat leisurely, one ankle resting on the other knee, with leather boots and close-fitting leggings crossed with leather thongs, and he could see the standard-issue Militis mail on the lower body, although the upper was hidden in shadow. A hand came down to rest on the boot and Nitesco saw the distinctive oak leaf tattoo on the right wrist.

"Who are you?" he asked, his senses clearing and beginning to tell him something was not right.

The figure leaned forward as he said with a smile: "I think you know who I am, Libraris." A lock of hair curled on his forehead, and as he realised which wrist the tattoo was on, Nitesco recognised who it was.

It was Gavius.

A smile formed on Nitesco's face before the full realisation sank in, and he stood and stepped towards the knight before he caught himself. He stared, his smile fading. "But you are..." his voice trailed off.

"What?" Gavius prompted, teasing.

"Dead," said Nitesco matter-of-factly.

Gavius shrugged. "Life is not black-and-white, Nitesco. One is not just alive or dead. It is a matter of degrees. You should understand that better than anyone."

Nitesco did not understand, but he nodded anyway. His heart pounded, but he was afraid to move or say anything to express his alarm, in case the knight vanished. Eventually, he stated, "They said you activated the Node before...before..."

Gavius nodded. His eyes were a bright blue, like a piece of the sky that had been hidden for so long. "It was magnificent," he breathed. "I saw the Green Giant – he rose up out of the earth and spoke to me. The energy, Nitesco, you would not believe the energy that flowed through me."

Nitesco nodded, suddenly finding tears in his eyes. "What are you doing here?"

Gavius blinked. "I am here to help you."

"Me?" Nitesco's breathing quickened. "You mean with the fifth Node?"

"Yes."

"You know where it is?"

"Yes." Gavius smiled.

Nitesco opened his mouth to ask him a Question, but a movement in the shadows caught his attention, and the words melted in his mouth like soft pastry. Something was crawling across the floor. He stared as it writhed towards him, slow and insidious like a snake. Was it a snake? He couldn't take his eyes off it, and he couldn't move. His feet felt glued to the floor, his limbs frozen. He looked up at Gavius in alarm, but Gavius just continued to smile at him and did not rise to help.

The thing on the floor crawled closer, and suddenly Nitesco realised it wasn't a snake. It did not appear to be animal at all. It was something from a plant, like a creeper, or a tree root...

The root crept up to him and wrapped itself around his legs. Frozen as he was, he could only watch as it curled up his calves, then his knees, then around his thighs. It reached his waist, and then, suddenly, it tugged.

It took him by surprise and he lost his balance. He fell backwards onto the floor. The root tightened and contracted, and he clawed at the floor as he was dragged towards Gavius. The knight was still smiling, but Nitesco was suddenly frightened, and he scrabbled for a hold on the floor, his fingers clawing earth and loose stones, but he could not get a grip. Slowly, he slid across towards the Militis. The root dragged him all the way to Gavius's feet. Nitesco lay there like a dog, panting, looking up at the knight in confusion. Why was Gavius not helping him? Why was he just sitting there, that cool, curious smile on his face?

Then, suddenly, he felt himself sink into the earth.

"No!" Finally finding his voice, he yelled at Gavius, but the knight did not move to help him. His sky-blue eyes fixed on Nitesco and just watched as the Libraris was sucked slowly into the earthen floor. Nitesco felt as if he were stuck in quicksand. No matter how much he struggled, he could not seem to break free. His alarm was growing now, and no longer did he believe he was in no danger. His arms flailed to either side as he tried to find something to grab onto, but there were only books and pieces of parchment on the floor.

Finally Gavius leaned forward. His blue eyes looked deeply into Nitesco's. "Let it take you," he breathed.

Nitesco stared at him. So this was all part of the plan? It went against all his instincts to not struggle, but, believing in Gavius, he took a deep breath, closed his eyes and let the ground suck him down.

Eventually, the sinking sensation stopped. He lay there for a minute, afraid to open his eyes, but lifted the lids slowly. Astonished, he sat up. He was still in the Cavum, and both Gavius and the tree root had gone. He was sitting on the floor, books scattered around him, and there was no hole, nowhere through which he could sink.

He pushed himself to his feet and stood, staring down at the chest where Gavius had been sitting. Had it just been a dream? It had seemed so real. But then, how could it be real? Gavius was dead! He rubbed his eyes tiredly. He was overworked and had had too little sleep. His brain was playing tricks on him.

Then his eyes alighted on the chest. He remembered the way the coffer in the Armorium had covered the entrance to the Cavum. His heart began to pound as he went across to it and began to pull on one of the handles. It was heavy, filled with books, but he was too impatient to take them all out. Putting all his weight behind it, he dragged it slowly away from the wall.

When it was a few feet away, he went around the back and stared at the floor. He brushed away the centuries-old dirt covering it. There was a large piece of board fitted into the floor. He bent down and began to scrape away the dirt at the edges, trying to get his fingers beneath the sides. After a while his fingers bled and his nails broke, but he carried on and eventually lifted the board, heaving it up against the wall. Then he looked down again.

There was a hole in the floor.

His head spun. It had been a vision; Gavius really had appeared to show him the way.

He retrieved the lantern from the table where he had been reading and brought it over to the hole. Looking down, he could see steps leading into the darkness. The air smelled musty but not bad. He wondered whether he should go and get one of the other Militis to go with him, but his curiosity overrode his caution.

His booted feet treading uneasily on the earthen steps, he descended into the darkness. The steps curled around and down, and he walked slowly, afraid of slipping and falling. He counted the steps as he descended. After twenty, he raised his lantern and tried to peer further down, but the darkness was like thick, soft mud, dense and sticky, and the light seemed unable to break through it.

After fifty steps, his foot found flat ground and he stumbled, putting his hands out to steady himself. He raised the lantern. He was in a small chamber, neater than a cave, with strange, archaic etchings on the walls in a language he did not recognise. They looked old, very old.

On the opposite side of the chamber was a wooden door. It was plain with an iron handle. Nitesco drew his sword. He was impulsive but not stupid. Swallowing, he walked over, turned the handle and opened it.

Stale air filled his nostrils, but nothing waited behind the door. He stepped into a passageway at right angles to the door. The passageway curved to both the left and the right. He chose left and walked along the earthen tunnel. After about twenty yards, it split into two more passages. He hesitated. Was he in some sort of maze? He chose left again, walked a short distance and once again found himself at a fork. That confirmed it: he was definitely in a labyrinth, a maze that appeared to be right under the Temple, maybe even right under the Arbor. Looking closely at the sides of the passage, he could see tree roots embedded deep within them, as if the tree itself was holding up the walls. He could not go any farther without the risk of getting lost. Turning, he went back up the tunnel. He would get himself a long rope and tie it to the door or search for some other way to leave a trail so he could find his way back.

He went down the corridor, went right, then right again. He walked twenty yards, thinking about where he could go to get some rope.

Then he stopped.

The door wasn't where it should be. Instead, in front of him was another fork.

Nitesco froze on the spot, his heart hammering. When he had entered the maze, he had gone left, then left again. So right and right again should have brought him back to the door. Shouldn't it?

Perhaps he had been mistaken. He took the right fork and walked a bit further. The door, however, did not appear. After another twenty yards, the passageway forked again, each tunnel looking exactly the same as the others.

Nitesco cursed himself loudly. He should have marked the tunnels with his sword as he walked. But deep inside, he knew it wouldn't have mattered. He knew the way he had walked should have returned him to the door. It was a magical labyrinth, a maze that could not be solved with logic.

He was going to have to find some other way out.

IV

After the swamps and quagmires of the open fields of Laxony, the Forest of Blades to the south of Heartwood was a welcome change for Beata and Teague. It was still wet in there, of course, as some of the trees were not yet in leaf, but there were enough evergreens to provide some shelter from the downpour, and the ground wasn't quite as soggy as that which they had been travelling on the past few days.

Beata glanced over her shoulder to check Teague was still with her and hid a smile at the sorry sight he presented. Slouched forward on the horse, he looked like a sodden mass of clothes dumped on top of the saddle. His beautiful black hair was plastered to his head like a helmet, and he showed the beginnings of a black beard where he had not shaved for several days because she would not loan him a blade.

Looking down, she checked his wrists were still cuffed to the saddle and the rope that joined his horse to hers was tied to the reins. She turned back in the saddle. She did not want to look at him. Every time she gazed into those golden eyes, she was reminded of what she had done, and her shame was overwhelming.

The horses' hooves squelched through the soggy leaves. She wondered what had happened to the bandits that had attacked them on their way from Heartwood, a lifetime ago. There had been no sign of them since they entered the forest. She remembered the attack, and how poor Erubesco had been wounded. She had not had time to call in and pick her up on her way back to Heartwood.

She kicked her heels into her horse's sides, trying to get it to move more quickly, but it was difficult in the undergrowth; the mare stumbled repeatedly on broken branches and clearly disliked the atmosphere of the forest, where the trees whispered and played with her mane as she passed under them.

Behind her, Beata felt a tug on the rope that joined her to Teague. She ignored it at first; it was a game they played; he would keep doing it and she would ignore it until she lost her temper and shouted at him.

This time, however, it was different; she felt the tension on the rope tighten and her mare pranced impatiently in the leaves in response. Beata twisted in the saddle and whispered furiously over her shoulder, "Will you stop that!"

In reply, Teague put his fingers to his lips and motioned for her to stop. She did so, wondering what the matter was now. He kicked his horse forwards until it stood beside hers and leaned closer to her. She watched him carefully, waiting for a trick.

"We are being watched," he said quietly.

She glanced around the forest, but could see nothing. "Bandits?" she whispered, her heart rate increasing a little.

Teague's golden eyes flickered around the trees, then returned to her, his steady gaze making her shiver. "No. They are Komis."

"Komis?" Beata was confused. "What are you talking about? What would Komis be doing here?"

"I do not know. I do not understand it myself. But they are here; they are in the trees."

"Have they come to rescue you?"

Instead he laughed. "I sincerely doubt it."

"Have they seen us?"

"I am not sure. But either way, we will not be visible much longer."

"We won't?"

His eyes glittered. "I have ways of blending in with nature. But to hide you too, I'll have to get on your horse with you."

She stared at him for a moment, not trusting him at all. Why on earth would Komis be hiding in the woods? Surely it was just a ruse, a way to try and escape?

But then why try and get on her horse? Surely he would have done better to increase the distance between them, not shorten it? She looked around the forest again, her heart thumping, but still could not see anything.

"They are coming closer," he said matter-of-factly.

With a sigh, she leaned forward and unlocked the manacles chaining his hands to the saddle. Smoothly, he slipped off his horse. Untying the rope binding them together, he turned the horse and smacked its rump. The horse trotted off a short way and then turned to look at them. Teague ignored it. "I cannot disguise her as well." Coming up to Beata's mare, he lifted himself up behind her.

Beata felt the warmth of him against her back. Every muscle tensed as she waited for him to hit her over the head or try and strangle her or something, but he didn't; he put his arms around her waist, took a deep breath and let it out slowly. He was quiet for a moment, and through the whispering leaves and pattering of rain she heard him deepen his breathing, concentrating.

After a few moments, the strangest thing began to happen. Around them, the air started to shimmer and blur, as if the forest had been recently painted and the water was starting to smudge the edges. The effect ended about three feet from them in any direction, as if they had been encased in a giant bubble.

"It is done," he whispered in her ear. His soft breath made her tingle all over, and she closed her eyes and swallowed. Every nerve was aware of his warmth pressed tightly against her back.

Now was not the time to get lost in foolish daydreams, she scolded herself, and, kicking the mare's sides, she began to guide her forward through the forest.

"Why cannot the Komis see through your disguise?" she asked.

"All Komis have some connection with the land, but mine is stronger than most."

"Why?"

"I do not know."

Beata lapsed into silence, aware that if indeed there were people hiding in the woods, they might still hear them even if they couldn't see them. She thought about his strange talent and wondered why it was so strong in him but guessed maybe it was just one of those things, like being able to sing, or carve wood. Sometimes you were just born with it.

They had only gone a few hundred yards when there was some rustling in a tree above her head, and Beata looked up with a gasp to see a figure sitting on a branch, sharpening a sword. It was clearly a Komis: the dark hair and gold eyes were distinctive. She held her breath as the horse passed underneath, but the figure did not move, and she realised they truly could not be seen.

They passed several other Komis on their journey through the forest, but each time they moved unseen, and Beata gradually began to relax. However, it still did not solve the Question of why they were there. She felt very uneasy at the thought of all those warriors so near to Heartwood.

She had calculated they were perhaps five minutes from the far edge of the forest when they came upon a small clearing in which there were a group of about ten Komis deep in discussion. Beata edged the horse around the outside of the clearing to avoid them and held her breath when the mare stepped on a twig that snapped loudly, but although one of the warriors looked over, he clearly saw nothing of interest and soon returned to the discussion.

As they moved away, she whispered to Teague: "Could you hear what they were saying?"

"Yes," he murmured into her ear. "They were talking of the rising waters. Apparently, the Flumen has burst its banks."

"Oh, no." Beata bit her lip. The flood, and the fact that it looked like there was a large Komis army camped outside Heartwood, would mean they would have closed the gates. There was no chance of them accessing the secret passageway into the grounds, either, as the Komis were camped out at the forest entrance, which they had passed along the way.

Even as she sat worrying about how to get in, the trees thinned and the countryside opened up before them. Beata reined in the mare, and they both stared silently at the vista in front of them.

The road and fields were so flooded, it almost looked like one big river between them and Heartwood. The few small pockets of high ground that were left were filled with Komis soldiers, and Beata sensed they wouldn't last much longer. The continual downpour made the air look like there was a thick fog. She still didn't know why the Komis were there, but there was no way a war could be waged in such conditions.

"What shall we do?" she said softly, her spirits sinking.

Teague sighed softly in her ear. "We shall have to keep as close to the mountains as possible. I can give us some protection, but it will not be as good out in the open as it was in the forest. We shall have to be prepared in case we are seen."

"There is nothing else we can do," said Beata. She had managed to bring Teague all this way, and yet it still seemed as if there was so far to go. She could not see how they could possibly make it to Heartwood, and even if they did, how were they to get into the complex? They would have to take it one step at a time.

"Ready?" she asked Teague.

"I am ready."

They both pulled the hoods of their cloaks well over their heads. Then, nudging the mare forward, they left the sanctuary of the trees and went out into the open.

Instantly, they were struck by how hard it was raining: the downpour seemed to have increased since they entered the forest only hours before. Beata edged the horse towards the mountain side of the road, but she was beginning to doubt the Komis would be able to see them, anyway – how could anyone see anything in this rain?

It was not far to Heartwood, but it was hard going. The mare splashed through the puddles and shied occasionally at the deeper water lying across the road. The nearer they got, the deeper the puddles were getting, and as Heartwood began to loom out of the foggy atmosphere, Beata could see the roads out the front were completely under water. That meant the moat was already overflowing.

"What are we going to do?" Teague asked as she pulled the mare to a halt just south of Heartwood's walls.

Beata remained silent for a moment. It was clear they could not go any further on the mare. How could they get into the complex? With the river still rising, there was no way Valens would open the gates, even if she jumped up and down and told them she had the Virimage with her. Briefly, she wondered if it was flooded inside; after all, the channel ran right through the centre of the Baillium. She remembered they had cut off the inlet at the source.

And then suddenly she realised how they could get in.

"We will have to swim for it," she said. "Get down."

"Are your brains addled?" said Teague, swinging his right leg back over the horse and dismounting. "Where are we going to swim to?"

"Aim for the wall," she said, dismounting as well. "Help me take off my armour."

She waited for him to make a comment but he said nothing as his fingers began to fumble at the fastenings holding her cloak in place. Removing it, she laid it across the horse's back and then got him to lift the heavy mail shirt over her head. She placed that on the horse too, shivering in the cold as her leather tunic quickly became wet. She unbuckled it and stood in just her linen tunic, shivering. "Take off anything that will weigh you down," she ordered.

He removed his cloak but was not wearing any armour. Finally, they both stood there, shaking with cold. Beata turned the horse and smacked it on the rump, and it set off back to the forest with a whinny.

She turned to Teague. His arms were crossed across his chest and he looked positively miserable. "Now," she said firmly, "we are going to swim across the moat to the wall. At the bottom is the culvert where the channel that runs through Heartwood leaves the Baillium. The channel has been diverted, so although the opening will be underwater, we should be able to make it through into the Baillium." She sighed. "I am going to have to trust you will not just swim away. You have nowhere to go, unless you wish to try and make it back to your kinsfolk, which doesn't sound like a good idea to me. You can see clearly there is more than meets the eye here – the Darkwater Lords are on their way, and unless we stop them, the whole of Anguis is eventually going to succumb to them. So your only option really is to come with me to try and help me save the Arbor. I will not tie us together. I am trusting you will do the right thing."

"I did not think you trusted me," he said, teeth chattering.

"I don't. I just do not have any option."

She began to wade into the water. It was freezing, and the shock of it striking her legs through her breeches made her gasp. "Come on!" she snapped to Teague, who stood on the patch of higher land.

He said nothing, just looking at her, shivering. For a brief second she thought he was going to flee.

Then, suddenly, an arrow came out of nowhere and thudded into the ground next to him. They both jumped, and he spun around. The Komis had spotted them; someone was yelling, and there was movement in the mist.

Without any further encouragement, Teague plunged into the water. He gasped as she had. Turning, she began to wade towards the wall. With her feet, she felt for the edge of the moat. When her toes tipped over the edge, she took a deep breath and plunged in.

The icy water immediately seeped right through her tunic and soft breeches and put cold hands all over her skin. It was hard to get her breath. Beside her, she heard a whizz and a splash as another arrow hit the water. She could not see Teague and did not know if he had followed her. Please don't let him be hit by an arrow, she pleaded. Not now they had got this far.

Kicking out, she crossed the moat and stopped by Heartwood's wall. Treading water, she looked up as she heard raised voices. Someone was leaning out over the parapets, but she could not see who it was; they had spotted her, however, and whoever it was yelled to someone inside. They would be watching out for her, she realised. The thought gave her renewed energy.

The entrance to the channel was just below the surface of the water. Taking a deep breath, she ducked her head under, looking for it. The water was moving and there wasn't much light, and it took several attempts to find it. But she did find it, and she surfaced with a gasp.

As she did so, however, there was another whooshing sound, and then to her horror, she felt the arrow thud into her shoulder.

She screamed. Immediately, she went under and swallowed mouthfuls of water. She surfaced, coughing, but her arm was numb, and she could not keep herself afloat. Where was Teague? Had he left her? It was only what she had expected, she thought, but still, she had somehow hoped he would change...

The pain in her shoulder was excruciating, the cold numbing. Unable to keep her head above water, Beata went under for the last time.

V

Dolosus swam out of Darkwater, keeping as close to the sides of the cavern as possible, staying in the shadows. It might be pointless trying to stay invisible, but there was also no sense in drawing attention to himself. He swam quickly but steadily, knowing it was a long way back to Heartwood, and he was still not as comfortable in his form as the Darkwater Lords obviously were.

Still, he thought he might have a while, as he was sure Thalassinus wouldn't bother to send just a few guards after him, and certainly wouldn't come after him himself on his own. The big attack had been imminent, and Dolosus guessed once the High Lord realised Dolosus had got the Pectoris, he would call for the attack to begin. He would send the whole force of Darkwater after his wayward son.

He slipped through the green curtain and out into the wild ocean. The currents were strong around him, and he realised the High Moon must be rising in the sky. The Pectoris weighed heavy on his back, but the Darkwater army would be wearing armour and might be similarly weighed down.

He wondered how the Arbor's heart was faring in his backpack. He was surprised it had survived its extraction from the tree and also that it was still beating after being taken so deep in the ocean. It should therefore survive the journey back, he thought. But would it mend the tree? Would that horrible rent in the Arbor's trunk close up around its heart if it was placed back in it?

The ocean was dark and silent, and Dolosus felt strangely lonely as he swam, even though he passed shoals of fish and the large, shadowy shapes of sharks and whales in the deep. For the first time, he wondered what the others had thought of his disappearance on the beach. Procella and Chonrad – what had they thought when he suddenly vanished? Had they guessed he had continued down to Darkwater on his own, or had they assumed he had perished along the way?

And would they have guessed at his betrayal? In spite of the cold, his cheeks burned. He hoped none of them – especially Valens – would ever find out he had so nearly defected.

After several hours, and what he estimated was about halfway back to the coast of Anguis, Dolosus stopped swimming and took a quick rest. Though he did not have muscles as such, still his limbs ached and burned with the exertion of swimming so far so fast. He turned and looked back the way he had come, towards Darkwater. And then he saw something that made his very soul seem to freeze.

In the distance was a huge dark mass. He stared at it for a moment, not sure what he was seeing, thinking maybe it was a whale on the seabed. And then he realised. It was the Darkwater army, with soldiers so numerous they seemed to cover the sea floor.

Immediately, he turned and started swimming towards the shoreline. His heart was in his mouth. Of course, he had known they would come after him, but to actually see it was so chilling that for a while, it seemed as if he had to warm his limbs up again to get them swimming properly.

Eventually, he reached a rhythm, however, and soon was swimming quickly and evenly. Occasionally, he risked a glance over his shoulder, and in time, he saw the mass was growing. After a while, he began to make out individual shapes, and he knew they were getting closer. But all the time, he was getting closer to the shore, too.

As he swam he gave some thought as to what he was going to do when he reached the shore. He did not expect Chonrad and Procella and the others to be waiting for him; they would have returned to Heartwood, as he would have done if he was in their position. So therefore, if he came ashore at Vichton, what would he do? He would have to find a horse and ride to Heartwood, and that would take too long.

Therefore, he decided he would not get out of the ocean at Vichton, but would instead try to find the mouth of the Flumen and then swim up it, right to Heartwood if possible. Of course, it meant Thalassinus would probably find it easier to catch him if he stayed in the water, but he thought it was worth the risk to cut travelling time.

It was not long before he began to sense the seabed shallowing, and sure enough, before long the coastline of Anguis reared up before him. He swam along the coast, searching for the mouth of the Flumen. He came upon it more quickly than he had anticipated. He purposely wasn't accessing Damaris's watery instincts, as he was afraid the water elemental might take him over once again.

Before long he was swimming up the Flumen, finding it strange to be out of the open sea. He could see the sides of the river channel and beneath him the river bed. The water was different, too; it was fast-flowing due to all the extra rain ,and its pace slowed him down as he was swimming against the current all the time.

Still, he could feel the miles passing. Occasionally, he risked a glance over his shoulder, and it wasn't until he thought he was about halfway up Isenbard's Wall that he saw his first glimpse of Darkwater.

In the far distance was the dark mass of figures swimming up the channel behind him. And in the front, he thought he saw a glitter of a golden sash. Thalassinus.

Well, that was a battle that would need to be fought, he thought grimly, but for now he was still ahead and needed to get to Heartwood before they did. He had come so far; he couldn't fail now. But he was getting tired, and the Pectoris seemed to be getting heavier the nearer he got to its source.

The last half of the journey up the Flumen was the hardest of all. His watery muscles burned, and he felt so tired, he was sure any moment he would feel Thalassinus's sword slicing through his tail. But although the Darkwater Lords were clearly closing in, they had not reached him by the time he saw the western end of Isenbard's Wall.

The volume of water made it clear to Dolosus the river had burst its banks. He was able to swim up and out of the Flumen's channel and across the land into Heartwood's moat. He swam right up to the end of it, then back, trying to think furiously about what would be the best way in.

Then he saw her – a figure floating motionless in the water. Her light brown hair drifted around her face in the water, and he could see an arrow protruding out of her shoulder. He could also see a dark-haired man trying desperately to drag her up to the surface.

He swam up to them. The man stared at him in alarm, bubbles rising from his mouth, but he did not let go of the woman. He blinked and Dolosus saw a pair of bright golden eyes. Komis?

Dolosus looked at the woman, and his heart missed a beat. It was Beata. He did not think he had ever seen her without her armour and had not recognised her with her hair all around her face. She looked beautiful floating there, and he had to shake himself mentally to remind himself she could not breathe underwater like he could.

He did not have to think what to do next. Grasping her under the arms, he hauled her easily upwards. It was only as he neared the surface he saw the hole in the wall above him and realised where he was. He swam for the hole, the Komis swimming next to him.

They passed under Heartwood's solid wall, and then they were in the Baillium. Dolosus saw several pairs of hands reach down and haul Beata and the Komis out of the water. He hesitated, suddenly unsure of what to do. How did he change back into his earth spirit? Nitesco hadn't explained that part.

He swam back to the wall as he thought about it. Outside, in the moat, he looked down towards Isenbard's Wall. And what he saw frightened him more than anything in his life so far.

Thalassinus waited in the gap between the moat and the overflowing Flumen by Isenbard's Wall. Clearly, he was waiting for the rest of his army to catch up with him. Gradually, more and more warriors were lining up behind him. He saw Dolosus looking at him, and he smiled. He was huge and terrifying, and immediately, Dolosus turned and fled.

He swam through the hole in the Wall and, before he could think about it, headed down the channel to where the water level shallowed. In one fluid move, he leapt straight out of the water. In midflight, he felt himself begin to change. Time seemed to stop. His earthly self emerged and engulfed his watery one. Damaris screamed but was forced down deep inside. It was agonising, and he twisted in the air, thinking for a moment he was going to die. But by the time he landed back on the ground, it was his feet, and not his tail, that fell to the earth, and the transformation was complete.

Immediately, he felt the points of several swords on his body. "It is me!" he panted, holding up his hands.

Before him, Procella gradually lowered her sword. "It is Dolosus!" she said in amazement. Behind her, Valens's face lit up.

Dolosus nodded. "It is I." He looked to his left and saw Beata turn onto her side and vomit water onto the ground. Relief surged through him that she was all right. Beside her, the Komis looked up at him with those strange golden eyes. Briefly, he remembered she had been sent to try and find the Virimage. Was this he?

Suddenly, he remembered what he had travelled so far to recover. "I have it," he said, raising the handle of his bag over his head and handing it to Procella. "The Pectoris is in there. I think it is still alive."

"You brought it back?" said Chonrad, coming up behind him. "Roots of the Arbor, you brought it back!"

Around him, everyone was suddenly laughing and clapping, celebrating the fact that both he and Beata had returned. Chonrad clasped Dolosus to him in a breathtakingly hard embrace, and then someone else reached over and kissed him. He felt a flood of warmth inside, of delight at the thought that they were pleased to see him. He went to grab them and, as he did so, suddenly became aware of his missing arm. The loss hit him like a bolt of lightning and drew him out of his dream homecoming.

He glanced over his shoulder. "There is no time for celebrating. Quick, we must block the entrance to the channel."

He gaze took in all the knights crowded around him. And when he spoke, his fear was plain for all to see.

"They are coming!"

PART THREE

CHAPTER SIXTEEN

I

Following Dolosus's words of warning, Valens yelled to a handful of Custodes to bring over some large rocks, and they very quickly blocked up the hole that led out into the moat. Valens nodded when he saw it done and said, "That should keep them out."

Dolosus looked at the rocks and wasn't so sure. They didn't really have a clue just how many or how strong the Darkwater Lords were. Should he tell them? Or was it pointless now they were here, as Heartwood would shortly be finding out for itself, anyway?

Valens beckoned him over. The great Imperator clasped him by the shoulders and stared at him for a moment. Dolosus met his gaze, and felt as if Valens's eyes were like great torches, burning and seeing right through him. Before he knew what he was saying, he blurted, "I am sorry."

Valens nodded, and Dolosus suddenly thought: he knows. He knows about the dream. But then Valens smiled and clasped his foster-son to him, and Dolosus gasped as he felt he had been forgiven.

He turned to look at the Komis who was kneeling on the ground beside Beata. Several guards stood over him, swords pressed to his neck.

"Who are you?" Valens demanded, towering over him. "Are you part of the army who attacked Heartwood?"

The Komis shook his head. "I am Teague. The one they call the Virimage."

There was a collective gasp. Nobody could believe at the same moment both the Virimage and the Pectoris had been found.

"Come," said Procella impatiently. "We must replace the Pectoris."

"The Darkwater Lords were right behind me," Dolosus reminded everyone urgently.

Valens nodded. "The guard on the wall will tell us as soon as there is a breach. Quick, we must sort the Arbor out first, or all else is pointless."

Dolosus turned and knelt by Beata's side. The arrow still protruded out of her shoulder, and she was pale and sweating in spite of the rain. "Can you carry her inside?" he asked Chonrad, who was kneeling by her.

Chonrad scooped her up into his arms. Together, they all walked towards the Castellum. Dolosus cast a nervous glance back at Heartwood's huge walls and giant Porta. How long would it keep them out?

The Quad was awash with water, and they all had to splash through it to get to the oak doors. The two Custodes standing guard opened the doors, and they entered the Temple.

Chonrad laid Beata on the floor to one side. He went to try to pull out the arrow, but she pushed him aside impatiently, gesturing towards Procella. The Dux was opening the bag she had been carrying and, with a gasp, she took out the Pectoris. Everyone stared at the organ that lay in her hands.

"Is it still beating?" asked Valens hoarsely.

Procella looked up at him, her bottom lip trembling. "I cannot tell."

"Give it to Silva."

The Custos of the Arbor was waiting by the tree. She took the Pectoris from Procella, held it in her hands and closed her eyes. Dolosus looked across at Teague and saw him watching Silva curiously, the first time he had seen another of his own kin inside the walls.

Silva looked over at Valens, relief evident on her face. "It is alive."

There was a collective sigh, quickly hushed as she went over to the Arbor. Dolosus stared at the holy tree. It looked dead. There was no sign of movement in the branches or roots.

She reached over the massive split in its trunk and carefully placed the Pectoris in the middle of the hole. She spent a moment making sure it was secure, then stepped back.

They all waited.

Nothing happened.

Silva put her hands on the tree and closed her eyes. Dolosus strained his eyes to look for some sign of movement. Did the twigs and branches just flutter a little, or was it his imagination? Eventually, Silva turned, her face drawn. She looked straight at Teague.

"Can you help?" she asked.

Teague shook his head as everyone turned to face him. Dolosus could see the panic in his eyes. "I do not know what I can do," he said defensively.

"But Beata travelled across Anguis for you," blurted Procella. "Look at her, at what she has suffered. You were supposed to be able to help us."

Valens put a warning hand on her arm. He walked over to Beata and knelt awkwardly by her side. "How are you, Beata?" he said softly.

She was breathing shallowly, and her face was very white. She was also shivering noticeably. "I am not sure," she said with a weak smile.

"We need to get that arrow out of you."

She nodded. Valens called for someone to bring some water and a cloth.

Dolosus came over. Emotion rushed through him at the sight of Beata lying there, pale as milk, sweat beading on her forehead, her long hair lank and matted around her face. To see her so weak and helpless filled him with rage and frustration, and he came forward and knelt beside her. Teague leaned over her, stroking her hair and muttering soothing words. Dolosus watched him with an amused smile. The Komis spoke tenderly and clearly had some affection for her.

Valens took hold of the arrow shaft in his right hand. He put his left on her shoulder and Dolosus did the same. "Ready, Beata?" She nodded, her breathing coming rapidly.

"Now," he said. He pulled as Dolosus pushed down. The arrow came out with a sucking noise, and Beata screamed. Dolosus grabbed the cloth and pressed it down on her shoulder. He gritted his teeth. It was always hard to see someone else in pain and know you could do nothing, but somehow it was worse with the beautiful, gentle Beata. He wanted to comfort her, but Teague was stroking her hair while she sobbed, and suddenly he felt as if he were intruding.

He stood, watching as Teague tended to her, binding the wound and putting her arm in a sling. It was only then he turned to Valens as the Imperator pulled him slightly away from the others.

"It is good to see you back," Valens said in his deep, gruff voice. His dark brown eyes, so like Dolosus's own, were calm and forgiving.

"It was a long journey," said Dolosus. Suddenly, he didn't have the words to explain what had happened to him down in Darkwater. "I... There was..." His voice faltered.

Valens placed a hand on his shoulder. "There will be time for tales later," he said. "When the battle has been won."

"Yes." The two knights looked at each other, and each saw in the other's eyes their true beliefs.

"It has been good knowing you," said Valens. His grip tightened on Dolosus's shoulder.

"And I you," said Dolosus, meaning it. "They will break through the walls, you know."

"Yes, I know." Valens's arm dropped. He turned and looked over at the Arbor, which still showed no signs of life.

"Do you think it is dead?" asked Dolosus.

"No," said Valens immediately. "Silva insists there are still signs of life within it, although honestly, I cannot see it. But she says she would be able to feel when it died, and I believe her – she has a strong connection to the tree."

"And the Virimage?" Dolosus asked, looking across at Teague, who was still curled around Beata, refusing to move. "What about him? Why is he not helping us?"

Valens glanced over. "You know as much about the situation as I. But I think it is time we spoke. I am not happy with him being quite so close to our Dean."

He walked over to Teague and Dolosus followed, curious about the Virimage Beata had travelled all over Anguis to find. "Komis," Valens said in a commanding tone. "We have to talk."

Teague looked up. He saw who was speaking, then looked away. "I have nothing to say to you."

"I just want to talk."

"I have nothing to say to you," repeated Teague stubbornly.

Dolosus drew his sword and lowered it until it touched the Komis's throat. "Get up," he said flatly.

Teague looked at the blade. Then, carefully, he put a hand under Beata's head and extricated himself from her, leaving a Militis to take his place. He stood and lifted his chin defiantly. "I am sorry Beata has been wounded, but her journey was in vain. I cannot help you."

Valens frowned. "How do you know unless you try? Do you mean you cannot, or will not?"

Teague said nothing.

Valens gestured to the Arbor. "Perhaps Beata did not explain to you fully the situation."

Teague did not look at the tree. "She explained everything to me – more than once. I know what you want me to do. I am telling you I am not able to do it!"

"And again I say: how do you know unless you try? Why do you not go over to the tree? Place your hands upon it like Silva does? Even a little of your power might be enough to bring the tree back to life."

Teague risked a quick glance at the Arbor. To Dolosus's surprise, the Komis shuddered. "This is not my battle," he said stubbornly. "I have no interest in the affairs of Heartwood."

"Of course you do," said another voice. Dolosus turned and saw Silva pushing through the people who were all now listening to the conversation. She came to stand before her compatriot, her golden eyes flashing. "Where do you think your power comes from? The Arbor, of course! Without the Arbor you would have nothing."

"If only wishing made it so," Teague snapped, turning away in frustration. He spun back, lips curled in a snarl. "All my life, I have been cursed with the Greening, and never have I wanted it. I have been brought here, dragged across half of Anguis, all against my will…"

His voice tailed off as Silva stepped towards him. She carried no weapon, but there was no doubt her manner was menacing. "I do not care," she said in a low voice. "But you will help the Arbor, whether you want to or not."

His eyes narrowed. "You know you cannot force me to do the Greening. You of all people should know that."

She grabbed his hand. He resisted, but found with alarm he could not pull away. Everyone watched in shock as, suddenly, vines began to grow from the adjoined hands of the Custos and the Virimage. They sprouted from their fingers and curled down their arms, leaves unfurling, twisting and twining themselves around their body.

Teague tore himself from Silva with a gasp. Silva's eyes, too, were wide. "You see," she panted, "I can make you, and I will!"

"What was that?" demanded Valens. "I have never seen you do anything like that before!"

Silva turned to face Valens. "His power is far greater than mine. I just forced him to channel it. But you can see what he is capable of. We must make him do it!"

At that moment, however, there was a commotion from the oak doors at the front of the Temple. Everyone turned as Solum rushed in. He came straight up to Valens. "Imperator," he gasped, face white with shock. "You must come with us. The water... It is rising up the walls!"

II

Valens's breathing quickened at the panic on Solum's face. The knight quickly explained to everyone the river had now risen so much it was starting to creep up the sides of Heartwood.

"So is the water level rising all over Anguis?" asked Valens, confused, picturing the whole land ten feet under water.

"No. There seems to be an invisible wall on the other side of the moat. The water is only rising on this side of it. It is the most peculiar thing I ever saw." Solum's eyes conveyed his fear, although his voice was calm.

Valens looked across at Dolosus and Chonrad, who stood side by side. They met his eyes with the same look of resignation. Valens nodded. It was time. There was nothing else to be done.

Turning, he leapt as nimbly as his leg would allow onto a nearby upturned box. "My friends!" he called out, waiting until everyone had quietened. "My friends," he began again, hoping his tone implied he truthfully considered those in the Temple to be in that category. "There is no more time. The Darkwater Lords are here. We have done everything we could possibly do, and I am amazed at what we have achieved.

"Dolosus travelled to the depths of the ocean to retrieve our precious Pectoris, which might yet prove to be the deciding factor in our war with Darkwater." Dolosus met Valens's eyes. The Imperator thought of his dream and wondered just what had happened to the knight when he vanished into the sea.

"Not only did Beata traverse the whole of Laxony for the Virimage, but she found him and brought him here, although the cost to her may have been great and his usefulness unknown." His eyes lingered on the wounded Militis. She had pushed herself up to a sitting position, and at his words her eyes flicked to Teague, who still sat by her side. Teague looked away. Valens smiled to himself; from that look, he knew her business with Teague had not yet finished. Between her and Silva, there was still hope they could get him to help the Arbor.

He continued, "Four brave knights and their companions have travelled the length and breadth of the four countries in Anguis. Their task was to activate the four Nodes. I do not think any of us anticipated just how difficult that would be. We thought it would be a physical act – we did not realise it would be an emotional one, too. Each knight has, in his or her own way, had to deal with a personal crisis, and each has shown his or her inner strength by dealing with that crisis, and coming through the other side.

"Gravis, for maybe the first time in his life, travelled without his twin to the Node at the Henge in Laxony, and confronted his own inner fears to activate it." He looked down at Gravis, who had returned only days before, tired, exhausted, but triumphant at his success. Gravis nodded his head in response, giving a small smile, although his gaunt face was an echo of the horrors he had faced on the journey. He had told Valens everything that happened to him on his travels, and although Valens knew Gravis's problems stemmed from his close relationship with his brother, nevertheless he knew learning of Gavius's death had been a great shock to him, and it would not be something from which he would recover easily.

"Grimbeald gathered his courage to descend into the Tumulus in Wulfengar and fought old terrors to open his Node." The Wulfian warrior raised a hand in recognition. He had spoken little since his return, spending all his time tending to Tenera, who was still suffering from an unidentifiable sickness. Valens had in fact been surprised to see him come back; he had thought he might stay in Wulfengar to defend his own lands. But he was pleased to see the gruff Wulfian return; Grimbeald had shown his courage and his worth, and Valens knew he would defend the Arbor to the death.

"Fionnghuala faced her past and opened the Node in Hanaire." The Hanaireans had been the last to return, only days before. Valens did not know the full extent of what Fionnghuala had had to undergo to open her Node; the Hanaireans were a private people, and he had not wanted to force her to tell him. But he could see from the way Bearrach touched her hand gently, the two of them had grown close, and clearly, he had supported her throughout the ordeal she had had to undergo.

"And Gavius triumphantly opened his Node in Komis before his life was so abruptly taken from him." Gavius, of course, was not there to explain what had happened on his journey. Only Niveus had returned out of his party, and she now met Valens's eyes, her own filled with tears at the memory of what she had endured.

Valens paused. His eyes took in all the people in the room. There were his own Militis, both those who lived in Heartwood and those in the Exercitus who had returned to try and save the Arbor; the Laxonians and Hanaireans, who remained because they felt such a powerful need to defend the tree; and perhaps most especially the Wulfians, who had braved the antagonism and resentment from everyone because of their loyalty to the tree they loved.

Everyone who mattered to him was there: Procella, his courageous and faithful Dux, who would stand by his side until one or both of them fell; Dolosus, who he thought of as his son, and who had undergone who knew what horrors to retrieve the Pectoris; Beata, whom he had a soft spot for, although he would never admit it to anyone; and Chonrad, the knight who had been rejected by Heartwood so long ago, and yet remained to defend it, proving himself a loyal and noble companion.

They all looked weary, some of them were wounded, and although none of them would admit to being scared, he knew the thought of the Darkwater Lords pounding on the doors of Heartwood would strike fear into any heart.

"It is time," he said firmly. "Time to make a stand. Time to show Darkwater we are not just going to step aside and let them take Heartwood. We have done everything we could to try to protect ourselves against this invasion. There is nothing more to do. It is time."

He indicated Beata, who was now struggling to sit up. "There will be many more injured by the end of the day. We shall clear an area behind the Arbor, and this will serve as our Infirmaria. All wounded are to be brought here and treated. Silva, perhaps you could organise bedding and medicines in preparation for our first arrivals." Silva nodded.

"Fionnghuala and Bearrach, I would be grateful if you could please organise the materials ready for barricading the oak doors." They nodded, faces pale. "We will make the Temple our last stand. Our last breath, the last stroke of our swords, must be spent defending the Arbor." He drew his own sword. "I do not know what the end of the night will bring. Many of us, if not all of us, will die. But we are holy knights – we live to defend the Arbor. And defend it we will, though it may cost us our lives."

Chonrad drew his sword. "To the death."

"To the death." Dolosus drew his.

"To the death." Procella, Gravis, Grimbeald, all the knights who had accompanied them on their missions, and all those who had remained at Heartwood, drew their weapons.

It was only then Valens became aware they were all bathed in an icy white light. He looked around, puzzled, but it was only when Silva said, "Look!" and pointed upwards that he, and everyone else, looked up.

The clouds had parted. And right above the Temple was the High Moon, white as snow, cold as ice.

Valens stared at it. It had been raining for so long that for a moment he almost felt confused to see the sky. He looked at the

Moon, felt its pinky-white light like cool water on his skin. He supposed it should be fear he was feeling; after all, the High Moon marked the highest point of the tides and was the moment the Darkwater Lords would be strongest. No doubt they had made it appear to strike fear into their hearts.

But strangely, he did not feel fear, but instead a seed of hope planted itself within him. He looked across at the Arbor. Was it his imagination, or was the tree moving in the white light, as if it were reaching up to soak the light into its branches?

"The tree is alive!" He whispered the words, and yet as one, everyone turned to the Arbor and gasped. It was true; the branches were moving, only gently, but it proved to them the Arbor was not yet dead, and that was the final thing they needed to send them into battle.

Valens smiled. "Let us do it."

Outside, it was still raining, and as they stood in the Quad and looked up, the clouds were heavy and grey, showing no signs of abating. They were used to the wet now, though, and hardly gave it a thought as they made their way across the Baillium to the walls.

Valens had spent weeks strengthening the fortifications, and there was little more they could do now. Procella and Chonrad behind him, he climbed as quickly as he could up the Porta and looked over the parapet. Solum was right; the water level was rising rapidly and was now almost two thirds of the way up Heartwood's walls. It was as if there were an invisible wall on the other side of the moat. Beyond this, he could see the Komis army milling about uneasily. The Flumen was still rising, and it wouldn't be long before the landscape in front of Heartwood was completely covered in water.

He looked at the shadows stirring in the rising water. They were going to come right over the top, he thought suddenly. He looked down into the murky depths of the water. Hundreds of shadows moved inside: the Darkwater army, preparing to invade.

"We must withdraw," he decided suddenly. He turned to Procella. "They are going to come right over the wall. We cannot fight them until they become corporeal, so it is pointless having people stationed here. This is no ordinary siege. Our high walls give us no advantage. We must form a front line halfway between the walls and the Temple. We will defend as far as we can, then withdraw into the Temple."

Procella nodded. Immediately, she started ordering the Custodes away from the walls. Chonrad turned to him, however. "Are you sure about this?" he said, eyes narrowed. "We will have no advantage just waiting for them to come at us."

"There is nothing I can do about that. It will be suicide to just wait up here."

"Is it worth us setting up a line of pikes at the top, ready for when they cross?"

Valens thought about it. "My guess is they will wait to transform until the water is pouring down the other side of the wall. I do not think any of our defences will work now." He thought Chonrad was going to argue with him, but the Laxonian just nodded, and together they headed back down the stairs.

In the Baillium, Procella was already organising the Exercitus into lines, facing Heartwood's outer walls, halfway between the walls and the Temple. Her archers flanked either side of the central army, formed from Exercitus, Laxonians, Hanaireans and the few Wulfians that were left. She turned as Valens and Chonrad walked up to her. "Lord Barle," she said, placing a hand on his arm, "I wondered whether you would like to lead a cavalry charge. I thought maybe you could take a group of cavalry around the Barracks and come around the back of the Darkwater army once battle has engaged."

Chonrad nodded. He felt a pang of disappointment at not being at her side in battle, but his horse skills were unparalleled, and he knew he was the person to do this.

Valens held up a hand as Procella started to tell him to stay at the rear. "My place is beside yours," he told her firmly. "I cannot stand aside while Heartwood itself is under attack, and I know you understand this. The time has gone, my dear Dux, for playing games. This is war, and we shall all stand together." He looked across at Dolosus, who stood to one side. Dolosus nodded back.

"Let us do it."

Chonrad grasped his hand quickly, resting his left hand on Valens's wrist, and Valens did the same. Then the Laxonian turned to Procella. Valens watched something unseen pass between them, although they did not speak or touch. Then Chonrad marched off to find his horse.

Valens smiled at his companions, walking to the front line and taking his place beside his Dux and his foster-son.

He looked up at the wall in front of them. For a moment he did not understand what he was seeing, and then he realised. A shimmer of water ran along the top edge of the wall, silver in the light of the rising Light Moon.

III

After the majority of the knights had left, inside the Temple there was a flurry of commotion as everyone prepared to make the Temple ready for the last stand.

Fionnghuala and Bearrach and the few remaining Hanaireans headed the organisation, ferrying around large pieces of wood and stone ready for when they had to barricade themselves in. Meanwhile, Silva cleared an area behind the Arbor and began spreading out bedding, while Niveus brought medicinal supplies and bowls of clean water ready to bathe wounds.

Teague sat sullenly to one side, Beata propped up in a chair nearby, and watched the commotion. He felt no compulsion to take part. This was not his battle, after all, he reminded himself. If there had not been a whole army of Komis outside, and a whole army of mysterious underwater warriors, he would have disguised himself and made a run for it. But he had a feeling he wouldn't make it more than a few yards from Heartwood.

He thought about the way the knight they called Dolosus had suddenly appeared beside him in the moat. He had been struggling to get Beata to the surface, and then Dolosus was there, a shadowy shape in the water, with a tail instead of legs and a silver shimmer to his face. Teague had never seen anything like it in his life. Now, for the first time, he wondered exactly who these Darkwater Lords were, and why they were attacking Heartwood.

Clearly, they wished for the downfall of the tree, he thought. He did not understand his gift with the Greening, did not want it, but he did know he was connected with the earth, and obviously the Darkwater Lords had an affinity with water.

He looked across at Beata to find her watching him. She said nothing, but her eyes were hurt, accusing. He looked away.

He could not put into words why he did not want to help her. He didn't even know himself. He just knew he was frightened.

He cast a quick glance over at the tree. He had been shocked when he first came into the Temple. Beata had spoken to him of the wonder of the Arbor, of their glorious tree. And of course, he knew all about the stories of Animus from his childhood. But he could hardly believe this was the same tree as that of the golden myth.

How could anyone revere such a decrepit specimen of nature? Teague was repulsed, disgusted and – he had to admit – disappointed by it. Holy tree? He had seen better, greater oaks in the forest. He could not ever imagine worshipping this drooping, torn example.

He looked away. The two Hanaireans were beginning to make headway with their preparations. There were piles of wood and stone on either side of the doors, ready to barricade the army in when the time came. All furniture and precious objects had been stowed, moved or hidden, although lit candles still circled the room, as it was now almost completely dark outside, except for the Moon, which kept peeping out behind the rainclouds. The Temple sat in a complex pattern of light and shadows, cast by the eerie glow from the Moon.

Teague could feel Beata's eyes on him, as if they were two red-hot irons branding the back of his neck. He ignored her for the moment, however, as he was gradually becoming aware of the sound of crying. It was very soft and in the distance, and he couldn't tell if it was male or female, but although it was subdued as if someone was trying to hide their misery, nevertheless there was such unhappiness in the sobbing it wrenched at his heart.

He looked around the Temple. Everyone seemed busy. He could not see anyone huddled in a corner. There did appear to be individual cells in the outer ring, so maybe the noise was coming from there, he thought. He stood, intending to walk over there, but immediately as he did so, he realised the sound was coming from the centre of the Temple, not the outside.

He was at that moment in the outer ring, close to the fence that usually kept out visitors to the inner part of the Temple. He started walking around the fence, searching for some sign of the distraught soul. The inner circle was deserted, however; on the western side, near the Domus, Silva was setting up the Infirmaria, but she was busy in the outer circle.

Teague walked all the way around, then came to a stop not far from where he had started. The crying was, if anything, louder, and laden with such misery it almost made him want to cry himself. His hands gripped the top of the fence. Surely, it couldn't be… His eyes flicked around the room, looking for another source of the sound. But there was no other, and suddenly he realised the truth.

The tree was crying.

Teague froze to the spot, feelings as if his hands were stuck to the fence. In all his years exploring the Greening, his contact had always been through touch and the sixth sense of "feeling" nature around him. He had never heard any plants or trees speak to him, and he had certainly never heard any of them crying.

He stared at the Arbor, his heart pounding. Why was the tree crying? Because it was hurt? Or because it was so upset at what was happening to Heartwood? He looked frantically around the room. Could nobody else hear it? But it was so loud!

He started as someone touched him on the arm, and he spun around, but it was just Beata. Her face was as pale as the moonlight on the flagstones, but she seemed steady on her feet, and her eyes were clear. "What is the matter?" she asked, eyes narrowed as she stared searchingly into his own.

Teague swallowed. He was not about to admit to her he could hear the tree crying, or she would assume the connection meant he could help it. Instead, he just shrugged. "How are you feeling?"

"I will live." She glanced over at the Arbor, then looked back at him. "I did not drag you from one end of Anguis to the other for nothing, you know."

He glared at her. His golden eyes usually unsettled people, and he waited for her to look away, but this time she didn't, meeting his gaze directly and firmly. "You cannot make me do anything," he said.

She smiled. "Oh, I think we both know that is not true."

"You think you can still best me one-handed?" he scoffed.

She raised an eyebrow. "I do not think so; I *know* so."

Teague knew he had to raise his game. She was clearly going to try to use force to make him go closer to the tree, and he had to do everything he could to stop her doing that. If he could just distract her until the invasion started, maybe then she would leave him alone, and he would somehow be able to disguise himself and slip away.

He took a step closer to her. He knew how to get under her skin. "You seem to think you are the one in control," he said softly. "If that is so, then you must bear full responsibility for what happened between us that evening. Can you do that, Beata? Can you accept you were as responsible as I for the seduction that occurred?"

"I..." For the first time she faltered. Two bright spots of pink appeared on her cheekbones, the only colour on her pale face apart from her blue eyes. She took a step backwards, clearly unnerved at his proximity. "Do not come any closer," she warned.

Teague ignored her. He continued to walk forwards, and she continued to back away until she bumped into the cells and could retreat no further.

He fixed her there with his golden eyes, moving closer until their bodies touched. She could easily have pushed him away with her good arm, but she seemed unable to move, although her chest rose and fell quickly with her rapid breathing. She seemed entranced by his eyes, and indeed, that was what he had intended. He knew others found them beguiling, but this time, there was more to Beata's inability to move than fascination with the colour of his eyes. Like him, she was remembering what had transpired between them.

His gaze fell to her lips. He remembered the feel of them beneath his own, their softness as he had pressed his mouth onto hers. Suddenly, he wanted to kiss her more than anything in the world. The urge was irresistible. If he had been clearer in his thoughts, he may have realised something magical was at work, but his senses had overridden his mental processes, and all he could think about was Beata and the touch and taste of her.

He placed one hand on either side of the cell behind her and leaned forward.

Their lips touched. He closed his eyes and gave himself up to the kiss.

He had forgotten about distracting her, about the tree, about anything except the feel of her in his arms and the memory of their lovemaking. Carefully avoiding her wounded shoulder, he wrapped his arms around her and pressed her to him, his left hand threading through her hair, cupping the back of her head. He could feel her heart pounding against his own ribs. She softened in his arms, leaning into the kiss, her good arm moving around his waist, and he felt her sigh, although whether from bliss or resignation he couldn't tell. All thoughts of distraction fled from his mind. There was just Beata, and her beautiful, soft lips.

It was only when something fell on his cheek that he blinked and opened his eyes, then lifted his head. Like people awaking from a dream, they looked around in surprise. Soft rose petals were falling from the sky. The ceiling of the Temple was still intact; the petals were materialising out of thin air, falling throughout the room, landing on the heads and shoulders of those standing around, who, Teague suddenly noticed, were all staring at the couple caught up in their embrace.

Teague looked down at Beata and felt a sudden stab of fear at the look on her face. Rage, white and hot, burned in her eyes, and she pushed him with her good arm in the chest so hard, he stumbled. "You would try to seduce me here, of all places!" she hissed. Before he could say anything, before he could move, she drew her arm back and suddenly her fist met his chin with a loud crack, and then he was his back on the floor.

"It was not me," he said truthfully, turning as she aimed a kick at his groin, and she missed and hit his thigh. She ignored him and tried again, but he curled into a ball, yelling as she whacked his shinbone. "Beata!" How could he explain he hadn't been responsible for the petals?

"Beata!" This time the voice came from Beata's side. He waited until the kicks had stopped and then unfurled slightly to see who it was. Fear clenched his stomach. It was Silva.

Beata glared at the Custos of the Arbor, her fury making her more beautiful than ever. "He... he..." She seemed unable to put her anger into words.

"I know," said Silva calmly. "I saw. He tells the truth, Beata; it was not him. He has a connection to the Arbor; I could feel it. It was the tree who wanted him to kiss you. It was the tree that sent the petals."

"It was the Arbor?" gasped Beata, puzzled.

Silva's golden eyes were unreadable. "It read what was in your hearts and interpreted it in the only way it knows: the natural world."

Beata reddened. "If it could read my heart, it would send thunder and lightning, not rose petals."

Silva's gaze was unrelenting. "That is what you want to feel, not what you truly feel. You can deny it to yourself, Beata, but you cannot deny your true feelings to the Arbor. It sees all."

Beata turned. Clearly, Silva's words had not made her feel better. "I have had enough," she spat. "It is time. Let us take him to the tree."

"No!" Teague yelled, and turned onto his knees, intending to make a run for it, but he wasn't quick enough, and Beata's foot came down on his backside, forcing him forward onto his face. He turned and felt her firm hand on his arm, dragging him to his feet. He twisted, trying to wrench himself from her grip, but she was so strong it surprised him, and then Silva too had his arm, and although he struggled, he could not shake them off.

Half-dragging him, half-carrying him, they brought him through the gate in the fence and across the channel to the inner circle. Beata threw him down in front of the tree so he sprawled on the ground amongst its roots. She towered over him, still furious, although whether it was just with him or also with herself he wasn't really sure.

"No!" he yelled, then, more pleadingly, "Please, do not make me do this."

For a moment she didn't speak. Then, more softly, she said, "I have no choice. We all have a destiny to fulfil Teague, and this is yours."

Then she stepped back, and let the tree loom over him.

IV

Chonrad sat quietly on his horse at the head of the Equitas and watched the water slowly seep through the parapets of

Heartwood's outer walls. He shivered. It was a terrifying sight. It was so unnatural, seeing water at that height. His grandfather, who also came from Vichton, had once seen a tidal wave during a great storm. Although only six feet high, it had swept in from the ocean and destroyed most of the town, killing several thousand people. His grandfather must have felt what he was feeling now, thought Chonrad, watching the first splashes reach the grass in the Baillium. Part of the terror came from the unfamiliar, from not knowing how to react or what to do in that situation.

He looked over his shoulder, checking everyone was ready. The Heartwood Equitas, or cavalry, had its own commander, a sturdy rider called Aquila, whose horse now stood beside Chonrad, chomping impatiently at the bit, but he had been glad of Chonrad's offer of help. Chonrad's own battle steed pawed the ground, and he patted its side, speaking to it softly. No doubt it was picking up on his tension: horses could always sense the battle to come, almost as if they could see into the future, he often thought.

He looked across at the front line, the knights of which were facing the walls, waiting for the first onslaught of Darkwater warriors. He could not see Procella and Valens from where he was, but he could see the faces of some of the knights. They showed the same mix of emotions he had seen the whole of his life on Isenbard's Wall: nervousness at the thought of their lives coming to an end that day, determination to prove themselves worthy knights and eagerness to engage the enemy and end the waiting.

He wished he had Fulco at his side. Not as a bodyguard, although it had always been nice to know someone was there to protect his back, but as a companion, a friend to watch over and to watch over you when all around you the enemy were baying for your blood.

Once again, he found himself wondering just what he was doing there, in Heartwood. The outcome seemed inevitable, and he faced almost certain death. If that was the case, shouldn't he be at home, in Vichton, trying to save the people who looked to him for security, as well as looking after his family? He thought about the beach he had stood on only days before, when Dolosus had vanished into the sea. Presumably, that would soon be under water when the Darkwater Lords invaded. They would storm the city and take his castle, and Arbor knew what they would do to his children.

His hands tightened on the reins. He should be there. He should not be amongst these knights who lived a life he could not comprehend, with their rituals and services and strange deference to the dying tree that made shivers run up his spine.

Then he remembered Fulco's last "words". *You are the key*, he had signed. Chonrad shifted in the saddle, aware once again of this feeling of fate, that somehow he was destined to play a part in this struggle, a part he had not yet fulfilled. He wanted to scoff at such a fanciful notion, but as a battle commander, he had learned to rely on hunches and gut feelings, as they had saved his life more than once. And now his gut feeling was telling him his job in Heartwood was not yet done.

Not that it would have made a difference if he had wanted to leave, Chonrad thought wryly as the flow from the top of the battlements increased. It was too late now. The tide had turned, so to speak, and it was only moments before Darkwater struck.

The water level outside had clearly almost reached the top of the wall. Water was pouring through the crenellations, adding to the already-large puddles in the Baillium, but he could see it was nothing compared to what was about to come over the wall.

He glanced along the front line again and suddenly saw Procella as she stepped forwards and yelled something to her army. He gave a half smile. She was stunning, not an ounce of fear on her face, her sword glinting in the moonlight.

And then the water reached the top of the wall.

There was a moment when time seemed to freeze, and Chonrad thought that was it; the water was not going to go any higher. They had won; the Darkwater Lords would go away and leave them alone.

Then, when it happened, it happened suddenly. A stream of water started pouring down the wall, producing a tremendous waterfall, all the way round the wall from one end where it met the mountains to the other. And as it touched the ground, Darkwater warriors leapt out from the water, materialising in solid form and immediately coming forward, swords drawn.

Procella yelled something, although he couldn't hear her over the rush of the water and the battle cries of the army. The archers pulled back their strings, and the continual rain was joined by a torrent of arrows. They thudded down into the water warriors, and hundreds of them stopped, shuddered and then dissolved in water, but immediately there were more to take their place, splashing through the remains left by their kin. Another hail of arrows flooded down, then another, and then the water warriors were too close to the Exercitus, and so the archers drew their swords, and battle was engaged.

Chonrad gritted his teeth, holding the reins of his horse tightly. He wished he had refused to follow her directions and had stayed with her on the front line. It was his usual role, and he did not enjoy this waiting game. Though she was Dux, she was not his captain, and he should have ignored her. But it was too late now.

She wanted him to wait until the last of the Darkwater army was over the wall and then move in behind them, effectively closing them in a pincer movement, but the Darkwater warriors just kept on coming. There was no sign of them stopping. He looked over at Aquilas, whose pale face echoed his own fear; there was no end to the army, just as there was no end to the fish in the sea, and they would be waiting there all night if they waited for the end.

Chonrad raised an eyebrow at Aquilas, who nodded firmly. Drawing his sword, Chonrad kicked his heels into his mount. The horse reared, then charged out from the Barracks, straight into the side of the Darkwater army.

Very early on in his life, Chonrad had learned a well-trained cavalry could turn a battle in an instant. Not only did a cavalry knight have the advantage of height from which to see the battle, the horse itself was both a weapon and a shield, protecting him from the occasional blow and yet able to crush enemies beneath its huge hooves.

Thunder, his own horse, was a stallion standing at seventeen hands high, built and bred for war, a horse that sensed blood in the air and got the battle fever in his eyes.

Thunder crashed into the Darkwater Lords on their left flank, crushing bodies beneath his hooves as Chonrad swung his heavy sword on either side of him, slicing through green skin and limbs. The stallion ploughed through the Darkwater army with the rest of the cavalry on his tail, cutting a swathe through the green warriors like a plough in a field of corn.

As before when Darkwater first attacked in the Curia, Chonrad was struck by how powerful the warriors were. They were all tall and broad-shouldered with bulging muscles, and although he seemed to hack limbs off all over the place, his sword just rang off the strange seashell armour they wore.

And still they kept coming. He reached the other side of the Baillium and turned the horse, both of them sweating, the stallion's eyes wide with excitement. Aquila reined in beside him, and they looked over at the walls to see more and more of the water warriors materialising. The flow of the waterfall from the battlements did not seem to be easing, either. With a sinking heart, Chonrad realised they were vastly outnumbered.

He caught himself there, however. Had he really thought they stood a chance? He had already known his death was written for that day. He was not going to spend his last minutes getting depressed. He was a warrior, and he was going to fight to the death.

"For Anguis!" he yelled, hoping his children would meet a quick death.

"And for Heartwood!" yelled back Aquila.

That too, thought Chonrad, with slightly less enthusiasm.

He charged back into the fray. This time, the bodies seemed more compact and he did not cut such a swathe through, finding himself jammed in about halfway across the Baillium. He slashed with the sword as hands reached out to grab him, but it was only minutes before he realised it was no good; if he didn't dismount they would pull him off the horse, and then he would probably be crushed under its hooves.

Pulling sharply on the reins, he leaned forward as Thunder reared and then crashed down on several bodies, bones snapping under his weight. Kicking his feet free of the stirrups, Chonrad dismounted neatly, slapping Thunder on the rump so the stallion skittered off, scattering warriors as it ran.

With one hand, he pulled the hood of his mail coat over his head, and then someone was on him, and he was swinging his sword with all his might as the Darkwater warrior slashed at him with his curved weapon.

He killed that one, then another, realising that although they were strong and powerful, his years of training and battle experience made him more than a match for most of the water warriors. However, there were so many of them, he soon realised it was sheer numbers that were going to be the problem.

Out of the corner of his eye, he saw Procella. She was fighting easily, seemingly with two warriors at once, and Valens was at her back, the two of them circling in a kind of horrific dance, Valens clearly favouring his injured leg. But as he neared, he saw her glance repeatedly at the wall, and he knew she was thinking the same as him: there was no way they could hold out against those kinds of numbers.

He reached her side, and she gave him a brief flash of a smile before they continued to fight. "I am sorry I could not do more with the cavalry," he shouted above the noise of swords on armour and the screams and yells of battle. "They were too many."

"And they are still coming," she yelled back. "We shall fall under this number. We are going to have to retreat."

He fought off a particularly big Darkwater Lord whose sword just managed to nick him in the face before he thrust his own blade down into his neck, and Chonrad cursed as blood poured down his cheek. It was a small wound but one of those which would bleed profusely; just what he didn't need.

He looked around briefly, knowing in battle the balance of power was like a ball tossed into the air; it would continue to climb, and then it would reach its peak and seemingly hang there for a moment before it began its descent, and he wondered whether this battle had reached the peak yet.

All around him, the Exercitus were battling hard. Darkwater warriors were falling, dissolving into water as they hit the ground. The whole of the Baillium was now ankle-deep in water, and rising. Though the Exercitus were holding their ground, the water warriors were still increasing in numbers, pressing forward all the time, and friendly bodies littered the ground all around him. He saw one Heartwood warrior fall and then another as their foes seemed to double in number, coming forward in droves.

It had happened, he thought. The ball was on its way down.

"Retreat!" yelled Procella at the same time, obviously realising the battle had reached its turning point at the same time as he had. Behind her, someone sounded the horn, which echoed above the clashing of battle. "Retreat!"

The Exercitus started to move backwards towards the Temple. Chonrad stumbled several times on bodies, although he did not have time to check who they were. There was no time either to pick up the bodies or take them with him. He fought continuously, and began to realise he was starting to use defensive tactics more than aggressive ones. The Darkwater warriors were growing more confident, sure of success. They scented blood.

Under the water, which was now a foot deep, gravel scrunched, and he realised he was in the Quad. Exercitus were pouring through the oak doors into the Temple, and he joined Procella and Valens at the front, digging his heels deep into the ground and holding off the onslaught while the army retreated. Gradually, they were pushed back. Beside him, Solum fell, speared like a pig in the stomach, but although he cursed, he could not stop to help because he was being pushed back, and he was slipping in the water.

"Get back!" yelled Valens, and turned to see only a handful of knights remained in the Quad, surrounded on all sides by the Darkwater army.

Chonrad stumbled on a fallen knight and could not regain his balance; he fell backwards, landing heavily in the water. Cursing, he rolled onto his knees, expecting any moment to feel a blade cut into his spine, but suddenly, Procella was there, heaving him to his feet with one hand under his arm, and she pushed him through the doors, which were already closing as the last knight filtered through.

"Procella!" he yelled as Bearrach put his weight on one side and Fionnghuala leaned on the other, and the doors slammed shut. "She is still out there!"

Valens strode to the door. Bearrach pulled it open a crack, and Valens stuck his arm through, grabbed Procella's mail hood and yanked her back. She landed inside the Temple, sprawled on the floor, and then the doors were shut and the two Hanaireans placed huge oak beams across, barricading them in, piling stones and wood against them.

V

Chonrad walked over to Procella where she lay sprawled on the floor and extended his hand. For a moment, he thought she was going to refuse it and get angry with him as she had on the way back from Vichton. Then, to his surprise, she burst out laughing.

"What is so funny?" he asked, bemused and amused at the same time.

"I am sorry." She wiped her face. "That was a close one." She accepted his hand, and he pulled her onto her feet. They both looked over at the doors as a thundering sound echoed from the wood.

"How long will they last?" asked Chonrad warily, expecting Darkwater to come crashing through at any moment.

Bearrach put a last piece of stone on top of the pile in front of the doors and said, "Should be a while. There is not even any water coming through yet."

It was true, Chonrad noted; there was not even a trickle of water through a crack in the door. Clearly though, it was just a matter of time before they found a way in.

"How many made it in?" he asked Valens as the Imperator scanned the crowd inside the Temple.

Valens counted silently, then looked at him. "Maybe three hundred."

"Three hundred? Out of three thousand!"

"I know." Valens beckoned to Procella. "We need to get any wounded who managed to get in over to Silva. Then organise the remaining knights into groups, one on the Temple doors, one over by the Domus, one by the Arbor. Make sure there is food and drink for everyone. Try to get them to rest, if only for a few minutes. Darkwater will break through, and they need to be ready."

"Yes, sir." Without further bidding, Procella went off. Chonrad watched her go, thinking how marvellous she was; she had just nearly died out there, and yet there had been no dramatics, no regaling of stories on how she had been brave and heroic; she had merely put her mind to the next task and continued on as if nothing had happened. She was amazing.

Looking round, he saw Valens watching him, a small smile on his face. Chonrad felt embarrassed. "Do not get the wrong idea," he warned, cleaning his sword on a piece of cloth; "I was only admiring her talents as a general; that is all."

"Of course," said Valens in a tone that suggested he wasn't convinced. "She is a fine knight. A noble heir." He sighed. "Of course, I had hoped Dolosus would take over from me one day, but that idea faded like a rainbow when he lost his arm."

Chonrad suddenly realised he hadn't seen the Militis since he came in. "Is he... Did he make it?"

"Oh, yes. Even with his disability, he is a powerful knight." Valens nodded over to the Arbor, and Chonrad saw Dolosus there, talking to Beata.

"I cannot believe he went all the way down to Darkwater and brought back the Pectoris," he commented. "That was truly a great achievement."

Valens nodded. "For all the good it did." He frowned, looking at Beata and seeing Teague on the floor in front of her. "What is going on there?"

Together, they walked over to the Arbor, which remained unchanged as far as Chonrad could see. The Komis lay among the roots of the tree and Beata was standing over him, kicking him occasionally.

"What is happening here?" Valens demanded.

"He can help us," Beata snapped, "but he refuses. He is an idiot."

"He is not an idiot," said Chonrad, frowning as he looked at Teague's white face. "He is scared."

"Scared?" Beata stared at him. "Of course he is scared. We are all scared!"

"Not scared of Darkwater. Scared of the Arbor."

Beata and Valens's gazes were blank. "Scared of the Arbor? That does not make sense."

"You have grown up with it since you were a child," Chonrad tried to explain. "To you, watching the tree is as normal as riding a horse, or swinging a sword. But to those of us who do not belong in Heartwood, the Arbor is mysterious and not a little terrifying."

He looked at Valens. "Let me talk to him," he pleaded. After all, he thought, I know what he's feeling.

Valens nodded, ignoring Beata's startled outburst of indignation. "We have things to do," he told the Dean, taking her good arm and leading her away. "And you need to rest. Come, you have not yet told me about your journey."

Chonrad watched them go and then turned back to the Komis, who lay watching him sullenly. He held out his hand to help him up, but Teague ignored it and pushed himself to his feet.

"Come and sit over here," Chonrad suggested, leading him over to one of the cells. He sat on a bench, and Teague joined him. Chonrad left the door open, but it was quieter in the cell, and he felt more relaxed. He had the strange feeling it was because the Arbor couldn't see him.

He stretched out his legs and rubbed the thigh muscle. It had not yet healed from the wound he received on the way back from Vichton, and it was aching now. His face was stinging, too.

"You are hurt," said Teague.

Chonrad sighed. "It is nothing." He eyed the Komis thoughtfully. "How are you feeling?"

"I am fine," Teague grunted. He was still wet through from his swim, though, and shivering a little. Chonrad went out and fetched him a blanket. He brought it back and handed it to the shivering Komis. Teague stared at it, then reached out and took it, wrapping it around him.

"Thank you," he said, somewhat grudgingly.

Chonrad nodded, wondering what he could say that would convince Teague to help the Arbor. He could not think of anything. It was not really his place, he thought, to tell Teague what to do. He understood Teague's reticence about the tree. Instead, he decided to ask him a Question.

"Why are you frightened?"

Teague pulled the blanket tight around his neck, shivering, although whether from the cold or his fear, Chonrad couldn't tell. Teague gave a sigh. "The tree... I can feel it. I can hear it. It is so powerful."

Chonrad frowned. "What do you mean, hear it?"

"I can hear it crying. And it whispers to me." Teague looked up at him. He frowned. "It is telling me you are the key. What does it mean by that?"

A shiver ran from the nape of Chonrad's neck down his back, as if someone had poured icy water down his spine. He remembered Fulco's last gesture, the turning motion of a key. "I do not know, but you are not the first to tell me that."

Teague shrugged. His golden eyes rested on Chonrad's cut cheek. Sighing again, he said, "Come here." As Chonrad moved closer, frowning, the Komis took his face in his hands. He closed his eyes. He took a deep breath and let it out slowly. Then suddenly, his hands stared to grow warm.

The warmth spread right through him, from the top of his head to his toes. He grew suddenly sleepy and closed his eyes. He felt as if he were melting into the ground. His legs seemed to sink into the earth, as if he were putting down roots and becoming part of the natural world around him.

Then all of a sudden, Teague lifted his hands. Chonrad opened his eyes. The ache in his leg had disappeared. When he touched his face, the cut had vanished.

"You can heal," Chonrad said, astonished. "Why did you not heal Beata?"

"She was too busy kicking me."

Chonrad shrugged. "I can understand that. But my thanks, anyway." He rubbed his leg, amazed the deep wound had healed. Teague's gaze had drifted off into the distance, and Chonrad turned to see the Komis staring at Beata, who was talking to Valens. "You have feelings for her," he stated.

Teague snorted. "Yes: irritation, annoyance and vexation."

"They are three things that mean the same."

Teague stared at him and then smiled a little. "Yes, I suppose they do." He ran his hands through his wet, black hair. "She is the most annoying and yet most beautiful person I have ever met. I cannot stop thinking about her – and the Arbor can see that. It knows what I am feeling."

Chonrad looked out at the tree, wondering if it could also see his feelings for Procella. Would it be angry, because the Militis were denied relationships? Or would it understand?

Teague sighed. "Are you not going to give me a lecture on why I should help Heartwood? Is that not why you brought me here?"

"No," said Chonrad. "I thought you were being treated unfairly and you should be given a chance to think about it."

Teague's eyebrows rose, making his golden eyes seem even bigger than ever. "You are an honourable knight," he observed. "Which is more than I can say for some of these warriors." He cast a glance out of the door.

Chonrad sighed. "The whole world is at stake. If the Arbor falls, Anguis will fall. That is how I understand it, anyway."

Teague looked sulky. "No pressure or anything."

Chonrad smiled. "You must make your own mind up about what you should do. I think we are very similar, young Komis. We are both here, even though we wish to be at opposite ends of the world. I have young children back in Vichton."

"Then why are you here?"

"Truly? I have no idea." They both looked over at the oak doors as something crashed against the outside of them, but the doors continued to hold.

Teague rolled his eyes. Then he continued. "How do you have children if you are a Militis? I did not think they were allowed to have relationships."

"I am not from Heartwood," said Chonrad.

Teague looked confused. "But the Arbor…" his voice tailed off. "What?"

Teague sighed. "The Arbor implied you belonged to it. That you served it. I could not distinguish between its feelings for you and its feelings for Beata, for example."

Chonrad's heart missed a beat. "I do not understand."

"Neither do I." Teague leaned forward, putting his hands over his eyes. "I can still hear it crying. Why will it not stop crying?"

Chonrad stood and looked outside, marvelling at the lack of pain in his leg. He looked over at the Arbor, which still sagged forlornly. "Well, that must hurt."

Teague shook his head. "It is more than that. But I cannot see…"

"Why do you not come over and speak to it?" Chonrad said gently. "It will answer all your Questions, and I am sure you will be able to hear it, too."

Teague looked up then, fear plain on his face. "I cannot. Please, do not make me do it!"

"I will not," said Chonrad, partly understanding, "but Beata might." He had seen the Dean striding across the Temple towards them, a face like thunder. "I am sorry," he finished before she could reach them. "I do not think you should be forced to help, but I do think you should offer it." And with that, he slipped out of the cell.

He stopped Beata just outside by catching her good arm. She had pinned up her hair again and someone had helped her back into some mail, and a sword was on her hip. Her arm was still bandaged to her chest, though. She was beautiful, he thought, more beautiful than Procella, but she was like the moons, cold and forbidding, whereas Procella was like the sun, warm and fiery. He knew which Militis he preferred.

Beata looked up at him, her blue eyes sharp as knives. He released her arm but stood in the door of the cell so she could not pass. "Slow down," he said.

"Get out of my way." She stepped forward, clearly intending to push him to one side.

He held up his hands. "I will move. Just listen to what I have to say."

She heaved an exaggerated sigh but stepped back. He lowered his hands. "I understand why you feel the need to force him," he said gently. "But he is deeply scared. Something about the Arbor is frightening him. He is not doing it to spite you, Beata. He has true feelings for you. I do understand some of his worries about the tree. I... feel them too, to a lesser extent, I think. Just try to put yourself in his shoes; that is all I am asking."

Beata stared up at him. Then she frowned. "Five minutes ago, your cheek was pouring blood. What happened?"

Chonrad stepped aside. "I think you should ask him about that." And then he left her to it.

CHAPTER SEVENTEEN

I

Chonrad left Beata and Teague, too tired and exhausted to deal with their argument. He walked over to the outer ring, where someone had placed a supply of food and drink, and helped himself to a piece of bread and cheese, and a cup of water. He found himself standing next to Gravis, who was limping slightly but appeared otherwise unscathed.

Chonrad nodded to him, enjoying the food and drink and feeling it rejuvenate him. Suddenly, though, he had a thought and stared at the piece of bread in his hand. "Should we be rationing the food?" he asked, wondering how much they had stored in the Temple.

Gravis shrugged. "I think they have kept some back, just in case. But somehow I do not think Darkwater's plan is to starve us out." As if to confirm his thoughts, there came a massive crash on the oak doors. The two of them spun around, but there was plenty of stone and timber barricading the doors, and they did not move. As if the Darkwater Lords had realised this, it fell silent outside.

The two knights' gazes met. "I suppose they are going to try and think of another way in," said Chonrad.

"Where do you think they will try next?"

Chonrad looked around. The door to the Domus was also very soundly reinforced. He found his eyes drawn upwards, to where the High Moon shone her peaceful light through the beautiful coloured glass. "I wonder whether they will try and come through that way."

"How?" asked Gravis, puzzled. "The dome is not just that shape for aesthetic purposes; it is sloped purposefully so invaders could not climb onto it with ladders."

It was Chonrad's turn to shrug. "I did not think the water level would rise to the top of the Porta either, but it did."

Gravis blinked. "You think they will cause the water level to rise up to the top of the Castellum?"

"I am beginning to think anything is possible now."

They fell silent, eating their small meal as they watched everyone scurrying about the Temple. Gradually, the knights seemed to be settling down as they realised it was going to take a little while for Darkwater to find a way into the Castellum. Chonrad used the moment's peace to look around, realising the Temple was more like a keep than he had previously thought. The walls were clearly several feet thick, and the doors were easily reinforced. Though the dome was beautiful, the glass was only fitted in the highest part, meaning it would be very difficult to climb and break in that way. And although the Temple could be accessed via the Domus, it was clearly designed so it could be isolated, as if the builders had known one day Heartwood would be invaded.

Chonrad looked at the Arbor, for the first time thinking how strange it was to have a tree growing inside a building. He knew the history of Heartwood and understood how the Castellum had grown around the Arbor in order to protect it, but when you thought about it, it was quite unnatural; the tree had no access to the wind and rain, and the only sunshine it received was that which came through the small panes of glass in the dome.

After he had eaten, Chonrad clapped Gravis on the back and wished him luck, then wandered over to where Procella and Valens were talking to several other Militis, Grimbeald, Fionnghuala and Bearrach. As he came up, they turned, and he realised they had been talking about him.

"Did you have any luck with Teague?" Valens asked.

Chonrad shrugged. "I think I gave him something to think about." Or more likely the other way around, he thought wryly, but he didn't say the words.

Valens nodded. "We must do our best to get him to help the Arbor. It is incredible that we have achieved so much. Retrieving the Pectoris, finding the Virimage, activating four of the Nodes... I feel we are so close to solving the problem, and yet the final pieces of the will not fall into place."

"Speaking of Nodes," said Procella, "how is Nitesco?"

Valens stared at her, stricken. "Nitesco! By the Arbor, I had forgotten him completely. We have barricaded the door and left him in the Domus."

Fionnghuala and Bearrach exchanged a glance and then said, "Please let us go and see if we can find him, Imperator. We should be able to open the doors enough to slip out, and you can barricade them immediately behind us."

Valens looked over at Procella. She gave him a small smile. "We cannot leave him out there. He is so young."

Valens did not reply, but Chonrad could sense what he was thinking: that they would probably all be dead before sunup whether they were inside the Temple or not. But he didn't say so. Instead, he sighed and nodded. "I would be most grateful, thank you."

They all went around the outer circle and through the temporary Infirmaria where Silva was tending to some of the wounded, to the doors leading to the Domus. They had been well sealed and were at that moment heavily guarded. Everyone prepared themselves in case the Darkwater Lords were waiting outside. But when the doors were opened a crack, there was nothing there.

"When you return, give three long knocks, two short and three long," said Valens. "That will be the code to let you in."

Fionnghuala and Bearrach nodded. Then, without a sound, they slipped through, and the doors were shut behind them.

Chonrad and Procella exchanged a glance. "What do we do now?" he asked wryly, feeling strangely useless.

"Wait," she said simply. She looked over at the Arbor. "Walk with me."

He didn't really want to go closer to the Arbor, but he did want to spend some time with the Dux, and so he followed her as she crossed the outer ring and the dry channel to the inner ring beyond. They stopped just in front of the Arbor. He watched as she touched her fingers to her chest, lips and forehead.

"You are an enigma," he said, smiling. "You are so devout; I would not have expected you to be so."

She turned her large brown eyes on him, and for a moment he worried he had offended her, but she just smiled and said, "Why so?"

He shrugged. "You are such a competent warrior – no, that does not come near to explaining you in the least – you are an amazing warrior, a fearless knight, and yet you are also like a priestess, so holy."

"But that is the very nature of the Militis," she said. "We are holy warriors; that is what we do."

"I know." He wasn't explaining himself very well, he thought. "But I feel for some of you, the religious bit comes a poor second to the defensive role – Dolosus, for example."

"Dolosus is not the best example you could quote," she said wryly.

"I suppose not. Well, what about Valens, then? I feel his devotion to the Arbor is second to his defense of it."

She looked uncomfortable at discussing the Imperator in such a manner but said, "He was Dux for many years. I suppose it is natural for those who spend their time on the Wall that defence comes first."

"Do you think you will change as the years go by?"

She smiled sadly. "Do you really think that is a Question I need to answer? Are we likely to see the sun rise?"

Chonrad shrugged. "The Darkwater Lords have done some truly amazing things I never thought to see – but so have we. My whole perception of the world has changed since I came to Heartwood for the Congressus. I realise how little I know about my religion and the world I inhabit. Teague, for instance, just laid his hands on me and healed me. I would never have thought possible a few months ago."

She looked astonished. "Truly?"

"Truly. I would have said he will be a great asset when people are injured, but I think he has bigger fish to fry." He looked pointedly at the Arbor.

Procella nodded. "There is still time for him to help."

"He needs to come to that decision himself, or I feel he will be useless to us." Chonrad thought of the Virimage's words, that echoed Fulco's last sign before his death, and he frowned.

"What are you thinking?" Procella asked, sensing his mood.

He sighed. "Before Fulco died, he signed, *you are the key*."

"Oh?"

"I did not have a clue what he was referring to. Well, when I first talked to Teague, he said the Arbor had spoken to him, and had also told him I was the key."

Procella's eyebrows rose. "The key to what?"

"If I knew that... He also said the Arbor thought of me as a Militis."

She smiled. "I am not surprised."

He looked at the tree and shivered. "I am. I do not consider myself in the same league as you at all."

To his surprise, she put a gentle hand on his arm. "Though the Abbatis turned you away at the Allectus, I think maybe the Arbor did not. Perhaps we should have let it have more of a say in who was chosen. My guess is it has thought of you as its own from the beginning."

Chonrad stared at her. He was surprised for two reasons: that she would consider criticising an age-old practice, and also that she might be right.

Was it possible? That although he thought himself rejected, the Arbor had considered himself one of its protectors since he was seven?

His thoughts were interrupted by a cry from the back of the Temple. They spun, realising the Hanaireans had returned. Together, they ran over to the group gathering around the panting Fionnghuala and Bearrach.

"He is not there," said Fionnghuala. "We went into the Armorium and found the steps down to the Cavus. We went down, and found another hole in the floor in that room, with more steps leading down. We descended these and found ourselves in a small room with a door in the opposite wall."

"The door was open," continued Bearrach, "but as we approached it, it slammed shut. I do not know how, because there was no wind. We stepped back, and then suddenly saw on the door some words had appeared. They said: You need the key."

A shiver ran down Chonrad's back. Everyone started talking at once, but across the crowd, he felt Procella's eyes on him. She stepped forwards, her eyes never leaving him. "Valens," she said quietly. "Chonrad should go."

He turned to look at her, frowning. "Why?"

She explained, and gradually everyone fell quiet as she spoke. All eyes turned to Chonrad, and he grew increasingly uncomfortable.

When she had finished explaining what Fulco and Teague had foretold, Valens shook his head. "We need all healthy warriors up here, in the Temple. It is only a matter of time until Darkwater breaks through. We cannot afford for one of our most able allies to disappear at such a time."

"He is more than that," Procella insisted. "He is special."

Valens glared at her. "You are a Militis, a defender of the holy tree," he snapped. "I do not expect you to bring your private feelings into a matter concerning the Arbor's safety."

Procella went white. Everyone else looked shocked. Chonrad closed his eyes briefly, wishing the ground would just open up and swallow him.

"If you were any other knight, I would strike you down where you stand," Procella said quietly. "But you are my Imperator. I respect you because you are fair and just, and until now you have always listened to my opinion."

Valens said nothing. Chonrad opened his eyes. The face of the leader of the whole of Heartwood was impassive, but Chonrad had a feeling he might be regretting his words.

Procella continued. "Chonrad has been told by the Virimage the Arbor thinks of Chonrad as its own. We all know it is not the Arbor that chooses its guardians at the Allectus; it is the Imperator and the Abbatis together. Perhaps this time they were wrong – perhaps the Arbor chose Chonrad for one of its defenders, and Heartwood sent him away."

Valens's jaw tightened. "Even if that were so, why would that make Lord Barle the person to go and find Nitesco? Surely any Militis could fulfil that role?"

Procella lifted her chin, and Chonrad's heart missed a beat – she was beautiful, noble, intelligent, commanding and brave. At that moment, he could not have loved her more. "It can be no coincidence both Fulco and Teague called Chonrad the 'key'." She sighed and suddenly reached out and took Valens's hand in her own, a surprisingly tender gesture. "Great leader, I think we have to think bigger than just throwing bodies at these Darkwater Lords. We have to think about how to save the Arbor, and I do not think we will do that by just killing the enemy now. There are too many of them. I believe Nitesco found the fifth Node down in the Cavus, and I think if Chonrad can go down there and activate it, there might just be some hope he can save us all."

"No pressure," said Chonrad wryly, echoing Teague's words and causing everyone else to start laughing with relief at the break in the tension.

Procella dropped Valens's hand and turned to him. "Will you go and try for us?"

Suddenly, Chonrad was past caring what everyone else thought. He reached out and took Procella into his arms, wrapping her firmly in his grip. He buried his nose in her hair. She smelled of rain and the fresh cool air, making him think of summer showers and afternoons spent down by the river in Vichton, picking daisies.

He lifted his head. "I will. But I must warn you – if we survive this day, I am going to ask you to marry me."

He did not wait to hear what she had to say, nor to read the astonished look on Valens's and indeed everyone's faces. He kissed her swiftly and then turned, and walking over to the oak doors leading to the Domus, said to Niveus firmly, "For Arbor's sake, if you hear three knocks, then two, then three again, let me in, won't you?"

II

Beata stood in the doorway of the cell, looking down at Teague. For a moment neither said anything. Then she said, "Chonrad insinuated you can heal."

Teague said nothing.

"Why did you not tell me?"

"You did not ask." His golden eyes were accusing, wary, and suddenly she regretted the way she had treated him earlier. Why had she reacted in such a way? He just made her so mad, that was all!

She had to ask. She continued, rather hoarsely. "Could you have... Peritus..."

"I cannot raise the dead, if that is what you are asking," he said flatly.

She bit her lip, his words stabbing like knives. "You can be so cruel," she said softly. "I do not know why you have the power to hurt me."

He put his head in his hands. "That is the last thing I want. I just want to be left alone."

He looked so young then, and so vulnerable. Unbidden, the memory came to her of him in her arms that night in Henton, the night she had given herself to him, and had really experienced love for the first time.

Had it been love, she wondered? Or just a sexual act? It was true he had clearly never been short of female partners. But she had sensed at the time their bonding had been more than that; there had been something magical about it, something that transcended time and space and duty and all the other things that made her feel guilty afterwards.

Or was she just being fanciful, trying to create something beautiful out of something functional, like trying to make a silk purse out of a sow's ear?

She came into the room and sat beside him. He looked up at her suspiciously, but she just gave him a small smile. "Chonrad told me you are scared of the Arbor."

He couldn't stop his eyes stealing out to the tree. He shivered. His eyes flicked back to her. "It talks to me. I can hear what it is feeling. It is in such pain, Beata; you could not conceive it. It is crying." He put his head in his hands again. "I cannot bear it."

She stared at him, shocked, and then looked out at the Arbor again. She gazed at the old tree, at the sagging branches and split trunk. Of course, she had always known the Arbor was special, holy, a symbol of Animus's love for them all, and the channeller of the energy flowing around Anguis. But now, for the first time, she saw it as Teague saw it: not just a tree, inanimate and emotionally blank like any other natural feature, and not as a mechanical thing like a dam that diverted water, but a living, breathing organism, something that could think and feel, and that interacted with the world around it, a sentient being, as much alive and aware of its surroundings as she and Teague – maybe even more so.

She turned back to him, knelt before him and took his hand. "Then why do you not do something to help it?" she asked earnestly. "We do not have much time. I travelled across Anguis to find you, because we thought you were the only one who could help."

When he looked at her, his eyes were wet, and there was panic hiding inside them. "You do not know what you are asking of me."

It was only then she really saw how deep his fear went. Still, she could not understand why he was not doing anything. Militis were taught to conquer their fear, or at least to keep on fighting in spite of it, and she could not understand why he remained seated when the Arbor outside faded slowly away.

But she said nothing. She merely sat on the seat beside him and looked out at the tree. She suddenly felt very tired. Her shoulder throbbed, and the strength she had drawn on to get her back home, to bring Teague to Heartwood, dissipated.

She closed her eyes, just for a moment she thought, to rest. She felt so tired. When had she last eaten? She honestly could not remember. She sank into the seat as she dozed. No, she wasn't sinking into the seat; she was sinking into the ground. It was soft, like dough, and her feet were plunging deep into that softness; in fact, it was almost as if she were melting, becoming part of the dough, blending into it…

With a gasp, she opened her eyes. Teague's hand rested on her shoulder and his eyes were closed, but they opened as she sat up, and he smiled at her. She stared at him, shocked. The pain in her shoulder had gone. She tore off the sling and slipped her hand inside her mail tunic, trying to feel beneath the bandage. She could feel no gaping wound, no soreness.

"You healed me," she said softly.

"It might not be completely gone," he warned; "it was a deep wound."

She flexed her arm and opened her mouth to speak, but no words came out as, suddenly, a deep groaning noise echoed around the Temple.

"What in the Arbor's name was that?" They both stood and went outside the cell. All around the Temple, people were looking up at the walls and ceilings as the groaning noise echoed again.

"Chonrad was right – they are raising the water levels outside," shouted Gravis. "It is the walls moving under the pressure."

Instinctively, everyone began moving away from the walls to the centre of the room. Valens and Procella left the doors where they had been waiting for news of Chonrad and walked up to the group that now formed at the edge of the outer ring. Together, they looked up at the ceiling.

"I think we need a change of plan," said Procella. "They are not going to come in through the doors. They are going to come in through the ceiling, if the walls do not fall first."

Valens nodded. "I think we should abandon the doors. We will make a ring around the outer circle and another around the inner circle."

"What about the injured?" Beata asked softly.

Valens shook his head. "We will have to leave them where they are; we cannot afford for them to get in the way while we are fighting. Let us start organising this."

The group split, and everyone began preparing themselves for the last stand. Furniture was moved well out of the way against the walls, and the knights organised themselves into two rings, one in the inner circle, the other in the outer. Beata took Teague's hand and pulled him into the inner circle. He tried to resist her, but this time, she refused to release him. "There is nowhere left to go," she said. "This is it. Now, do you have a weapon?"

"Yes, I have a short sword. I am not skilled at warfare, though."

"It is for self-defence," she announced. "You will not be fighting. You will only need it after they have come through me."

She drew her own sword and started checking the lacings and buckles of her armour. Around them, the Temple groaned and creaked again. She had the terrible image of a wall of water climbing up the Temple, washing over the bodies of the knights who had fallen, sweeping them away as they continued their relentless attack.

What would be worse, she wondered: falling to a sword or drowning? She thought about the panic that had engulfed her when she had been shot in the water. She had always expected that if she didn't die of old age, she would die in battle; it was the nature of the role she had played all her life. But drowning was such an alien concept. Though they learned to swim in the Flumen, few of the Heartwood knights were comfortable in water, and she suspected the thought of being unable to breathe under water was as frightening to everyone else as it was to her.

She finished tightening the buckles on her belt and turned to see Teague staring her. "I should help," he said, clutching the hilt of his sword, looking strangely vulnerable without the heavy armour she was used to seeing around Heartwood.

"I thought this was not your fight." She wasn't accusing him; she just stated the fact. He looked confused, and turned and looked up at the Arbor. The point of his sword dropped slowly to the floor, and the hilt hung loosely in his hand. His gaze went unfocussed.

Beata frowned. "Teague?" He did not reply. She went over to him. The sword fell from his hand. Still he did not look away from the tree. "Teague?"

It was no good. Something had happened to him: he had been entranced by the tree. Her heart gave a funny little flip. Perhaps it wasn't all over, she thought. Perhaps there was something he could do.

"Look!" someone yelled, and she turned to see people looking up at the ceiling. She blinked, finding it difficult to see in the moonlight. Was she imagining it, or was water lapping at the glass in the top of the dome?

"Arbor, help us." She said the words under her breath, leaving Teague and backing towards the ring of knights who had all drawn their swords and were waiting nervously.

The water level crept up the glass panes set into the stone. Higher and higher it rose, and then finally it was at the top, and the Temple was covered.

Beata held her breath.

When the first pane broke it made her jump, the splintering of glass sounding loud in the silence of the Temple. The fragments fell to the floor like glittering snowflakes, another danger they would have to think about. Water seeped through the crack, running down the Temple wall. They all watched it trailing down the bricks, where it pooled on the flagstones.

Through the rest of the panes Beata could see the High Moon. Coloured by the glass and its surface fragmented by the water covering the dome, it was a strangely surreal picture, giving her the impression she was actually at the bottom of the sea. She looked across at Dolosus, wondering if he was remembering how it felt to be a water elemental in the ocean. To her surprise, he was smiling slightly. It unsettled her, and made her grow cold. Surely he was not working for Darkwater?

Her attention was distracted then by another pane breaking, then another. Water now began pouring down in streams, then in torrents. All around puddles formed on the floor, and the knights tightened their formation, raised their weapons. How long would it take for the elementals to take physical form? Beata was sick of the waiting. Now she wanted to get on with it, wanted to fight.

She cast one last glance over her shoulder. Teague had not moved at all, even when the glass broke; he was still staring at the Arbor, seemingly lost in a dream. She could not do anything for him now, she thought, except try to keep him safe until the very end.

III

When the Darkwater Lords rose out of the water, they rose as one, about a hundred warriors, green-skinned and broad-shouldered, dressed in their beautiful shell armour.

Dolosus hefted his sword in his right hand, waiting for them to approach. His sword was a little lighter than the usual Militis broadsword, as he had adapted his fighting manner following the loss of his arm. Before, he had used the standard thrust and parry, relying on his size and weight to gain control over his opponent, but now he kept his fitness at a higher level and his weight down and moved more quickly, relying instead on his speed and a greater variety of sword movements to keep ahead.

He felt healthy and ready for this battle. Though the swim from Darkwater had been long and tiring, his transformation back into earth elemental had somehow rejuvenated him, and he felt stronger and more alive than he had in months.

He looked along the line of knights, seeing Procella, Valens, Grimbeald, Gravis, Niveus, the Hanaireans and all the others he had known in his time at Heartwood who were still alive, all there readying themselves for the first contact, and pleasure surged through him that he was included in their ranks, that he was one of them. This was why he had returned, he thought: for the companionship and the feeling of belonging he just hadn't had in Darkwater.

The first group of Darkwater warriors advanced quickly, engaging the ring of Heartwood knights in the outer circle, and then suddenly more emerged from the water that had fallen on the inner circle, and in seconds one came towards him, and their swords met with a mighty clash.

One of the water warriors landed right in front of Dolosus, and he prepared himself to fight: feet spread wide, knees bent a little, sword across his body, on the balls of his feet so he was ready to move in any direction. The warrior turned to him and drew back his sword, and then… He stood, dropped his sword arm and stepped back.

Dolosus did not waste the opportunity and swung at him, cutting deep into the weak space between the warrior's helmet and shoulder guard, biting into his neck. The warrior shuddered, then melted into a puddle at his feet.

Dolosus stared at the water, puzzled, but there was no time to think on the matter because there was another warrior, and another, springing up in front of him.

He turned and did the same: spread his feet, readied himself for a blow; but again, the same thing happened. The warriors turned, saw him and stood to attention, lowering their weapons. Again, he took the advantage and swung his blade; the first he cut through the arm and then stabbed in his stomach, just below the shell breastplate, the second he got in the top of the thigh. Both warriors melted away, leaving him standing, hardly even out of breath. He swung his sword, growling, not satisfied by the easy deaths. He wanted a fight!

Ahead of him, across the channel, a vicious battle was going on, with the knights in the outer circle engaged in bloodthirsty fights, and so he pushed his way through, swinging his sword and cutting down water warriors until he found himself in the middle of the fray.

He yelled at the warrior nearest to him and the warrior turned, raised his sword. But then he saw who he was fighting and lowered his sword, stood to attention. Dolosus swung his weapon, cut up into the invader's armpit. Again the enemy gurgled and died.

"Fight me!" he yelled, spinning and approaching someone else, but every time it was the same. They would prepare to fight, see who it was and then lower their weapon, even though it meant certain death.

Dolosus roared, a flailing fury in the centre of the outer circle, warriors falling every which way from his blade. He fought for a long time, but every time he felled one of them it seemed two more sprung up in his place, and none of them would fight him.

After a while, he stopped fighting. He stood in the centre of the invaders and watched while they attacked his friends, but he found he could not raise his sword to help them. He felt sickened by the killing fury he had just experienced. There was no joy in taking a life in such way, no satisfaction. He could slay these

Darkwater warriors forever, and still they would rise up and defeat Heartwood.

One of them rose up beside him, and he turned, saying, "I will not fight you." Then he stopped as he looked at the golden sash across the warrior's chest.

"Father," he gasped.

Dolosus stared at the High Lord of Darkwater, feeling all the energy and enthusiasm he had received on returning to Heartwood drain from him.

"What, not happy to see me?" said Thalassinus, with absolutely no humour in his voice at all.

"Are you here to kill me?" Dolosus asked, conscious that all around them were the sounds of battle, and yet feeling as isolated from his companions as surely as if there were a brick wall between them and him. He kept his weapon across his body, his weight on the balls of his feet. If Thalassinus intended to strike, Dolosus was not going to stand there like the High Lord's warriors and take it without fighting back.

"Of course not," said Thalassinus mildly. "You are my son; why would I want to kill you?"

Dolosus's eyes narrowed. "I am not going to stand by and let you destroy Heartwood."

Thalassinus gestured to the warriors fighting around him and said, "They will not stop you; you have seen that already. Why do you not continue to hack them down where they stand?"

Dolosus said nothing. He realised Thalassinus was banking on the fact that he would have no stomach for a mindless slaughter.

The High Lord looked pointedly at the sleeve of Dolosus's tunic, where it had been tucked under and sewn just above his elbow. "Are you enjoying being a cripple again?"

Dolosus flushed. He swung his sword at Thalassinus, who met it with a parry that made the two weapons ring. "I am not a cripple," Dolosus snapped. "I can fight as well as any knight in the Temple."

"As well as when you had two arms?"

Unbidden, the memory flooded his head of how he had felt when he first transformed into a water elemental. He remembered looking down and seeing his hand back in place, and the thrill that had run through him at the thought that he was whole again. He looked at Thalassinus, who was smiling slightly, and he wondered whether the warrior had somehow stimulated the memory to return.

"Do you want me to show you how well I fight?" Dolosus asked, raising his sword.

Thalassinus just smiled, however. "Do you really want to kill your father?"

Dolosus felt Damaris stir within him, and he knew he would not be able to bring himself to do it.

Inside him, he felt something flicker, like the sun filtering through clouds, or a candle flame fluttering in the wind. It was Damaris, fighting to get out and take hold of his form and change it to a water elemental. "No!" he cried, trying to concentrate on the ground beneath his feet, but all he could think of was water, the feeling of cool blue liquid flowing through his fingers, and the beautiful green of the deep.

Dolosus felt Damaris shifting inside him. He felt his loyalties being torn and twisted between Thalassinus, his real father who had promised him a kingdom and who had the power to make him whole, and Valens, his adopted father who had taken him in and given him a place he could think of as his own.

He felt completely divided. How could he fight against his natural father? How could he turn his back on the chance to rule Darkwater, that beautiful, glittering jewel under the ocean? And how could he pass up the chance to have his arm back again?

And yet, the thought of leaving Valens to die made him ache inside. He could see him now, fighting in front of the Arbor. The Imperator was clearly favouring his right leg, and Dolosus's trained eye could see his reactions were slower than the other knights fighting around him. Still, his experience kept him ahead of the game, and Darkwater knights fell continually to his sword.

Thalassinus stood in front of him, the first signs of anger showing on his face as he saw Dolosus looking at Valens. Damaris pushed his way through briefly, and his body contorted as the two elementals fought for dominance.

Through his pain, Dolosus saw Thalassinus turn away from him and march towards the Arbor. Heartwood knights stepped in front of him to stop him, but he swept them away with one swing of his sword. Dolosus watched, frozen with pain and indecision, as the High Lord of Darkwater crossed the channel to the inner ring. Someone stood in front of him – was it Gravis? But Thalassinus swung his sword and cut him down.

"No!" Dolosus twisted inside and fell to his knees. He saw Thalassinus walk up to Valens.

Valens wouldn't know this was the High Lord of Darkwater, Dolosus realised. He tried to shout to him, but Damaris clenched his throat, forced him to keep quiet.

Valens turned and saw the warrior approaching and spread his feet, his injured right leg slightly behind him. He raised his sword, ready for battle.

IV

The moment the oak doors of the Temple shut behind him, Chonrad felt he was in a different world. The Temple had been unusually busy and noisy, the atmosphere filled with nervous tension, but here in the corridor between the Temple and the Domus, it was completely quiet, the only noise a muffled knocking as the doors were barricaded from the other side.

Chonrad hefted his sword in his hand, taking a few moments to let his eyes adjust to the darkness. He did not have a torch with him, as he did not want to attract attention, just in case there were any Darkwater Lords lurking around. After a while, he began to make his way along the corridor, feeling for the door to the Domus once he realised it didn't matter how long he waited; he wasn't going to be able to see any better in the inky blackness.

When his hand finally rested on the handle, he listened at the wooden planks and then, hearing nothing, quietly opened the door.

The Domus was empty, the moonlight that peered from behind the clouds shining bright on the puddles lying on the grass square in the centre. He moved silently along the colonnade, watching carefully for any signs of movement, but there was nothing. He was completely alone.

He made his way around the loop of the colonnade to the Armorium and paused in the doorway. Seeing no sign of movement inside, he walked into the Armorium. A lamp burned over near the steps leading down to the Cavus, and he guessed Fionnghuala and Bearrach had left it on for whoever came next.

Picking the lamp up, he quietly descended the stairs, his leather boots treading carefully on the uneven steps. His heart was thumping so loud he thought anyone hiding nearby would easily be able to hear it.

At the bottom he found himself in the Cavus, which was also empty, save for the piles of books and parchments that were scattered over the floor. He saw the hole in the floor immediately, though, and went over and bent down, shining the lamplight onto the steps. There was no sign of movement. He began to descend once again, the steps spiralling deep underground.

His boots made no noise on the steps. Everywhere was silent.

It was only when he reached the bottom he realised he had been holding his breath, and he let it out with a rush. He was in a small room, with nothing in it except a door on the opposite side. He went over, seeing as he approached the words Bearrach had described: You Need the Key.

He stood before the door. There was no handle. He stared at the letters, wondering how he was to open it. He put his hand onto the door.

The moment his fingers touched the wood, a glow emanated around the edges. He snatched his hand back, and the glow faded. Cursing, he took a deep breath and let it out slowly. Then he put his hand back.

The glow appeared immediately. It deepened, the door seeming to vibrate under his hand, as if it were humming gently. Then, slowly, the door swung towards him.

He stepped back, removing his hand and letting the door fall completely open. He waited for a moment, heart pounding, then went forward and looked through the door.

In front of him was a corridor leading to the left and right, disappearing into darkness. He listened, but could not hear a thing.

Where was Nitesco, he wondered? Had he been down this way? If that was the case, if he, Chonrad, was supposed to be the key, how had Nitesco got the door to open? Lifting the lantern high in his left hand and holding his sword in his right, he stepped into the corridor.

Left or right? Right, he thought. He walked down the corridor, making sure the door remained open behind him.

He walked twenty yards or so, the corridor bending to the left around the corner. In front of him was a fork in the corridor. He took the right again and went down another twenty yards. He came to another fork. Here he stopped, holding the lamp aloft and peering down the corridor. Was he going to find another fork twenty yards down here?

A rope, he thought. He should tie a rope to the door and then he wouldn't lose his way.

He turned and went back up the corridor. He kept to the left, then left again. He turned into the tunnel where the door was.

Except the door wasn't there. He ran up the tunnel and stood in front of the wall. Definitely no door. He looked up and down the corridor. Had he come the wrong way?

But he knew he hadn't. He turned to look back down the corridor. He forced himself to stay calm. If this was indeed the fifth Node, then from what he had heard from the others who had activated the Nodes, there would be some sort of trial he would have to undergo. And no doubt this was part of it – a conquering of his fear of being lost underground in a giant maze. There was no point in panicking. The door had disappeared, and giving in to his fear would not open it again.

He turned and sighed. Left or right? He decided he would pick right again and keep choosing the right path. As he began walking, he wondered whether Nitesco was lost somewhere in the labyrinth. Would he be able to find the young Libraris? He sincerely hoped so; he didn't like the thought of him being left in such a dark and lonely place.

As he walked, he began to think about what he might find at the end of the maze, presuming he did eventually find his way to the middle, or the end, whichever came first. If the fifth Node was down here somewhere, what would it look like? The others had said the spirit, or whatever it was in the Node, had appeared as members of their family, or figures from their past. Who would appear to him?

He did not think he had any terrible issues with people that needed resolving. He had had a good-enough relationship with his parents and got on well with his children. He supposed it could be his dead wife, Minna, who would come to talk to him, but he didn't think they had unresolved issues. Their marriage had been pleasant enough, and he did not think she had been disappointed; he had never been unfaithful to her, had been kind and gentle, and although he had never fallen in love with her, he knew she hadn't with him, either. Theirs had been a marriage of convenience that had suited them both at the time, and he could not imagine she would reappear now to accuse him of anything.

The corridor forked again and he continued right. Logically, he thought, this should mean he was following the outside of the maze which, if it didn't eventually lead him back to the beginning, should take him further in. Of course, that would not work if this wasn't a logical puzzle, which of course it wasn't, because the door had disappeared when he had gone back to find it. He sighed. Presumably, then, it didn't matter which way he went.

Still, at the next fork he continued to go right.

He walked for about fifteen minutes. The corridor continued to bend around to the left, and he took the right fork each time. The maze showed no sign of ending, and he had no idea how far he was from the beginning, or if indeed he was just circling and had passed the hidden doorway several times.

Eventually, he stopped. He checked the lamp, making sure it wasn't going to go out on him. There were still a few hours of burning time left, he calculated. He walked until he came to a fork. He sighed. There seemed no point in continuing to try to be logical. Logic was clearly not the way to the centre of this maze.

He chose the left fork, and started walking.

He began to lose track of time. He felt as if he had been walking for hours, but the candle did not seem to burn any lower. His legs began to ache, and he wished he had thought to bring a drink with him. His mind wandered, and he started to feel as if he was in a dream. It was quite stuffy in the passages, and he wondered if it was the lack of air that was making his head fuzzy.

After a while, he stopped and decided to sit down for a while. He had to think of another way to get through the maze, he told himself, but he was so tired he could barely keep his eyes open, and he couldn't seem to get his brain to function. Breathing seemed difficult, and he wondered if there were some sort of poison in the air.

He was going to die in the maze, he thought. He was going to die, and the knights who were probably engaged in battle above his head would all die, and that would be the end of that. He thought briefly of Procella, and wondered if he would ever see her again.

It was then he noticed the tiny pinpoint of light ahead of him. He stared, blinking, trying to get his brain to work. The light danced, moved away from him, then moved back. It seemed to want him to follow it, he thought.

He pushed himself to his feet. It was difficult to move, as if the air had grown thick and he was swimming through honey, but eventually he stood, and he began to shuffle down the corridor towards the light. As he neared, it danced away again, and he continued to follow it down the tunnels, no longer thinking about whether to go left or right, but just blindly hoping the light was not an attempt to lure him farther away from his goal but was in fact someone or something trying to help him.

After a while, the tunnels seemed to change. The slope of the ground began to lead downwards, taking him farther into the earth. They still twisted and turned, however, and he thought he was still going round in circles, just going deeper and deeper.

He turned a corner, and then stopped with a gasp.

He stood in a chamber. It was about as big as the Temple, although not quite as high. The ceiling and walls were made of earth and appeared to be reinforced with thick, uneven beams. He walked over to one and touched it, and gasped. It was a tree root. The whole cavern was thick with them. He looked up at the ceiling, suddenly realising where he was.

He was standing right underneath the Arbor.

The floor was also made of packed earth and was empty, apart from a figure lying right in the centre, motionless. He ran across to it and turned it over and realised it was Nitesco. He put his hand on the Libraris's chest. He was still alive. Chonrad shook him gently, but Nitesco did not rouse. Clearly, he was in some sort of induced slumber.

Chonrad turned and looked around him. The only other thing in the chamber apart from Nitesco was a wooden tablet set into one of the walls, about four feet square in size. He went over to it and touched it. It was highly polished and dust-free, although clearly nobody had been down there in years. The surface was empty of marks or carvings, and there was nothing on it to explain what it was doing there.

He looked up at the roots above his head, thinking about the fact that he appeared to be standing right under the holy tree. His fingers touched the tablet again. "Are you something to do with the Arbor?" he murmured to himself.

And then something happened that made him jump back as if he had been burned. One word appeared on the wooden tablet as if an invisible hand had etched the letters there with a chisel.

Yes.

V

Teague wasn't sure if he was dreaming or merely under some kind of spell. He could hear the sounds of battle echoing around him, but he could not turn around; his feet were rooted to the ground, his body limp and unresponsive.

His gaze was fixed on the Arbor. He could not take his eyes off it. He could still hear it crying, but the sound was now far off in the distance, like an echo. What was drawing his attention more was the soft whisperings of a conversation, audible even over the clashes of swords on shields and armour in the background.

He strained his ears to hear what the voices were saying but could not quite make them out. He frowned, concentrating. The more he concentrated, the more he began to make out individual voices.

"…for so long…"

"…they have forgotten…"

"…can hear us. Call for him…"

"…growing dark. Growing dark…"

He shivered. The voices sounded lost, forlorn, like figures at the bottom of a well, calling to be found. Part of him wanted to run to them, to try to help them, but the other part of him just wanted to flee and get as far away from the tree and Heartwood as he could.

"I do not want this," he whispered, although he wasn't sure to whom he was talking. "Please, leave me alone."

The voices continued to whisper: "…he has engaged Valens…"

"…the Militis will fall…"

"…she is hurt, she is hurt…"

The last words struck a chord within Teague, and he stirred and roused from his dream, the voices dying and the sounds of battle growing louder around him.

His vision cleared. To one side of him, Beata stumbled from a blow to her left shoulder. He had told her the wound might not have completely healed, and he had been right. She grimaced, her body twisting, dropping her guard.

Teague screamed, wrenching himself free of whatever force was holding him in place, and ran to her, but he was too late. The Darkwater warrior took advantage of her exposed left flank and thrust his sword, and it entered her right side just under her armpit, skewering her through her ribcage.

Behind her, Procella had turned at Teague's scream and now bellowed as she swung her sword, slicing the water warrior's head clean from his body. But Teague hardly even noticed. He caught Beata as she slowly collapsed, and he fell to the ground with her on top of him.

"No!" he sobbed, gathering her in his arms, trying to place his hands on the wound. They slipped on her armour, which was already thick with blood, and he cursed. He locked his fingers behind her back so she couldn't slip out and closed his eyes. He searched for the seed of light within her so he could link it to the ground and feed it energy.

But it wasn't there.

His heart swelled with horror. He searched again, and again, looking for some sign of life.

There was, however, none to find.

He sat there for a while, soaking in her blood, while Procella and Fionnghuala and Bearrach fought around him, protecting him from the Darkwater warriors who continued to fall through the holes in the roof. He could not believe she was dead. Beautiful, vibrant Beata, with her fiery temper and frighteningly accurate battle skills. She had travelled across the world to find him; she had cajoled and argued and bullied him all the way back, and got herself shot for the effort. All along he had fought her, and now she was gone and he could have his way and go home.

He remembered seeing her at Henton, elegant in her dress, like a real lady, quiet and so unlike a warrior, he would never have realised the truth. And then he remembered the day she had found him at the Harlton Forest, and the terror he had felt when he saw how she had changed, and realised what she was really like.

He still found it difficult to marry up the two Beatas: the gentle, elegant lady and the fierce, aggressive warrior. It was hard to think of them as the same person. And then there was also Beata the lover, who had given herself to him freely. He knew part of that had been curiosity, that she had been intrigued to find out what it was all about, but he thought it had also been more than that. There had been something between them, like lightning, quick and fierce, and damaging if you got caught in it, but beautiful nevertheless.

And now she was gone.

He bent and kissed her gently on the forehead, then pushed her carefully to one side onto the ground and got up. He stared around him like one who had woken from a dream. The knights were still in front of him, trying to keep him safe from the Darkwater Lords who now definitely outnumbered the standing Militis, but Teague could see it wouldn't be long before they fell, too. Fionnghuala bled profusely from a cut on her neck, and Bearrach was holding his left arm in a strange way, as though it had been numbed with a strike. Valens was now fighting a magnificent, powerful Darkwater Lord and could barely defend himself again his blows. Dolosus was motionless, on his knees in the midst of the warriors in the outer circle. And all around, knights were falling like felled trees. Only Procella remained unhurt and magnificent in her fury, but Teague could see that eventually the number of the Darkwater warriors would overwhelm her. The tide had turned. The element of water was on the rise.

"…come to us…"

"…Teague…"

Slowly, he turned to face the Arbor. The tree was calling him. He could hear the voices, tens, maybe hundreds of them, whispering to him, beckoning him.

He swallowed. He could not reason why, but he was afraid, more afraid than he had ever been in his life. Still, he thought of Beata lying on the floor, and he began to walk slowly forwards.

When he was just a few feet from the trunk, standing with his feet amongst the roots and his head just being touched by the drooping branches, he stopped. In front of him, the great rent down the middle of the trunk was obvious, and from this position, he could just see the Pectoris, pulsing slowly in the middle.

Once again he felt himself begin to grow sleepy. This time, however, he did not fight it.

He closed his eyes.

Immediately, the sounds of battle around him grew dim, and the voices in the tree grew louder. This time, however, he could hear them more clearly.

"Teague… You have come to us!"

"I am here," he whispered. "What do you want me to do?"

"Come closer…" echoed the answer.

His heart pounded. His eyes still shut, he walked forwards the few feet until his hands met the trunk.

"Closer…" whispered the voices.

He pressed himself against the wood, his cheek to the bark, and wrapped his arms around the torn trunk. He slowed his breathing.

Gradually, he reached out with his senses, the way he had always been able to do since he was a child. All Komis had some ability to do this, but he had never met anyone who was able to do it in the same way he could. He could not explain how he did it, however. It was like physically reaching out with your hand to take an object from someone's grasp, but you did it instead with your mind, stretching out with your thoughts, to touch what he thought of as the energy of Anguis, which seemed to flow beneath the land as the rivers flowed on the surface.

Immediately, warmth and light flooded him. He gasped, shocked at the amount of power that flowed through him. If previously he had felt the energy he had contacted was like a river, then this was the ocean, vast and awe-inspiring, terrifying in its strength and size.

It overwhelmed him like a tidal wave, and for a moment, he thought he was going to drown in the energy. Then, just as quickly, it dimmed.

When the voices spoke, they were as clear as if they were standing beside him.

"Teague..."

"You came..."

"I am here," he repeated. "What do you want me to do? How can I help you?"

As an answer, he received in his head a series of images. They were pictures of people, male and female, young and old. He watched them play through his mind, not understanding what he was being shown. "Who are these people?" he asked. "What do they have to do with the tree?"

"They are us..." the voices whispered. He frowned, watching the images in his head. It was if he were looking out from the point of view of the Arbor, seeing these people standing before him. Behind them, he could see the Temple, the imposing walls rising above them.

Gradually, however, as the pictures continued flashing by, the background began to change. Suddenly, the Temple as he had seen it vanished, and it was replaced by a smaller, square wall with no roof. Then, after maybe fifty more images of people, even that wall disappeared, and the tree was left in the open air, exposed to the elements.

Teague gasped. "You are taking me back in time!" He watched the people standing in front of the Arbor, looking up at him. "All these people have stood before you, from the days before the temples were built."

"Yes…"

He frowned. There must be some reason the tree was showing him these people in particular. He could see nothing about them that linked them; they were Wulfian, Laxonian, Hanairean and even Komis, the further back in time they went. "I do not understand," he said urgently. "What are you trying to tell me? Who are these people?"

Suddenly, the pictures slowed down and stopped. Gradually, he watched as time reversed itself and began to run forward again, but this time the flashing images were speeded up, and he gasped as, in seconds, the last thousand years sped by in front of his eyes.

As time caught up with itself, the images slowed once again. Standing before him was a slightly blurry figure, and he realised as he looked closely it was actually every single figure he had seen merged into one, like the layers of an onion or a rose's petals.

Then, taking his breath away, the thousand-figures-as-one stepped forwards into him. As the Arbor, he felt himself embrace the figure and welcome its energy into himself. And suddenly, he understood.

The people he had seen standing before the tree were sacrifices who had given themselves willingly to the Arbor, who been embraced by it and who had become part of it, part of its heart. These people *were* the Pectoris, their essences hidden within its beating form.

And it was his turn to be next.

CHAPTER EIGHTEEN

I

Locked in the argument between the two elements, the Militis and water warrior who was both Dolosus and Damaris could only watch the battle raging between Thalassinus and Valens.

Though the High Lord of Darkwater was the younger and stronger foe, Valens had a tremendous amount of experience in battle and years of training, and this showed clearly while the two were fighting. But he was also wounded, and after a while he began to favour his weaker leg, and Thalassinus soon spotted this and started to press his attentions on that side. The High Lord was strong and fearless, shining like a beacon in his gold sash.

Dolosus/Damaris twisted in agony where he knelt on the ground, torn with indecision. Part of him wanted to run and help Valens, but the other half admired the impressiveness of his real father, and wanted to be part of his world.

Feeling his earth counterpart giving ground, Damaris the water spirit crowed triumphantly. It was Valens's undoing. The Imperator heard the call and turned slightly. He saw the figure kneeling on the ground amidst the water warriors who were still rising from the puddles on the floor, and he saw his form flicker, and the semi-transparentness of the water elemental coming through.

And in that second of his distraction, Thalassinus took the chance to pull back his sword and thrust at his opponent's stomach. The blade entered Valens above his right hip, skewering him completely. His head snapped back and he stared at his assailant with surprise. He coughed, blood appearing on his lips, then gradually slid to his knees as Thalassinus withdrew the blade.

It was the worst thing the Darkwater High Lord could have done, for in that moment, Dolosus knew what really mattered to him, and with a resounding: "No!" he pushed himself to his feet, and crushed the water elemental inside him, where his voice was heard no more.

Dolosus covered the distance between the two of them in seconds. He caught Valens in his arm as the older knight fell forwards, and lowered him gently to the ground. He stared into his eyes, and brushed the hair back from his forehead gently.

Valens opened his eyes. "Dolosus?" he queried.

"It is I, Father." He heard a snarl from Thalassinus but did not look up.

Valens smiled. "You know I have always thought of you as my son," he whispered.

"I know. And I have always thought of you as my father. I just did not know it until now." Tears came into his eyes. "I am sorry I realised it too late."

Valens tried to raise his hand to touch Dolosus's face, but he was too weak. Instead, he just nodded. "It is not too late," he said, his voice fading with his body. "Kill him, Dolosus."

Dolosus swallowed. "I will, Father." He waited for Valens to reply, but the old knight's eyes grew dim, and Dolosus realised he would be saying no more.

Slowly, he pushed himself to his feet. He realised he had left his own sword behind, and picked up Valens's instead. Thalassinus stood in front of him, green eyes dangerously bright, all trace of humour gone. "You think you can take me, boy?"

"I do not think it – I know it," said Dolosus, swinging the sword around his body, testing its weight. To his surprise, it was almost as light as his own. Valens had clearly realised his strength was waning and had attempted to compensate by using a lighter weapon.

He faced Thalassinus, and they circled each other warily. Thalassinus hefted his sword in his hand. "Do you really think you can best me?" he asked silkily. "With your one arm and your split loyalties?"

Dolosus said nothing. Thalassinus was trying to distract him, to make him angry and force him to lose his control. Well, he wasn't going to do that. He was past letting other people control him.

He spun his sword around his body, getting used to the feel of the grip, the balance and the weight. He eyed Thalassinus as he did so. Though the water warrior was big and sturdily built, Dolosus had the advantage of being more used to fighting on land. Thalassinus was used to the water currents helping him to follow through on some sword strikes, and occasionally his swing fell short. Dolosus would use that to his advantage.

He began to test the other's sword skills, thrusting first to one side, then the other, testing for weaknesses, finding where Thalassinus left flesh exposed, and where he kept a tight defence. The High Lord did not return the thrusts but parried easily, talking all the while, taunting Dolosus with cruel words, but Dolosus shut him out, concentrating only on the clash of swords and feeling his body begin to loosen up as he moved around.

Gradually, he began to increase the pressure of his thrust and swipes, poking and prodding at Thalassinus's weaknesses as if trying to prise a winkle out of a shell. Slowly, Thalassinus's taunts stopped, as all his attention focussed on not getting hurt. The game stopped being a game when Dolosus's sword slipped through the High Lord's guard and nicked his arm. Thalassinus drew back with a hiss and looked down at the green blood that marked his arm.

Dolosus turned his sword in his hand and smiled. "Do I have your attention now?"

Thalassinus growled and began to fight properly, putting his weight behind his thrusts and slashing back rather than just accepting the blows. Dolosus kept on the balls of his feet and met each blow as it came, still probing the weak spots. It became harder as Thalassinus also warmed up, and he soon realised they were an even match.

They swung, parried, thrust and stabbed, circling around the Arbor, oblivious to those who fought around them, and those who lay dead or injured on the floor. All that mattered was the moment, that one instance in time with the two of them locked in combat.

Gradually Dolosus grew tired, and yet the water warrior grew, if anything, stronger and stronger. He could not allow Thalassinus to beat him! The thought kept him going, but he could feel his muscles beginning to strain, his brain tiring with the constant effort of keeping alert. Thalassinus seemed to be sensing it, too, and let out a triumphant bellow as he pressed forward, the number and force of his blows increasing. Dolosus fell back gradually, finding himself more and more on the defensive, and a slither of fear crept into his stomach: he was going to lose this fight.

And then it happened. Thalassinus forgot he was fighting on land and let a sword swing carry too far; the momentum carried him farther than he had meant, and he twisted slightly, exposing his side and under his arm. Dolosus did not pass on the opportunity; he brought up his sword, thrusting it into the flesh.

Thalassinus shuddered, stumbled and fell to the floor. Dolosus was on him instantly. Thalassinus knocked away his sword and they fought with fists. Dolosus hit him squarely on the jaw, dislodging his helmet, which rolled away down the steps. He grabbed his dagger from his waistband and brought the point up to the warrior's neck.

For the first time, he found himself looking into the earthly translation of Thalassinus's face. He could see elements of himself, and he blanched at the clear similarity between the two of them.

Thalassinus gasped, more green blood flowing from his side, but he still managed to smile up at Dolosus. "Can you really bring yourself to kill me? Your own father?"

With the dagger pressed to Thalassinus's neck, Dolosus looked into his eyes.

II

Chonrad stared as the word that had appeared on the wooden tablet slowly disappeared. His heart was pounding. "You are connected to the Arbor?" he repeated, wanting confirmation.

Yes.

He could barely believe he was about to say the words, but before he could think better of it, he said: "Are you the Arbor?"

Yes.

He sucked his breath in through his teeth. He was actually talking to the holy tree. Fear washed over him. Was the tree angry with him? Did it know how he felt about it? Or had it brought him here?

"Are you the one who wrote the message on the door?" he whispered. "About me being the key?"

No, said the Arbor.

That surprised him. If the message wasn't from the Arbor, then who had written it?

"What do I have to do to activate the Node?" he asked.

Nothing happened. No more words appeared. He racked his brain, trying to think what to ask.

"Where is the Node?"

Nothing.

"What do you want me to do?"

No reply.

Frustration built inside him. He was not asking the right Question but could not think how else to phrase it. His brain seemed sluggish, refusing to work properly. And even if it had been, he was no scholar, he thought disconsolately. He was a knight, someone who used his hands, his strength. Not his brain!

Despondency swept over him. The Arbor was not the one who had written the words on the door. The tree probably did not want him there at all. It needed someone like Nitesco, or any of the Militis – one of its own. He was an intruder. He should not be there.

And then, suddenly, just as he was about to turn and try and wake Nitesco up again, something appeared on the tablet.

This time, there were four words, and they were not carved but seemed burned in the wood, written by an unseen hand.

You are the key.

He stared, instinctively realising it was not the Arbor talking. "Who is writing this message?"

One word appeared. *Gavius.*

Wonder flooded through him. The spirit of the knight had returned to help him. Gavius was trying to tell him it was indeed he who could help. All he had to do was find the right way to do it.

He studied the wooden tablet with renewed enthusiasm, trying to think what attributes he had the Arbor needed. He did not have the ability to make things grow like Teague. Teague was the one who could help the most, the one the Arbor needed to regenerate. And yet Gavius had told him he was the key, and that he could help.

He thought about the tree, and the way it was drooping. Maybe what Teague could do was channel the energy. But as yet, there was no energy for the tree to channel.

Energy was the key. And yet he could not access the energy until the Node was activated.

How could he activate the Node? He could not think what he should do. Concentrate, he told himself firmly. The answer lay within this wooden tablet. He had to ask the right Question.

Then he realised. He thumped his forehead, feeling stupid. So far, the Arbor had only answered a Question that had a yes or no answer.

Clearing his throat, he said, "Arbor, am I the key?"

Yes.

His heart pounded. "Can I help save you?"

Yes.

He racked his brains, trying to think about what to ask next. "Do I have everything I need to help you?"

Yes.

So it wasn't as if he had to collect something. Whatever he needed, he had it within him already.

"What do you need from me?" he whispered, although he knew it wouldn't answer such a Question. What did the Arbor need?

Strength and energy. Two things he had a lot of.

"Do you need my strength?" he asked softly.

Yes.

"Do I have to move something?"

No.

He frowned. So it wasn't physical strength. It was strength of the heart.

And suddenly, he knew what was needed. He was a modest man, unaccustomed to showing off, but still, he knew others saw him as kind and just, compassionate and loyal. But so many others had those qualities, too. Why had the Arbor not called on any of its Militis?

Then he remembered what Teague had said: the Arbor chose its own followers, and thought of him as one of them. He also remembered what Procella had suggested to Valens: the Militis had done the wrong thing in choosing the knights themselves, that they should have let the Arbor do it.

Nitesco had made the point very early on that he thought something had been lost over the centuries. Oculus had written the same. Was it possible somehow the Militis had got it wrong? And it was the very fact that he was not a Militis that meant he had a closer connection to the Arbor?

He forced his brain to think on the problem, aware that with each minute that passed, his companions above ground were dying. Why would he have a closer connection with the Arbor than the Militis, who prayed to it every day, who worshipped it?

Unless it did not want to be worshipped. The thought came to him suddenly. The tree was the centre of all energy through Anguis, but still, it was also just a tree. Maybe the deification of the Arbor was completely wrong; maybe all along, it should have been treated as just a tree.

What the Arbor needed was a connection. It no longer felt connected to the land, because it had lost its connection with people. People thought of themselves as something separate from the land and the tree, but they weren't. In their raising of the tree to a holy emblem, a symbol of Animus's love, they had separated themselves from it. What they now needed to do was reconnect themselves and the tree to the land.

Teague was, of course, the one who could do this, and suddenly Chonrad saw what was needed. A sacrifice, someone to give themselves freely to the Arbor.

He recoiled at the thought. "I cannot help Teague to his death," he whispered.

Yes, said the Arbor.

"Is there no other way?"

No.

But he knew the answer already. His mind seemed to be expanding – he seemed to be understanding more and more. He knew what he had to do.

He stepped forwards and put both hands on the wooden tablet. Immediately, his hands stuck to the wood. They grew warm. Strength and energy. That was what the Arbor needed, that and the connection the Militis did not have have; a connection to the earth.

He closed his eyes.

••••

III

Teague recoiled at the realisation of what the Arbor wanted from him.

"No," he said hoarsely. "I cannot. Please, do not make me."

"Yes," the figures whispered. "We need you, Teague. You are the only one who can help."

"I do not want to die." He was near to sobbing. He wanted to move and run away, but his arms were locked around the tree, his cheek pressed to the bark so tightly he could feel it cutting into his flesh.

"No, no!" laughed the figures. "It is not dying. You will live forever!"

Teague tried to calm his breathing. Live forever? "What do you mean?"

He could feel the figures around him, touching him, calming him. "For those of us who carry the secret of the Greening, we are unhappy out in the world. This is where we feel at home, Teague. Here. In the arms of the Arbor."

Tears flooded his eyes. Their compassion rolled over him in waves. They understood. They knew what it was like to not fit in. To always feel like an outsider. To fear your gift, when you should be embracing it.

"If I say yes, will you get better?" he asked.

The figures smiled. One of them reached out and touched his face. "If you join with us, we will be reborn."

Where his face pressed into the bark, he felt the skin break. Blood ran down his face and onto the trunk. He gasped as the tree shuddered in his arms.

"Beata," he whispered.

"She will join with you forever," the figures told him. "Draw her into the Arbor, Teague, and you will never be parted."

He sighed. Slowly, he began to send out his senses.

Warmth flooded into Chonrad's hands. His eyes were closed. He concentrated on the wood beneath his fingers, imagining it as

part of the Arbor. We are one, he thought. Earth and tree, tree
and earth. One and the same.

Suddenly, his fingers sank into the wood. He almost pulled
back, alarmed, but he forced himself to stay, in spite of the frantic
beating of his heart. His fingers continued to sink, and then the
palms of his hands were in, and then he was up to his wrists.

One and the same. Only he understood. Only he could help
the Arbor.

A rumbling began beneath his feet. He shuddered, tremors
running up through his body via his bones. He concentrated on
his hands, picturing himself joining with the tree, becoming one
with the trunk.

Beneath his eyelids, the room began to glow with light. He
kept his eyes tightly shut, afraid of being blinded as the light
continued to grow, becoming so bright it was as if the very sun
had fallen to the earth.

The trembling continued. He felt as if he were shaking with
it. Briefly, he thought of Nitesco and wished he had pulled him
further from the tablet, but it was too late now. He thought of
Procella, and Valens, and Gavius who had shown him the way.

Suddenly, a burst of light shot through him. Pain, sharp and
quick, burned him, firing every nerve ending, every cell and
bone. His back arched and his head fell back as he tried to scream,
but no sound came out.

IV

Teague felt the energy begin to build within the Arbor as soon as
he stretched out his senses, like fingers reaching for an object just
out of his reach. Something had happened. The fifth Node, he
thought somewhere in the deep recesses of his mind. The Node
had been opened. The key had been found. The circle of energy
was complete.

He tightened his grip on the trunk instinctively. The furrows in
the bark cut into his skin, but he tightened his grip still further.

Gradually, he joined with the tree. Where his toes touched the base of the trunk, the Arbor reached out, the roots entering his boots, creeping into his flesh. They pushed themselves into his feet, crept up his calves, then his thighs. It was both agony and ecstasy at the same time. They entered his chest cavity, locked around his heart. His face had merged with the trunk, his eyes already part of the wood. As he was absorbed into the tree, he felt his heart pulled towards the Pectoris. It joined with the thousand other hearts that formed it.

The tree crept into his head, into his brain.

He screamed, but it just turned into a whisper of leaves.

V

Dolosus held the blade of his knife to his father's neck. He pushed until he felt the flesh resist. He took a deep breath, ready to thrust the blade through.

Suddenly, however, the ground trembled violently under his feet. Startled, he began to stand and then lost his footing, falling to the floor. Thalassinus laughed and rose, but something caught his attention, and Dolosus turned to follow his gaze as he saw the horrific look on the High Lord's face.

He stared, shocked. The Arbor was growing. Roots crawled along the ground towards him, and he scrambled to his feet, backing away. The great split in the trunk was disappearing as the two halves merged back together. He stared at something caught between the parts of the trunk. It was a figure; he could just see long, dark hair disappearing as the wood closed together. Suddenly, he realised who it was: Teague. The Virimage was working his magic.

His form disappeared into the wood. The tree continued to grow. The trunk lengthened, thickened. Branches hardened and strengthened, gradually lifting so they began to stretch up towards the top of the dome rather than drooping on the floor.

Dolosus watched the remaining knights back away as the ground trembled again. The water warriors looked as frightened as he felt. Thalassinus was the only one who stood his ground, roaring in rage as the tree arched above him.

The tree stretched, spread, as if it were taking a gigantic breath, opening its arms to the world. Something was appearing on the branches. He gasped as he realised it was buds.

The buds unfurled and grew into waving leaves. There were hundreds of them – no, thousands. Still, the tree continued to grow.

The ground trembled again, violently this time, and suddenly, light seemed to emanate from amongst the roots, so bright he put his hand to his face to protect his eyes.

He could still see Thalassinus standing under the tree. The High Lord of Darkwater had taken his sword to the Arbor and was hacking at the tree as he howled with rage. The tree groaned and shuddered, and then the earth shook, and beneath Dolosus a wave of energy spread out like a spilt pot of paint. Thalassinus howled. The Darkwater Lords around the Temple shuddered. And then as one they melted back into the water, their screams of frustration becoming the whisper of thousands of leaves.

The tree continued to grow at a rapid pace. The air was filled with a creaking, groaning noise, the sound of splitting wood and rustling leaves. Dolosus looked down, startled as something moved beneath him, and he saw the roots of the Arbor were extending, widening as a base for the gigantic tree now filling the Temple.

And still it grew. The branches reached the top of the Temple, the remaining panes of glass shattering as the twigs and leaves pushed through. And then the tree was breaking open the Temple roof, and masonry began to fall around them, and Dolosus scrambled to his feet, joining the mad rush of those knights who were able enough to walk, others helping those who could not.

They fled through the oak doors and then outside, stopping when they reached the edge of the Quad. It had stopped raining, Dolosus realised, and it was growing lighter: the sun was coming up. He looked back at the Temple, shocked to see it crumbling as if made of parchment. The branches of the Arbor had pushed through the roof, and now the walls were disintegrating too, the roots dislodging the foundations, bit of stone and wood and mortar dropping to the floor as the whole building collapsed.

And at that moment, the first rays of the rising sun appeared over the horizon. The tree shivered and seemed to grow even faster, its branches now huge and heavy with leaves, arching over the whole Temple site.

Dolosus turned his face to the sun, not realising how much he had missed its rays. The tree seemed to be doing the same. Gradually, its growth rate slowed, and instead it filled out, its leaves now a canopy of green above his head.

And then the rumbling began again. Fear grew inside him as the ground trembled. The light brightened around the tree and spread outwards, engulfing anyone who stood in its way. He tried to scramble to his feet, but he wasn't quick enough; the light was on him, bathing him in its brightness, and he stood still, realising it was too late to run.

The light spread through him, burned up inside him. The warmth spread, his head hurt, and the stump of his missing arm throbbed. He groaned as pain shot through him, then, just as suddenly, it was gone. The light faded. The world came back into focus.

All around him, knights were staring in amazement at each other. Dolosus realised all their wounds had been healed. All gashes, scrapes, bumps and bruises had vanished.

He looked down at himself and gasped. He had two arms, two hands. The Arbor had somehow managed to grow back the missing limb.

The tree shook gently over his head, the leaves shivering in the early morning breeze.

EPILOGUE

Chonrad turned his face up to the sun and welcomed the warmth on his cheeks. The light was bright through his eyelids. He knew he shouldn't stand there for too long or he would get burned, but even though four months had passed since the Rains, as they had come to be called, he still felt grateful every time the sun came up.

After a while, he sighed and opened his eyes. He stood atop the Porta, looking down on Heartwood, much as he had that first day before their adventures had begun. Now, as then, Procella stood at his side.

The Baillium looked very different. The Castellum was gone, that which wasn't destroyed by the Arbor cleared by the knights who had survived the Last Stand. The Barracks, too, were in the process of being removed. Many of the other buildings that had stood in the Baillium had also fallen, and the rubble from these had also been taken away.

The only part of Heartwood that still remained was its wall and the Porta. Procella had organised for these to be repaired and strengthened but had acknowledged these were now the only defences to remain at Heartwood, and the Arbor was not to be enclosed again.

Chonrad looked at the great tree in the centre of the complex. It was truly magnificent, everything he had ever dreamed about as a child. Twenty times bigger than the average oak tree, the Arbor was tall and strong, its greenery thick and lush. He had been amazed when he finally climbed his way out of the Cavum, the just-awakened Nitesco stumbling behind him, emerging into daylight to find the Domus had collapsed.

The first thing he had done was to find Procella, who had been sitting on the ground some distance from the tree, eyes closed, feeling the sun on her face. When he stood before her, casting a shadow and blocking the sun, she had opened her eyes and looked up at him, and then she had arisen and put her arms around him. There had been no need for words.

They had stood there, arms around each other, for some time, watching everyone starting to move around, talking to each other, showing their healed wounds, laughing at their triumph over the Darkwater Lords.

It was only when Dolosus came over that they broke apart, exclaiming in amazement as he held both hands up to them, grinning. Chonrad thought something had changed Dolosus on a very deep level; his bitterness and resentment seemed to have completely vanished, and he sensed it was down to more than just the reappearance of his limb.

Together, they had walked over to the Arbor, right up to the trunk, which was now so wide that the three of them, holding hands, would not have been able to reach around it. Dolosus explained to them what he had seen and how Teague had merged with the tree. And then he walked them around the other side of the trunk, and they had both gasped.

Two figures stood proud of the trunk, their wooden features highly polished and intricately carved. It was Teague and Beata. He had his arms around her, and she was leaning her head on his chest, smiling slightly. The two of them joined, forever.

After they had got over their amazement, the three of them had started to clean up the area and work out who had survived the Last Stand and who had not. The Komis army had vanished – those who were not swept away had returned to their land, and those at Heartwood suspected they would not bother anyone again for a while.

More of their good friends had survived than they had expected. Gravis, Grimbeald, Fionnghuala and Bearrach, Niveus, even Nitesco.

But the casualties were many, including of course Valens, the great Imperator. Now there was time to mourn, Procella wept as she cleaned his face of blood and laid him carefully at the base of the tree. Dolosus spent some time with him, saying his goodbyes before the tree took him within, absorbing his energy.

They had organised the clean-up together, and then they had prepared a great feast under the tree, which had lasted well into the night as they wept and laughed and wept again, and discussed every move of the battle, every slash of the sword.

Everyone told their story; Nitesco related what had happened in the Labyrinth; Chonrad how he had activated the Node; Dolosus told of his journey to Darkwater. And then they had slept soundly under the shade of the tree, Procella in Chonrad's arms, and he didn't think he had ever been so happy.

The next day they discussed the future and what was going to happen to Heartwood. Chonrad had led this discussion, making it clear the Arbor did not want to be worshipped or defended, pointing out it was clearly capable of defending itself. Procella suggested keeping the outer wall and the Porta, mainly to control the flow of traffic to and from the Arbor. The Exercitus were to remain on Isenbard's Wall as a peacekeeping force.

It was decided that those who wished to remain in the Militis could stay in Heartwood, but Chonrad suggested they no longer be a holy, celibate, defensive force, but instead a group concentrating on controlling the flow of pilgrims to the Arbor. Though the Arbor did not wish to be worshipped, people would still wish to come and visit the glorious tree when they heard what had happened to it, and they would need a place to stay and somewhere to buy food. He suggested they concentrate the new settlement outside of the walls, and leave the tree the space inside to breathe.

The rest of the time since then had been spent clearing up. Fionnghuala and Bearrach had helped for a while and then had returned to Hanaire. Though they had not discussed their plans, Chonrad suspected they would be giving up their places on the Council to move in together, as they had certainly seemed very close.

Grimbeald, too, had left eventually, and with him Tenera, who had been healed by the Arbor and was now inseparable from the gruff Wulfian. He also seemed to have changed since his initial arrival at Heartwood. He made it clear to everyone that he was going to do his best to bring peace to Wulfengar and had already called a meeting of all of the Lords of the Five Lands to discuss how to begin this plan. His was not an easy task, thought Chonrad; violence was a way of life in Wulfengar, and his ideals were certainly not common. However, he seemed determined, and Chonrad felt if anyone could convince the other lords, it was the stouthearted Grimbeald, with the sensible and level-headed Tenera at his side.

Gravis announced he had decided to become an emissary for Heartwood, with the intention of travelling to all four lands to encourage them to be at peace with one another. He said he knew it would not be an easy task, but Gavius would always be with him, and with his help, he hoped he could do some good.

Dolosus and Procella had talked for some time about what was to happen with those Militis who stayed behind. Chonrad had left them to it, feeling that once he had offered his opinions, it was not his place to say. When they eventually finished, it was Dolosus who came over to tell him it had been decided he would run the new settlement with the help of some of his old friends: Niveus, Terreo and the newly arrived Erubesco, to name a few. They had drawn up plans for buildings and lists of ideas on how to make it work, and he seemed enlivened by the idea and strangely pleased to be concentrating on something other than fighting.

"You are truly a great heir to Valens," Chonrad had told him, and Dolosus's great smile had explained his feelings more fully than any words could have.

When Dolosus finally walked away, Chonrad had looked at Procella curiously. Perhaps for the first time since he had met her, she looked uncertain, her large brown eyes glancing up into his, then looking away.

"What about you?" he asked curiously. "Are you not going to stay and help run the settlement?"

She looked back at him then. "Do you remember what you said to me before you left to go to the Cavum that day?"

He smiled at her. "Of course I do. I said I was going to ask you to marry me, if I came back."

He cocked his head at her, watching her watch him. "What?"

She laughed, embarrassed. "Well, are you going to ask me?"

A warm glow flowed through him. "I did not think for a moment you would say yes!"

"Does that change whether you ask the Question or not?"

He smiled and dropped to one knee before her, taking her hand in his. "No, of course not. Procella, will you marry me and come and live with me in Vichton?"

"Yes, Chonrad, I will."

And so they had been married in a simple ceremony under the Arbor, and now Chonrad leaned forwards and placed his arms around her, feeling the slight swelling of her stomach, which announced the fact that she was pregnant with his child. The one night they had spent together in Vichton had been enough for their love to make a new life. He had worried she might not want the child; after all, the life of a Militis had been deeply ingrained in her, but she seemed genuinely thrilled, and he sensed she was looking forward to the chance to create life, after spending so long taking it away.

And now they were saying goodbye to the Arbor. Chonrad knew they would be back; there was no way Procella would be able to leave the Arbor forever, and Chonrad would not expect her to. Neither did he expect her to be the sort of wife who stayed at home and embroidered cushions. She was still going to take an active role with the Exercitus on the Wall, and she also wanted to help Grimbeald to try to make peace in Wulfengar. But her heart was with Chonrad, and for that he was glad.

He was looking forward to returning home. As soon as he was able after the Last Stand, he had sent a rider to Vichton enquiring about the health of his children, and had received word they were safe and well, though Vichton itself had taken some damage from the Darkwater Lords. But he had been away long enough.

He looked at the Arbor. His feelings towards the tree had changed dramatically, and now he only felt peace and love towards it; but still, the thought of its power and how for a short while he had been the source of it still unsettled him. He was pleased the tree was healed, but he was not disappointed to be leaving it behind.

It was time. He gave one last glance at the two figures of Beata and Teague carved into the trunk, locked in their eternal embrace. Then he took Procella's hand and led her down the stairs.

Though his eyes no longer saw in the way they had when he was alive, Teague watched Chonrad and Procella leave. He stretched, feeling his leaves rustle and his branches sway in the wind. If he concentrated, he could feel through his roots to the very ends of Anguis. The energy was now being channelled to all four corners of the realm, and the land was flourishing.

Everything had ended well, he thought. He was strong and in control, and for once he felt as if he belonged. The Darkwater Lords were contained in the sea, where they would remain, eternally bound within their watery chains. The world was at peace, and the element of earth was in the ascendant.

For now.

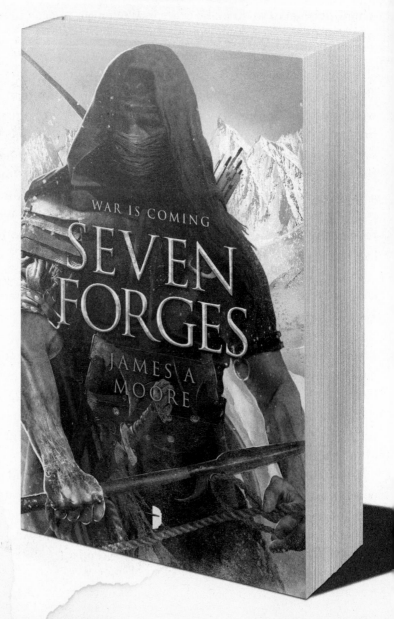

"Political intrigue, brutal fighting, beguiling magic and assassinations... Seven Forges has the WOW factor."
The Book Plank

WAR IS COMING

SEVEN FORGES

JAMES A MOORE

"This is how historical fantasy gets dirty."
Douglas Hulick, *author of* Among Thieves

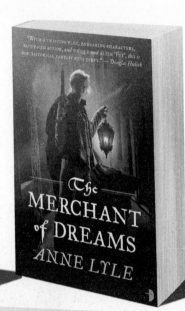

The world has collapsed, and there are no heroes any more

The complete Courts of the Feyre saga.
Urban Fantasy at its best.

"Sword and sorcery at its rollicking best."
Library Journal

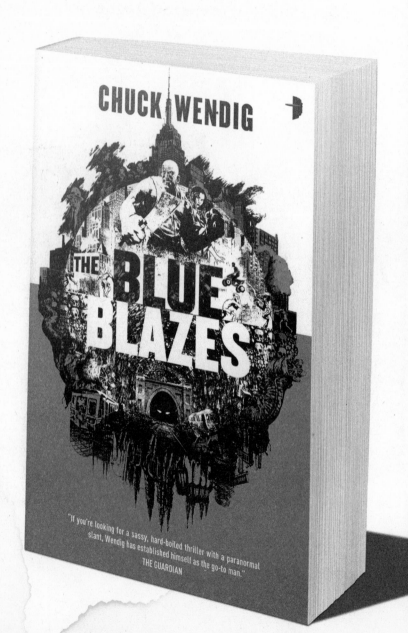

"Violent and funny and noir."
Tor.com

CHUCK WENDIG

THE BLUE BLAZES

"If you're looking for a sassy, hard-boiled thriller with a paranormal slant, Wendig has established himself as the go-to man."
THE GUARDIAN